Donated
To The Library by

Family and friends

In memory of

Jane Bennett

Reckless

Also by Amanda Quick
in Thorndike Large Print ®

Ravished
Scandal

This Large Print Book carries the
Seal of Approval of N.A.V.H.

Reckless

Amanda Quick

Thorndike Press • Thorndike, Maine

Library of Congress Cataloging in Publication Data:

Quick, Amanda.
    Reckless / Amanda Quick.
        p.   cm.
    ISBN 1-56054-657-3 (alk. paper : lg. print)
    ISBN 1-56054-882-7 (alk. paper : lg. print : pbk.)
    1. Large type books.   I. Title.
[PS3561.R44R43   1993]   92-42499
813'.54—dc20   CIP

Thorndike Large Print® Romance Series edition
published in 1993 by arrangement with Bantam Books, a
division of Bantam Doubleday Dell Publishing Group, Inc.

Cover photo by Thayer Smith.

The tree indicium is a trademark of Thorndike Press.

This book is printed on acid-free, high opacity paper. ∞

To Yook Louie, whose artistic talent and vision never cease to amaze me. I am truly grateful.

Chapter 1

Moonlight suited him.

Cloaked in the silver light that illuminated the meadow, Gabriel Banner, Earl of Wylde, looked as mysterious and as dangerous as a legend that had come to life.

Phoebe Layton brought her mare to a halt at the edge of the trees and held her breath as Wylde rode toward her. She tried to steady her hands as she gripped the reins. This was no time to lose her nerve. She was a lady on a quest.

She needed the services of a knight-errant and it was not as though she had a great deal of choice. Indeed, Wylde was the only candidate she knew who had the proper qualifications. But first she had to talk him into accepting the position.

She had been working on that project for weeks. Until tonight the solitary, reclusive earl had steadfastly ignored all but deliberately intriguing letters. In desperation, she had resorted to other tactics. In an effort to lure him forth from his lair, she had baited a trap using the one tempting morsel she knew he could not resist.

The fact that he was here tonight on this lonely country lane in Sussex meant that she had at last succeeded in provoking him into a meeting.

Wylde did not know who she was. In her letters she had signed herself only as The Veiled Lady. Phoebe regretted the small deception, but it had been a necessary maneuver. If Wylde had been aware of her true identity at the start of the venture, he would most certainly have refused to help her. He had to be persuaded to take up the quest before she dared reveal herself. Phoebe was certain that once he understood everything, he would comprehend the reasons for her initial secrecy.

No, Wylde did not know her, but Phoebe knew him.

She had not seen him in nearly eight years. At sixteen she had imagined him a living legend, a noble, valiant knight straight out of a medieval romance. In her young eyes all he had lacked was the shining armor and a sword.

Although Phoebe clearly recalled the last time she had seen him, she knew Gabriel had no recollection of it at all. He had been too busy plotting to run off with her sister,

Meredith, at the time.

Phoebe tensed with curiosity now as he rode toward her. Unfortunately, the combination of the veil she was wearing and the pale moonlight made it impossible to tell just how much he had changed over the years.

Her first thought was that he seemed larger than she remembered. Taller. Leaner. Harder, somehow. His shoulders appeared broader under the caped greatcoat he wore. Snug breeches outlined the strong, muscular lines of his thighs. The curled brim of his hat cast Wylde's features into a forbidding, impenetrable shadow.

For an unsettling moment Phoebe wondered if this was the wrong man. Perhaps she was about to encounter a genuine villain, a highwayman or worse. She stirred uneasily in the saddle. If she came to grief this night, her poor, beleaguered family would no doubt feel justified in having her tombstone engraved with something fitting. SHE FINALLY PAID THE PRICE OF HER RECKLESS WAYS would do nicely. As far as her overprotective clan was concerned, Phoebe had spent her entire life getting into one scrape after another. This time she might have taken one chance too many.

"The mysterious Veiled Lady, I presume?"

Gabriel inquired coldly.

Relief washed over her. Phoebe's doubts as to the man's identity were instantly resolved. There was no mistaking those dark, gritty tones even though she had not heard them in eight years. What startled her was the small thrill of anticipation they sent through her. She frowned briefly at her strange reaction.

"Good evening, my lord," she said.

Gabriel brought his black stallion to a halt a few feet away. "I received your most recent note, madam. I found it extremely irritating, just as I did the others."

Phoebe swallowed uneasily as she realized he was not in a cheerful mood. "I had rather hoped to pique your interest, sir."

"I have a strong distaste for deception."

"I see." Phoebe's heart sank. *A strong distaste for deception.* She suddenly wondered if she had made a serious tactical mistake in dealing with Wylde. Just as well she had been careful to go veiled tonight, she thought. She certainly did not want him to discover who she was if this night's work came to naught. "Nevertheless, I am pleased you decided to accept my invitation."

"Curiosity got the better of me." Gabriel smiled faintly in the moonlight, but the curve of his mouth held no warmth and his shad-

10

owed gaze revealed nothing. "You have become a thorn in my side during the past two months, madam. I expect you are well aware of that fact."

"I apologize," Phoebe said earnestly. "But the truth is, I was becoming quite desperate, my lord. You are a difficult man to see. You did not respond to my initial letters and as you do not go into Society, I could think of no other way to gain your attention."

"So you decided to deliberately provoke me to such an extent that I would finally bestir myself to meet you?"

Phoebe took a deep breath. "Something like that."

"It is generally considered dangerous to annoy me, my mysterious Veiled Lady."

She did not doubt that for a moment, but it was too late to retreat now. She had come too far to call a halt to this night's venture. She was a lady on a quest and she must be stouthearted.

"Is that so, my lord?" Phoebe tried for a cool, amused tone. "The thing is, you left me no alternative. Never fear, I am certain that once you have heard what I have to say, you will be glad you finally agreed to meet me and I know you will forgive my small deception."

"If you have summoned me so that you

can gloat over your latest triumph, I should warn you I do not like to lose."

"Triumph?" She blinked behind the veil and then realized he was talking about the bait she had used to draw him here tonight. "Oh, yes, the book. Come, now, my lord. You are as eager to see the manuscript as I am. Obviously you could not resist my invitation to view it, even though I am the new owner."

Gabriel stroked his stallion's neck with a gloved hand. "We appear to share a mutual interest in medieval manuscripts."

"True. I see that it annoys you that I am the one who located *The Knight and the Sorcerer* and discovered that it was for sale," Phoebe said. "But surely you are generous enough to give me credit for the cleverness of my investigations. The manuscript was right here in Sussex, after all, practically beneath your very nose."

Gabriel inclined his head in acknowledgment of her skills. "You seem to be rather lucky in that regard. This is the third such manuscript you have gotten to ahead of me in recent weeks. May I ask why you didn't simply snatch it up and carry it off the way you did the others?"

"Because as I explained in my letters, I wish to speak to you, sir." Phoebe hesitated and then admitted in a soft rush, "And because, to be quite honest, I decided it might be wise to take an escort with me tonight."

"Ah."

"I have come to the conclusion that Mr. Nash is a very odd sort of man, even for a book collector," Phoebe continued. "The stipulations he put on the time at which he would turn over the manuscript made me rather uneasy. I do not like doing business at midnight."

"Nash sounds somewhat more than merely amusingly eccentric," Gabriel agreed thoughtfully.

"He claims to be nocturnal, rather like a bat. He says in his letters that his household is run on a schedule that is opposite to that of the rest of the world. He sleeps while others are awake and works while others sleep. Very strange, is it not?"

"He would no doubt fit very nicely into the Polite World," Gabriel said dryly. "Most of the *ton* stays out all night and sleeps during the day. Still, you were probably right to be careful about meeting him alone at midnight."

Phoebe smiled. "I am glad you approve of my plan to take an escort."

"I approve, but I confess I'm surprised by your concern," Gabriel said with the precision of a swordsman sliding his blade home. "You have not thus far demonstrated much inclination toward caution and prudence."

Phoebe's cheeks burned at the sarcasm. "When one is on a quest, one must be bold, my lord."

"You consider yourself on a quest?"

"Yes, my lord, I do."

"I see. Speaking of quests, I should tell you that I am here tonight on a small one of my own."

A chill of apprehension seized Phoebe. "Yes, my lord? What would that be?"

"It was not just the prospect of viewing Nash's manuscript before you take possession of it that brings me here, my Veiled Lady."

"Really, my lord?" Perhaps her scheme had actually worked, Phoebe thought. Perhaps she had truly piqued his interest, just as she had hoped to do. "You are interested in what I have to say?"

"Not particularly. But I am interested in making the acquaintance of my new opponent. I believe in knowing one's enemy." Gabriel watched her coldly. "I do not know who you are, madam, but you have been leading me a merry dance for some time now. I have had enough of your games."

A fresh flicker of uneasiness dampened Phoebe's rising spirits. She was still a long

14

way from the successful completion of her quest. "I expect we shall encounter each other again in the future. As you said, we are interested in collecting the same books and manuscripts."

Saddle leather creaked softly as Gabriel urged his stallion a few steps closer. "Have you enjoyed your little victories recently, my Veiled Lady?"

"Very much." She smiled in spite of her nervousness. "I am quite pleased with my recent acquisitions. They make excellent additions to my library."

"I see." There was a slight pause. "You do not consider it a bit reckless to invite me along tonight to witness your latest coup?"

It was all far more reckless than he could possibly know, Phoebe thought ruefully. "The thing is, my lord, you are one of the few people in all of England who is capable of appreciating my recent find."

"I certainly do appreciate it. Very much, in fact. And therein lies the danger."

Phoebe's fingers trembled slightly on the reins. "Danger?"

"What if I decide to take the manuscript from you by force after you have collected it from Mr. Nash?" Gabriel asked with lethal softness.

Phoebe stiffened abruptly at the threat.

She had not considered that possibility. Wylde was an earl, after all. "Do not be ridiculous. You are a gentleman. You would not do any such thing."

"Mysterious veiled ladies who scheme to deprive gentlemen such as myself of much-desired objects should not be too surprised if said gentlemen become impatient." Gabriel's voice hardened. "If Nash's manuscript is a genuine fourteenth century legend of the Round Table as he claims it is, I want it, madam. Name your price."

Tension crackled in the air between them. Phoebe's courage faltered briefly. It was all she could do not to wheel her mare around and gallop back to the safety of the Amesburys' country house, where she was staying. She wondered if knights-errant had been so bloody difficult in medieval times.

"I doubt that you could meet my price, sir," she whispered.

"Name it and we shall see."

Phoebe licked her dry lips. "The thing is, I have no intention of selling it."

"Are you certain of that?" Gabriel edged the stallion a step closer. The great beast tossed his head and blew heavily, crowding Phoebe's mare.

"Quite certain," Phoebe said quickly. She paused for effect. "However, I might consider giving it to you."

"*Giving* it to me?" Gabriel was clearly taken aback by that remark. "What the devil are you talking about?"

"I will explain later, sir." Phoebe struggled to soothe her nervous horse. "May I remind you it is nearly midnight? I am due at Mr. Nash's cottage in a few minutes. Are you coming with me or not?"

"I am most definitely going to fulfill my duties as your escort this evening," Gabriel said grimly. "It is far too late to get rid of me."

"Yes, well, shall we get on with the business, then?" Phoebe gave the signal to her mare to move off down the moonlit lane. "Mr. Nash's cottage should be a short distance from here, according to the directions I received in his last letter."

"I would not want you to keep him waiting." Gabriel turned his stallion to follow her.

The sleek animal fell into step alongside Phoebe's mount. Phoebe wondered if her mare was feeling as nervous as she was. Gabriel and the stallion both loomed large and forbidding in the moonlight.

"Now that we have met at last, my Veiled Lady, I have some questions for you," Gabriel said.

Phoebe slanted him a wary glance. "As you have been ignoring my letters for the past two months, I'm surprised to hear that. I had gained the impression that I was not a subject of any great interest to you."

"You know damn well I'm interested now. Tell me, do you intend to continue going after every obscure medieval book that I happen to want?"

"Probably. As you have noted, we appear to share similar tastes in such matters."

"This could get very expensive for both of us. Once the word is out that there are two rival bidders for every old volume that comes to light, the prices will go very high, very quickly."

"Yes, I imagine they will," Phoebe said with studied carelessness. "But I can afford it. I receive a very generous allowance."

Gabriel sent her a speculative, sidelong glance. "Your husband does not mind your expensive habits?"

"I have no husband, sir. Nor am I eager to acquire one. From my observation, husbands tend to limit a woman's adventures."

"I'll grant that few husbands would countenance the sort of nonsense that you are engaged in tonight," Gabriel muttered. "No man in his right mind would allow a wife to traipse around alone in the country or anywhere else at this hour."

Neil would have allowed her to do so, Phoebe thought wistfully. But her fair-haired Lancelot was dead and she was on a quest to find his killer. She put the memories aside and tried to suppress the little wave of guilt she always felt when she thought of Neil Baxter.

If it had not been for her, Neil would never have gone off to the South Seas to seek his fortune. And if he had not gone off to the South Seas, he would not have been murdered by a pirate.

"I am not alone, sir," Phoebe reminded Gabriel. She tried desperately to keep her tone light. "I have a knight-errant to accompany me. I feel quite safe."

"Are you referring to me, by any chance?"

"Of course."

"Then you should know that knights-errant are accustomed to being well rewarded for their tasks," Gabriel said. "In medieval days the lady bestowed her favors upon her champion. Tell me, madam, do you intend to repay me for this night's work in a similar fashion?"

Phoebe's eyes widened behind her veil. She was shocked in spite of herself. Surely he had not meant to imply that she should reward him with favors of an *intimate* nature.

19

Even if he had become a recluse and no longer felt obliged to honor the polite rules of Society, she could not bring herself to believe that Gabriel's basic nature had changed that much.

The noble knight who had set out to rescue her sister from an arranged marriage all those years ago was at heart a gallant gentleman. Indeed, in her sixteen-year-old eyes he had been worthy of sitting at the Round Table itself. Surely he would not make blatantly unchivalrous advances to a lady.

Would he?

She must have misunderstood him. Perhaps he was teasing her.

"Remind me to give you a bit of ribbon or some such frippery as a gift for your efforts tonight, my lord," Phoebe said. She could not tell if she sounded suitably sophisticated or not. She was nearly twenty-five years old, but that did not mean she had had a great deal of experience with ill-mannered gentlemen. As the youngest daughter of the Earl of Clarington, Phoebe had always been well protected. Too much so at times, as far as she was concerned.

"I do not think a bit of ribbon will be sufficient payment," Gabriel mused.

Phoebe lost her patience. "Well, it is all you are likely to get, so do stop provoking me, my lord." She was relieved at the sight of a lamp-lit window ahead. "That must be Mr. Nash's cottage."

She studied the small, ramshackle house revealed in the moonlight. Even at night it was possible to see that the cottage needed attention. There was a general air of neglect about the place. A broken gate barred the overgrown garden path. The glow from within the house revealed a small, fractured windowpane. The roof needed patching.

"Nash does not appear to be doing particularly well in the manuscript trade." Gabriel drew his stallion to a halt and swung lithely to the ground.

"I do not believe he sells a great number of manuscripts. I got the impression from his letters that he has a large library but that he is loath to part with any items from it." Phoebe halted her mare. "He is selling *The Knight and the Sorcerer* to me only because he is in dire need of funds to purchase a volume he considers more important than a frivolous medieval romance."

"Now, what could be more important than a frivolous romance?" There was a faint curve to Gabriel's mouth as he raised his hands and clasped Phoebe around the waist.

She gasped as he lifted her effortlessly down from the sidesaddle. He did not set her on her feet, but continued to hold her in front of him, the toes of her half boots an inch off the ground. It was the first time he had ever touched her, the first time she had been so close to him. Phoebe was shocked at her own reaction. She was breathless.

He smelled good, she realized with surprise. His scent was indescribable, all leather and wool, and all male. She knew suddenly that she would never forget it.

For some reason the strength in his hands unnerved her. She was conscious of just how small and light she was compared to him. It was not her imagination; he *was* larger than she remembered.

Eight years ago Phoebe had admired her sister's would-be rescuer with a young girl's innocent, idealistic admiration.

Tonight she was startled to discover that she might very well find herself attracted to him in the way a woman is attracted to a man. She had never before felt this way about any man, not even Neil. Never had there been this immediate, shattering sense of awareness.

Perhaps it was only her imagination at work, she assured herself. Too much moonlight and tension. Her family was forever warning her to subdue her imaginative mind.

Gabriel set her on her feet. Confused by

the dizzying effect he was having on her senses, Phoebe forgot to steady herself firmly on her right leg before putting weight on her left one. She stumbled and clutched at Gabriel's arm to catch her balance.

Gabriel's brows rose. "Do I make you nervous, my lady?"

"No, of course not." Phoebe released his arm and quickly shook out the skirts of her riding habit. She started determinedly toward the broken gate. There was no way to conceal the slight limp that marred her walk. She had grown accustomed to it long ago, but others were forever noticing it.

"Did you twist your ankle when I set you down?" There was genuine concern in Gabriel's voice now. "My apologies, madam. Here, let me assist you."

"There is nothing wrong with my ankle," Phoebe said impatiently. "My left leg is somewhat weak, that is all. The effects of an old carriage accident."

"I see," Gabriel said. He sounded thoughtful.

Phoebe wondered if the obvious weakness in her left leg bothered him. It had certainly put off other men in the past. Few men invited a woman with a limp to join them in a waltz. Normally she was not bothered by such reactions. She was used to them.

But she discovered that it hurt to think that Gabriel might be one of those males who could not tolerate imperfections in a woman.

"If I seem a trifle nervous," Phoebe said gruffly, "it is because I do not know you all that well, sir."

"I'm not so certain about that," Gabriel said with a hint of amusement in his voice. "You are about to steal your third manuscript from me. It would seem you know me very well, indeed."

"I am not stealing from you, my lord." Phoebe reached up to the brim of her small hat and lowered the second layer of the dark veil. One layer might not be enough to conceal her features inside the cottage. "I consider us rivals, not enemies."

"There is little difference when it comes to this sort of thing. Be warned, madam. You may have pushed your luck too far with this night's work."

Phoebe knocked quickly. "Do not fret, Wylde. I am certain there will be other opportunities for you to win in this game."

"No doubt." Gabriel's eyes were on Phoebe's heavily veiled face as footsteps sounded on the other side of the door. "I shall certainly make it a point in the future to provide you with more of a challenge than I have thus far."

"I have been quite satisfied with the challenge to date," Phoebe said as the door was unlatched inside. Sparring with Wylde was akin to dragging a chunk of raw meat in front of a tiger. A dangerous business, to say the least. But she must keep him intrigued, she reminded herself. If he lost interest, he might simply vanish into the night. Once again she could only regret the current shortage of knights-errant. Selection was limited.

"If you are satisfied with the challenge thus far," Gabriel said, "it is only because you have been winning. That is about to change."

Chapter 2

The door of Nash's cottage opened and a stout, middle-aged housekeeper in a dingy cap and apron peered out.

"Who be you?" the woman demanded in a suspicious tone.

"Kindly tell your master that the person to whom he recently sold a medieval manuscript has arrived to collect it," Phoebe said. She glanced into the hall behind the woman. Floor-to-ceiling bookcases lined the walls. Each shelf was crammed full with leatherbound volumes. More books were stacked in piles on the floor.

"So he's sold off another one, eh?" The housekeeper nodded with obvious satisfaction. "Well, now, that's a blessing. He's behind on me wages again. Owes me a packet, he does. I'm goin' to see to it he pays me afore he settles up with the tradesmen this time. Weren't nothin' left by the time he got around to me last quarter."

"Nash sold an item from his collection to pay his bills last quarter?" Gabriel asked as

26

he strode into the tiny hall behind Phoebe. His heavy coat swirled around the tops of his beautifully polished Hessians.

"Egan finally talked him into it. You'd have thought Mr. Nash was gettin' a tooth pulled." The housekeeper sighed as she closed the door. "The master cannot bear to part with any of them old books of his. They're all he cares about."

"Who is Egan?" Phoebe asked.

"The master's son. Comes by to see to things once in a while, thank the lord, or else nothin' at all would get done around here." The housekeeper led the way down the hall. "Don't know what we'd have done if Egan hadn't convinced Mr. Nash to sell off one or two of them dirty old books. Starve to death, more'n likely."

Phoebe glanced covertly at Gabriel, who was examining the shabby, book-filled hall. He had removed his hat. She studied him with the new, heightened awareness that he had ignited in her. In the dim glow of the flickering candlelight his hair was still as black as midnight, just as she remembered. There was a faint trace of silver at the temples. But then, he was thirty-four now, she reminded herself. And the silver was oddly attractive.

Eight years ago she had thought him rather

old. Now he seemed exactly the right age. Her gloved fingers tightened around a fold of her purple riding habit. She lifted the small train to clear a pile of books. The rising sense of anticipation inside her had nothing to do with collecting the manuscript or convincing Gabriel to help her in her quest to discover Neil's murderer.

It had everything to do with Gabriel himself.

Dear heaven, this was getting dangerous indeed, Phoebe thought. This sort of emotional complication was the last thing she needed at the moment. She must keep a clear head and remember that Gabriel had no reason to feel any affection for any members of her family.

Gabriel's face was half averted as he read the spines of some of the books stuffed higgledy-piggledy into the nearest case. Phoebe gazed at the hard line of his jaw and the arrogant angle of his cheekbones. For some reason she was startled to see that he still had the face of a raptor.

Her stomach fluttered nervously. She had not expected that the passage of the past eight years would soften those fierce features. It was unsettling, however, to see that they had become harsher and more unyielding than ever.

As if he could read her mind, Gabriel suddenly turned his head. He looked straight at her, pinning her with predatory green eyes. For a nerve-racking moment Phoebe had the impression he could see beneath her heavy veil. *She had forgotten about his eyes.*

As a young girl on the brink of womanhood, she had not understood the impact of that intense green gaze. Of course, she had only had a few brief glimpses of it. Those occasions had occurred when Gabriel had come to her father's town house along with all the other young bloods of the *ton* to pay court to her lovely sister, Meredith.

The only man in the crowd who had interested Phoebe had been Gabriel. She had been curious about him from the start because she had avidly read the books and poems he had given to her sister. Gabriel had wooed Meredith with Arthurian legends rather than flowers. Meredith had not been interested in the ancient tales of chivalry, but Phoebe had devoured them.

Every time Gabriel had come to call, Phoebe had made it a point to observe as much as possible from her hiding place at the top of the stairs. In her naïveté, she had thought the glances he had given Meredith were deliciously romantic.

Now she realized that *romantic* was far

too soft and frivolous a word to describe Gabriel's glittering gaze. No wonder her sister had found him terrifying. For all her razor sharp intelligence, Meredith had been a gentle, timid creature in those days.

For the first time since she had begun the reckless quest to lure Gabriel into helping her, Phoebe felt momentarily overwhelmed by the challenge. He was right. He was not a man with whom an intelligent woman played games. Perhaps her scheme was not going to work, after all. She sent up a silent prayer of thanks that she was still safely concealed behind her veil.

"Is something wrong?" Gabriel asked softly. His eyes skimmed over her bright purple habit. He looked amused.

"No. Nothing." Phoebe lifted her chin as she turned away from him to follow the housekeeper. What did it signify if the purple shade of her habit was a trifle livid in tone? She was well aware that her taste was not appreciated by many. Her mother and sister were always lecturing her about her love of what they termed inflamed colors.

The housekeeper showed them into a small room that was even more crowded than the hall. Bookcases took up all the available wall space. Each was filled to overflowing. Volumes were stacked waist high on the floor,

forming meandering paths. Heavy trunks, lids open to reveal more books and papers, were stationed on either side of the hearth.

A portly man dressed in overly snug breeches and a faded maroon coat sat at a desk piled high with books. He was hunched over an aging volume. Candlelight illuminated his bald head and thick gray whiskers. He spoke without looking up from the page in front of him.

"What is it, Mrs. Stiles? I told ye I was not to be bothered until I have finished translating this text."

"The lady has come for her manuscript, sir." Mrs. Stiles did not seem perturbed by her master's gruff manner. "Brought a friend with her, she has. Shall I make tea?"

"What's this? There's two of 'em?" Nash threw down his pen and surged to his feet. He turned toward the door and glowered at his visitors through a pair of silver-framed spectacles.

"Good evening, Mr. Nash," Phoebe said politely as she stepped forward.

Nash's scowling gaze was drawn briefly to Phoebe's left leg. He refrained from commenting on her limp, however. His already florid face turned a darker shade of red as he looked at Gabriel. "Here, now. I'm only sellin' the one manuscript tonight. How come

31

there's two of ye?"

"Do not concern yourself, Mr. Nash," Phoebe said soothingly. "This gentleman is with me merely because I did not like the thought of coming out alone at this hour."

"Why not?" Nash glared ferociously at Gabriel. "No harm will come to ye in this neighborhood. Nothin' ever happens around this part of Sussex."

"Yes, well, I am not as familiar with the local situation as you are," Phoebe murmured. "I am from London, if you will recall."

"About the tea," Mrs. Stiles began firmly.

"Never mind the damn tea," Nash growled. "They won't be stayin' long enough for it. Take yerself off, Mrs. Stiles. I've got business to attend to."

"Yes, sir." Mrs. Stiles disappeared.

Gabriel's gaze was speculative as he surveyed the room full of books. "My compliments on your extensive library, Nash."

"Thank you, sir." Nash's gaze followed Gabriel's. Pride gleamed briefly in his eyes. "Rather pleased with it, if I do say so."

"You would not, by any chance, be in possession of a particular copy of Malory's *Morte d'Arthur* would you?"

"What copy?" Nash asked suspiciously.

"A 1634 edition. Rather poor condition.

Bound in red Moroccan leather. There is an inscription on the flyleaf that begins 'To my son.'"

Nash frowned. "No. Mine is an earlier edition. Excellent condition."

"I see." Gabriel looked at him. "Then we had best be getting on with our business."

"Certainly." Nash opened a desk drawer. "I expect ye'll be wantin' to see the thing afore you take it away, won't ye?"

"If you don't mind." Phoebe cast a swift glance at Gabriel.

He had picked up a fat book from a nearby table, but he put it down at once when he saw Nash lifting a wooden box out of the desk drawer.

Nash lifted the lid off the box and reverently removed the volume inside. The gold on the edges of the vellum sparkled in the candlelight. Gabriel's eyes gleamed a very brilliant shade of green.

Phoebe almost smiled in spite of her new fears. She knew exactly how he felt. A familiar rush of excitement shot through her as Nash placed the manuscript on the desk and carefully opened the thick leather covers to reveal the first page.

"Oh, my goodness," Phoebe whispered. All of her immediate concerns about the wisdom of asking Gabriel's assistance in her quest faded as she looked at the magnificent manuscript.

She moved closer to get a better view of the four miniatures placed together on the top half of the page. An intricate ivy-leaf border surrounded the ancient illustrations. Even from this distance the illuminations glowed like rare jewels.

"It's a beauty, right enough," Nash said with a collector's pride. "Got it from a book-seller in London a year ago. He bought it from some Frenchman who fled to England on account of the Revolution. Makes me bilious to think of all the fine book collections that must have been broken up or destroyed on the Continent during the past few years."

"Yes," Gabriel said quietly. "War is not good for books or anything else." He walked over to the desk and stood gazing intently down at the illuminated manuscript. "Bloody hell. It is quite remarkably beautiful."

"Wonderful." Phoebe studied the glittering miniatures. "Absolutely fantastic." She glanced at Nash. "May I examine it more closely?"

Nash hesitated and then shrugged with obvious reluctance. "Ye paid fer it. It's yers. Do what ye like."

"Thank you." Phoebe was aware of Gabriel hovering over her shoulder as she reached into her skirt pocket for a clean lace handkerchief. The intense, controlled eagerness in him amused her because it was so similar to her own emotions in that moment.

She and Gabriel were as one in this particular passion, she reflected. Only another book collector could appreciate a moment such as this.

She used the handkerchief to turn the vellum pages. *The Knight and the Sorcerer* was a richly decorated manuscript. It had obviously been commissioned by a wealthy medieval French aristocrat who had appreciated the illuminator's art as well as the story the scribe had set down.

Phoebe paused to study some of the old French, noting the exquisite script. When she got to the final page, she concentrated intently for a moment to translate the colophon.

"Here ends the tale of *The Knight and the Sorcerer*," Phoebe read aloud. "I, Philip of Blois, have told only the truth. This book has been created for my lady and belongs to her. If anyone takes this book from this place, he shall be cursed. He shall be set upon by thieves and murderers. He shall hang. He shall be condemned to the fires of hell."

"I'd say that covers everything," Gabriel

said. "Nothing like a good old-fashioned book curse to make one think twice about engaging in a bit of book theft."

"One can hardly blame the scribes for trying everything possible to keep these gorgeous works of art from being stolen." Phoebe carefully closed the volume. She glanced up at Mr. Nash and smiled. "I am well satisfied with my purchase, sir."

" 'Tis only a romance of the Round Table," Nash muttered. "A foolish story written down for some spoiled court lady. Not as important as the copy of the *Historia Scholastica* that I picked up at the same time, of course. Still, 'tis a pretty thing, ain't it?"

"It is quite outrageously beautiful." Phoebe carefully replaced the manuscript in its box. "I will take excellent care of it, Mr. Nash."

"Well, ye'd best take it and be gone." Nash tore his gaze away from the box containing the manuscript. "I've got work to do tonight."

"I understand." Phoebe picked up the heavy container.

"I'll take that for you." Gabriel deftly removed the manuscript box from Phoebe's hands. "Somewhat awkward for you to manage, don't you think?"

"I can manage it very well, thank you."

"Nevertheless, I'll be happy to carry it

for you." Gabriel smiled enigmatically. "You have engaged my services as an escort tonight, if you will recall. It is my privilege to be of service to you. Shall we go?"

"Yes, yes, take yerselves off," Nash grumbled. He sat down at his desk and picked up his pen. "Mrs. Stiles will see you to the door."

Unable to think of any alternative, Phoebe was obliged to walk past Gabriel and out into the crowded hall. She did not like the taunting look in his eyes.

Surely he would not actually attempt to take the manuscript from her by force, she assured herself. She refused to believe for one minute that her gallant knight had turned into a genuine villain. He was teasing her, she thought.

Mrs. Stiles was waiting at the front door. She eyed the box in Gabriel's hand. "Well, that'll be one less book to dust. 'Course, the master will probably go out and buy ten more to replace it. I'll be lucky to get my wages this quarter."

"The best of luck to you, Mrs. Stiles," Gabriel said. He took Phoebe's arm and guided her out into the night.

"Once I am mounted, I can handle the manuscript," Phoebe said quickly.

"You do not trust me to keep it safe for you?"

"It is not a matter of trust." She refused to allow him to make her any more anxious than she already was. "I know you are a gentleman, after all."

"So you keep telling me." He put the box down on a stone, grasped Phoebe around the waist, and swung her up onto the sidesaddle. His hands lingered around her as he looked up at her veiled face. "You seem to think you know a great deal about me."

"I do." She realized she was clutching his shoulders. Hastily she jerked her fingers away and picked up the reins.

"Just how much do you know, madam?" Gabriel released her to collect the stallion's reins. He vaulted lightly into the saddle and proceeded to secure the manuscript box beneath the heavy folds of his greatcoat.

The time had come to talk. Phoebe chose her words carefully as they started down the lane. She had lured the solitary knight out of his keep, but she had not yet accomplished her goal. She wanted him intrigued and curious enough to commit to the quest before she revealed herself.

"I am aware that you are only recently returned to England after an extended stay abroad," she said cautiously.

"An extended stay abroad," Gabriel repeated. "That is certainly one way of putting it. I was out of the country for eight bloody long years. What else do you know about me?"

She did not like the new tone in his voice. "Well, I have heard that you came into your title rather unexpectedly."

"Very unexpectedly. If my uncle and his sons had not all been lost at sea a year ago, I would never have inherited the earldom. Is there more, my Veiled Lady?"

"I know that you have a great interest in chivalry and legends."

"Obviously." Gabriel looked at her. His green eyes were colorless in the moonlight, but there was no mistaking the challenge in them. "Anything else?"

Phoebe took a grip on her nerves. She had to use more potent weapons, she decided. "I know what a great many members of the fashionable world would kill to discover. I know you are the anonymous author of *The Quest*."

The effect of that announcement was immediate. Gabriel's controlled anger was palpable. His eyes narrowed swiftly. "Damnation. You have indeed been busy. How did you learn that?"

"Oh, I have my sources," Phoebe tried to say lightly. She could hardly tell him the full truth. Not even her family knew her deepest, darkest secret.

Gabriel abruptly reined in his stallion. He shot out a hand and caught hold of Phoebe's wrist. "I asked you how you came by the knowledge. I will have an answer, madam."

A tremor went through Phoebe. His fingers were locked tightly around her wrist and his face was stark in the shadows. She knew he meant exactly what he said. He would have his answer.

"Is it such a great offense?" she asked breathlessly. "Everyone is wondering about the identity of the author of the most popular book of the Season."

"Did my publisher tell you who it was? Bloody hell, madam, did you bribe Lacey?"

"No, I swear I did not." She could hardly tell him that she was the mysterious backer who had rescued Josiah Lacey's faltering bookshop and publishing business last year. She had done so using money she had saved from the generous quarterly allowance provided by her father and the income she had made selling some of her precious books to other collectors. No one knew the truth, and Phoebe knew it had to stay that way. Her family would be horrified to learn that she was, for all intents and purposes, in trade.

The arrangement she had made with Lacey worked very well, for the most part. Phoebe selected the manuscripts to be published and Lacey handled the printing of them. Between the two of them and with the assistance of a young solicitor and a couple of clerks, Lacey's Bookshop was flourishing. Their first big success had been *The Quest,* which Phoebe had insisted on publishing the instant she had finished reading the manuscript.

"You must have crossed Lacey's palms with silver," Gabriel said. "But I did not think that old drunken sot such a fool. He knows better than to cross me in this matter. Surely he is not stupid enough to risk the future profits he intends to make on my next book."

Phoebe looked down at the leather-gloved fingers clamped around her wrist. Perhaps this really had all been a dreadful mistake, she thought frantically. Gabriel was not behaving in the least like a knight of ancient times. The hand that gripped hers felt as unyielding as a steel manacle. "It was not his fault. You must not blame Mr. Lacey."

"How did you discover I was the author of The Quest?"

Phoebe groped for a reasonable answer. "I had my solicitor look into the matter for me, if you must know." She tried unsuccessfully to free her hand. "He is extremely clever." That much was true, she reflected. Mr. Peak was an extremely intelligent, extremely accommodating young man anxious to make his way in the world. So anxious, in fact, that he was willing to do business with the youngest daughter of the Earl of Clarington without bothering to notify her father of that fact.

"Your solicitor." With a sharp oath, Gabriel released her. "I grow weary of this game you are playing, madam. I have told you I have no patience with deception and illusion. Who are you?"

Phoebe moistened her lower lip. "I cannot tell you, sir. Not yet. It is too soon. Furthermore, if my plan is not going to work at all, as I am beginning to conclude, then I would just as soon not risk my reputation any more than I already have. I am certain you will understand."

"What plan? I am to listen to your scheme and commit myself to it before I learn your true identity? What sort of an idiot do you think I am?"

"I do not think you are an idiot at all. Merely extremely difficult," Phoebe retorted. "I would rather you did not know my identity until you have agreed to help me. Once you have given me your oath that you will assist me, I shall feel free to confide in you. Surely you can appreciate my desire for secrecy."

"What the bloody hell is this all about?"

Gabriel had clearly reached the end of his patience. "What is this silly scheme of yours?"

Phoebe gathered herself and took the plunge. "I am involved in a serious and important quest, sir."

"You're after another manuscript?" he asked derisively.

"No. Not a quest for a manuscript. A quest for justice. Your background gives me reason to believe you could be of great service to me."

"Justice? Good God, what is this foolishness? I thought I made it clear I am not interested in playing any more games."

"It is not a game," she explained desperately. "I am trying to find a murderer."

"A *murderer*." There was a stunned silence from Gabriel. "Hell and damnation. I am out here in the middle of the night with a madwoman."

"I am not a madwoman. Please, just listen to me. That is all I ask. I have spent two months trying to gain your attention. Now that you have finally emerged from your cave, surely you can at least hear me out."

"I don't live in a damn cave." He sounded offended.

"You might as well do so, as far as I am concerned. From what I have been able to discover, you stay holed up on your estate like some sort of troglodyte most of the time. You refuse to see anyone or have anything to do with Society."

"That is an overstatement," Gabriel muttered. "I see whom I wish. I happen to like my privacy and I have no love for the Social World. It defeats me why I should explain my habits to you, however."

"Please, sir, I need your help in securing justice for someone who was once very close to me."

"How close?"

Phoebe swallowed. "Well, to be perfectly precise, at one time he wished to marry me. My family was against the match on the grounds that he had no fortune."

"Not an uncommon situation," Gabriel observed grimly.

"I am aware of that. My friend went off to the South Seas to make his fortune so that he could return and ask for my hand. But he never came back. I eventually learned that he was murdered by a pirate."

"Christ. You want me to help you track down a damn pirate? I have news for you. It would be an impossible task. I have spent most of the past eight years in the South Seas and I can assure you that that part of the world has more than its share of murderers."

"You do not understand," Phoebe said. "I have reason to believe the killer has returned to England. At the very least, someone who may know the killer has returned."

"Good lord. How did you come to that conclusion?"

"Before he left to seek his fortune, I gave my friend one of my favorite manuscripts as a keepsake. I know he would never have sold it or given it away. It was all he had to remind him of me."

Gabriel stilled. "A manuscript?"

"A fine copy of *The Lady in the Tower*. Do you know it?"

"Bloody hell."

"You *do* know it." Phoebe was excited now.

"I am aware of the existence of a few copies," Gabriel admitted. "Was yours French, English, or Italian?"

"French. Beautifully illuminated. Even more lovely than *The Knight and the Sorcerer*. The thing is, my lord, I have heard a rumor that the book is back in England. Apparently it is now in someone's personal library."

Gabriel eyed her sharply. "Where did you hear that?"

"From a bookseller in Bond Street. He had it from one of his best customers, who had it from an odd little collector in Yorkshire."

45

"What makes you think it is your copy?"

"The bookseller told me that it is the French version of the tale and that the colophon at the end gives the scribe's name as William of Anjou. My copy was created by him. Sir, I must locate that manuscript."

"You believe that if you find the book, you will find the man who killed your lover?" Gabriel asked softly.

"Yes." Phoebe blushed furiously at hearing Neil described as her lover. But this was not the time to explain that Neil had not been her paramour, but her most virtuous and devoted Lancelot. His love had been pure and noble. He had kept himself always at a chivalrous distance, asking only to serve his lady in the manner of a true knight of old.

The fact that she had never felt more than a warm affection for Neil was one of the reasons she harbored guilt about his death. If she had truly loved him, she would have defied her family to marry him. But she had not loved Neil and Phoebe could not abide the thought of a marriage that was not based on true love.

"What was the name of this man who meant so much to you?"

"Neil Baxter."

Gabriel sat unmoving for several seconds.

"Perhaps the present owner of the book merely happened to purchase it somewhere along the way," Gabriel suggested coldly. "Perhaps he knows nothing about your lover's fate."

Phoebe shook her head firmly. "No, I do not believe that to be the case. You see, Neil wrote to me occasionally after he left England. In one of his letters he mentioned a pirate who was harassing shipping in the islands. He said the man was not a normal sort of villain, but an English gentleman who had turned to piracy and had become the scourge of the South Seas."

"He would not have been the first to do so," Gabriel pointed out dryly.

"My lord, I believe that such a villain would have taken *The Lady in the Tower* as booty after killing Neil."

"And now that there is a rumor the book is back in England, you assume this gentleman pirate has also returned?"

"I think it is very likely. Possibly he has returned with enough stolen loot to set himself up in the Social World. He may even be a member of the *ton*. Just think, sir — who would know he had been a pirate? Everyone would assume he had simply made his fortune in the South Seas as others have and now has returned home."

47

"Your imagination is breathtaking, madam."

Phoebe gritted her teeth. "It seems to me, sir, that you are rather lacking in imagination. My notion is quite plausible. However, even if, as you suggest, the present owner of the book is not the pirate, he might very well know the identity of the pirate. I must find him."

The sound of something large crashing through the underbrush alongside the lane interrupted the rest of Phoebe's hurried explanations.

"What the devil?" Gabriel steadied his stallion as a horse and rider plunged out of the trees and onto the road.

"Stand and deliver," the newcomer roared from behind a mask. A black cloak swirled around him. Moonlight gleamed on the pistol in his fist.

"Bloody hell," Gabriel said wearily. "I knew I should have stayed in bed tonight."

Chapter 3

Gabriel realized at once that the Veiled Lady did not immediately comprehend what was happening. Then she apparently caught the glint of light on the barrel of the pistol in the highwayman's hand.

"What on earth are you about, sir?" the Veiled Lady demanded as if she were dealing with a clumsy servant.

Gabriel hid a quick grin. The lady had more than enough courage to suit a respectable knight-errant. He did not know many females who would have handled a highwayman with such withering scorn. But then, he did not know any females at all who bore the least resemblance to his irritating Veiled Lady.

"Your money or your lives." The highwayman swung the pistol back and forth between Gabriel and his companion. "Be quick about it, now. It'd be just as simple to shoot ye dead and be done with the trouble."

"I only have a few coins with me," the

Veiled Lady announced. "And I am not wearing any jewelry."

"I'll take whatever ye got." The highwayman peered at Gabriel over the edge of his mask. "Expect yer carryin' a pistol somewheres on ye. Take yer coat off and throw it on the ground."

"As you wish." Gabriel shrugged and began to unfasten the greatcoat.

The Veiled Lady was instantly alarmed. "No, you must not remove your coat, my lord. You will catch your death of cold." She turned back to the highwayman. "Please, sir, I pray you. Do not make my friend remove the garment. He has a very weak chest. His doctor has told him he must never go about without a coat on."

Gabriel gave the lady an amused look. "How kind of you to think of my health at this rather tense moment, madam."

"His chest will be a great deal weaker if I put a bullet through it," the highwayman snarled. "Hurry it up, now."

"Wait. You must not take off the coat, my lord," the lady said desperately.

But it was too late. Gabriel was already free of his greatcoat. The manuscript box was revealed beneath his arm.

"Here, now, what's that?" The highwayman urged his mount closer to Gabriel's stallion. "That looks interestin'."

"It's just an old box," the lady said repressively. "Nothing of value. Is that not right, my lord?"

"It is definitely an old box," Gabriel agreed.

"I'll take it." The highwayman held out a hand. "Give it to me."

"Do not dare hand it over to him, Wylde," the lady commanded. "Do you hear me?"

"I hear you." Gabriel handed the box over very carefully. He tossed a few coins on top.

Clearly outraged, the Veiled Lady whirled again to confront the highwayman. "Do not touch it. I demand that you give it back at once. That box belongs to me."

"Well, now, I cannot rightly do that," the highwayman said.

"Stop him, Wylde," the Veiled Lady ordered. "I shall never forgive you if you let him get away with this."

"I pity ye, havin' to put up with that mouth of hers," the highwayman said sympathetically to Gabriel.

"One gets used to it," Gabriel said.

"If ye say so. Well, thank ye very much and good evenin' to ye both. Pleasure doin' business."

The masked man swung his horse around, kicked hard, and sent the beast galloping off down the lane.

The Veiled Lady watched as the highwayman disappeared. Then she rounded on Gabriel. He braced himself for the onslaught. It was obvious she was not pleased with his performance as a knight-errant.

"I do not believe this, sir," she said furiously. "How could you give up my manuscript without so much as a single attempt to defend it?"

Gabriel slanted her a meaningful glance as he dismounted to retrieve his greatcoat. "Would you rather I had let him put a hole in my already weak chest?"

"Of course not. But surely you could have dealt with him. You are a gentleman. You must know about pistols and such. He was nothing but an uncouth highwayman."

"Uncouth highwaymen are capable of pulling the trigger of a pistol just as easily as any gentleman who has trained at Manton's." Gabriel vaulted back into the saddle and collected the reins.

The Veiled Lady groaned in frustration. Gabriel thought he heard her swear under her breath.

"How could you let him just take it like that?" she asked. "I brought you along for protection. You were supposed to be my escort tonight."

"It seems to me I did my job. You are quite safe."

"But he took my manuscript."

"Exactly. *Your* manuscript. Not mine." Gabriel urged his horse forward down the lane. "I learned long ago not to risk my neck fighting for something that does not belong to me. There is no profit in it."

"How dare you, sir? You are certainly not the man I believed you to be."

"Who did you believe me to be?" Gabriel called back over his shoulder.

The lady urged her mare after his stallion. "I thought that the man who wrote *The Quest* would be at least as noble and as valiant as the hero in his book," she yelled.

"Then you are a fool. Chivalry is for novels. I admit it sells well, but it is useless in the real world."

"I am exceedingly disappointed in you, my lord," she announced in ringing accents as her mare drew alongside his stallion. "Apparently everything I believed about you is nothing more than an illusion. You have ruined everything. *Everything.*"

He glanced at her. "What did you expect of me, my Veiled Lady?"

"I expected you to put up a fight. I expected you to protect that manuscript. I did not expect you to give it up so easily. How could you be so cowardly?"

"How badly do you want that manuscript back, madam?"

"Quite badly. I paid a great deal of money for it. But that is the least of my concerns at the moment. What I really need is a genuine knight-errant."

"Very well, I will get the manuscript back for you. When I bring it to you, I will tell you whether or not I will accept your quest."

"What?" She was plainly dumbfounded. At the same time, Gabriel sensed her renewed hope. "You mean you will think about taking on the task of helping me find the pirate who has my copy of *The Lady in the Tower*?"

"I will give the matter my closest consideration. But I must warn you, my Veiled Lady, that if I do undertake the quest and if I am successful, there will be a price."

That news appeared to startle her. "A price?"

"Yes."

"As it happens," she said, sounding disgruntled, "I had intended to give you that book you just handed over to the highwayman, as I'd hinted. It was to be a sort of memento of the quest. If we were successful, that is."

"I'm afraid the price will be a great deal higher than that, madam."

"You expect me to *pay* you to help me bring the villain to justice?" she demanded.

"Why not? When you send a man out on a quest, it is only fair to reward him."

"You should be ashamed of yourself," she shot back. "This is a matter of justice and honor. It is not as though I am asking you to help me find a lost treasure or a cache of jewels."

"Justice and honor are commodities that can be bought and sold just as freely as jewels and gold. I see no reason why I should not be paid for finding them."

She drew a breath. "You are very cynical, my lord."

"I am very practical, madam."

"I see. Very well. If you prefer to do business as a common tradesman rather than as a chivalrous knight, so be it." Her chin came up proudly. "What is the cost of your services?"

"As I do not yet know how much trouble this particular quest will cause me, I cannot set the price in advance. I must wait until the task is completed," Gabriel said.

After weeks of growing fascination with this outrageous female, he was feeling well satisfied with himself at last. He had finally gained the upper hand. A useful advantage, he thought. He would certainly need it, judging by what he had learned of her thus far.

"You will not name your price in advance? That's ridiculous. What if I cannot afford your fee?" she said.

"Never fear. You will be able to afford my price. The question is whether or not you will be honorable enough to pay it. Can I trust you to be true to your word, madam, or will you continue to play your little games?"

She was incensed. "How dare you question my honor, Wylde?"

"You certainly have not hesitated to question mine. You went so far as to call me a coward a few minutes ago."

"That's different," she sputtered.

"Is it? Men have been known to kill each other for less insult. But I am prepared to let bygones be bygones."

"How very decent of you," she got out in a choked voice.

"Do we have a bargain, my Veiled Lady?"

"Yes," she said instantly. "But first you must recover *The Knight and the Sorcerer*. I seriously doubt that you will be able to do so."

"I appreciate your confidence in my knightly prowess."

"That highwayman will be miles away by now with my manuscript." She paused.

"Good heavens, I just realized something."

"What's that?"

"Remember the curse at the end of the book?"

"What about it?" Gabriel asked.

"Well, if I recall correctly, it began with the statement that whoever took the book would be set upon by thieves and murderers. We were definitely set upon by a thief, my lord."

"Who fortunately did not turn into a murderer, thanks to my clever handling of the situation."

"You mean thanks to your ineptitude," she grumbled.

"Whatever you say, madam. In the meantime, you and I must seal our pact." Gabriel drew the stallion to a halt and held out his hand.

The Veiled Lady hesitated and then reluctantly put out her own gloved hand. "Are you really going to think about accepting my quest?"

"Rest assured, I am going to think about little else until I see you again."

"Thank you, my lord," she said stiffly. "If you are indeed serious, you cannot know how much this means to me."

"Perhaps you should demonstrate the extent of your gratitude." Gabriel's fingers closed around hers.

Instead of clasping her hand in a ritual handshake, however, he used his grip to pull her close. Before she realized his intent, he lifted the veil of her hat, exposing her startled features to the pale glow of the moon.

The lady gasped and then froze in stunned shock.

Gabriel raked the upturned face of his sweet tormentor with the fierce curiosity that had been burning within him for weeks. The need to know her identity had become as powerful a force as any physical desire. It had been growing steadily since he had opened the first letter from her.

One glance at the elegant handwriting and he had not needed the cryptic signature of the Veiled Lady to recognize that he was dealing with a female. And a very reckless, impulsive one at that. Which was why he had bided his time, allowing her to make all the initial moves.

Gabriel took pride in the iron control he had become skilled at exerting over his own passions during the past eight years. He had learned his lessons the hard way, but he had learned them well. He was no longer the naive, idealistic man he had been in his youth.

It had taken all of his control to restrain himself during the past two months, however.

It seemed to him that the Veiled Lady had been deliberately attempting to drive him mad. She had very nearly succeeded. He had become obsessed with discovering her identity.

He had pored over the handful of tantalizing letters he had received from her as intently as he had ever studied any of his precious medieval manuscripts. The only certainty he had been able to glean from them was the knowledge that the Veiled Lady was as well versed in chivalric lore as he was.

Her uncanny ability to predict his taste in books had almost persuaded Gabriel that he must have met her at some time in the past.

But tonight as he looked at her in the glow of the moon, he realized that she was a stranger. She was a woman of mystery, as enthralling as the rare, exotic dark pearls that were found in the secret lagoons of the South Seas.

Her skin was the color of rich cream in the silvery light. She stared up at him, her soft, full lips parted in startled surprise. He had a glimpse of a bold, aristocratic little nose, fine cheekbones, and huge, astonished eyes. He wished that he could see the color of those eyes.

She was a striking woman, not merely a

pretty one. The strong lines of her nose and chin saved her from the kind of weak, passive beauty that Gabriel associated with weak, passive females. He liked the feel of her, he realized. She was small and sleek and shimmering with feminine energy.

At Nash's cottage he had been able to see the color of her hair. Drawn back in a neat chignon beneath her veiled hat, the glossy dark stuff appeared a deep brown that was almost black. The candlelight had revealed intense dark red highlights in it. Gabriel had experienced an almost overpowering need to see those tresses loose around her shoulders.

He could not quite believe he finally had his hands on his Veiled Lady. As he gazed down at her, all the strong emotions she had aroused in him crystallized into a white-hot desire. He wanted her.

Even as anger began to replace the astonished shock on her face, Gabriel bent his head and took her mouth.

In the beginning he did not ask for a response. The kiss was hard and commanding in retribution for all the trouble she had caused him. Then her lips trembled and he felt the shiver of fear that went through her entire body.

Gabriel hesitated for an instant, nonplussed by her panicky reaction to his kiss. She was not a child. The chit appeared to be in her early twenties and she had been deliberately challenging him. Furthermore, she had apparently been one of Neil Baxter's paramours. Baxter had been a master at seduction. Even Honora Ralston, Gabriel's fiancée in the South Seas, had succumbed to Baxter's lures and lies.

But whatever else she was, it was immediately obvious the mysterious Veiled Lady was not the accomplished flirt he had assumed from the start. She had goaded him into kissing her, yet she seemed completely disconcerted by the response she had drawn.

Gabriel's curiosity, already straining at the leash, broke free of the last vestiges of his self-control. He suddenly needed to know if he could make her respond to him.

He softened the kiss, sliding the edge of his tongue along her lower lip, urging her to open her mouth. He wanted to taste her more than he had wanted anything in a very long time.

He knew the instant the feminine fear in her dissolved beneath a wave of desire. The Veiled Lady made an achingly sweet, soft sound against his mouth. Gabriel swallowed up the tremulous cry as if he were a starving man being offered food. He immediately craved more.

A deep satisfaction flared in him as he felt the undeniable stirring within her. She trembled. Her free hand was on his shoulder now, clutching at the heavy wool of his greatcoat. He felt her lean forward as if she wanted to be closer to him.

The hint of passion in his Veiled Lady sent a shudder of heightened desire through Gabriel. His own body was throbbing with an urgent need to possess her. He had definitely been too long without a woman. His arm tightened around her.

"My lord?" She sounded dazed.

"There is a chill in the night air," Gabriel muttered hoarsely against her throat. "But I vow that when I lay you down on the ground over there in the woods, you will soon be warm enough. I shall use my coat to make a bed for us, my Veiled Lady."

In the blink of an eye the spell was broken. The Veiled Lady shuddered as if she had been burned. Suddenly she was pushing at him, trying to wrench herself free of his grasp.

Gabriel fought a battle with his clamoring senses and won. He reluctantly released the lady. With a muffled exclamation, she sat back, grabbed at her veil with fumbling fingers, and lowered it hastily. He could hear her unsteady breathing. The knowledge that her nerves and passions were unsettled gave him some satisfaction.

"You had no right to do that, sir," she whispered in almost inaudible tones. "That was most unchivalrous. How could you be so ungallant? I thought you an honorable man."

Gabriel smiled. "You seem to have acquired some very odd notions of my sense of chivalry based on your reading of *The Quest*. It goes to show the critics are right, I suppose. Young ladies should be prevented from reading tales of that sort. Their emotional natures are too easily influenced."

"Rubbish. You are deliberately trying to provoke me." The strength was returning rapidly to her voice now. This was not a woman who was easily overset.

"You have been deliberately provoking me for the past several weeks," he reminded her. "I have already told you that I'm extremely annoyed with you, madam."

"You do not understand," she wailed. "I was trying to capture your interest, not make you angry. I thought you would enjoy the adventure of it all. It was the sort of mystery the hero of your book would have enjoyed."

"The hero of *The Quest* is a much younger man than I am," Gabriel said. "He still has a decidedly unhealthy amount of knightly idealism and youthful naïveté."

"Well, I like him that way," the Veiled Lady flung back. "He is much nicer than you are, that is for certain. Oh, never mind. It has all gone wrong. I regret I ever embarked on this stupid venture. What a disaster it has been. A complete and utter waste of time. I do not even have *The Knight and the Sorcerer* to show for all my efforts."

"The next time I see you," Gabriel said softly, "I shall return your manuscript and give you my decision concerning your quest."

The Veiled Lady urged her mare away from Gabriel's stallion. "You do not know who I am. You will not be able to find me."

"I shall find you." He knew even as he spoke the words that he was making a vow to himself and to her. Tonight's venture had done nothing to satisfy his curiosity about the Veiled Lady. Indeed, it had only whetted his appetite. He had never met a woman like her and he knew now that he would not be content until he had possessed her. "It is you who began this business, madam, but be assured that I am the one who will end it."

"I am convinced you have already ended it," she said bleakly. "I must tell you again that you are a grave disappointment thus far, my lord."

"I am, of course, stricken to hear that."

"It is not amusing, damn you." The Veiled Lady struggled to calm her mare. The beast was reacting nervously to the emotion in her rider's voice. "I do not know why I ever started this."

"Neither do I," Gabriel said. "Why don't you try explaining it to me?"

"I thought you were another sort of man altogether," the Veiled Lady said accusingly. "I thought you were a true knight who understood about things like quests. You may recall that when I first wrote to you, I mentioned the possibility of an important venture. But you were completely unresponsive to my initial inquiries."

"Hardly surprising, considering all I had were a couple of cryptic letters from an unknown woman who asked me if I wanted to play knight-errant. When I ignored those, I found myself dueling with the lady for every medieval romance I wished to acquire. The entire experience was extremely irritating."

"I told you, I wanted to create a mystery that you would wish to solve."

"You achieved your goal, madam. But the mystery is still not entirely solved, even though I have seen your face. I don't know your name."

"And you are never going to discover it," she assured him. "I am finished with this nonsense. I shall pursue my quest by myself. I find I do not need or want your help, after all. Good night, my lord. I apologize for bringing you out at midnight on a fool's errand."

The Veiled Lady abruptly gave a signal to her mare. The horse leaped forward at full gallop and tore off down the moonlit lane.

Gabriel waited a moment before following at a more sedate pace. He could hear the mare's hoofbeats pounding away in the distance, but he made no effort to catch up to his quarry. He did not want to overtake her, but merely keep track of her until she was safely home. He had a fairly good notion now of where she was going.

A few minutes later he rounded a bend in the lane and saw that his hunch was correct. He sat watching from the shadows as the Veiled Lady and her mare turned into the drive of the massive country house belonging to Lord and Lady Amesbury.

From the number of carriages in the lane, it was apparent the Amesburys were holding one of their famous house parties this week-end. Music and light poured from the open windows of the great house. Lady Amesbury never invited less than a hundred guests to her affairs.

It was obvious his Veiled Lady had slipped unseen away from the ball to keep her midnight rendezvous. It would have been easy enough to do in that crowd, Gabriel thought. Most of the guests were no doubt roaring drunk by now. She would not be missed.

It was clear that there was no simple way to learn the identity of the Veiled Lady by finding out who had attended the ball tonight, Gabriel realized. The guest list would include a number of the important people of the *ton* and most of the local gentry.

Gabriel was not disappointed. There were other ways of learning the name of the lady. But first he had to attend to the small matter of recovering *The Knight and the Sorcerer*. He turned his stallion around and cantered back up the lane.

Chapter 4

Twenty minutes later he brought the stallion to a halt in the trees near Nash's cottage. He was not surprised to see that a light still burned in the window.

He secured the stallion to a branch and made his way through the woods to the small barn at the rear of the cottage. When he opened the barn door, a horse whickered softly in the darkness. He saw the vague outline of an equine head as it turned toward him.

"Easy, lad." Gabriel left the door open so that a shaft of moonlight lit the interior of the barn. He walked over to the stall. The horse blew softly and thrust its head out over the gate.

"You've had a busy night of it, haven't you?" Gabriel took off his glove and stroked the horse's damp neck and shoulder. "You're still warm from that last gallop. How do you like being a highwayman's nag? Lots of excitement in the job, I imagine."

Gabriel gave the animal's neck a last pat

and then made his way back out of the barn. As he walked toward the rear door of the cottage, he removed the pistol from the pocket of his coat.

He was mildly surprised to find the door unbarred. The highwayman had evidently been in a hurry when he had returned from his business on the road. Gabriel opened the door and stepped into the kitchen.

Mrs. Stiles was at the sink. She whirled around in shock at the sound of the door. Her eyes widened in recognition and then her mouth opened on a scream.

"Hush. Not a word, if you please, Mrs. Stiles." Gabriel did not bother to point the pistol at her. He held it quietly at his side. "I merely wish a few words with your master. You needn't bother with tea. I will not be staying long."

Mrs. Stiles's lips snapped shut. "I knew no good would come of this mad scheme. Told him so meself."

"Yes. Well, now I am going to tell him the same thing. We shall see if my advice makes a more lasting impression."

Mrs. Stiles gave him a beseeching look. "Ye won't have the master arrested, will ye? He only did it on account of he needs the money and he cannot bear to part with those books of his. If they send him to prison,

I don't know what I'll do. Work is hard to come by in these parts. Mr. Nash don't always pay me my wages, but there's plenty to eat and he lets me take some home to me family."

"Do not concern yourself, Mrs. Stiles. I have no intention of putting you out of work. Is Nash still in the parlor?"

"Yes, sir." Mrs. Stiles's hands twisted in the folds of her apron. "Are you certain you don't plan to have him arrested?"

"Reasonably certain. I understand Mr. Nash's dilemma and I sympathize. Still, I cannot allow him to get away with his little scheme in this instance. The lady was most upset."

Mrs. Stiles sighed. "I cannot see why the lot of ye bookish types set so much store by them old manuscripts and such. Nothin' but useless trash, if ye ask me. Waste of time readin' and collectin' them dirty things."

"The desire to collect old books is difficult to explain," Gabriel admitted. "I suspect it is an affliction of sorts."

"Too bad there ain't a remedy."

"Perhaps. On the other hand, it is not an unpleasant ailment."

Convinced that the housekeeper was going to stay out of the matter, Gabriel nodded politely to her and made his way down the hall. The door of the parlor was closed, but he could hear loud voices from inside the room. The first voice was that of an irate young man.

"Damnation, Pa, I did it just like we planned it. Just like we did it the last time. How was I to know she'd have that big cove with her? What does it matter, anyhow? He didn't give me any trouble."

"Ye should've backed off when ye saw there was a gentleman with her," Nash growled back in response.

"I told ye, he didn't even put up a fight." There was a snort of derision. "Handed the damn box over as nice as ye please. It was the lady I was worryin' about. I swear, if she'd had a pistol, I'd have been done for. Stop frettin', Pa. We got the manuscript and the money the lady paid for it."

"I cannot help but fret," Nash retorted. "I did not like the looks of that gentleman who accompanied the lady. Something about him made me uneasy. Strange eyes. Green as emeralds, they were. And just as cold. Had a dangerous look to 'em. Never saw a man with eyes like that."

"Calm yourself, Pa. I told ye, he wasn't a problem."

Gabriel opened the door quietly. Nash was seated at his desk, his head in his hands. A thickset young man with heavy features was striding angrily back and forth across the small space left between aisles of books. A dashing black cape lay across a chair.

"I fear I am going to be something of a problem, after all," Gabriel said gently. He kept the pistol at his side, visible but not overtly threatening.

Both men whirled to face him. The young man's expression was one of dawning horror. Mr. Nash, after a brief start, looked gloomily resigned to his fate.

The young man recovered rapidly. "Here, now, what do ye mean by walkin' in on us without so much as a by yer leave? This is trespassin'. I'll have ye taken up by the magistrate for this."

Gabriel glanced at him without much interest. "You must be Egan. The helpful son who sees to things around here."

Egan's eyes bulged. "How did ye know that?"

"Never mind." Gabriel looked at Nash. "How often have you played this particular trick?"

"This was only the second time." Nash sighed wearily. "Worked bloody well the first time."

"So you decided to try it again."

"Had to." Nash gestured with his hand. "Out of money, ye see. And there's a book-

72

seller I know who's offering an absolutely splendid copy of Guido delle Colonne's *Historia Trojana*. What could I do? I was desperate."

"I see your point," Gabriel said. "And I quite understand. Naturally you did not wish to part with a rather choice item from your own collection in order to finance the new purchase, if you could avoid it."

Nash's eyes flickered. "I knew when I saw you with the lady that there was going to be trouble."

"A bit," Gabriel conceded. "But if it's any consolation to you, I have been put to a great deal more trouble than you have. In fact, I have come to the conclusion that the lady is nothing but trouble."

"Right fierce little thing," Egan muttered. "Worried me, the way she kept badgering you to put up a fight."

"It worried me, too." Gabriel glanced at the box on Nash's desk. "I congratulate you on your scheme, gentlemen. Unfortunately, you picked the wrong victim this time. I really must insist that the lady's manuscript be returned. She is desolate at its loss. Surely you can understand."

"I suppose yer goin' to summon the magistrate?" Nash said.

"I see no reason to go to extremes." Gabriel

walked forward and picked up the box. He kept the pistol in full view. "I shall be content as long as I get what I want."

"Well, you've got it," Nash muttered. "Take yerself off."

"There's one more thing," Gabriel murmured.

Nash glowered at him. "If ye want the lady's money back, yer too late. She paid in advance and I already sent off an order to that bookseller I told ye about."

"You're welcome to keep the money," Gabriel assured him. "What I want is the name and direction of the lady."

"Huh?" Egan stared at him. "Ye don't know her? But ye was with her."

"She is something of a mystery, I'm afraid. I was only along to protect her and the manuscript. She did not tell me her name."

"Bloody hell." Egan looked amazed.

Nash frowned. "Can't help ye. Don't know her name."

Gabriel eyed him intently. "She corresponded with you regarding the purchase of this manuscript. And she sent you a draft on her account to pay for it. You must know who she is."

Nash shook his head. "All the correspondence was through a solicitor. He deposited the funds at my bank. I never dealt with the lady direct until she showed up here tonight."

"I see." Gabriel smiled. "The name of her solicitor will do, then."

Nash shrugged. Then he opened a desk drawer and pulled out a letter. "This is the last message I had from him. Said to expect her tonight. Man's name is Peak."

Gabriel glanced at the London address. "This will do. My thanks, sir. And now you must excuse me. I have a great deal of work ahead of me."

"Work?" Egan looked more alarmed than ever. "What work? Are ye goin' to summon the magistrate, after all?"

"No, I have a far more pressing task awaiting me." Gabriel placed the letter carefully in his pocket as he strode toward the door. "Like it or not, I appear to be involved in a quest."

Five days later Gabriel sat alone in the tower room he used for his writing. His right shoulder ached, but that was not unusual when he sat at his work for extended periods of time. The old wound sometimes reacted to damp weather and the strain of long bouts of writing.

The important thing was that the words were flowing freely this morning. His second novel, which he had titled *A Reckless Venture,* was taking shape nicely. His pen moved across the foolscap with easy assurance as he sent his latest hero into combat against an evil villain. At stake was a magnificent inheritance and the love of a fair maiden.

In the tales Gabriel wrote, the fair maiden always went to the noble fool who was naive enough to fight for her.

Gabriel was well aware that in real life things seldom worked out that way. A man who trusted in the promises of a fair maiden was an idiot.

He had learned long ago that money, a title, and social standing were far more important assets than a noble heart and a chivalrous nature for a man who was hoping to interest a fair or even an unfair maiden. The beautiful Meredith Layton, daughter of the brilliant, powerful Earl of Clarington, had taught him that. He had never forgotten the lesson.

The earl had punished Gabriel very thoroughly for the crime of attempting to save Meredith from an arranged marriage to the Marquess of Trowbridge. Within days after the ill-fated rescue attempt, Clarington had set about destroying Gabriel financially.

The men Gabriel had convinced to back him in a small but potentially lucrative shipping venture mysteriously reneged on their agreements after Clarington spoke to them. They demanded that the money be repaid immediately. At the same time, the loan that Gabriel had obtained to finance the purchase of some London property suddenly came due early. Clarington had advised the investor to withdraw.

The combined effect had been disastrous. Gabriel had been forced to sell off virtually everything he owned, including his beloved books, in order to repay his debts. In the end he had been left with barely enough money to purchase passage on board a ship bound for the South Seas.

Knowing that there was no future for him in England, Gabriel had sailed for the islands where a man could dream new dreams.

He took a grim satisfaction now in knowing that he had spent the past eight years ridding himself of such unnecessary encumbrances as a noble heart and a chivalrous nature. Vowing he would never again be at the mercy of his own emotions, he had sweated blood to secure a fortune in the South Seas pearl trade, and he had been extraordinarily successful. The venture had nearly cost him his life on more than one occasion, but he had survived and flourished.

While in the islands he had encountered

the aggressive, ambitious Americans, whose ships now traded in every corner of the globe. Using those contacts, he had built a shipping empire. His vessels now routinely plied the trade routes between England and America.

During his time in the South Seas Gabriel's lessons in reality had continued. He had learned that illusion was the rule, not the exception in the real world. People were rarely what they seemed and few men honored the code of conduct that had governed the fictional knights of King Arthur's court.

The real world, Gabriel had discovered, was a place where cutthroats masqueraded as gentlemen and women betrayed the men they had sworn to love.

Survival amid such perils required ice in one's veins and realistic expectations of human nature. Only a fool put his trust in others. And an intelligent man did not make the mistake of putting either his trust or his honor, let alone his heart, into a woman's hands. A man who intended to survive in the real world had to be cautious.

But that did not mean he could not enjoy what pleasures the world had to offer. As long as he kept his heart and his emotions out of the matter, Gabriel reasoned, he could allow himself a harmless dalliance with an intriguing woman such as the Veiled Lady.

He could even allow himself a wife.

In fact, a wife was a necessity.

Gabriel frowned at the thought. It was true that one of these days he must marry, not only because of his duty to the title, but because he had grown weary of his self-imposed solitude. He needed a woman to bear his heirs and warm his bed. He wanted someone to talk to in the evenings.

But he saw no reason why he could not manage a wife with the same coolheaded, detached approach that he would use with a mistress.

A vision of the Veiled Lady as both mistress and wife stole into Gabriel's head and wrapped itself around his thoughts. He put down his pen and gazed unseeingly out the tower window.

The Veiled Lady as his wife? Gabriel's mouth twisted wryly even as he felt the stirring in his groin. It was a crazed notion. He could not possibly consider making one of Baxter's castoffs the Countess of Wylde. A man in Gabriel's position was expected to marry a woman with an unblemished reputation. A virgin.

But virgins were no more trustworthy than experienced ladies of the night, Gabriel knew. Thus, virginity would not be the chief criteria he would use when it came time to select a wife. There were other, more important assets to look for in a woman.

The Veiled Lady did not meet those criteria, either.

Gabriel had decided long ago that when he eventually chose a wife, he would take care to select a biddable female, one who would respect a husband's authority.

A woman who had been raised to honor a man's right to be master in his own home would be more manageable than an independent, reckless hoyden such as the Veiled Lady. A woman who had been brought up with proper notions of female duty would be easier to protect from the risks and temptations of the world.

Even if he managed to find that pearl among women, a manageable, obedient female, Gabriel knew he would always remain cautious. He might indulge her, but he would certainly never make the mistake of trusting her completely.

When it came to dealing with females, he had concluded, it was better to be safe than sorry. An ounce of prevention was worth a pound of cure.

The matter of choosing a wife was a problem to be dealt with in the future, however. Gabriel turned his thoughts back to the Veiled Lady. Locating her was his first priority.

Unfortunately, finding the Veiled Lady meant going into Society. Gabriel swore at the thought. He did not much care for the Social World. He had not bothered to go into Society since his return to England a few months ago.

But the Veiled Lady obviously moved in the best circles of the *ton*. If he was going to hunt her, he, too, would have to go into the world of the Haute Monde.

Gabriel allowed himself a slow smile as he envisioned the expression on the Veiled Lady's face when she realized he had pursued her into the heart of the Social World. The huntress was about to become the hunted.

He got to his feet and stretched, working out the stiffness in his muscles. He rubbed his right shoulder absently with his left hand. He had been at work since shortly after dawn and it was now nearly eleven. He needed a long walk along the cliffs.

His gaze fell on the manuscript box he had collected from Nash. The sight of it sitting on a nearby table amid a stack of papers and books made him grin with anticipation. Soon he would have the pleasure of returning *The Knight and the Sorcerer* to its owner.

And then he would tell her that he would accept her quest. He had no interest in helping her discover Baxter's killer, but he definitely wanted the lady. He freely admitted to himself that her reckless, daring ways intrigued and fascinated him even as he condemned them. Perhaps it was his fate as a lover of ancient legends to respond to a woman whose bold manner bespoke a courage that was both rare and dangerous in females. A troubadour could have created a very interesting legend based on the Veiled Lady.

Whatever the reason for his compelling desire for her, it was clear that the only way to obtain the lady was to pretend to become involved in her mad scheme. It was bound to be an interesting task, to say the least.

After all, he already knew who owned the manuscript of *The Lady in the Tower* she sought. The trick would be to keep her from discovering that fact while he lured her into his bed.

Gabriel paused beside a row of bookcases that contained some of the most interesting items in his collection. He opened the glass doors, reached inside, and removed a volume bound in thickly padded leather.

He carried the surprisingly heavy book over to the desk. There he put it down carefully and undid the tiny lock that secured the thick covers around the gilded vellum pages.

He opened the book carefully and turned to the last page.

For a moment he stood gazing thoughtfully down at the colophon, which was in Old French:

Here ends the tale of The Lady in the Tower. I, William of Anjou, have written only the truth. A curse on he who would steal this book. May he drown beneath the waves. May he be consumed by flames. May he spend an eternal night in hell.

Gabriel closed *The Lady in the Tower* very carefully and put it back in the case. The game he intended to play with his Veiled Lady was not without its risks. He wondered how she could have ever thought herself in love with Neil Baxter.

She must still care a great deal for the bastard, Gabriel reflected with a frown. That was unfortunate. Baxter had not been worthy of such a spirited female.

But Baxter had had a way with women, as Gabriel knew to his cost.

He decided his initial goal would be to make the Veiled Lady forget her previous lover. Gabriel looked forward to the challenge.

He let himself out of the small tower room

and went down the narrow spiral staircase. His booted heels rang on the old stone.

He was aware of a chill in the empty rooms of the third floor as he walked down the hall. It was almost impossible to keep Devil's Mist properly heated. When the castle had been built, the comfort of its occupants had not been a high priority. There was no getting around the fact that Gabriel had a monstrosity of a house on his hands. Refurbishing it would take years.

He consoled himself with the knowledge that at least there was plenty of room for his books. There was also room to house his father's magnificent library, which Gabriel was in the process of rebuilding. And the castle certainly provided a suitable setting for his growing assortment of medieval armor.

Nevertheless, the devil alone knew why he had succumbed to the whim that had made him buy the crumbling pile of stone here on the Sussex coast. The place was huge and he had no one to share it with except the members of his staff.

Not that being alone was anything new to Gabriel. He had spent most of his life alone. His father had been a brilliant scholar who, after the death of Gabriel's mother, had devoted himself to the treasures in his library. He had been kind enough in his fashion, but there was little doubt but that he had preferred his books to the task of rearing a motherless son.

Left to his own devices and the care of servants, Gabriel had learned early to create his own private world. He had done so from the age of five, populating it with a cast of characters from the Arthurian legends. When he had devoured all the tales he could find that dealt with the glories of ancient knighthood, he had begun writing his own.

He had not kept any of his childish scribblings. They had been disposed of along with most of the rest of his worldly possessions when he had left England. But two years ago, when he had decided to make a serious attempt to write a real novel, he had recalled those early efforts.

The knights of the Round Table had been good company for a young man. Unfortunately, they had not been able to teach him life's hard, realistic lessons. Those he had been forced to learn on his own.

Gabriel had purchased Devil's Mist shortly after returning to England. Something about the magnificent towers, turrets, and ramparts had appealed to him. When he looked out of the narrow windows, he could almost see knights in full battle armor mounted on huge destriers riding through the massive gates.

Devil's Mist was not a rich man's architectural folly, like so many other grand houses. Built in the thirteenth century, it had once been a working castle whose lord had apparently had a taste for secret passages and doors that were operated by hidden mechanisms. After taking up residence, Gabriel had spent weeks exploring the catacombs beneath the castle. The project had given him much inspiration for his newest novel.

Gabriel went down another twisting flight of stone steps and strode into the vast hall. Rollins, the butler, materialized from a side door.

"My lord, the post has arrived." The salver Rollins held out with grave formality contained only a single letter. Devil's Mist did not receive a great deal of mail. Most of the letters recently had been from the Veiled Lady.

Gabriel paused beneath a particularly fine thirteenth century battle shield that was one of several hanging from the hall ceiling. "Thank you, Rollins. I'll read it on my walk."

"Very good, sir." Rollins turned and moved off between two stately rows of highly polished armor suits. At the far end of the hall he opened the huge doors.

The motto carved into the stone over the doors had not been there when Gabriel had purchased the castle. He had ordered it engraved shortly after moving into Devil's Mist. Gabriel was rather pleased with it. It was succinct and to the point.

AUDEO. Latin for "I dare."

It was not the traditional motto of the earls of Wylde. There was no traditional Wylde motto. Gabriel had invented this one for himself and for his heirs. Now that the title had come to his side of the family, he had every intention of keeping it there.

It occurred to him that whatever else might be said about the Veiled Lady, she certainly suited the Wylde motto.

Gabriel examined the letter he had received as he walked out the door. A flicker of excitement coursed through him. It was from his London solicitor. With any luck it would contain the information for which he had been waiting.

The world of solicitors was a small one and money talked loudly in it, just as it talked in every other world. Gabriel had been certain his man would know Peak, the solicitor who handled the affairs of the Veiled Lady. There could not be that many women in London who collected medieval books.

He tore open the letter as he went down the stone steps and out into the chilly April sunshine. The name that leaped off the carefully penned page made him stop short. He stood gazing down at it in a gathering fury.

Lady Phoebe Layton, youngest daughter of the Earl of Clarington.

"Hell and damnation." Gabriel could not believe his eyes. Rage poured through him. His mysterious, illusive, fascinating Veiled Lady was none other than Clarington's youngest chit.

Gabriel crumpled the letter savagely in his fist.

The youngest daughter. Not the one who had begged him to save her from an arranged marriage eight years ago. Not the one who had nearly gotten him killed in a duel with her brother. *The other one.* The one he had never met because she had still been in the schoolroom at the time.

She would have been no more than sixteen when Clarington had destroyed Gabriel financially and forced him out of England. She would have been a mere girl when Gabriel had been forced to sell off the contents of his father's library, the only legacy he had from his parent, in order to survive.

Eight years ago. The Veiled Lady was not more than twenty-four at the most. Yes, it all fit.

"Bloody hell," Gabriel said through his

teeth. He stalked across the courtyard and out through the old stone gate. Another Clarington chit. As if he had not already had enough of Clarington women to last him a lifetime.

She had a hell of a nerve playing her games with him, he thought. Did she assume she could follow in her sister's footsteps? Did she believe she could safely amuse herself with him?

"Damnation."

Gabriel paced to the edge of the cliffs and stood gazing down into the churning sea. The desire that had burned in him for the Veiled Lady was as hot as ever. He would have her, he promised himself. Yes, he would definitely have her. But on his own terms.

How did she dare try her wiles on him after what her family had done to him? he wondered. Was she really so reckless or so arrogant? The frustration and fury he had felt eight years ago roared back into life as if it had all happened yesterday.

But it had not happened yesterday, he thought grimly. He was not the same idealistic, penniless fool he had been then. Lady Phoebe's father could not protect her this time the way he had protected his other daughter eight years ago.

The Veiled Lady was more vulnerable than

she could have possibly imagined. *And so was her family.*

The wealth Gabriel had brought back with him from the South Seas was more than a match for the Clarington fortune. And that wealth was now coupled to a title that was the equal of Clarington's. With that kind of fortune and status came power. Great power.

Of course, Gabriel reminded himself suddenly, the Veiled Lady had no inkling of just how wealthy he was. No one knew him or anything about him. He was as anonymous to the Social World as he was to the readers of his novel.

Lady Phoebe Layton wanted his assistance on a quest. Gabriel's hand closed into a fist. Very well, she would have it. And the price she would pay for his services would be high, indeed.

He would use her to punish Clarington for everything that had happened eight years ago.

Chapter 5

The Marchioness of Trowbridge set a delicate stitch in the hem of a little muslin dress. "You need not be quite so cool with Lord Kilbourne, you know, Phoebe. I am certain he is going to offer for you soon. You may give him some encouragement now without fear of anyone thinking you overbold."

Phoebe poured another cup of tea and made a face. Her sister did not notice. Meredith was too busy concentrating on the flower she was embroidering onto her daughter's tiny gown.

It occurred to Phoebe, not for the first time, that anyone looking at Meredith saw a paragon of wifehood and motherhood. It was not an illusion. Meredith was a paragon. But few people outside the immediate circle of her family were aware of the amazing talent for business and financial matters that lay beneath the breathtakingly perfect surface. In addition to being a devoted wife and mother, she was an active advisor to her husband in his many investments.

An inclination for such matters was a common trait in Phoebe's family. Her father, the earl, was a mathematician who loved to apply his principles to both his investments and his scientific experiments. Her brother, Anthony, Viscount Oaksley, had inherited his father's abilities. He now ran the Clarington empire, freeing the earl to concentrate on his experiments.

Phoebe's mother, Lydia, Lady Clarington, was also skilled with numbers. But unlike the others, she preferred to apply her talents at the card tables of her friends. Most of the time she won. Occasionally, however, she did not. In either event she was careful to keep her lord uninformed about her activities. Clarington would have been shocked to know of his wife's predilection for games of chance.

Phoebe, the youngest in the family, was the only one who had not shown any ability in the fields of mathematics or investments. Early on it had become obvious to everyone including Phoebe that she had not inherited the family talents.

The others loved her dearly, but they did not know quite what to make of her. She was different, and that difference frequently baffled everyone except her mother, who generally seemed unfazed by Phoebe's ways.

Phoebe was the changeling in the family. The others reached conclusions based on logic. Phoebe used intuition. She read novels while the others studied the stock exchange summaries in *The Gentleman's Magazine*. She was reckless where the others were cautious. She was enthusiastic where the others were wary. She was eager where the others tended to be disinterested or disapproving. And she was, of course, the youngest.

The result had been an overprotective attitude toward Phoebe from everyone else in the family except her mother. They all spent a great deal of time fretting about her impulsive ways. That attitude had intensified after the carriage accident that had left her with a badly injured leg.

The accident had occurred because of Phoebe's reckless attempt to save a puppy from being crushed by the vehicle. It was Phoebe, not the pup, who had ended up beneath the carriage wheels.

The doctors had gravely informed Clarington that his youngest child would never walk again. The family had been devastated. Everyone had hovered. Everyone had worried. Everyone had tried to keep eight-year-old Phoebe confined to a sickroom.

Phoebe, being Phoebe, had resisted the efforts to turn her into an invalid. She had defied the doctors by secretly teaching herself to walk again. To this day she still remembered the pain of those first tottering steps. Only her determination not to be bedridden for the rest of her life had made the effort possible. Her family, unfortunately, had never quite recovered from the shock of the accident. For them it was only one incident, albeit the most memorable, in a series of incidents that proved Phoebe needed to be protected from her reckless ways.

"I do not want Kilbourne to offer for me," Phoebe said. She propped her slippered feet on a small footstool and absently massaged her left leg, which was a bit sore from riding that morning.

"Nonsense. Of course you want him to offer for you." Meredith set another stitch. She was two years older than Phoebe and the two were as opposite in both appearance and temperament as night and day. Blond, blue-eyed, and as dainty as a piece of fine porcelain, Meredith had once been a shy, timid creature who had quaked at the thought of the intimate embrace she would encounter in the marriage bed.

Years ago when she had been on the brink of her debut into Society, Meredith had confided quite seriously to Phoebe that she wished to take religious vows in order to escape the demands of a husband. Phoebe had agreed that joining a holy order might be quite interesting, provided one got to live in an ancient, haunted abbey. The notion of encountering a few genuine ghosts had a certain appeal.

It was just as well Meredith had not followed her religious inclinations, Phoebe decided. Marriage had been good for her. Today Meredith was a cheerful, contented woman who reveled in the adoration of her indulgent husband, the Marquess of Trowbridge, and the love of her three healthy children.

"I'm serious, Meredith. I do not wish to marry Kilbourne."

Meredith looked up, her crystal-clear blue eyes wide in surprise. "Good heavens. What on earth are you saying? He's the fourth in the direct line. And the Kilbourne fortune is at least as large as Trowbridge's. Certainly it is equal to Papa's. Mama is so thrilled at the possibilities."

"I know." Phoebe sipped her tea and gazed gloomily at the magnificently stitched hunt scene on the wall. "It will be a coup for her if Kilbourne makes an offer. She will have another wealthy son-in-law to act as a private banker for her on those occasions when her luck runs low at the card tables."

"Well, we both know she can hardly ask Papa to cover her debts of honor. He would never approve of her gaming. And you and I cannot continue to go to her rescue. Our allowances are not large enough to cover some of her losses." Meredith sighed. "I do wish she were not quite so enamored of cards."

"She usually wins."

"Yes, but not always."

"Even the most skilled of gamesters has a bit of bad luck now and then." Phoebe was inclined to be far more sympathetic with her mother's enthusiasm for gaming than Meredith was. From her own experience in the world of rare books, Phoebe understood what it was to be cursed with expensive passions.

Meredith bit her lip. "I fear Trowbridge was a little impatient the last time I asked him to oblige her."

Phoebe smiled ruefully. "Hence Mama's fervent wish to marry me off to Kilbourne. Poor man. He has not the least notion of what he is attempting to take on. Perhaps I should tell him about Mama's weakness for gaming before he makes his offer."

"Don't you dare."

Phoebe sighed. "I had hoped Mama and Papa had quite given up on getting me married off. I am getting rather advanced in years."

"Nonsense. Twenty-four is not so very old."

"Be honest, Meredith. I am dangerously close to twenty-five and you and I both know that the only reason I'm still attracting the occasional offer at my age is due entirely to the size of my inheritance."

"Well, you cannot accuse Lord Kilbourne of being interested in you solely because of your fortune. He has estates scattered from Hampshire to Cornwall. He does not need to marry for money."

"Ah-hah. So why is he interested in me when he can have his pick of the new crop of beauties available this Season?" Phoebe demanded.

She pictured Kilbourne in her mind, studying the image closely in an effort to decide just why she was not particularly attracted to him.

Kilbourne was tall and distinguished with cool gray eyes and light brown hair. She had to admit he was handsome in an aloof, dignified manner. Given his stature in the *ton*, he was a catch any ambitious mama would relish. He was also a crashing bore.

"Perhaps he has developed a *tendre* for you, Phoebe."

"I fail to see why. It is not as though we

have a lot in common."

"Of course you do." Meredith selected new thread and started a leaf on the flower she was embroidering. "You both come from good families, you both move in the best circles, and you both have respectable fortunes. What's more, he is of a proper age for you."

Phoebe cocked a brow. "He's forty-one."

"As I said, a proper age. You need someone older and more stable than yourself, Phoebe. Someone who can provide you with mature guidance. You know very well that there are too many occasions when we all quite despair of your impulsive nature. One of these days you will get into more trouble than you can handle."

"I have survived very nicely thus far."

Meredith sent a pleading glance toward heaven. "By luck and the grace of the Almighty."

"It's not that bad, Meredith. In any event, I believe I'm maturing very nicely on my own. Just think, in a few more years I'll be forty-one myself. If I can hold out long enough, I will be as old as Kilbourne is now and I won't need his guidance."

Meredith dismissed Phoebe's small attempt at humor. "Marriage would be good for you, Phoebe. One of these days you really must settle down. I vow, I cannot comprehend how you can be content with your life. Always gadding about, chasing after those silly old books."

"Tell me truthfully, Meredith, do you not find Kilbourne a trifle cold? Whenever I am talking to him and happen to look straight into his eyes, I get the impression there is nothing of substance behind them. No warm emotion, if you take my meaning. I do not think he has any strong feeling for me at all."

"What an odd thing to say." Meredith frowned delicately. "I do not find him cold. It is merely that he is a very refined sort of gentleman. He displays a very nice sense of the proprieties. Your problem is that you have been reading far too many of those books you collect."

Phoebe smiled bleakly. "Do you think so?"

"Yes, I do. All that nonsense about chivalry and knights-errant dashing about slaying dragons to win their ladies cannot be good for your brain."

"Perhaps not. But it is amusing."

"It is not in the least amusing," Meredith declared. "Your fondness for old legends has not only made your imagination far too active, it has given you an unrealistic view of the married state."

"I do not think it unrealistic to want a marriage based on true love," Phoebe said quietly.

"Well, it is. Love comes after the wedding. Just look at Trowbridge and myself."

"Yes, I know," Phoebe agreed. "But I do not want to take such a risk. I want to be certain that I am being married for love and that I can return that love, before I commit myself to something as dreadfully permanent as marriage."

Meredith slanted her an exasperated glance. "You do not want to take the risk? That is rather humorous, coming from you. I know of no female who takes more risks than you do."

"I draw the line at a risky marriage," Phoebe said.

"Marriage to Kilbourne is not a risk."

"Meredith?"

"Yes?" Meredith set another stitch with exquisite precision.

"Do you ever think about that night you ran off with Gabriel Banner?"

Meredith gave a start. "Oh, dear. I have pricked my finger. Would you hand me a handkerchief, please? Quickly. I don't want to get blood on this dress."

Phoebe put down her teacup and got to her feet. She handed her sister a linen handkerchief. "Are you all right?"

"Yes, yes, I am fine. What were you saying?" Meredith set aside her embroidery and wrapped the handkerchief around her finger.

"I asked if you ever thought about Gabriel Banner. He is now the Earl of Wylde, you know."

"I understood he has returned to England." Meredith picked up her tea and took a dainty swallow. "And to answer your question, I try very hard never to think of the appalling events of that night. What a little idiot I was."

"You wanted Gabriel to rescue you from marriage to Trowbridge." Phoebe sat down again and propped her feet back on the footstool. The skirts of her bright lime-green muslin gown flowed over her ankles. "I remember it all very well."

"You should," Meredith said dryly. "You not only encouraged me in my foolishness, you helped me knot the sheets I used to descend from my bedroom window."

"It was so exciting. When Gabriel raced off with you into the night, I thought it was the most romantic thing I had ever seen."

"It was a disaster," Meredith muttered. "Thank God Anthony discovered what had happened and came after us immediately. I vow, I have never been so glad to see our dear brother in my life as I was that night, although he was in a towering rage. I had come to my senses by the time we reached the outskirts of London, of course, but Gabriel was still intent on saving me from Trowbridge."

"Even though you had changed your mind?"

Meredith shook her head. "You would have to have known Gabriel to understand how difficult it was to deflect him from his chosen course of action. When I asked him to turn the carriage around and take me home, he thought I was merely succumbing to my own fears. I suppose I cannot blame him for that conclusion. I was such a timid little wren in those days. I still cannot believe I actually agreed to run off with him in the first place."

"You were very frightened of marriage to Trowbridge."

Meredith smiled reminiscently. "So silly of me. Trowbridge is the finest husband a woman could ever hope to have. The problem was that I did not really know him at that point. Heavens, I had only danced with him on one or two occasions and I was quite awed by him."

"So you asked Gabriel to save you?"

"Yes." Meredith wrinkled her nose. "Unfortunately, his notion of saving me was somewhat different than my own. Gabriel made it quite clear after we were under way that he intended to marry me at Gretna Green. I was horrified, naturally. I had not realized that was his plan."

"What did you think he intended when he agreed to save you?"

"I'm afraid I had not thought very far ahead at all. I was merely bent on escape and Gabriel was the sort of man one instinctively turned to for help in an adventure. He gave one the impression he could manage such things."

"I see." Gabriel had apparently changed over the years, Phoebe thought grimly. He had certainly not managed that business with the highwayman in Sussex very well. Still, she had to admit her adventure with him had been exciting.

"I soon realized that in agreeing to run off with Gabriel, I had jumped from the frying pan into the fire," Meredith concluded.

"You do not regret coming back home that night?" Phoebe asked carefully.

Meredith glanced around the elegantly furnished sitting room with deep satisfaction. "I thank God every morning of my life that I escaped being carried off by Wylde. I am not entirely certain Papa and Anthony were correct when they said he was only after my fortune, but I am convinced he would have made me a perfectly dreadful husband."

"Why?" Phoebe asked, unable to stop herself.

Meredith gave her a look of mild surprise. "I am not precisely certain, to be perfectly truthful. All I know is that he frightened me. He displayed no proper notion of gentlemanly behavior. He quite terrified me during that dreadful trip north, if you must know. Within the first few miles I had taken a complete disgust of him. I was in tears."

"I see." Phoebe recalled the one brief moment she had spent in Gabriel's arms. Angry though she had been at the time, she had certainly not been in the least disgusted by the threat of his embrace.

In fact, all things considered, Gabriel's kiss had to rank as the most thrilling moment of her entire life. Phoebe had lain awake until dawn thinking about that searingly sensual embrace. The memories still haunted her.

"Do you think that, now he is back in England and has a title, he will ever venture into Society?" Phoebe asked softly.

"I pray he does not." Meredith shuddered. "For the past eight years I have feared his return. The very thought of it is enough to give me the vapors."

"Why? You are safely wed to Trowbridge now."

Meredith gave her a direct look. "Trowbridge knows nothing of what almost happened eight years ago, and it must stay that way."

"I realize that," Phoebe said impatiently. "No one outside the family knows anything about it. Papa hushed up the matter very nicely. So why are you frightened at the thought of Wylde's return?"

"Because I would not put it past Wylde to humiliate us all by somehow resurrecting the events of that night," Meredith whispered. "Now that he has the title, he would soon command the attention of the gossips of the *ton*, were he to enter Society."

"I take your point," Phoebe murmured. Meredith was right. As an earl, even an earl without a fortune, Gabriel would not go unnoticed in Society. If he chose to spread tales about the wife of the Marquess of Trowbridge, there would be plenty of people who would listen.

"I could not bear to have Trowbridge embarrassed by my actions eight years ago," Meredith said tightly. "At the very least I am certain he would be deeply hurt to know that I had tried to run off to avoid marriage to him. Papa would be enraged to have the scandal made public. Anthony might take it into his head to risk his neck in another duel."

"I do not believe it would be all that bad," Phoebe said. "Surely Wylde would not tell tales. He is a gentleman, after all." She bit her lip, reminding herself silently that she could no longer be certain of that. The stark truth was that Gabriel had changed during the past eight years. Her illusions of him had received a severe blow the other night in Sussex.

"Wylde is no gentleman. Still, we must look on the bright side." Meredith picked up her embroidery. "I seriously doubt he will attempt to enter Society. He never had much taste for it, and he certainly does not have the money for it."

"His financial situation might have changed by now." Phoebe frowned thoughtfully. She knew very well that the income he was receiving off the sale of *The Quest* would not be enough to enable him to go about much in Society. But there was all that time he had spent in the South Seas. And Gabriel had an undeniable air of competence.

"Everyone knows there was no fortune to go with the title he inherited," Meredith said crisply. "No, I think we are reasonably safe."

Phoebe thought of the expression on Gabriel's face as he had reluctantly freed her from his kiss. *Safe* was not a word that came to mind.

Deep inside she was afraid that he might make good on his vow to find her, return the manuscript, and accept the quest. And equally afraid that he might not.

Meredith eyed her sharply. "You are in an odd mood today, Phoebe. Is it because you are thinking about how to deal with Kilbourne's offer?"

"I have already decided how to deal with it. Assuming he makes one."

Meredith sighed. "Surely after all this time you are not still hoping that Neil Baxter will miraculously return to England with a fortune and sweep you off your feet."

"I am well aware that Neil has been dead for over a year."

"Yes, I know, but you have not been able to accept that, have you?"

"Of course I have. But I fear his death will be on my conscience for the rest of my life," Phoebe admitted.

Meredith's eyes widened in alarm. "You must not say that. You had nothing to do with his death."

"We both know that if it had not been for me, Neil would never have gone off to the South Seas to seek his fortune. And if he had not gone to the islands, he would not have been killed."

"Dear heaven," Meredith whispered. "I had hoped you had put aside your foolish sense of responsibility. Neil chose his own destiny. You must not continue to blame yourself."

Phoebe smiled sadly. "It is easier said than done, Meredith. I think the fact that I considered him a friend, not a potential husband, is what makes it all so very difficult. He never accepted that all I wanted was friendship from him."

"I remember how he called himself your own true Lancelot and how he claimed he had dedicated himself to your service." There was strong disapproval in Meredith's voice. "He was rather attractive. I'll give you that much. But other than his looks, I do not know what you saw in him."

"He danced with me."

Meredith gazed at her in amazement. "Danced with you? What on earth do you mean by that?"

Phoebe smiled ruefully. "We both know that very few men ever ask me to dance. They fear I will make an awkward partner because of my bad leg."

"They do not wish to see you embarrassed

on the dance floor," Meredith said firmly. "They refrain from asking you to partner them out of gentlemanly consideration."

"Rubbish. They don't want to humiliate themselves by being seen with a clumsy partner." Phoebe smiled reminiscently. "But Neil did not give a fig for his own appearance on the floor. He waltzed with me, Meredith. He actually waltzed with me. And he did not mind that I was a bit clumsy. As far as I was concerned, he really was my own true Lancelot."

The only way she would find any peace of mind, Phoebe knew, was if she found Neil's murderer. She owed him that much. Then, perhaps, she would be able to put the past to rest.

"Phoebe, regardless of how you feel about Kilbourne, I beg you to wear something a bit more subdued in color than you usually do tonight. There is no sense putting him off entirely with one of your more inappropriate gowns."

"I was planning on wearing my new chartreuse and orange silk," Phoebe said thoughtfully.

"I was afraid of that," Meredith said.

"Have you read The Quest, by any chance, my lord?" Phoebe looked up at Kilbourne as he led her sedately back to the ballroom from the cold buffet. Out of sheer boredom she had just consumed three lobster patties and some ice cream.

"Good lord, no." Kilbourne smiled his most condescending smile. He was looking very distinguished, as usual, in his immaculately tailored evening clothes. "Such tales are not to my taste, Lady Phoebe. Don't you think you're getting a little old for that sort of thing?"

"Yes, and getting older by the minute."

"I beg your pardon?"

Phoebe smiled quickly. "Nothing. Everyone has read the book, you know. Even Byron and the Regent." Primarily because she had made a point of having Lacey send them copies, Phoebe thought smugly. She had known she was taking a chance in doing so, but she had been fortunate. Both Byron and the Regent had read *The Quest* and told their friends that they had enjoyed it. When word got out, the book had been catapulted to the heights of success.

Kilbourne had to be one of the few people in London who had not read Gabriel's book.

Whenever she envisioned marriage with the stuffy Kilbourne, she foresaw a lifetime of irritating conversations such as the one she was having now. Marriage between herself and Kilbourne would never work. She could only hope he would not offer for her and thus oblige her to refuse him. What a tempest in a teapot that would create. Her whole family would be aghast.

"I must say I am surprised at the popularity of that ridiculous novel." Kilbourne surveyed the crowded ballroom. "One would have thought Society had more edifying things to do with its time than read such nonsense."

"Surely one cannot complain about the high-minded tone of *The Quest*. It is a tale of adventure that draws its inspiration from notions of medieval chivalry. It deals with honor and nobility and courage. And I must tell you that the subject of love is handled in a very inspiring fashion."

"I imagine our ancestors were every bit as practical as we are when it came to the subject of love," Kilbourne said. "Money, family, and property are the important factors in matrimonial alliances. Always have been. And as for honor and nobility, well, I suspect that such notions were considerably less refined in medieval times than in our own."

"You may be correct. But it seems to me that the important thing is the idea of chivalry. Perhaps it never really did exist in a perfect state, but that does not mean the notion should not be encouraged."

"It is all a lot of foolishness suitable only for the minds of young women and children. Now, then, Lady Phoebe, perhaps we could change the subject. I wonder if I might have a word with you out in the garden." Kilbourne's fingers tightened under her arm. "There is something I have been meaning to discuss with you."

Phoebe stifled a groan. The last thing she wanted was an intimate discussion out in the garden with Kilbourne. "Some other time, if you don't mind, my lord. I believe I see my brother. There is something I must say to him. Please excuse me."

Kilbourne's jaw tightened. "Very well. I will escort you over to your brother."

"Thank you."

As Clarington's only male heir, Anthony held the title of the Viscount Oaksley and was in line for the earldom. He was thirty-two and cut a strong, athletic figure. In addition to his gift for mathematics and business, he had inherited his father's fair hair and strong-boned features.

Anthony had also inherited the cool aristocratic self-confidence that came from knowing he had several generations of wealth, breeding, and power behind him.

Phoebe was quite fond of her brother, but there was no denying that Anthony could

112

be almost as autocratic and overbearing as Clarington himself. She tolerated both of them with good humor, for the most part, but there were occasions when their overly protective attitudes toward her were more than she could bear.

"There you are, Phoebe. I was wondering where you had got to. Evening, Kilbourne." Anthony nodded pleasantly at the older man.

"Oaksley." Kilbourne inclined his head politely. "Your sister says she has a message for you."

"What's that, Phoebe?" Anthony reached for a glass of champagne as a liveried servant walked past with a tray.

Phoebe thought quickly, searching for some remark that sounded reasonable. "I wanted to know if you are planning to attend the Brantleys' masquerade on Thursday. Mama and Papa are not going, and neither is Meredith."

"And you need an escort?" Anthony chuckled indulgently. "I know how much you love masquerade balls. Very well. I shall stop by for you at nine o'clock. Won't be able to stay, however. Got other plans for the evening. But don't worry, I shall make arrangements with the Mortonstones for you to be taken home in their carriage. Will you be there, Kilbourne?"

"I had not planned on it," Kilbourne admitted. "I do not care for fancy dress balls. All that dashing about in a mask and cloak is very irritating, if you ask me."

Nobody had asked him, Phoebe thought resentfully.

"But if Lady Phoebe is planning to attend," Kilbourne continued magnanimously, "I shall, of course, make an exception."

"There is no need to disturb yourself on my account, my lord," Phoebe said hastily.

"It will be a pleasure." Kilbourne inclined his head. "After all, we gentlemen must humor the whims of our ladies. Isn't that right, Oaksley?"

"Depends on the whim," Anthony said. He started to smile at Phoebe, and then his glance fell on the staircase that descended into the ballroom from the balcony. His smile vanished in an instant. "Well, I'll be damned." His blue eyes turned icy cold. "So the rumor is true. Wylde is in town."

Phoebe froze. Her eyes flew to the red-carpeted stairs. *Gabriel was here.*

She could hardly breathe. Surely he would not recognize her. He could not possibly have had a clear view of her face in the moonlight the other night in Sussex. He'd had no way of discovering her name.

Still, he was here. Right here at the very

same ball where she was. It had to be a coincidence. At the same time she knew in her heart it could not be a coincidence.

She watched in stunned fascination as he came down the steps into the crowd. There was such dangerous arrogance in him. Phoebe's stomach was churning with excitement. Perhaps she should not have eaten so many lobster patties, she thought.

Gabriel was dressed all in black with only a brilliant white cravat and a pleated white shirt for contrast. The stark color suited him. It emphasized his fierce, aquiline features and the predatory grace of his movements. His ebony hair gleamed beneath the chandeliers.

At that moment Gabriel looked out across the room full of elegantly dressed people and captured her gaze.

He knew who she was.

Excitement soared through Phoebe. The only reason Gabriel could possibly be here tonight was that he had decided to accept her quest.

She had found herself a knight-errant.

There were a few potential problems, to be sure. Judging from her recent experience with him, she was forced to conclude that Gabriel's armor badly needed polishing, to say nothing of his manners and his attitude.

But in her relief at seeing him, Phoebe was not about to be cast down by such trivial details. Knights-errant were extremely scarce on the ground these days. She would work with what was available.

Chapter 6

"Look at him," Anthony growled. "One would think the man had inherited the title at birth rather than come into it through a flukish accident."

"He certainly seems at home with his new status," Kilbourne agreed. He was clearly no more than mildly interested in the new-comer. "What do you know of him?"

"Not much," Anthony said shortly. He shot a warning glance at Phoebe. "Surprised to see him here, that's all. Didn't think he had the blunt to move in Society."

"The man's recently come into a respect-able title," Kilbourne observed with a shrug. "That makes him valuable to certain host-esses."

Anthony's eyes narrowed. "There's only one reason why he would be prowling through ballrooms this Season. He's hunting a fortune."

In spite of her fluttering stomach, Phoebe glared at Anthony. "You cannot be certain of that. As I understand it, no one knows very much about Wylde."

Anthony's mouth hardened. It was obvious he wanted to argue further but could hardly do so in front of Kilbourne. The events of eight years ago were a dark family secret.

"Lady Phoebe has got a point," Kilbourne said. "No one knows much about Wylde. Understand he's been out of the country for years."

"So one hears," Anthony muttered. "Damnation. I believe he's coming this way."

Phoebe squeezed her eyes shut for an instant and fanned herself rapidly with her Chinese fan. For the first time in her entire life, she felt light-headed. *He had found her.* Like a bold and valiant knight straight out of a medieval legend, he had come in search of her and he had found her.

She was going to have to reassess his skills as a knight-errant, Phoebe told herself happily. Perhaps he was better at this sort of thing than she had concluded after the events in Sussex. He had, after all, been able to locate her here in London with the aid of very few clues.

"If you will excuse me, I believe I shall go have a chat with Carstairs," Kilbourne said. He bowed over Phoebe's gloved hand. "I shall look forward to seeing you Thursday night, my dear. What sort of costume will you be wearing?"

"Something medieval, no doubt," Anthony said dryly.

Kilbourne grimaced as he released Phoebe's hand. "No doubt." He swung around on his heel and marched off into the crowd.

"Damn that man. He always did have the devil's own gall," Anthony said half under his breath.

"I would not call it gall, precisely," Phoebe mused as she watched Kilbourne disappear. "But he does tend to be rather pompous, does he not? One shudders to think what it would be like sitting across from him at the breakfast table every morning of one's life."

"Don't be an idiot. Kilbourne is a perfectly decent sort. I was referring to Wylde."

"Oh."

"Hell, he really is going to approach us. Talk about raw nerve. I shall deal with him, Phoebe. Go and find Meredith. If she is aware of his presence, she will be extremely anxious."

"I do not see what all the fuss is about," Phoebe said. "And in any event it is much too late to send me packing. He is practically upon us."

"I do not intend to introduce you to him," Anthony said grimly.

Gabriel came to a halt in front of Phoebe and her brother. Ignoring Anthony, he looked down at his prey with clear challenge in his brilliant green eyes. "Good evening, Lady Phoebe. It is certainly a pleasure to see you again."

So much for waiting for an introduction from his old enemy, Phoebe thought. She had to give Gabriel credit. He knew how to take the bold approach.

"Good evening, my lord," she said. Out of the corner of her eye she saw the storm gathering on her brother's face. She smiled brightly. "Anthony, I believe I forgot to mention that his lordship and I have already been introduced."

"I'd like to know when and where." Anthony gazed coldly at Gabriel.

"It was at the Amesburys' country house, was it not, my lord?" Phoebe looked straight up into Gabriel's glittering gaze. "You remember I spent the week in the country, Anthony."

"So you did," Anthony rasped. "And you're quite right. You definitely did forget to mention that you had met Wylde while there."

"It was a very large crowd," Phoebe murmured. She realized Gabriel's expression was one of savage amusement. He was enjoying himself. She had to get him away from Anthony before there was bloodshed. "I expect you would like to ask me to dance, would you not, my lord?"

"*Phoebe.*" Anthony was truly scandalized, in spite of the tense situation. Ladies did not ask gentlemen to dance under any circumstances.

"Do not concern yourself, Oaksley." Gabriel took Phoebe's arm. "Your sister and I became very well acquainted at the Amesburys'. Perhaps it is because I have spent the past eight years in exile from Polite Society or perhaps it is just my nature. Whatever the reason, I find I am not in the least put off by what some men might consider fast behavior in a female."

"How dare you imply my sister is fast?" Anthony snarled.

"Well, she certainly is not slow." Gabriel led Phoebe out onto the floor before Anthony could find a civilized way to stop him.

Phoebe nearly laughed aloud at the look on her brother's face. And then she heard the strains of a waltz and sobered quickly. She looked anxiously up at Gabriel, wondering how he felt about being seen with her on the dance floor. She wondered if it had occurred to him that she might embarrass him.

"Perhaps we should content ourselves with a quiet conversation, my lord," Phoebe suggested, feeling a bit guilty for having more or less forced him into this situation.

"We'll get to the quiet conversation eventually," Gabriel vowed. "But first I intend to have this dance."

"But my lord — "

He gave her a knowing look. "Don't worry, Phoebe. You may trust me to catch you if you lose your balance."

A glorious sense of relief and joy welled up inside Phoebe as she realized Gabriel did not give a damn about how she made him look on the dance floor.

Gabriel swung her into a whirling turn. She would have lost her footing on the first step if he had not been holding her so tightly. As it was, her slippers barely touched the floor. The silk skirts of her chartreuse and orange gown swung wide.

The dazzling lights of the chandeliers spun overhead as Gabriel swept her across the floor. Phoebe saw a band of iridescent color form around her. She realized vaguely that it was the pastel gowns of the ladies merging into a rainbow.

Exhilaration sang through Phoebe. She could not recall feeling like this before in her life.

Even Neil had never danced with her like this. Her noble Lancelot had always taken care to choose slow, measured steps that she could safely follow. But there was nothing safe about the way Gabriel was dancing. Yet he seemed to sense whenever her balance was threatened. When her left leg faltered, he caught her and carried her through the swirling turns. Phoebe felt as though she were flying.

She was breathless as the music swept toward a ravishing crescendo. The only solid thing to hang on to in this spinning, chaotic world was Gabriel. Instead of resting her fingers lightly on his shoulder, she clutched at him. His firm grasp made her feel safe even in the most outrageous, sweeping turns.

She was vaguely aware that the music had stopped, but her senses were still spinning wildly out of control. She clung to Gabriel as he led her off the floor.

"My lord, that was truly wonderful," she gasped.

"It is only the beginning," he said softly.

A moment later she was aware of the cool evening air on her face. She realized he had brought her over to the row of open French doors that lined the ballroom.

Without a word, he took her by the hand and led her out into the night.

"Now we shall have our quiet conversation,

Lady Phoebe." He drew her into the deeper shadows of the garden.

Phoebe was still breathless, but she knew it was no longer because of the excitement of the dancing. She could hardly believe Gabriel had found her.

"I must tell you, I am most impressed with your questing skills, my lord." Phoebe looked at him. "How did you discover my identity? I vow I gave you no clues."

He stopped in the deep shadow of a hedge and turned to face her. "I found you by using the same technique you used to discover that I was the author of *The Quest*. I contacted a solicitor."

She felt herself turning red. It was most unfortunate she'd been obliged to mislead him on that point, she reflected. But she really had no choice. She simply could not tell him the truth. "That was very clever of you."

"It was necessary," he said. "There is unfinished business between us. You were in rather a rush to leave me the other night, if you will recall."

Phoebe studied the severe folds of his white cravat. "I trust you will forgive me, my lord. I was somewhat overset at the time. The adventure had not gone as I had planned it."

"You made that very clear. Neither the

adventure nor I had lived up to your expectations, apparently."

"Well, to be perfectly frank, no."

"Perhaps you set your expectations too high," Gabriel suggested.

"Perhaps." She wished she could see his eyes and the expression on his face. His voice gave her no clue as to his mood, but she sensed a grim tension in him. It was as if he were preparing for battle. "Then again, perhaps not. May I ask why you have gone to the effort to find me?"

"I would have thought you'd have guessed the answer to that. I have something to return to you."

Phoebe caught her breath. "You found *The Knight and the Sorcerer*?"

"I told you I would get it back for you."

"Yes, I know, but I never dreamed you'd actually be able to do it."

"Your great confidence in my knightly prowess is truly inspiring."

She ignored the sarcasm. "My lord, this is so exciting. How did you find the highwayman? How did you force him to turn over the manuscript?" Phoebe blinked as a thought struck her. "You were not obliged to shoot him, were you?"

"No. Mr. Nash and his son were quite cooperative."

Phoebe's mouth fell open. "Mr. Nash? He was the one who stole the manuscript from us?"

"It seems he could not bear to part with it. At the same time he desperately needed the money. So he and his son concocted a scheme whereby they could have both the manuscript and the money. The ever helpful Egan played the part of the highwayman."

"Good heavens." Phoebe frowned. "Actually, it was a rather clever plan and I can certainly understand Mr. Nash's dilemma. It must have been very hard for him to sell the manuscript. How did you tumble to the truth?"

"I thought it was pushing coincidence a bit far to get robbed within ten minutes of leaving Nash's cottage. The highwayman showed only a rather casual interest in our purses, but he got quite enthusiastic about the box containing the manuscript."

"So he did." Phoebe's eyes widened. "You knew who the highwayman was when he appeared?"

"I had my suspicions."

"How utterly brilliant of you." Phoebe was awed. "No wonder you did not resist at the time. You knew exactly where to go to collect the manuscript later. My lord, I take back all those nasty things I said about you."

"I am relieved to know you do not consider me a complete failure as a knight-errant."

Phoebe realized she had injured his pride. She touched his arm in a small, earnest little gesture of apology. "I assure you I never actually thought you a *complete* failure."

"You called me a coward, I believe."

"Yes, well, my temper was somewhat frayed at the time. I trust you will make allowances?"

"Why not?" Gabriel's tone was dry. "I suppose ladies who send knights out on quests have the privilege of being demanding."

Phoebe smiled. "And I suppose knights who are asked to risk their necks are entitled to be somewhat temperamental."

"We are in agreement on one topic, at least." Gabriel took a step closer and caught her chin on the edge of his gloved hand. His strong thigh brushed against the silk skirts of her gown.

Phoebe shivered. His touch instantly re-ignited everything she had felt that night on the road when he had taken her into his arms. She had never been so acutely conscious of a man before in her life. There was danger in this kind of masculine power, she realized suddenly. But it was also incredibly alluring. She drew a deep breath and tried to compose herself.

"My lord," she said, "I must ask you if you have come here tonight because you have decided to assist me in my quest."

"I think you know the answer to that."

Phoebe gazed up at him in gathering excitement. "Then the answer is yes? You will help me locate the murderous pirate who stole *The Lady in the Tower*?"

Gabriel's mouth curved faintly. "Rest assured, Lady Phoebe. You will know the identity of the owner of your book before the Season is over."

"*I knew it.*" Overcome with joy, she threw her arms around Gabriel's neck. "I knew you would not be able to resist such a bold quest. I do not know how to thank you, my lord." She stood on tiptoe and brushed her lips across his cheek. Then she stepped back quickly. She felt the heat in her face as she realized what she had done.

Gabriel narrowed his eyes. He touched the side of his face briefly. "That will do for starters. But I think I should warn you that these days when I set out on quests, I make certain I get properly rewarded for my efforts."

"I understand. You said there would be a fee for your services." Phoebe straightened her shoulders. "I am prepared to pay it."

"Are you, indeed?"

"If it is within my means," Phoebe amended quickly.

"It will definitely be within your means."

Phoebe searched his unreadable face. "What is your fee, sir?"

"I am still calculating it."

"I see." Phoebe did not know how to take that. She cleared her throat cautiously. "I, myself, have never been very good with calculations and such."

"I am very, very good with them," he assured her softly.

"Oh. Well, then, you must let me know as soon as you have settled upon a sum. In the meantime, I shall give you some preliminary instructions."

Gabriel eyed her. "Instructions?"

"Yes, of course. This quest is a very serious matter and I would have you proceed carefully and, above all, discreetly." Phoebe took another step back and began to pace up and down in front of him. She frowned in thought. "First of all, we must maintain absolute secrecy."

"Secrecy." Gabriel considered that for a moment. "Why?"

"Don't be a dolt. Secrecy is necessary or we shall risk warning our quarry that we are on his trail."

"Ah."

Phoebe held up her hand and raised one finger. "Secrecy is the first requirement. No one must know that we are working together on this quest." She raised another finger. "The second requirement is that you keep me informed of your progress."

Gabriel's brow rose. "You want regular reports?"

"Yes. That way I shall be able to guide and coordinate your work. I shall make certain you are covering all the obvious avenues of inquiry."

"You do not trust me to be able to find all those particular avenues on my own?" Gabriel asked.

"No, of course not. You have been out of Society for eight years, my lord. There is much you do not know. I shall be able to give you a great deal of valuable information about certain book collectors and booksellers. You will, in turn, be able to apply that information while you are investigating."

"Phoebe, I agreed to this quest of yours, but you had better understand from the beginning that I am not some damn Bow Street Runner you may order about as it suits your whim."

She paused in her pacing to give him a placating smile. "I am well aware you are not a Runner, my lord. This matter is well beyond the scope of a mere Runner. You are a knight-errant. *My* knight-errant. In a very real sense you will be working for me, my lord. You do comprehend that, do you not?"

"I am starting to grasp your notion of how this partnership is supposed to work. But I don't think you have got a proper concept of how a knight-errant functions."

She peered at him in surprise. "What do you mean, my lord?"

"Knights-errant are notorious for going about their quests in their own fashions." Gabriel slowly stripped off his gloves. His eyes gleamed in the shadows as he leaned over her. "Do not misunderstand me. They are happy to serve their ladies, but they do so as they see fit."

She frowned. "Be that as it may, you will find my guidance quite necessary, my lord. Not only can I supply information, I can also secure the invitations you will need."

"Hmm. I cannot argue with you on that score," Gabriel conceded. "With your contacts, you can get me invited to the same parties and soirees that you will be attending."

"Precisely." She gave him an approving smile. "And you will find me very useful in other ways, too. You see, my lord, we must work closely together on this. I don't mean to put too fine a point on it, but the fact is the quest to find my book is my idea. Therefore, it stands to reason that I should be in charge."

Gabriel caught her face between his bare hands. "Something tells me that reason does not have a lot to do with this entire affair." He bent his head.

Phoebe's eyes widened. "My lord, what are you doing?"

"I am going to kiss you."

"I am not at all certain that is a sound notion." Phoebe was violently aware of her racing pulse. Visions of his last unnerving kiss flashed in her head. "I believe knights-errant are supposed to admire their ladies from afar."

"Now, that is where you are quite wrong." Gabriel's mouth brushed across hers with tantalizing slowness. "Knights-errant did everything in their power to get as close as possible to their ladies."

"Nevertheless, it might be best if we — "

The rest of Phoebe's half-strangled protest was lost as Gabriel's mouth came down on hers. She clutched at his shoulders, riveted by the intensity of feeling that was washing through her.

The first time he had kissed her, he had

been wearing gloves. Tonight the unexpected roughness of his palms against her skin startled her. *Not the hands of a gentleman,* she thought. *Dear heaven, these are the hands of a warrior.*

Gabriel deepened the kiss swiftly, his mouth fierce and demanding. Phoebe felt herself respond with a sudden urgency that took her by surprise. She moaned softly. Her fan fell from her hand as she moved her arms up to circle his neck.

She was even more dazed and breathless now than she had been when he had danced with her. Gabriel was consuming her and at the same time creating a shattering hunger within her. His lips moved on hers, seeking a response that matched his own. Phoebe hesitated, uncertain how to handle the still unfamiliar and utterly devastating sensuality he ignited within her.

Then she felt Gabriel's callused thumb at the corner of her mouth. She realized he was coaxing her lips apart. Uncomprehending, she obeyed. In an instant he was inside, groaning heavily as he plundered her softness.

Phoebe had been kissed before by the occasional overly bold suitor. Such embraces, frequently snatched in gardens outside a crowded ballroom such as this, had been hurried and generally uninteresting. They had filled her with nothing more than a desire to return to the ballroom. Neil Baxter had also kissed her once or twice, but never like this. Neil's kisses had been chaste and polite and Phoebe had never desired more than what he offered.

With Gabriel she knew she was experiencing passion. This was the stuff of legend, she told herself exultantly. This was what she had always sensed was waiting for her somewhere with the right man.

This was exceedingly dangerous.

Gabriel's rough hand moved lightly over her bare shoulder. His finger slipped beneath the edge of the tiny sleeve of her gown. He started to slide it down her arm.

Phoebe surfaced from the shock of the embrace. Her mind was still reeling. She moistened her lips with the tip of her tongue, trying to find her voice. "My lord, I really don't think — "

Without warning there was a movement in the darkness behind Gabriel. Phoebe went cold as she heard Anthony's voice slice harshly through the night.

"Take your goddamned hands off my sister, Wylde," Anthony said. "How dare you touch her?"

Gabriel's smile was cold in the moonlight as he turned slowly to face Anthony. "We seem to have played this scene once before, Oaksley."

"And it will end the same way it did the last time." Anthony came to a halt a few paces away. His hands were clenched in fury.

"I think not," Gabriel said far too gently. "Things are a little different this time."

Phoebe was horrified. "Stop it, both of you. Anthony, Gabriel and I are friends. I will not allow you to insult him."

"Don't be a fool, Phoebe." Anthony did not look at her. "He is plotting to use you somehow. You may depend upon it. I know him well enough to guarantee that he is after either money or revenge. Probably both."

Meredith's voice called out anxiously from the shadows. "Anthony? Did you find them?" A second later she appeared from behind a row of topiary. When she saw Gabriel, she stopped short, a stricken expression on her lovely face. "Dear God. So it is true. You are back."

Gabriel glanced at her. "Did you think I would not return eventually?"

"I prayed you would not," Meredith whispered brokenly.

Phoebe was getting angrier by the minute. "This is all a grave misunderstanding. Anthony, Meredith, I insist you be polite to Gabriel."

Meredith looked at her. "Anthony is right, Phoebe. Wylde is here for only one reason. He wants revenge."

"I do not believe it," Phoebe declared. Defiantly she took a step closer to Gabriel. She looked up at him, frowning severely. "You won't discuss what happened eight years ago, will you?"

"None of you need be unduly alarmed," Gabriel said. He looked amused. "I have no intention of discussing ancient history." His eyes flickered across Meredith's face. "Especially such exceedingly dull ancient history."

Meredith gasped.

Anthony took a menacing step forward. "Are you insulting my sister, sir?"

"Hardly." Gabriel smiled blandly. "I was merely commenting on Lady Trowbridge's impressive virtue. A subject I can speak on with some authority."

Phoebe scowled at her brother and sister. Anthony looked frustrated and furious. Meredith just stood there, an ethereal, tragic figure with her hand at her throat.

Phoebe had had enough. She stepped in front of Gabriel, putting herself between him and the other two. "There will be no more of this nonsense. Do you hear me? I will not tolerate it. What is past is past."

"Stay out of this, Phoebe." Anthony glowered at her. "You have caused enough trouble already."

Phoebe raised her chin. "Gabriel has given his word that he will not gossip about what happened eight years ago, and that is that. From now on, you will treat him as you would any other respectable member of Society."

"The devil I will," Anthony growled.

"Dear heaven, this is a disaster," Meredith whispered.

Gabriel smiled. "Do not concern yourself, Lady Phoebe." He tugged his gloves on. "You need not protect me from your family. I assure you that this time I can take care of myself."

With a polite inclination of his head that was directed solely at her, he turned and walked into the shadows.

Chapter 7

Topaz.

Gabriel smiled with a curious sense of satisfaction as he opened the newspaper. At last he had the answer to what had become a pressing question during the past few days. Phoebe's eyes were the warm, golden color of fine topaz.

She reminded him of the brilliant fish in the lagoons of the South Seas. Phoebe was a creature of bright colors and shimmering hues. Last night the chandeliers had gleamed on her dark hair, causing the red fire buried there to blaze. Her vivid gown had reminded him of an island sunrise. And when he had taken her into his arms on the dance floor, he had been keenly aware of the sensual excitement that burned within him.

He wanted her more than ever. The fact that she was Clarington's daughter could not alter that. But it did not affect the situation, either, he assured himself. He could have both the woman and the revenge.

Gabriel made an effort to concentrate on

his newspaper. His club was quiet this morning. The majority of such establishments were usually quiet at this hour. Most of the members were still sleeping off the effects of a late night and a prodigious quantity of alcohol. It had been eight years since he had last been here, but little had changed. That very lack of change was the sign of a good club.

His gaze skimmed across the advertisements for theater productions, horses, and houses for rent. He paused briefly to read through the list of guests who had attended a soiree the preceding evening and mentally made a note of the names.

He needed to learn his way through the intricate and sometimes dangerous maze of the Social World as quickly as possible. It was not unlike the business of learning his way in the treacherous waters of the South Seas. Pirates, sharks, and hidden reefs were plentiful in both locales.

Phoebe was right about one thing: Her status in Society would instantly open important doors. To carry out his goal of revenge, he would need to move in the same levels of the *ton* in which Lord Clarington and his family moved.

Once he was inside those exclusive doors, Gabriel reflected, his title and fortune would secure him a virtually invulnerable position from which to carry out his assault on Clarington's clan.

"Wylde. So my son was correct. You're back."

Gabriel lowered his newspaper slowly, fighting back a wave of fierce satisfaction. Clarington was here. The battle had begun.

He looked up with polite resignation, as if it were the most boring task in the world. He found himself gazing at his old enemy. "Good day, my lord. Kind of you to drop by to welcome me back to Town."

"I see you are just as insolent as ever." Clarington sat down across from Gabriel.

"I would not wish to disappoint you."

Gabriel examined his old nemesis curiously. Like the club, the Earl of Clarington had changed little in the past eight years. Although he was at least sixty and had put on some weight around his midsection, he was still endowed with the air of pompous arrogance Gabriel recalled so well.

Clarington had been born and bred to the title. He had imbibed five generations of history and social status while still in his cradle and he was determined to make certain his entire family carried on in his footsteps. Gabriel knew that Clarington's guiding goal in life was to see to it that nothing disgraced the title.

Clarington was an imposing man physically. He was tall, almost as tall as Gabriel. His beak of a nose dominated a face that reflected unwavering determination and pride. His piercing blue eyes were filled with the keen intelligence that characterized the whole family. They were also filled with bottomless disapproval as he glared at Gabriel.

"I say, don't suppose you've done anything much to improve yourself while you've been out of the country," Clarington said.

"Now, why would I want to improve myself? So much easier to run off with an heiress."

"So that's your game." Clarington appeared grimly satisfied at having his worst fears confirmed. "Anthony said as much. He saw you virtually drag my youngest daughter into the garden last night."

"I did not precisely drag her out into the garden." Gabriel smiled briefly. "She went along quite willingly, as I recall."

"You, sir, took advantage of her somewhat impulsive nature."

"Somewhat impulsive? I'm not sure I'd characterize Phoebe as being merely *somewhat* impulsive. I'd say she has a definite talent for sheer recklessness."

Clarington's gaze turned glacial and his

whiskers twitched. "Now, see here, Wylde. Don't think I'll stand by and let you run off with my Phoebe. You won't get away with it any more than you did when you tried to carry off my eldest daughter."

"Perhaps I don't wish to run off with your Phoebe. After all, if I marry her, I'll be stuck with her for life, will I not? No offense, sir, but my impression of your youngest daughter thus far is that she would not make the most biddable and obedient of wives."

Clarington sputtered furiously. "How dare you make such a personal remark!"

"In fact," Gabriel continued thoughtfully, "I believe it would be safe to say that Lady Phoebe would be a definite handful for any man. No, I am not at all certain I wish to take on the task of marrying her. But who knows how I shall feel about the matter after I have had an opportunity to consider it more closely?"

"Damn you, Wylde. What are you up to?"

"I'm sure you will understand when I tell you I do not intend to discuss my plans for the future with you."

"You've got some foul scheme afoot, by God." Clarington's bushy white brows bounced up and down with the force of his anger. "I warn you, you'll not get your hands on my Phoebe or her inheritance."

"Why are you so hostile, Clarington? You must admit I'm a much better catch this time."

"Bah. Rubbish. You may have a title, but you haven't got a penny to go with it, have you? I know for a fact that there was no fortune or property left with the Wylde title. I checked into the matter."

"Very far-sighted of you, Clarington. But then, you always were a prudent man. You must have guessed you'd see me again one of these days."

Out of the corner of his eye, Gabriel saw the earl's son walk through the doors of the club at that moment. Anthony surveyed the uncrowded room, spotted his father and Gabriel, and hurried forward. He appeared as angry as he had been the preceding evening.

"I see you found him, sir." Anthony sank down into the chair beside his father. "Have you had a chance to ask him what he thinks he's up to hanging around Phoebe?"

"I know damn well what he's up to." Clarington's eyes snapped with rage. "Thinks he can run off with her just as he tried to do with Meredith. Thinks he'll get his hands on her inheritance that way."

Anthony glowered at Gabriel. "Give it up, Wylde. Go hunt some other innocent. There's always an heiress or two running about in Society whose father will trade her money for a title."

"I shall bear that in mind," Gabriel said politely. He picked up his newspaper and started to read.

"Damnation, man, is it just the money you want this time?" Clarington thundered softly. "Do you expect me to buy you off? Is that it?"

"Now, there's an interesting thought." Gabriel did not look up from the paper.

"If that's the case, then you are even more despicable than I had thought," Clarington rasped. "Last time at least you were too proud to accept money to stay away from one of my daughters."

"A man learns to be practical in the South Seas."

"Hah. Practical, indeed. You have truly sunk to the depths, Wylde. You are a disgrace to your title. Well, you won't be the first upstart I've paid to stay clear of Phoebe. She does seem to attract bounders of the worst sort. How much do you want?"

Gabriel looked up, immediately intrigued. "Who else were you obliged to buy off, Clarington?"

Anthony frowned. "I think that's enough on that subject. It's a family matter and does not concern you."

Clarington squared his shoulders. "My son is right. I don't intend to discuss such matters with you, sir."

"Was it Neil Baxter, by any chance?" Gabriel asked softly.

Clarington's expression of outrage was all the answer Gabriel required. Anthony swore under his breath and reached for a bottle of port that stood nearby.

"I said I do not intend to discuss such personal matters with you," Clarington repeated in a stony voice. "Name your price, man."

"There is no need to state it." Gabriel put down his newspaper, rose to his feet, and picked up the bundle he had placed on the small table beside his chair. "Rest assured, Clarington, you do not possess a large enough fortune to buy me off this time. Now, you must both excuse me. I have an appointment."

"Hold on, there, Wylde." Anthony set his glass down swiftly and got to his feet. "I give you fair warning. If you insult my sister, I will call you out, just as I did the last time."

Gabriel paused. "Ah, but the outcome might be considerably different this time, Oaksley. I find that I am no longer quite as indulgent as I once was."

Anthony turned a dull red. Gabriel knew the other man was recalling their dawn meeting eight years ago. It had been the viscount's first duel, but it had been Gabriel's third.

Driven as he was in those days by his naive sense of chivalry, Gabriel had already managed to get involved in two previous dawn appointments. On both occasions he had been defending a lady's name.

He had won both duels without having to kill his opponent, but he had begun to wonder how long his luck would last. He had also begun to wonder whether any woman was worth the risk. None of the ladies involved appeared to appreciate his efforts on their behalf. On that cold, gray October morning eight years ago, Gabriel had concluded that he'd had enough of duels over females.

Anthony had been resolute, but he had also been extremely nervous. He had been too quick off the mark that morning. The viscount had fired wildly. It was purest chance, not good aim, that had caused the bullet to strike Gabriel's shoulder, and both men knew it.

Anthony was also well aware that the only reason he was alive today was because Gabriel had held his fire after taking the bullet. The blood soaking through his white shirt and the stricken expression in Anthony's eyes had convinced Gabriel that three duels were three too many.

In disgust, he had aimed his pistol at the sky and discharged it. Honor had been satisfied and Gabriel had made a decision. He would never again allow his outmoded sense of chivalry to guide his actions. No woman was worth this kind of nonsense.

He smiled coldly now at Anthony, watching the memories in the viscount's eyes. Satisfied, Gabriel turned and walked off without a backward glance.

Behind him he could feel Clarington and his son staring at his back in helpless outrage.

It felt good. Revenge was an extremely gratifying sensation, Gabriel decided.

Lydia, Lady Clarington, put down her teacup and peered at Phoebe through a pair of gold-rimmed spectacles. She wore the spectacles only in the privacy of the elegant Clarington town house and when playing cards at the home of one of her cronies. She would have died before she allowed herself to be seen wearing them in public.

Lady Clarington had been declared a diamond of the first water in her younger days. Her golden hair had now faded to silver and her once lushly rounded figure had grown a trifle plump over the years, but she was still a very attractive woman.

Phoebe privately thought her mother looked charmingly maternal and endearingly innocent in her spectacles. Lord Clarington apparently suffered from a similar illusion and had done so for the entire thirty-six years of their marriage. The earl had never made any secret of his affection for his wife. As far as Phoebe could tell, her father was still blissfully unaware of the depths of Lydia's passion for cards.

As far as Lord Clarington knew, his fashionable countess merely liked to play the occasional hand of whist at the home of friends. The staggering amounts of some of her winnings and the extent of some of her losses was a topic with which he was entirely unacquainted.

"I don't suppose," Lydia said with the unquenchable optimism of the inveterate gamester, "that Wylde had the good sense to pick up a fortune while out in the South Seas?"

"Not as far as I can tell, Mama," Phoebe said cheerfully. "You must not delude yourself on that score. I expect he is not much richer now than he was when he left England eight years ago."

"Pity. I was always rather fond of Wylde. There was something rather dangerously attractive about him. Not that he would ever have done for Meredith, of course. Would have frightened her to death. And of course he would have made a perfectly useless son-in-law from my point of view."

"Lacking a fortune, as he did. Yes, I know, Mama. Your requirements in a son-in-law have always been quite simple and straightforward."

"One must be practical about such matters. Of what use is a penniless son-in-law?"

Phoebe hid a smile as she recalled the success of Gabriel's book. "Wylde may not be completely penniless. I believe he has a small income from certain investments he has made recently."

"Bah." Lady Clarington brushed aside the notion of a pittance. "A small income will not do. You must marry a man with a respectable fortune, Phoebe. Even if I were willing to make an exception, your papa is most insistent. You must form a suitable alliance. You owe it to your family name."

"Well, there is absolutely no point even speculating on Wylde's intentions toward me, Mama. I can tell you right now that he is not the least bit interested in marriage."

Lydia eyed her closely. "Are you certain of that?"

"Quite certain. It is true we became acquainted at the Amesburys' and discovered we have mutual interests, but we are merely friends. Nothing more."

"I fear it comes down to Kilbourne, then," Lydia mused. "One could certainly do worse. A lovely title and a lovely fortune."

Phoebe decided to seize the opportunity to put her mother off the notion of the proposed alliance. "I regret to tell you, Mama, that I find Kilbourne not only pompous but something of a prig."

"What does that signify? Your father is also pompous and quite capable of giving lessons to any prig in the *ton*. But I manage quite nicely with him."

"Yes, I know," Phoebe said patiently, "but Papa is not without feeling. He is quite fond of you and of his three offspring."

"Well, of course he is. I should not have married him if he had not been capable of such tender sensibilities."

Phoebe picked up her teacup. "Kilbourne, I fear, is not capable of such sensibilities, Mama. I doubt, for example, that he will approve of paying off his mother-in-law's occasional debts of honor."

Lydia was instantly alarmed. "You think

he will balk at the notion of making me the odd loan?"

"I fear he would, yes."

"Good heavens. I had not realized he was that much of a prig."

"It is definitely something to consider, Mama."

"Quite right." Lydia pursed her lips. "On the other hand, your father does approve of him and there is no denying it is a fine match. It is no doubt the best we can hope for, now that you are nearly five and twenty."

"I realize that, Mama. But I cannot get enthusiastic about marrying Kilbourne."

"Well, your father certainly can." Lydia brightened. "And there is every chance Kilbourne will mellow somewhat on the subject of loans after being married for a time. You can work on him, Phoebe. Convince him that you need a very sizable allowance to maintain appearances."

"And then turn around and make you loans from my sizable allowance?" Phoebe sighed. "I doubt it would be that simple, Mama."

"Nevertheless, we must not give up hope. You will learn to manage Kilbourne. You are a very managing sort, Phoebe."

Phoebe wrinkled her nose ruefully. "Thank you, Mama. Wylde implied much the same thing last night."

"Well, there is no doubt but that you have always been somewhat strong-minded, and the tendency has definitely increased as you have grown older. Women do that, naturally, but generally they are safely wed before such tendencies start to show."

"I fear it is too late for me, then," Phoebe announced as she got to her feet. "My managing tendencies are already quite plain for all to see. Now, you must excuse me."

"Where are you going?"

Phoebe moved toward the door. "Hammond's Bookshop. Mr. Hammond sent around a message saying he had some very interesting new items in stock."

Lydia gave a small exclamation. "You and your books. I do not comprehend your interest in those dirty old volumes you collect."

"I suspect my passion for them is not unlike your passion for cards, Mama."

"The thing about cards," Lydia said, "is that one can always look forward to the next winning streak. With books it is all money out the window."

Phoebe smiled. "That depends on one's point of view, Mama."

The message had not been from Mr. Hammond. It had been from Gabriel asking her to meet him at the bookseller's. Phoebe had

152

received the note earlier that morning and had sent word back immediately that she would be there promptly at eleven.

At five minutes to the hour she alighted from her carriage on Oxford Street. She left her maid sitting in the sunshine on the bench outside the shop and sailed eagerly through the doors.

Gabriel was already there. He did not see her come in because he was busy examining an aging, leather-bound volume that Mr. Hammond was reverently placing on the counter in front of him.

Phoebe hesitated for an instant, her attention caught by the way the sunlight filtering through the high windows gleamed on Gabriel's ebony hair. He was dressed in a dark, close-fitting jacket that emphasized the breadth of his shoulders and his flat stomach. His breeches and beautifully polished Hessians revealed the sleek, muscular contours of his legs.

For some reason Phoebe had felt obliged to spend an inordinate amount of time choosing her own attire this morning. She had found herself dithering between two or three gowns in a totally uncharacteristic manner. Now she was very glad she had worn her new squash-yellow muslin with its fuchsia-colored pelisse. Her bonnet was a confection of squash and fuchsia pleats and flowers.

As if sensing her presence, Gabriel looked up and saw her. A slow smile edged his mouth as he took in the sight of her in her vivid gown. His eyes were very green in the morning light. Phoebe drew a deep breath and acknowledged to herself that this was why she had spent so long in front of her mirror this morning. She had been hoping to see exactly that look of approval in Gabriel's eyes.

Even as the realization dawned on her, she tried to quell it. Gabriel had proven beyond a shadow of a doubt eight years ago that his taste in women ran to delicate blue-eyed blondes who favored soft pastels.

"Good morning, Lady Phoebe." Gabriel walked across the room to greet her. "You're looking very bright and cheerful today."

"Thank you, Lord Wylde." Phoebe glanced around quickly and decided no one could overhear their conversation. "I got your message."

"So I see. I thought you would be quite anxious to recover *The Knight and the Sorcerer.*"

"You have it with you?"

"Of course." Gabriel led her back toward the counter, where a manuscript-shaped bundle wrapped in brown paper was sitting next to the volume he had been examining. "Proof of my skills as a knight-errant."

"Wylde, this is wonderful." Phoebe picked up the bundle. "I cannot tell you how impressed I am. I know you'll be of great assistance in my quest."

"I shall do my best." Gabriel indicated the open book on the counter and raised his voice slightly. "You might be interested in this, Lady Phoebe. A rather fine copy of an early sixteenth century history of Rome. Mr. Hammond says he acquired it recently from the estate of a collector in Northumberland."

Phoebe realized instantly that Gabriel was attempting to provide a reasonable excuse for them to continue talking. No one in the bookshop would think it odd that they were studying an interesting old book. Obediently she bent her head to take a closer look.

"Very nice," Phoebe declared in a strong voice as she caught sight of Mr. Hammond out of the corner of her eye. "Italian, I see. Not Latin. Excellent illuminations."

"I thought you might appreciate it." Gabriel turned a page in the book and read silently for a moment.

Phoebe took another quick look around and leaned closer on the pretext of reading over his shoulder. "My family is a trifle upset about all this, Wylde."

"I noticed." Gabriel turned another page and frowned thoughtfully as he studied it.

"They know nothing of my quest, so they naturally assume you and I have formed a friendship of sorts."

"Something more than a friendship, Lady Phoebe. They are afraid we are forming an attachment." Gabriel skimmed another page of text.

Phoebe blushed and glanced quickly around the shop again. Mr. Hammond was busy with another patron now. "Yes, well, I can hardly explain the truth to them. They would never approve of my quest. But I want to assure you that you need not worry about their concerns."

"I see. How, exactly, do you intend to assure them that we are merely acquaintances?"

"Don't worry. I shall manage Papa and the others. I have had a great deal of experience with that sort of thing."

"Headstrong," Gabriel said under his breath.

"I beg your pardon?"

Gabriel pointed to a word on the page in front of him. "I believe this is Italian for headstrong."

"Oh." Phoebe studied the word. "No, I

do not believe so. I am quite certain that word translates as mule."

"Ah. Of course. My mistake. What was it you were saying?" Gabriel asked politely.

"You must not allow my family's suspicious notions to interfere with your investigations."

"I shall do my best to rise above their low-minded opinions, madam."

Phoebe smiled in approval. "Excellent. Some people can be quite put off by my father's somewhat dictatorial approach."

"You don't say?"

"He is really very nice, in his way, you know."

"No, I don't know."

Phoebe bit her lip. "I suppose your experience of him eight years ago cannot have left you with a pleasant impression."

"No, it did not."

"Well, as I said, you must pay him no heed. Now, then, let us get down to business. I have secured some important invitations for you. The first is for the Brantleys' masquerade ball on Thursday."

"I take it I am being ordered to attend?"

Phoebe scowled. "It is an important affair. I shall be able to introduce you to a great many people and you will be able to begin your inquiries."

Gabriel inclined his head. "Very well, my

lady. Your wish is my command."

"That's the spirit. Now, then, have you anything to report on your investigations thus far?"

Gabriel drummed his fingers on the counter. "Let me think. Thus far I have managed to secure a house for the Season. Not an easy task, I might add. I've also acquired a small staff. I have paid a visit to Weston's to order some new clothes, and I've been to Hoby's for boots. I think that about covers my accomplishments to date."

Phoebe glowered at him. "I was not speaking of those sorts of accomplishments."

"I must take care of such details before I can move about in Society, madam. Surely you realize that?"

Phoebe bit her lip. "You are quite right. I had not thought of such matters. Now that you have brought them to my attention, I must ask you a very personal question."

Gabriel slanted her a sidelong glance. "How personal?"

"Please do not take offense." Phoebe risked another quick look around before leaning very close. "Have you got enough money to cover your expenses?"

Gabriel paused in the act of turning another page. "That is indeed a very personal question."

Phoebe felt her face flame with remorse. Gabriel was a very proud man. She had not meant to humiliate him. Nevertheless, she had to be firm about this.

"Please do not be embarrassed, my lord. I am well aware that I am asking you to move in some very exclusive circles at the height of the Season, and I am equally aware that to do so you will need money. As I am the one who requested your assistance on this quest, I feel it is only fair that I cover some of your expenses."

"There is the income I received from the publication of *The Quest*," he reminded her.

Phoebe waved that aside. "I am well aware that the income a beginning writer receives from his work would not begin to finance a Season."

Gabriel kept his gaze focused on the old volume in front of him. "I believe I can handle my own finances without your assistance, madam. At least for the length of time it takes to complete this quest."

"You are certain of that?"

"Quite certain. I shall contrive to get by." Gabriel leaned one elbow against the counter and turned to study Phoebe with a sharp, assessing gaze. "It is my turn to ask a personal question, madam. How desperately did you love Neil Baxter?"

Phoebe stared at him in amazement. Then her eyes slid away from Gabriel's. "I told you that Neil and I were friends."

"How close was the friendship?"

"I do not see that it matters now."

"It matters to me."

"Why?" she shot back. "What difference does it make? Neil is dead. The only thing that matters now is finding his murderer."

"Murderers go unpunished every day of the week."

"This one shall not." Phoebe's hand tightened into a small fist on the counter. "I must find him."

"Why?" Gabriel asked softly. "Because you loved Baxter so much you cannot rest until justice has been done?"

"No," she admitted sadly. "I must find him because it is my fault he was killed."

Gabriel stared at her, clearly stunned. "Your fault? Why in God's name do you say that? The man died in the South Seas, thousands of miles away from England."

"Don't you understand?" Phoebe gave him an anguished look. "If it were not for me, Neil would never have gone off to the South Seas. He went there to seek his fortune so that he could come back and ask for my hand. I am to blame for what happened."

"Christ," Gabriel muttered. "That's an insane notion."

"It is not insane," Phoebe hissed, struggling to keep her voice low.

"It is an addlepated, idiotic, and totally irrational conclusion."

Phoebe felt a sinking feeling in the pit of her stomach. She searched Gabriel's fierce face. "I thought you of all people would understand my quest."

"It is foolishness."

Phoebe took a breath. "Does that mean you will not help me, after all?"

"No, by God," Gabriel said through his teeth. "I will help you find the owner of *The Lady in the Tower*. What you choose to believe about the man after you have located him will be your business."

"The man is a murderous pirate. Surely you will want to help me bring him to justice."

"Not particularly." Gabriel closed the book he had been examining. "I told you that night in Sussex that I am no longer overly concerned with idealistic notions."

"But you have agreed to my quest," Phoebe pointed out.

"It intrigues me. I am occasionally amused by such puzzles. But do not assume that I intend to help you punish the man who killed your lover."

Phoebe wanted to argue further, but at that moment a young lady dressed in the height of fashion and accompanied by a maid walked into the shop. She went straight to the counter and waited impatiently as Mr. Hammond hurried over to serve her.

"I wish to purchase a copy of *The Quest,*" the young lady announced in imperious tones. "All of my friends have read it, so I suppose I must read it also."

"I believe you will have to go to Lacey's Bookshop for that," Mr. Hammond murmured.

"What a nuisance." The young lady turned to Phoebe and Gabriel as Mr. Hammond disappeared into his back room. She looked at Gabriel through her lashes. "Have you read it, sir?"

Gabriel cleared his throat. He looked oddly ill at ease. "Uh, yes. Yes, I have."

"What did you think of it?" the young lady asked earnestly. "Is it really as clever as everyone says?"

"Well . . ." Gabriel looked helplessly at Phoebe.

Phoebe realized it was the first time she had ever seen Gabriel appear flustered. He was actually turning a dull red. She smiled at the young lady and coolly stepped into the breech.

"I am certain you will enjoy *The Quest*," Phoebe said. "In my opinion it represents an entirely new species of novel. It is full of adventure and incidents of chivalry and it does not rely on the supernatural element for effect."

"I see." The young lady looked dubious.

"The tone is very affecting," Phoebe continued swiftly. "The novel engages the most lofty of the sensibilities. Very inspiring treatment of the subject of love. You will be especially pleased with its hero. He is even more exciting than one of Mrs. Radcliffe's heroes."

The young lady brightened. "More exciting than one of Mrs. Radcliffe's?"

"Yes, indeed. I assure you that you will not be disappointed." Phoebe smiled and paused a second before adding the final touch. "Byron has read *The Quest*, you know. He recommended it to all his friends."

The young lady's eyes widened. "I shall go to Lacey's Bookshop at once."

Phoebe smiled with satisfaction. Another sale for Lacey's Bookshop. If she had not been standing in a room full of people, she would have rubbed her hands together in glee.

She might not have inherited her family's talent for mathematics and investments, but she could certainly pick successful novels out of a pile of manuscripts.

It was unfortunate that her family would not appreciate her peculiar version of the family talent.

Chapter 8

*It represents an entirely new species of novel
. . . does not rely on the supernatural element
for effect . . . very inspiring treatment of the
subject of love.*

Phoebe's words were still ringing in
Gabriel's head that afternoon as he strode
into Lacey's Bookshop. They were very familiar words. They were, in fact, almost the
exact words Lacey had used in his letter
saying he wished to publish *The Quest*. Gabriel had read that letter several times, com-
mitting the approving phrases to memory.

Ever since leaving Phoebe at Hammond's
Bookshop that morning, a suspicion had been
growing in his mind. At first it had seemed
too outrageous to even contemplate, but the
more he thought about it, the more he realized
it all made a strange sort of sense.

If his suspicion was correct, it would certainly explain how Phoebe had known so
much about him right from the start. It would
also mean there was no limit to Phoebe's
daring.

The man behind the counter inside the bookshop peered at him. "May I help you, sir?"

"Where's Lacey?" Gabriel asked bluntly. He had met Lacey once before, shortly after the beginning of their association. On that occasion Gabriel had made it clear that he expected Lacey to respect his request for anonymity.

The clerk blinked and then coughed discreetly. "I'm afraid Mr. Lacey is busy, my lord."

"You mean he's drunk as a wheelbarrow?"

"Of course not, sir. He's working."

Gabriel heard a noise from the room directly behind the front counter. "Never mind, I'll find him myself."

He walked around the counter, pushed open the door, and stepped into the room where Lacey housed his printing press.

The smell of ink and oil was thick in the air. The massive iron press stood silent. Lacey, a stout, bald man with a florid face full of overgrown whiskers, was in the corner. He was examining a bundle of paper. He wore a leather apron over his ink-stained clothes. A bottle of gin was poking out of one of the apron pockets.

"Lacey, there is something I wish to discuss with you," Gabriel said, closing the door.

"What's that?" Lacey turned his head and glared at Gabriel with rheumy eyes. "Oh, it's you, m'lord. Now, see here, if you've come to complain about not getting paid enough for your last book, you're wasting your time. I told you my partner has put all that sort of thing into the hands of a solicitor. I don't worry about the damned money anymore."

Gabriel smiled coldly. "It's not the money that concerns me, Lacey."

"Well, now, that's a relief." Lacey straightened and pulled the bottle out of his apron pocket. He scowled at Gabriel as he took a healthy swig of gin. "You wouldn't believe how many authors get difficult when it comes to money."

"What interests me is the name of your partner."

Lacey choked on his mouthful of gin. He swallowed frantically and then burst out in a fit of coughing. "Afraid I cannot discuss it, m'lord. Anonymous. Just like you."

"I want the name, Lacey."

"Now, see here, what gives you the right to pry into my private business?"

"If you don't give me the name of your partner, I shall see to it that my new manuscript, which is almost completed, is delivered to another publisher."

Lacey stared at him in horror. "You wouldn't do that, my lord. After all we've done for you?"

"I don't want to take *A Reckless Venture* elsewhere, but if you force me to do so, I shall."

Lacey sat down hard in a wooden chair. "You're a hard man, m'lord."

"I'm a cautious man, Lacey. I like to know who I'm dealing with when I do business."

Lacey squinted at him and wiped his nose on the back of his stained sleeve. "You won't tell her I told ye? She's real insistent on keeping her name a secret. Her family wouldn't approve of her getting involved in trade."

"Trust me," Gabriel said grimly. "I can keep a secret."

Thursday morning Gabriel sat at his desk and worked on the last scenes of *A Reckless Venture.* He was rather pleased with the story. In a few days he would have it delivered to his publisher.

He would then await the letter of acceptance or rejection. It would certainly be interesting to see what Lacey's *partner* had to say about the manuscript.

Gabriel reluctantly looked up from his work when his new butler, Shelton, opened the door.

"Two ladies to see you, sir." Shelton did not look as though he approved of the visitors. "They would not give me their names."

"Show them in, Shelton." Gabriel put down his pen and got to his feet.

He smiled to himself. The only woman he knew who would be bold enough to pay a call on a man was Phoebe. She no doubt wanted to give him more orders, directions and suggestions. He wondered whom she had brought with her. Her maid, no doubt.

He was aware of a sense of anticipation, just as he had been on Tuesday when he had met her at Hammond's Bookshop. The feeling was a decidedly sensual one. He had a sudden vision of himself making love to Phoebe right here in his library. It just might be possible, he concluded.

If the little fool was silly enough to risk her reputation by coming here today, he certainly had no qualms about putting her reputation even more at risk.

After all, the lady was a born deceiver. She had been weaving her illusions right from the start.

At that moment the door opened again and two elegantly gowned and heavily veiled women appeared in the doorway. Gabriel experienced a sharp stab of disappointment. Although he could not see their faces, he knew immediately that neither of them was Phoebe.

He would know Phoebe anywhere now, veiled or unveiled. It was not just her slight limp that marked her. There was something about the way she held her head, something about the way her colorful, high-waisted gowns framed her breasts and skimmed the contours of her hips that he would always recognize.

He slanted a wistful glance at the green velvet sofa near the hearth. So much for his budding plans to spend the next hour seducing his outrageous lady.

"Good morning, ladies." Gabriel quirked a brow as his two visitors took seats in front of the desk. "I see that a taste for the veil runs in your family. Perhaps all the Clarington females have a heretofore unacknowledged religious vocation."

"Don't be ridiculous, Wylde." Lady Clarington lifted her veil with gloved fingers and secured it on top of her clever little blue hat. "I have no more interest in the religious life than you do."

Meredith raised her veil also and fastened it atop her fashionable flower-trimmed bonnet. She gazed at Gabriel with reproachful blue eyes. "You always did have an odd sense of humor, Wylde."

"Thank you, Lady Trowbridge." Gabriel inclined his head. "I have always thought that some sense of humor was better than none at all."

Meredith blinked uncertainly. "I never did understand you."

"No, I am aware of that fact." Gabriel sat down and clasped his hands together on his desk. "Shall we continue to exchange amusing jests, or will you two ladies condescend to tell me the reason for this visit."

"I would have thought the reason for our visit was obvious," Lydia said with a sigh. "We're here about Phoebe, of course. Meredith insisted."

Meredith cast her mother a chiding glance and then turned her attention back to Gabriel. "We have come to plead with you, Wylde. We are here to throw ourselves at your mercy and beg you not to ruin Phoebe's life."

"Assuming that is your intention, of course," Lydia murmured. She peered intently around the library, unconsciously squinting. "Don't suppose you managed to pick up a fortune out in the South Seas, did you?"

Gabriel gave her a deliberately bland look of inquiry. "Why do you ask, Lady Clarington?"

"Would have made things so much simpler," Lydia said. "That way you could marry Phoebe and no one would bat an eye. We wouldn't be going through all this nonsense."

"Mama, please try to comprehend what is happening here," Meredith said tightly. "His lordship does not love Phoebe. He is plotting to use her."

"Doubt that will work," Lydia said bluntly. "Very difficult to use Phoebe unless she wants to be used. She's much too strong-minded for that sort of thing."

Meredith's dainty jaw was rigid. She folded her hands together in her lap and faced Gabriel. "Sir, I know that you have struck up this friendship with Phoebe so that you can use her to punish the rest of us. I beg you to consider that she had nothing to do with what happened eight years ago. She was a mere child at the time."

"You told me that night that she was the one who figured out how to tie the bedsheets together so that you could lower yourself out the window," Gabriel could not resist saying.

Tears shimmered in Meredith's lovely eyes. "Surely you would not punish her for that. She did not understand. She thought it was all a grand adventure. She had been reading those books you were forever giving to me and she had some childish notion that you

172

were a modern-day knight of the Round Table. Heavens, I think she saw you as King Arthur himself."

Lydia looked suddenly alert. "Do you know, I believe you may be on to something, Meredith. Looking back on it, I do believe that was about the time Phoebe developed her lamentable enthusiasm for medieval legends and such. Yes, it all makes sense now." She frowned at Gabriel. "It is all your fault, Wylde."

Gabriel gave her a sharp look. "My fault?"

"Yes, of course." Lydia squinted thoughtfully. "You were the one who got her started on that nonsense. As far as I am concerned, you have already very nearly ruined her life.

"Now, hold on one minute here." It occurred to Gabriel that he was losing control of the situation. "I have done nothing to ruin Phoebe's life. Not yet, at any rate."

Meredith's eyes widened in shock as the implication of his last words sank in.

"Yes, you have," Lydia said, ignoring the implied threat. "She has never married because of you. I blame her current status as a spinster entirely on you."

"Me?" Gabriel stared at Lydia, trying to follow her crazed logic. "You can hardly blame me for the fact that you have not been able to marry her off."

"Yes, I can. Her interest in that medieval nonsense caused her to become far too particular when it came to suitors. None of them could equal the knights in those silly stories she was forever reading."

"Now, see here," Gabriel began.

"Furthermore," Lydia continued, "she has always complained that none of her suitors shared her interest in medieval lore. Except for that dreadful Neil Baxter, of course. Is that not right, Meredith?"

"Quite correct, Mama," Meredith agreed grimly. "But I do not think that is what we wish to discuss with his lordship. There are more pressing problems."

"Good heavens." Lydia frowned. "I cannot imagine anything more pressing than getting Phoebe married off to a suitable husband." She gave Gabriel a conspiratorial look. "In spite of the damage you have done, we still have great hopes for bringing Kilbourne up to scratch, you know."

"Do you, indeed?" Gabriel found the information irritating. Phoebe had not mentioned that Kilbourne was on the verge of making an offer. He discovered he did not care for the notion.

Meredith gave her mother a repressive look. "Mama, if Wylde ruins Phoebe, we shall never get her married off to anyone at all, let alone to Kilbourne."

"Oh, dear." Lydia squinted at Gabriel. "See here, you're not actually planning to ruin my daughter, are you?"

Meredith jerked a lace hankie out of her reticule and dabbed at her eyes. "Of course he is, Mama. That is what this is all about. It is his notion of revenge." She looked up at Gabriel, eyes brimming with crystal tears. "I beg you to give it up, my lord."

"Why should I?" Gabriel asked politely.

"For the sake of what we once had," Meredith cried.

"We did not have all that much, as I recall." Gabriel studied her beautiful, tear-filled eyes and wondered offhandedly what he had ever seen in Meredith. He reflected briefly on the narrow escape he'd had eight years ago and sent up a small prayer of gratitude to whichever saint watched over naive young men.

"Please, my lord. Think of Phoebe."

"It is difficult not to," Gabriel admitted. "She is a very interesting female."

"And an innocent one," Meredith put in quickly.

Gabriel shrugged. "If you say so."

Meredith stared at him in shocked outrage. "Are you implying otherwise, sir?"

"No." Gabriel thought about Neil Baxter,

wondering not for the first time just how deeply Phoebe had cared for the man. "Phoebe and I have never discussed the matter in detail."

"I should hope not," Lydia said sternly. "My daughter may be a trifle eccentric, sir, but she is a perfectly respectable young female. Her reputation is unstained."

"Eccentric? I would suggest she is more than a trifle eccentric," Gabriel retorted.

Lydia shrugged elegantly. "Very well. She has a few unusual interests, the blame for which I lay at your door. But I am certain those can be overlooked by the right man."

"It is not just her *unusual interests* that would concern me if I were responsible for her," Gabriel said.

"Oh, all right. I will admit she is a bit strong-minded on occasion," Lydia conceded. "Perhaps even a shade willful. And she does have a certain independent attitude that some might find objectionable, but there is nothing significant in that."

"Good lord." Gabriel realized Phoebe's family had no notion of just how outrageous she had become. He wondered what Lady Clarington would say were he to inform her that her youngest daughter had taken to meeting men at midnight and setting out on quests to find murderers.

Meredith gave Gabriel a piteous glance. "Sir, will you please give us your word that you will not continue to encourage this friendship with my sister? We both know you are not sincere in it."

"Is that right?" Gabriel asked.

Meredith sniffed into her hankie. "I am not a fool, sir. And neither are the other members of my family. We all know you have revenge in mind. I beg you on bended knee to reconsider that notion. Phoebe does not deserve to suffer for what happened."

"Perhaps not, but one must work with the material that is available," Gabriel said.

At ten-thirty that evening Gabriel propped one shoulder against the wall of the Brantleys' magnificent ballroom and sipped champagne. He was wearing a simple black mask and a black cloak over his evening clothes. Many of the guests, however, were dressed in amazingly elaborate costumes.

He had spotted Phoebe a few minutes ago, shortly after he had arrived. Given what he knew of her interests and her taste in colors, it had not been difficult to find her in the crowd.

She was wearing a high, wide medieval headdress and a gold half mask. Her sleek, dark hair was bound up in a net that glittered with gold thread. Her brilliant turquoise and gold gown was also medieval in style. Her gold satin dancing slippers sparkled as she moved through the crowd on the arm of a man in a brown domino.

Gabriel recognized her companion at once. The brown half mask and matching cloak did not do much to conceal Kilbourne's fair hair or the painfully polite expression on his face.

Gabriel smiled to himself. Phoebe was obviously having a good time, but it was apparent that Kilbourne was merely enduring the masquerade.

Gabriel's eyes narrowed as he watched Kilbourne attempt to pull Phoebe closer to his side. The sight of Phoebe's fingers resting on the earl's sleeve annoyed him. He recalled what Lady Clarington had said about the prospects of Kilbourne making an offer.

Gabriel put down his champagne glass and walked across the crowded room to where Kilbourne and Phoebe stood talking.

Phoebe looked up as he approached. He saw her topaz eyes flash with recognition behind her half mask. Her soft mouth curved into a delighted smile.

"Good evening, Lord Wylde," Phoebe said. "Are you acquainted with Kilbourne?"

"We've met." Kilbourne nodded brusquely.

"Same clubs, I believe."

"Good evening, Kilbourne," Gabriel said. He turned to Phoebe. "I wonder if I might have the next dance, Lady Phoebe?"

"Now, see here, sir," Kilbourne sputtered. "Lady Phoebe is not entirely comfortable on the dance floor."

"Rubbish," Phoebe declared. "I would love to dance." She smiled cheerfully at Kilbourne. "Perhaps I shall see you later, sir."

Kilbourne's irritation was obvious as he inclined his head politely over her hand. "I shall be eagerly awaiting another opportunity to converse with you, Lady Phoebe. As I was saying a moment ago, I would like to speak to you in private later this evening."

"We shall see," Phoebe said noncommittally as she accepted Gabriel's arm.

Gabriel felt a surge of satisfaction at having successfully removed Phoebe from Kilbourne's vicinity. He swung her into the first turn of the waltz, sensed her momentary awkwardness, and steadied her instantly. It was an easy task. She was as light as thistledown.

Phoebe glowed up at him. "I am pleased to see you here, my lord. Have you any news for me of our quest?"

Gabriel's hand tightened on her waist. "Is your quest all you can think about, Phoebe?"

"What else would you have me think about?"

"How about Kilbourne's impending offer? I should think that would be a subject of some interest to you."

Phoebe blinked behind her golden mask. "What do you know of Lord Kilbourne's intentions?"

"Your mother informed me today that she is hoping he can be brought up to scratch."

"Good heavens. My mother came to see you?"

"And your sister."

Phoebe chewed anxiously on her lower lip. "I do hope you were not put off the quest by anything they had to say, sir. I assured you I would manage my family. You must not let them intimidate you."

"Believe me, Phoebe, I am not intimidated by your family. But I was interested to hear that you are on the point of marriage."

Phoebe chuckled. "I am nowhere near the point of marriage, my lord. I can assure you that if and when Kilbourne gets around to making an offer, I shall politely refuse."

"Why?" Gabriel demanded. He realized he suddenly had to discover all he could about Phoebe's relationship with Kilbourne.

Phoebe rolled her eyes behind her mask. "If you have known Kilbourne for any length of time at all, you must see that he would make me an abominable husband."

Gabriel scowled. "He's a marquess and, from all accounts, an extremely wealthy one at that."

"The man is a prig. Believe me, I recognize the species and I have no intention of marrying one. I cannot imagine being tied to such a pompous, unbending creature for the rest of my life. It would be hell on earth."

"In other words," Gabriel said, "you fear he will not allow you to continue in your reckless ways, is that it? No more midnight meetings with strangers and no more quests."

"Kilbourne would not stop there. He is a very straitlaced, very disapproving sort of man. He tries to hide it now, because he is courting me, but I know that if we were to marry, he would try to choose my friends and dictate the cut of my gowns. I would have no freedom whatsoever."

"And you value your freedom?"

"Very much. Mama assures me that it is possible for an intelligent woman to manage a man such as Kilbourne, but I am not taking any chances." Phoebe smiled. "Do you know, my lord, that Kilbourne does not even approve of books such as yours? I believe he would actually try to prohibit me from reading them."

Something inside Gabriel untwisted. He smiled slowly. "In that case I must agree with you. Kilbourne would make you an abominable husband."

Phoebe laughed in delight and her eyes gleamed gold behind her golden mask. The glittering threads in her net twinkled in the light of the chandeliers. Gabriel looked down at her and wondered for an instant if he was holding a real woman or a sorceress.

He feared he was half bewitched. Desire pulsed in his veins. Instinctively he tightened his grasp on Phoebe. Most definitely she could not marry Kilbourne.

"My lord?" She tilted her head slightly, studying his masked face. "Is something wrong?"

"Let's go out into the gardens and get some fresh air," Gabriel muttered.

Phoebe did not resist as he swept her to a halt near the French windows. She lost her balance as he drew her out into the night.

"Not so fast, my lord." She grasped his arm to steady herself.

"I have you," he said quietly. He pulled her closer against his side. *And I am going to keep you,* he added silently. *At least until I have finished my business with your family.*

"The Brantley gardens are quite magnificent," Phoebe said conversationally as they walked along a graveled path. "Have you ever seen them?"

"No." Gabriel took a deep breath of the cool night air. He tried to quell the sensual need that was making his insides clench.

"They are quite extensive. There is an orangery and a maze and a pond with fish in it." Phoebe peered into the shadows. "One cannot see much at night, of course, but I have visited during the day and I was most impressed."

"Phoebe?"

"Yes, my lord?"

"I am not in the mood to discuss gardens."

"I knew it," Phoebe said with cheerful enthusiasm. "You have brought me out here to discuss your investigations, have you not? Tell me, sir, what have you learned? Are we any closer to our goal?"

"That depends on your point of view." Gabriel tugged her away from the lights of the house, deeper into the shadows of the large garden. "I think I can say with some certainty that success is probable."

"Excellent." Phoebe looked up at him. "What have you discovered? Have any of your bookshop contacts supplied you with new information? Have you learned anything in your clubs?"

"There are one or two avenues of inquiry which I intend to pursue." Gabriel realized they were out of sight of the mansion now. He slowed his pace.

Around them loomed great hedges cut into fanciful shapes. The moonlight revealed giant topiary figures in the form of mythical beasts. The graveled path wound through a night-shrouded forest of strange winged animals and snarling dragons.

"I am pleased to hear that, my lord." Phoebe hesitated, glancing around at the bizarre topiary. "This garden is truly spectacular, but it gives one chills at night, does it not?" She stepped closer to Gabriel. "During the day it is all very amusing, but in the darkness, one's imagination takes hold."

"Your imagination is more active than most," Gabriel said.

"You have no room to talk, sir. You are the one who makes a living writing imaginative books."

"Books that Kilbourne would no doubt try to prevent you from reading, were he your husband." Gabriel brought her to a halt in the deep shadows of a giant green Pegasus.

Phoebe smiled whimsically. "I have just explained that there is very little chance Kilbourne will ever become my husband.

Why do you harp on the subject, my lord?"

"Damned if I know." Gabriel felt himself giving in to his hunger. The lady had followed him willingly enough out into the night. She had no sense of decorum. She was reckless and overbold and she was Clarington's daughter.

She deserved what she got.

Gabriel pulled her abruptly into his arms and kissed her.

Phoebe's soft cry of startled surprise was quickly muffled. She did not resist the embrace. Instead, she moved tentatively closer.

Gabriel felt her arms steal slowly up around his neck, and a sense of triumphant excitement washed through him. *She wanted him.* He cradled the nape of her neck in one hand and deliberately deepened the kiss. He bent his head to kiss her throat. She shivered in response.

"Gabriel." Phoebe's voice was infused with a womanly excitement that captivated him.

Her fingers threaded through his hair, tightening with unmistakable urgency. Gabriel felt his already swollen manhood start to throb.

"Do you like this?" Gabriel asked, his lips on the warm skin of her throat. "Tell me you like this."

"Oh, yes." Phoebe sucked in her breath

as he closed his teeth carefully around her earlobe.

"Tell me how much you like it," he insisted. He was intoxicated with her response. She was trembling with it and her reaction made him shudder with his own need.

"I like it very much. I have never felt like this before, Gabriel."

He eased her deeper into the shadows of the looming hedges. His only thought now was to find as much privacy as possible. He could not wait to discover the treasures of her body.

Gabriel heard Phoebe's sharp little gasp of surprise when he lowered the sleeve of her gown. She turned her head into his shoulder, clutching at him as moonlight fell across her bared breast.

Gabriel looked down and thought he had never seen anything more lovely in his life. "Phoebe, you are perfect."

"Oh, Gabriel." She kept her face buried against his shoulder.

"Perfect." He cupped her sweet, apple-shaped breast in his hand and drew his thumb across the nipple. It budded instantly.

Gabriel bent his head and took the firm fruit into his mouth. Phoebe's reaction was immediate. She cried out softly and clung to him as if he were rescuing her from drowning.

Gabriel thought that he was the one who was drowning. He was lost in Phoebe's warmth and softness. Her scent filled his head, claiming his senses. He wanted to know the taste of her, the feel of her lying naked beside him. He ached to know what it would be like to be deep inside her. He longed to feel her shiver with release.

He had never wanted a woman the way he wanted Phoebe.

In the grip of a passion that he refused to deny, Gabriel pulled Phoebe deeper into the exotic greenery. He stopped, shrugged out of his cloak, and spread it on the grass.

Phoebe trembled, but she did not protest as he lowered her onto the cloak and came down beside her. She touched his face. His mask, like hers, concealed only his eyes. Her fingers were achingly gentle on his cheek.

"Gabriel, I think I must be dreaming."

"So am I. We will dream this dream together." He lowered his head and took her nipple gently between his teeth.

She arched herself against him, moaning softly. He stroked his hand down the length of her, reveling in the curve of her hip and thigh.

Gabriel found the hem of the turquoise and gold gown and raised it slowly. He moved his palm up the length of her leg, over her stockings, past the garter which was tied just above the knee. Then he explored farther, letting his fingers drift up the warm skin of her inner thigh. He could feel the heat of her and it nearly drove him mad.

Phoebe gave a small, muffled gasp when he closed his hand around the hot, damp place between her legs.

"Gabriel."

"Hush, love." He kissed her throat and then her breast again. "Let me touch you. You're already wet. I can feel your honey on my fingers."

"Oh, my God," she whispered. Her eyes were very wide in the moonlight and her lips were parted in wonder.

Gabriel raised his head to watch her masked face as he slowly and carefully opened the soft, plump folds that guarded her secrets. He saw her touch the tip of her tongue to the corner of her mouth. She clutched nervously at his shoulders.

When he gently eased one finger inside her, he almost lost what was left of his self-control. She was so tight. So hot. So ready for him.

Phoebe froze, her mouth open, her eyes glazed. "Gabriel?"

Gabriel knew for certain then that she had never been this intimate with a man. He felt a glorious thrill at the knowledge. Whatever Neil Baxter had meant to her, she had not allowed him to make love to her. He suddenly felt a fierce need to protect her even as he introduced her to her own passion.

"Calm yourself, sweet. I will be very careful with you." Gabriel sealed the solemn vow with a shower of small kisses across her breasts. "I won't hurt you. You're going to want me as much as I want you."

He moved his finger gently within her, easing it slowly out of her tight passage. She flinched in reaction, but she did not pull away from him. He entered her slowly again with his finger. Then he touched the tiny mound of sensitive flesh that was concealed within the soft thatch of hair. Phoebe stiffened and cried out against his jacket. He stroked her again.

"Gabriel, I do not . . . I cannot think . . ."

"This is not a time to think. This is a time to feel. Shall I tell you how you feel to me? You feel sweet. So sweet and soft and so responsive. My God, it's like touching liquid fire."

"I, oh, Gabriel, this is so strange. . . ."

He felt her body gradually begin to tighten demandingly around his finger. He continued to stroke her, enthralled by her response. When she began to lift herself against his hand, silently asking for more, he felt as if he had been handed a priceless treasure.

Phoebe was breathing more quickly now. Gabriel could feel her untutored body striving toward a release it did not yet recognize. He wanted to shout his own satisfaction from the rooftops. After tonight she would look at him as she had never looked at him before.

After tonight she would not dream of Neil Baxter.

Gabriel heard the soft crunch of shoes on gravel an instant before Phoebe went up in flames in his arms. He reacted instinctively, aware that Phoebe had heard nothing. She was too deeply enmeshed in the coils of the passionate spell he had woven for her. It was too late to call her back to the real world.

Gabriel did the only thing he could. He crushed Phoebe's mouth with his own just as she shuddered and convulsed in his arms. He barely managed to swallow her soft scream of release.

Then he swiftly pulled her close and wrapped the black cloak around her, holding her tightly as the small tremors rippled through her.

There was a moment of screaming silence and then Phoebe went limp.

Gravel crunched on the other side of the

hedge. Phoebe tensed in Gabriel's arms. He realized she must have heard the sound. She stilled abruptly and huddled against him.

"Lady Phoebe?" Kilbourne's voice called loudly in the darkness. "I say, are you out here?"

Gabriel felt Phoebe's stunned reaction. He leaned his head down and whispered soundlessly into her ear. "Hush."

She nodded frantically to indicate she understood.

Kilbourne's shoes came closer. Gabriel continued to hold Phoebe pressed against him. He glanced around and realized that they were surrounded by the green walls formed by the high hedges. With any luck, Kilbourne would not come this way.

The sound of footsteps on gravel drew closer. Gabriel held his breath, willing Kilbourne to move on. There was a muttered oath on the other side of one hedge. Then Kilbourne's footfalls receded into the distance. Gabriel relaxed as he realized Kilbourne was returning to the house.

Gabriel waited a moment longer until he was certain the marquess was out of hearing range. Then he unwrapped Phoebe from the folds of his black cloak.

She sat up looking delightfully bedraggled. Her elaborate headdress was askew and a lock of her hair had escaped the golden net that had bound it. Her mask had slipped down over her nose.

"Gracious, that was a close thing," Phoebe muttered as she attempted to adjust her head-dress. "I shudder to think what a disaster it would have been if Kilbourne had seen us."

Gabriel, his body still throbbing with desire and the battle-ready tension inspired by Kilbourne's approach, was inexplicably annoyed by the comment. "It's a bit late to be worrying about your reputation, madam."

Phoebe paused, her hands resting on the rim of the headdress. "I suppose you are right. It was a very narrow escape. Just think, if Kilbourne had seen us in that extremely compromising situation, you would have had to announce our engagement tomorrow."

Gabriel got to his feet and pulled her up beside him. "The thought of me announcing our engagement alarms you so much, madam?"

"Certainly it does." She looked up at him as she straightened her mask.

"Because your family would be outraged?"

"My family's reaction is not the issue. I am twenty-four years old and I do as I please. For the most part. The thing is, Gabriel, I have no overwhelming interest in marriage, although I see now that there are some benefits I had not fully comprehended."

"Hell and damnation."

"But if I were to marry," she continued relentlessly, "I would want to do so for love, not because I had been caught rolling about in the Brantleys' hedges."

Gabriel's outrage increased tenfold. He took a step forward and deliberately loomed over her. "It was a hell of a lot more than a matter of rolling about in the hedges, madam. And what, may I ask, makes you think I would have felt it necessary to announce our intention to marry if we had been caught?"

"Oh, you would have done the honorable thing, Gabriel. It's your nature."

"Your faith in me is sadly misplaced, madam. Once and for all, I am not the knight of your dreams. I am no King Arthur."

Phoebe smiled slightly at that. She stood on tiptoe and brushed her mouth across his. "Your armor may be slightly tarnished, but underneath I believe you are still the same man you were eight years ago. You would not be helping me in my quest if that were not so."

"Damn it, Phoebe — "

"I know that eight years ago you loved my sister, and I know that I am not in the least like her, so it is very unlikely you will ever love me."

"Phoebe, you don't know what you're talking about," Gabriel said.

"Yes, I do. I always know what I am talking about. Now, as I do not wish to marry a man who does not love me, and as I am well aware that a man of your nature would not wish to marry without love, either, we must have no more adventures together such as the one we shared tonight."

Gabriel stared at her, thunderstruck. "You expect me to just agree to that?"

"Do not misunderstand me, my lord," she said quickly. "It was all really quite pleasant."

"Pleasant!"

"Well, perhaps even better than pleasant. But I am certain you can comprehend the danger involved. Surely you do not wish to find yourself tied to me for the rest of your life because of a fleeting indiscretion."

"I don't believe this is the same woman who met me on that road in Sussex at midnight."

"Yes, well, it is. I know you find me reckless, but I am not a complete idiot."

"It strikes me that your mother has a sound point," Gabriel said. "She complained that you have been entirely too particular when it comes to your suitors. You don't want to marry a man like Kilbourne who will try to guide you — "

"Bully me is more like it. And no, I most certainly do not want to marry a man like him." Phoebe shuddered delicately.

Gabriel glowered at her. "And you don't want to marry any man who will not get down on his knees to vow his undying love — "

"Of course not."

"Your mother believes you're looking for a goddamned knight straight out of a legend."

She smiled brilliantly up at him. "Why should I settle for less?"

"You, madam, are too damn choosy for a woman of your advanced years. Good God. Why am I standing here talking to you of marriage?"

"I don't know. Why *are* you talking to me about it, my lord?"

"Never mind. We shall discuss this matter at another time. Rest assured that sooner or later we shall both repeat the experience we shared tonight. And a bit more into the bargain." Gabriel grabbed her hand and started down the narrow aisle shaped by the hedges.

"There is really nothing to discuss, Gabriel. I fear I must be quite firm about this matter. We must not take such risks in the future."

"There damn well is more to discuss. A great deal more. If you think that I am going to keep my hands off you after this, you're mad." He scowled as he realized he had come to the end of the hedge aisle and was facing another hedge. "What the devil?"

"Oh, dear." Phoebe glanced around at the looming walls of green. "I believe we have wandered into Lord Brantley's maze. He is quite proud of it. No one has ever found his way out on his own. Only Brantley knows the secret route."

Gabriel slammed his hand against the hedge in disgust. "Christ. This is all it needed."

"I fail to see the problem here, Gabriel." Phoebe smiled encouragingly at him in the moonlight. "I believe the hero of your book found himself trapped in a maze on page three hundred and four."

"So he did. What the hell has that got to do with anything?"

"He found his way out through some very clever reasoning, as I recall," Phoebe said. "I have complete faith that you can get us out of here using the same process. You had best hurry, however. We must return to the ball before someone else besides Kilbourne misses me."

Chapter 9

Later that night Gabriel stalked up the steps of the town house he had rented for the Season. He was not in a cheerful frame of mind. In fact, he was in a very strange mood.

The fact that Phoebe was now more convinced than ever that he was hero material only served to deepen his odd sense of gloom.

So what if he had been able to find his way out of Brantley's idiotic maze? It had not been all that difficult. He had simply put one hand on one wall of green and had not lifted his palm until he and Phoebe had arrived back at the entrance of the maze.

It was the same technique the hero of *The Quest* had used. Gabriel had read the advice for solving the puzzle of a maze years ago in some ancient medieval manuscript. He had never expected to have to apply the information in real life.

He had secretly been both exceedingly relieved and quite surprised that the method had worked.

Phoebe, of course, had taken the outcome

for granted. *There, you see? I knew you could do it, Wylde. This sort of thing is stock-in-trade for a man of your sort.*

Gabriel had been tempted to put her over his knee. Her blithe assumption that he was interchangeable with the hero of his novel was beginning to eat at him.

"Go back to bed, Shelton," he said to his sleepy-eyed butler when the town house door was opened. "I'm going to work for a while."

"Yes, my lord." Shelton obediently vanished through the door behind the staircase whence he had come.

Gabriel walked into the library, tossed his black domino onto a chair, and lit a lamp on the desk. He poured himself a glass of brandy from the crystal decanter on the small table near the hearth. The fiery liquid calmed his sense of frustration. His gaze fell on the folds of the black cloak he had worn earlier.

Hot memories of how Phoebe had looked in the moonlight as she burned in his arms exploded again in his head.

Matters were not working out quite as he had planned.

It was not that his scheme for revenge was going badly, he realized. It was that he was starting to have grave misgivings. What the devil was the matter with him? he wondered.

It had seemed so simple when he had left Devil's Mist. He would pursue and seduce Phoebe and in the process humiliate and outrage Clarington. In the end, when the reckless little wench had been well and truly bedded, Clarington would swallow his pride and beg Gabriel to marry her.

Gabriel had planned to look Clarington straight in the eye and decline the offer of his ruined daughter's hand in marriage. Only then would Clarington learn that Gabriel was no fortune hunter, and there was nothing he could do to force the marriage.

As for Phoebe, she would deserve what she got. She was an ungovernable hoyden, an impulsive, headstrong female who would learn the hard way that she had taken one too many chances, played one too many dangerous games.

Gabriel had consoled his uneasy conscience by telling himself that Phoebe was no green girl fresh out of the schoolroom. She was twenty-four years old and not averse to making arrangements to meet strangers at midnight on lonely country lanes.

He certainly did not intend to boast about his conquest once the deed was done. He had no intention of ruining the lady's reputation in Society. His only goal was to trample on the overweening pride of the

Earl of Clarington.

A simple, straightforward sort of vengeance.

Gabriel stared at the black cloak and recalled the feel of Phoebe as she responded to his touch. So sweet, so passionate. Bringing her to her first climax had made him feel like the all-conquering knight she believed him to be. When he had heard Kilbourne's approach outside the maze, his first instinct had been to protect her.

Gabriel took another sip of the brandy and thought about the glow of admiration that had lit Phoebe's eyes when he had found his way back to the entrance of the maze. He shook his head over her unwavering confidence that he would help her find Neil Baxter's killer.

It was all beginning to seem bloody damn complicated.

Hell, maybe he should just marry the little baggage and be done with it.

That thought shook him to the core.

"Damnation." Surely he was not going to weaken at this juncture. There was no point. He could have it all: the lady and the vengeance.

He thought of Phoebe's laughing eyes and innocent recklessness.

Gabriel went to the window and cautiously

allowed himself to consider the outrageous notion of making Phoebe his countess.

It would mean he would have to abandon his revenge against her family.

True, he could torment them for a while longer, but sooner or later they would learn that he was not the fortune hunter they believed him to be. They might not ever learn to like him, but they could not disapprove of him. He was, after all, everything they wanted in a husband for Phoebe.

It would mean he would have to find a way to handle a bold, adventurous wife who would no doubt lead him a merry dance for the rest of his days.

It would mean having Phoebe in his bed.

Gabriel realized he was smiling slightly at his own reflection in the window.

Bloody hell. He could do worse. She certainly lived up to the newly invented Wylde motto: *I dare.* She had courage. She would make a good mother for his sons.

Furthermore, Phoebe was the only woman he had ever met who might actually enjoy living at Devil's Mist. Any other respectable female of the *ton* would probably refuse to step foot inside the ancient, drafty castle.

Yes, he could do worse.

The realization that he was on the point of abandoning his revenge staggered him.

He would have to give the matter a great deal more thought before he made his decision.

Gabriel turned and walked over to his desk. He put down the brandy glass and reached toward the lamp. He hesitated as he glanced down at his desk. Something was wrong. One of the drawers was partially open, as if someone had been in a hurry and forgotten to close it completely.

He had left the drawers closed. And locked.

Someone had gone through his desk.

The writer in him nearly succumbed to panic. He yanked open the drawer that contained *A Reckless Venture* and hurriedly checked page numbers. He lowered himself slowly into his chair and swore in profound relief when he realized there were no missing pages.

Then common sense took over. Gabriel stood up again and calmly checked the contents of his small library. On close inspection it was clear several books had been moved about on their shelves, but nothing appeared to be missing. He glanced around the room, noting the furnishings. He wondered why the intruder had not taken the silver candlesticks or the handsome basaltware urn. Either could have brought the thief a nice price.

His library had been thoroughly searched, but nothing had been stolen. Gabriel knew he would have felt less uneasy if something of value had been taken. This situation raised the fine hairs on the back of his neck. It also raised questions.

In the morning he would interview the entire staff. If he was satisfied that none of the servants was involved, he would instruct Shelton to institute precautions so that this sort of thing did not happen again.

Three days after the Brantley masquerade Phoebe and Meredith were sitting in the drawing room of the Clarington town house when Lydia burst triumphantly through the door.

"He's rich, he's rich. And Kilbourne's in dun territory. Can you believe it? Kilbourne, of all people. Who would have dreamed it?" Lydia was crowing with excitement. "Wait until your papa hears this."

Phoebe stared at her mother in amazement. "What on earth are you talking about, Mama?"

"Kilbourne. And Wylde." Lydia ripped off her fashionable French bonnet and tossed it aside. She sat down on the yellow sofa with the air of Cleopatra sitting on her throne. "Someone pour me a cup of tea."

203

"Yes, Mama." Meredith reached for the green and white Worcester teapot.

"Better yet," Lydia said hastily, "see if there is any sherry in the decanter, Phoebe. I need something medicinal. This has all come as a monumental shock."

Meredith gave her mother a gently disapproving look as Phoebe rose and walked over to the sherry decanter. "Calm yourself, Mama. You are in a state."

"I should say so." Lydia snapped the sherry glass out of Phoebe's hand and took a swallow. "And with good reason. Wait until you hear the details."

Phoebe's brows rose as she sat down again. "Where did you hear them, Mama?"

"At Lady Birkenshaw's card party this afternoon. Nellie was so excited that she forgot to pay attention to her cards. Lost three hundred pounds to me before she even realized what had happened." Lydia paused to gloat briefly. "But after I heard the news, I was obliged to stop playing altogether. Simply could not concentrate."

"What news, Mama?" Meredith asked firmly. "What did you say about Kilbourne being in dun territory?"

"Under the hatches, done up, financially embarrassed. The man is virtually without funds." Lydia took a swallow of sherry. "Not that you'd know it, of course. He's managed to conceal it all Season, but Lord Birkenshaw stumbled on the truth this morning when his solicitor advised him not to go into partnership with Kilbourne."

"Ah-hah," Phoebe said. "So that's why Kilbourne has been pursuing me this Season. The man is looking for an heiress. I knew there was a reason he suddenly found me so eminently suitable to be his marchioness."

"Good lord." Meredith looked stunned. "Kilbourne was trying to latch on to Phoebe before anyone discovered the truth about his finances."

"Precisely." Lydia set down her glass. "Wait until your father hears about this. He will be outraged. Kilbourne was after Phoebe's fortune all along."

"And here I thought he would be such a sound, stable, mature influence on Phoebe," Meredith said regretfully. "What a pity."

Phoebe eyed her mother and sister. "There is no sense going into mourning over this. I have tried to make it clear all along that I was not interested in accepting an offer from Kilbourne."

"He is a marquess," Meredith reminded her.

"He is a prig," Phoebe said.

Lydia held up her hand. "Enough. It is

over. We have had a close call and that is the end of it. The good news is that we can now consider an offer from Wylde."

Phoebe and Meredith stared at her.

"Mama, what are you saying?" Meredith demanded.

Lydia smiled with smug satisfaction. "My dears, Wylde is as rich as Croesus."

Meredith gasped. "What on earth?"

"It's true." Lydia gave Phoebe a conspirator's smile. "As rich as your father. Always thought the boy would make something of himself out there in the South Seas."

Phoebe swallowed. "I don't believe it."

"Oh, it's all true enough. Nellie was certain of it. The solicitor who advised her husband not to get involved with Kilbourne suggested he consider investing in one of Wylde's ships instead."

"Ships?" Meredith was wide-eyed.

"Ships," Lydia repeated. "Plural. As in more than one ship. As in a great many ships that have extremely lucrative trading arrangements with America. Wylde has been extremely discreet about the state of his finances, but the extent of his fortune had to come out sooner or later. His business dealings are too extensive to be hidden for long."

"Good heavens," Meredith breathed. "Why has Wylde been so secretive? And why has he been taunting Papa by pretending he is interested in Phoebe?"

Lydia frowned. "I do not believe he is pretending an interest in Phoebe. I believe the man is quite serious. And as for taunting Clarington, I expect Wylde is merely getting some of his own back for what your papa did to him eight years ago."

Phoebe was horrified at the misunderstanding. "Mama, I must make it clear to you that Wylde and I are merely friends. There has been absolutely no talk of marriage. You must not delude yourself."

"There, you see?" Meredith poured herself another cup of tea. "I knew it. Wylde's intentions, whatever they may be, are definitely not honorable."

Phoebe turned on her sister. "Meredith, you must not say such things. Wylde is a very honorable man."

"If that were the case, why is he hanging around you and not showing any signs of offering for you?" Meredith retorted.

"Because we are friends," Phoebe said, feeling desperate. She could hardly explain about the quest to find Neil's killer. "We have interests in common. I assure you, that is all there is to it."

Meredith shook her head sadly. "I am so sorry, Phoebe. But you must be realistic.

There is only one reason why Wylde is continually in your company these days. He is plotting to ruin you in order to avenge himself on all of us."

Phoebe leaped to her feet. "You are wrong. I will not listen to any more of this nonsense. Wylde and I have no plans to marry. I am well aware that I am not his type. But we are friends and we intend to remain friends, and that is all there is to it."

Phoebe rushed out of the room and fled up the stairs to the privacy of her bedchamber. She closed the door and flung herself into the chair near the window.

So Gabriel was rich, after all. So what did that signify?

The fact that Gabriel was wealthy did not particularly surprise her. Gabriel was one of those amazingly competent men who gave one the impression they could do anything they set out to do. If he had set out to make his fortune in the South Seas, then it was not at all startling that he had succeeded.

His wealth or lack thereof had never been important to Phoebe. She had fallen in love with him for other reasons.

Love.

Yes, love. Phoebe closed her eyes and gripped the arm of her chair. She might as well admit it to herself. She had been in love with Gabriel since that night she had met him on that moonlit lane in Sussex.

Since the first time he had kissed her.

Perhaps even before that. Phoebe wondered sadly if she had fallen in love with him when she had read his first manuscript and realized the author was the man who had embodied her youthful ideal of knighthood.

She had instructed Lacey to write back immediately saying they would publish *The Quest*. She had dictated every sentence of that letter: . . . *A new species of novel. A very inspiring treatment of the subject of love*. . . .

Shortly after that, she had started to dream of him. When she realized she needed a knight-errant to help her track down Neil's killer, Gabriel had been the obvious choice.

There was no doubt about it. Gabriel had filled her thoughts for weeks and she had begun to realize he would haunt her for the rest of her life.

What a tangle it all was. There was Mama downstairs chortling over the notion of marrying Phoebe off to Wylde. Meredith was terrified that Gabriel was plotting to ruin Phoebe in order to avenge himself against the entire family. Anthony and Papa would no doubt fear something equally dire. Either that or they would begin to press Gabriel for an offer.

Phoebe groaned and dropped her head into her hands. No one listened when she tried to explain that Wylde was merely a friend. And they would not comprehend or approve if she tried to tell them he was merely assisting her in a quest to find a murderer.

The more she was seen in Wylde's company, the more her family would conclude that Gabriel was either plotting revenge or intending to make an offer.

Disaster loomed. How long could this state of affairs continue? she wondered.

The knock on the door of her bedchamber interrupted Phoebe's chaotic thoughts. "Come in."

One of the maids stepped into the room and made a small curtsy. "I've got a message for ye, ma'am." She held out a folded note. "A boy brung it around to the kitchens a few minutes ago."

"A message?" Surprised, Phoebe got to her feet. "Let me see it."

She took the note and frowned intently over the contents.

Madam: Allow me to introduce myself. My name is A. Rilkins. I am a bookseller with a small shop in Willard Lane. An excellent copy of a very rare medieval manuscript has just come into my possession. The illustrations are extremely fine and the tale concerns a knight of the Round Table. I am told you are interested in such books. I shall hold this volume until four o'clock this afternoon, after which time I shall be obliged to notify other interested parties.

Yours,
A. Rilkins

"Good heavens," Phoebe breathed. "Another tale of the Round Table has come to light. How exciting." She glanced up at the maid. "I want you to have one of the footmen dispatch a note for me."

"Yes, ma'am."

Phoebe went over to her escritoire, picked up a pen, and quickly jotted a message to Gabriel. He would be as interested in Mr. Rilkins's find as she was and would no doubt want to rendezvous at the bookshop to examine it with her. They could determine its value together.

Phoebe folded the note and handed it to the maid. "There. See that this is sent at once. Then send Betsy to me and have one of the footmen ask Morris to have the carriage brought around. I shall be going out this afternoon."

"Yes, ma'am." The maid curtsied again and hurried off down the hall.

Phoebe jumped to her feet and opened her wardrobe. She would be seeing Gabriel, so she wanted to look her best. She wondered if she should wear the golden yellow jaconet muslin or the new peacock-blue walking dress.

She decided on the muslin.

Phoebe and her maid set off within the hour for A. Rilkins's Bookshop. Both were a bit startled when they realized the route was taking them toward the river.

Betsy looked out the window and frowned anxiously. "This isn't a very good part of town, ma'am."

"No, it isn't, is it?" Phoebe reached into her reticule and pulled out Rilkins's note. "Willard Lane. I have never heard of it, have you?"

"No, but the coachman seemed to know where it was."

"Ask him to make certain."

Betsy obediently lifted the trapdoor in the ceiling of the carriage and shouted up to the coachman. "Are ye sure this is the way to Willard Lane?"

"Aye. Willard Lane's down by the docks.

Why? Has her ladyship changed her mind? I can turn the carriage around."

Betsy looked at Phoebe. "Well, ma'am? Would you like to go back?"

"No, of course not," Phoebe said. She had been in worse places than this in pursuit of a manuscript. A lonely lane in Sussex at midnight, for example. "I cannot miss out on an opportunity such as this merely because Mr. Rilkins cannot afford an establishment in a better part of town. We must press on."

Willard Lane proved to be a very narrow passage that was not much more than an alley. The stately Clarington town carriage would not fit into the entrance. The coachman brought the horses to a halt some distance away and the footman jumped down to escort Phoebe and her maid into A. Rilkins's Bookshop.

Phoebe glanced up at the barely legible sign over the entrance of the shop as she went through the door. It was obvious Mr. Rilkins was not a terribly successful bookseller. His premises were extremely shabby. The shop windows were so dusty she could not even see into the dark interior.

A dank, musty smell greeted Phoebe as she stepped into the shop. For a moment she could not make out any details in the gloom. Then a figure moved behind the counter.

A small wizened man with the face of a rat came around the corner. He squinted at her through a pair of spectacles and bobbed his head.

"Welcome to my humble shop, my lady. I expect you'll be the one who's come about the old manuscript, eh?"

Phoebe smiled. "Yes, that is correct." She glanced quickly around the tiny shop. It was virtually empty. There were no other customers about and there were only a handful of dusty volumes on the shelves. There was no sign of Gabriel. "No one else has arrived to look at it?"

"No one else." Rilkins cackled. "I am offering you the privilege of examining it before I notify any of my other regular patrons."

Phoebe realized Rilkins had probably calculated that he could get more out of her for the book than he could out of some of his regulars. "I appreciate your notifying me of your discovery, Mr. Rilkins. May I ask how you learned that I collect medieval volumes?"

"Word spreads among those of us who deal in books, madam. Word spreads."

"I see. Well, then, shall we get on with it? I am eager to see this manuscript."

"Right this way, madam, right this way. I've got it in my back room. Didn't want to risk putting something that valuable out in the front of the shop. Not the best of neighborhoods, you see."

"I understand." Phoebe started forward eagerly. Betsy followed.

Mr. Rilkins hesitated at the door behind the counter. "Your servants will have to wait out here, if you don't mind. Not enough room for all of us back here."

Phoebe glanced at Betsy and the footman. "I'll be right out," she assured them.

Betsy nodded. "We'll wait for ye outside, ma'am."

"That will be fine."

Mr. Rilkins opened the door into what appeared to be a tiny, darkened office. Phoebe swept through it, glancing around for the manuscript.

"I cannot tell you how much I appreciate this, Mr. Rilkins."

"My pleasure." Rilkins closed the door.

Gloom descended instantly. There was so much dirt on the tiny window that it blocked what little light might have filtered in from the alley.

"I'll light a candle," Mr. Rilkins said.

Phoebe heard him fumbling about behind her. She heard another sound, too. The slide of a booted foot across the wooden floor sent a chill of fear through her.

"Is there someone else in here?" she asked. She swung around quickly. Too quickly. Her left leg crumpled. Phoebe started to lose her balance. She grabbed at the edge of the desk.

A man's arm closed around her throat. A fat, filthy palm slapped across her mouth, cutting off her scream before it had even begun.

Terrified, Phoebe started to struggle. She lashed out with her reticule and connected with a man's shin. She heard an angry grunt from her captor. Encouraged, she kicked back. The toe of her half boot struck flesh again.

"Damme. The little wench is a fighter," the man hissed. "Get her feet, Ned. We ain't got much time."

Phoebe kicked out again, but this time a second man emerged from the gloom. He caught her ankles in two powerful fists. Phoebe was hoisted up off the floor between her two captors.

"Hurry, now. Hurry along there. He'll be waitin' for his lady, he will." Mr. Rilkins hastened across the small office and opened another door. This one fronted on a dark alley. He peered out and then nodded to the two men holding Phoebe. "No one about.

We'll meet this evening to settle up as planned."

"We'll be there, Rilkins," one of the villains growled. "Just make sure ye bring the blunt."

"I'll have it. His lordship is going to pay us very well for this day's work."

Phoebe groaned furiously and fought to free herself. It was useless.

Rilkins threw a dirty blanket over her and she was carted out into the foul-smelling alley as if she were a load of trash being removed from the bookshop.

Gabriel was relaxing in his club when Clarington approached with a thunderous scowl. Anthony was with him.

"Now, see here, Wylde, this game of yours has gone far enough," Clarington barked. He sat down abruptly. "What the devil is this about you being rich as Croesus?"

Gabriel looked up with a quizzical smile. "I'm surprised at you, Clarington. Talking about money is so very vulgar, don't you think?"

Anthony glowered. "Damnation, man, what's going on? Is it true you brought back a fortune from the South Seas?"

Gabriel shrugged. "I won't starve."

"Then what the bloody hell are you about?" Clarington demanded. "You won't be bought off and you haven't offered for Phoebe. Now we find out that you don't need her fortune, so apparently you ain't planning to run off with her. *So what are you about?*"

Anthony's gaze narrowed. "You've thought of another form of revenge, haven't you? It isn't money you want. You plan to seduce my sister. That's how you're going to avenge yourself on all of us. Damn it, man, have you no shame?"

"Very little," Gabriel admitted. "Strong morals are a luxury. One becomes extremely practical in a hurry when one finds oneself in the situation I was in eight years ago."

"You actually blame us for protecting her from an upstart fortune hunter such as you were then?" Anthony looked incredulous. "How the hell would you have felt if Meredith had been your sister?"

Clarington's bushy white brows snapped together. His face reddened. "Yes, by God, how would you have felt at the time if Meredith had been your daughter? You'll probably have a girl of your own someday. I'd like to see how far you'd go to protect her from fortune hunters."

A discreet cough interrupted Gabriel before he could respond.

"Ahem," the club's hall porter said. "I beg pardon, your lordships. I have a message for Lord Wylde. I am told it is important."

Gabriel glanced around and saw the note on the salver the porter was extending. He picked it up. "Who brought this, Bailey?"

"A young lad. He said he had been dispatched from your butler."

Gabriel opened the note and scanned the contents.

Sir: By the time you read this I shall be en route to A. Rilkins' Bookshop in Willard Lane to examine a manuscript that would appear to interest both of us. If you would care to view it, you may meet me there. But I warn you, when it comes to purchasing it, I have first crack at it.

Your friend,
P.

"Good God." Gabriel got to his feet. "Has anyone ever heard of Willard Lane?"

"Down by the docks, I believe," Anthony said, still scowling.

"I was afraid of that," Gabriel said. He knew every important bookseller in London and he had never heard of A. Rilkins. Trust Phoebe to go tearing off to a disreputable part of town in pursuit of a manuscript.

"Sit down, Wylde. We're talking to you,"

Clarington ordered.

"I fear we shall have to continue this fascinating conversation some other time," Gabriel said. "I must attend to a small, rather annoying problem that has come up."

He strode swiftly past Clarington and Anthony without a backward glance. It was time he reined in the headstrong young female he intended to marry.

Chapter 10

The hackney coachman knew the location of Willard Lane. Gabriel promised him a large tip if he made good time. The man was happy to oblige.

Gabriel sat back in the seat, arms crossed, jaw rigid, and contemplated what he would say to Phoebe. The closer the hackney carriage got to Willard Lane, the more annoyed Gabriel became. He eyed the grimy taverns and coffeehouses filled with dockside workers and seamen.

This was a dangerous part of town. Phoebe should have had enough sense not to come here on her own. But common sense was not one of Phoebe's strong suits, he reminded himself. She had obviously been overindulged by her family. She had been allowed to run wild.

Once she was his wife, he was going to put a stop to her reckless ways. There would be no more dashing about in pursuit of old books on her own. If she wanted to take chances, she could bloody well take them with him.

The hackney came to a halt in a narrow street. Gabriel got out.

"Sorry, m'lord. This is as close as I can get," the coachman explained as he took Gabriel's money. "The lanes ain't much wider than alleys in this part o' town. Too narrow for this carriage. Ye'll have to walk from here."

"Very well. Wait here. I shall return shortly."

The coachman nodded obligingly and reached for the flask he kept under the box.

Gabriel spotted the stately Clarington town coach half a block away when he rounded the corner. Painted maroon and trimmed in black, it was impossible to miss. Relieved to see it, he started to cross the narrow cobbled street.

He was partway across when he noticed another carriage parked at the entrance to a nearby alley. It was a small, sleek vehicle horsed by a pair of swift-looking grays. The expensive equipage was as out of place in this neighborhood as the Clarington town coach. Gabriel took a closer look and noticed that the crest on the carriage door had been deliberately obscured with a black cloth and that the curtains were drawn. He started toward it.

At that moment he heard commotion in

the alley. Ice-cold fingers gripped his insides. He had known this feeling before more than once out in the South Seas. He had learned not to ignore it.

Gabriel broke into a run. His boots rang on the cobblestones as he approached the alley.

Muttered curses and a muffled scream greeted Gabriel as he reached the narrow entrance. Two burly men were struggling with a squirming bundle wrapped in a large blanket.

Gabriel took in the scene before him in a single instant and leaped forward.

The two men were so busy trying to subdue their wriggling burden that they did not immediately see Gabriel. He grabbed the shoulder of the first, spun him around, and drove a fist straight into the man's florid, sweating face.

The man grunted, dropped his end of the bundle, and stumbled back against the alley wall.

"What the bloody 'ell?" The other man stared for an instant and then he, too, dropped his burden. The figure in the gray cloth landed ignominiously on the dirty stones.

The second man reached into his boot and came out with a knife. He grinned evilly at Gabriel. " 'Ere, now, mate. I'll teach you to interfere in a private business matter."

He lunged at Gabriel, who sidestepped quickly. Gabriel reached out as the man went past and shoved hard, increasing his assailant's momentum. The man lost his balance and his footing. His boots skidded on the slimy cobblestones. He fetched up against his cohort, who was just struggling to right himself. Both men went down. The knife skittered away.

Gabriel reached into his own boot for the knife he had carried there for nearly eight years. He had picked up the habit during his first few months in the islands. Old habits were hard to break. He walked forward and held the tip of the blade to the second man's throat.

" 'Ere, now, don't go gettin' excited, mate." The man smiled placatingly. The effect was somewhat spoiled by the mouthful of dark, rotting teeth that were revealed. "You want 'er, she's all yers. We was goin' to get a fair price for 'er, though from that gentry cove in the fancy carriage. Don't suppose you could make things even by meetin' 'is price?"

"Get out of here," Gabriel said softly.

"Right you are, mate. We're on our way." Both villains eyed the knife and the professional manner in which Gabriel held it. Then they eased back toward the alley entrance.

"No 'arm done," the first man said. "Like my friend says, she's all yers."

The two darted out of the alley and vanished.

Gabriel slipped the knife back into his boot and walked over to the flopping bundle. He was not particularly surprised when he caught a glimpse of a golden yellow muslin skirt. He reached down and extricated Phoebe from the folds of the blanket.

"Are you all right?" He surveyed her quickly from head to toe as he hauled her to her feet. She looked bedraggled but unhurt.

"Yes, I am fine. Oh, Gabriel, you saved me." Phoebe launched herself straight into his arms.

Gabriel heard the sound of carriage wheels outside the alley entrance just as his arms started to tighten around Phoebe.

"Hell." He released Phoebe and ran toward the front of the alley.

"Gabriel? What is it?" Phoebe hurried after him.

Gabriel did not wait for her. He saw the carriage with the obscured crest. The coachman was unfurling his whip, about to lash the team into full gallop.

"Hold," Gabriel shouted with the voice of authority he had once used to give orders in the South Seas. The coachman hesitated, turning his head to see who had given the command.

By the time the man realized Gabriel was in pursuit, it was too late. Gabriel had reached the door of the carriage. He jerked it open, reached inside, and clamped a hand around the arm of the occupant. He yanked the startled man out into the street.

Phoebe, clutching at her reticule and bonnet and hampered by her weak left leg, came to a startled halt. *"Kilbourne."*

Kilbourne did not look at her. He brushed off his sleeve with a disdainful movement and glowered at Gabriel with cool hauteur.

"I suppose you have an explanation for this unwarranted behavior, Wylde?"

"Of course." Gabriel kept his voice lethally soft so that Phoebe, who was still some distance off, would not overhear. "And I shall be happy to give it to you over a brace of pistols at dawn. My seconds will call on you this evening."

Kilbourne's composure faded rapidly. His face mottled with rage. "Now, see here, what do you think you're doing?"

"He is saving me from being kidnapped by you," Phoebe said furiously as she reached Gabriel's side. She was panting from her recent struggles and still frantically attempting to adjust her bonnet. "I know what this is all about."

"Phoebe, go back to your carriage," Gabriel ordered quietly.

She ignored him, her eyes bright with outrage as she glared at Kilbourne. "My mother told me this morning that it will soon be all over Town that you are done up, my lord. You knew my father would no longer be in the mood to entertain an offer for my hand if he learned you were penniless, did you not?"

"Phoebe," Gabriel said sharply.

"So you lured me here under false pretenses and tried to kidnap me," Phoebe continued triumphantly. "Well, you certainly did not get away with it, did you, sir? I knew Wylde would save me. He is very good at that sort of thing."

Gabriel clamped a hand around her shoulder and turned her to face him. "Not another word out of you, madam. Go back to your carriage and go directly home. We will discuss this later. Do you understand me?"

She blinked. "Well, yes, of course. You are quite clear, my lord, but I have a few things to say to Lord Kilbourne first."

"You will go home now, Phoebe." For a moment he thought she was going to argue further. Gabriel braced himself for the battle.

Then Phoebe shrugged and wrinkled her nose in disgust.

"Oh, very well." She shot Kilbourne one last gloating look. "You will be very sorry for this, my lord." She whirled around and marched off, her golden skirts a vivid blot of color against the gray landscape.

Gabriel waited until she was once more out of earshot. Then he inclined his head with mocking formality. "Until our dawn appointment, Kilbourne. I shall be looking forward to it." He turned and started toward the hackney coach.

"Damn you, Wylde, come back here," Kilbourne sputtered. "How dare you challenge me?"

Gabriel did not look back.

When he reached the hackney coach, he gave his instructions to the driver. "Follow the maroon carriage until it reaches a better part of town. Then take me back to St. James Street."

"Aye, m'lord." The coachman set down his flask and picked up the reins.

Thirty minutes later Gabriel stormed back into his club and discovered to his great satisfaction that Anthony and Clarington were still there. They were immersed in copies of *The Times* and *The Morning Post*.

Gabriel dropped into the chair across from the other two men and waited until they had lowered their papers.

"I see you're back," Anthony said. "Why in hell did you rush off like that?"

"I rushed off," Gabriel said evenly, "to rescue your sister from being kidnapped by Kilbourne."

Anthony stared at him. Clarington slammed his copy of *The Times* down on a nearby table. "What the devil are you talking about, sir? Explain yourself."

"The message I received earlier informed me that Phoebe was on her way to examine a manuscript that had been offered for sale by a certain A. Rilkins. When I arrived at Mr. Rilkins's establishment, I discovered Phoebe in the process of being carted out of an alley by two members of the criminal class."

Anthony looked stunned. "Now, see here. You cannot expect us to believe such a tale."

Clarington's mouth dropped open. "Good God. Is this some sort of joke, Wylde?"

"I assure you, it is no joke." Gabriel narrowed his eyes. "Kilbourne is apparently penniless. The word will soon be all over Town. He obviously realized his secret was out and he had no time left to court Phoebe, so he attempted to kidnap her."

"Good God," Clarington said again. He looked dazed. "She would have been ruined if he had succeeded in carrying her off. I would have been forced to agree to the marriage."

The three men stared at each other.

"Phoebe is safe?" Anthony's eyes were sharp with concern.

"She's on her way home, quite unharmed and with her reputation still intact." Gabriel reached for the claret bottle that stood on the table beside his chair. "Although one wonders for how long. At the rate she is going, disaster is inevitable."

"Damme," Clarington muttered, "I'll not allow you to talk like that about my daughter."

"Given that I have just saved her pretty neck, I shall talk about her in any way I like." Gabriel took a swallow of the claret. "Allow me to tell you, my lords, that I consider this entire debacle to be all your fault."

"Our fault?" Clarington bridled furiously.

"Yours in particular," Gabriel said. "As her father, you have allowed her to run wild. The woman is a menace to herself. She corresponds with strange men and arranges to meet them at midnight in remote country lanes. She goes haring off to the worst parts of London whenever she takes a fancy — "

"I say," Clarington interrupted.

Gabriel ignored him. "She is far too independent in her notions and she routinely courts disaster. One of these days she will almost certainly find it."

"Now, see here," Clarington growled. "This is my daughter we are discussing. What is this about corresponding with strange men and meeting them at midnight?"

"How the hell do you think I met her?" Gabriel asked.

Anthony stared at him, astounded. "Are you saying she struck up a correspondence with you? Arranged to meet with you?"

"Damn right," Gabriel said. "And it was pure luck that it was me she arranged to meet in Sussex. What if it had been some other man?"

Clarington stiffened. "What are you suggesting, sir?"

"I am suggesting that neither of you is capable of controlling Phoebe, much less protecting her from her own impulsiveness." Gabriel took another swallow of the claret. "Therefore I shall have to take on the task. There is obviously no other option."

"*You.*" Clarington glowered down the length of his beaked nose.

"Me." Gabriel put the empty glass on the

table. "I shall call on you tomorrow afternoon at three to discuss the matter. I want this settled at once."

"A moment, if you please." Anthony held up a hand. "Are you saying you intend to offer for Phoebe?"

Gabriel looked at him. "Would you prefer to wait until Kilbourne or some other fortune hunter makes another attempt to carry her off?"

"Don't be ridiculous. Of course we don't want her carried off." Clarington sighed heavily. "But it's damn difficult to protect Phoebe. More spirit than sense. Won't listen to sound advice. Thinks she can deal with the world on her own. Always been like that, ever since she was a little girl."

"It's true," Anthony said glumly. "She was forever exploring and getting into mischief. The more we tried to restrain her, the more adventurous she got." He looked at Clarington. "Remember how it was the day of the accident?"

"I shall never forget it as long as I live," Clarington declared. "Thought we'd lost her. Dashed out into the lane to save a damn hound that had darted in front of a phaeton. The hound made it safely across the road. Phoebe did not."

Anthony shook his head. "It was typical

of Phoebe. She's been reckless all of her life. But that time the results were nearly tragic. The doctors told us she would never walk again."

"Did they tell Phoebe?" Gabriel asked dryly.

Clarington nodded. "Certainly they told Phoebe. Told her she would have to take care not to exert herself. Told her she would spend the rest of her life as an invalid. Told her she must live a quiet life."

Gabriel smiled fleetingly. "But Phoebe, being Phoebe, refused to listen, I suppose."

Anthony looked at him. "I walked into her bedchamber one day three months after the accident and found her on her feet, clutching the bedpost. After that, there was no stopping her."

"Nevertheless," Gabriel said grimly, "you should have done a better job of protecting her. Devil take it, Oaksley. Do you realize she almost got kidnapped by a man who intended to force her into marriage in order to acquire her fortune? Her life would have been ruined if the ruse had worked."

Anthony raised his brows. "Now you know how it feels."

Gabriel stared at him.

"It's enough to make a man want to commit murder." Clarington was clearly still shaken

233

by the news of the near-disaster. "God knows it's a terrible feeling to discover one has failed to protect one's own daughter."

Gabriel could think of nothing to say. It struck him quite forcibly that the anger and fear he was experiencing at that moment were undoubtedly the very same emotions Clarington and his son had felt eight years ago on the night he had attempted to run off with Meredith.

For the first time he looked at the situation from their point of view. He acknowledged with grim honesty that he would probably have reacted in the same fashion as they had if he had been in their place. Clarington and his family had had no way of knowing that Gabriel had not been after Meredith's inheritance. To them he had looked as evil as Kilbourne now appeared.

"I take your meaning, Clarington," Gabriel finally said.

Clarington's eyes met Gabriel's. Understanding and a curious expression that might have been approval gleamed for a moment in the earl's piercing gaze.

"I believe you finally do comprehend my feelings at the time, sir." Clarington nodded, as if satisfied. "I also begin to believe you have some genuine affection for my daughter."

"I must confess my affection for her is somewhat tempered by the overriding fear that she will one day drive me mad," Gabriel said.

"A fate I have barely escaped myself." Clarington smiled slowly. "I gladly turn the responsibility of looking after her over to you, sir. I wish you the best of luck."

"Thank you." Gabriel looked at Anthony. "I shall need seconds."

Anthony studied him for a moment in silence. "You've challenged Kilbourne?"

"Yes."

"I'm Phoebe's brother. It is my place to handle this."

Gabriel smiled wryly. "You have already done your duty by one sister. I'll deal with this."

Anthony hesitated. "I'm not certain I should allow you to do so."

"As her future husband, it is most definitely my right," Gabriel said.

"Very well, I'll be one of your seconds," Anthony said. "I can arrange to find another. But you must be careful. If Kilbourne dies, you will be obliged to leave England and, knowing Phoebe, she would probably insist on going with you."

"I have no wish to leave England again," Gabriel said. "Kilbourne will live. Barely."

Anthony eyed him closely. Then his mouth curved ruefully. "Just as I did?"

"No," Gabriel said. "Not quite. I fully intend to put a bullet into the man. He will remember in future not to kidnap young ladies."

Three hours later, Anthony returned to the club to report back to Gabriel on the arrangements for the duel.

"You're out of luck," Anthony said. "Kilbourne has left London."

"Damn." Gabriel slammed his fist down on the arm of the chair in sheer frustration. "Are you certain?"

"His butler says he has gone north and no one knows when he will return. It certainly won't be anytime soon. The servants have instructions to close Kilbourne's town house. The word is all over Town that he is virtually penniless. Lost everything in a series of bad investments."

"Hell and damnation."

"Perhaps it's for the best." Anthony sprawled in a nearby chair. "It's over. There will be no duel and Kilbourne is out of the way. I, for one, am grateful."

"I am not."

"Trust me, you're luckier than you know." Anthony grinned. "If Phoebe had ever discovered that you intended to fight a duel in her honor, she would have been furious. I don't believe you have ever dealt with Phoebe when she is very angry. It's not pleasant."

Gabriel looked at him, aware that he and Anthony were forming a bond based on their mutual concern for Phoebe. "Thank you for agreeing to act as my second. I only regret you will not have the opportunity to perform your duties."

Anthony inclined his head. "As I said, it's over. Kilbourne has been well and truly humiliated. Let it go at that."

"I suppose I shall be obliged to do so." Gabriel was silent for a moment. "I know now how you felt eight years ago, Oaksley."

"Yes. I can see that you do. But I will tell you something, Wylde. I like Trowbridge, and Meredith seems quite happy with him. But I will admit that if I knew then what I know now about you, I would not have chased after you that night. I would trust either of my sisters in your care."

Gabriel raised his brows. "Because you have learned I am not penniless?"

"No," Anthony said. "My reasons have nothing to do with your financial status."

There was silence for a moment between the two men. Then Gabriel smiled. "Allow me to tell you that I am exceedingly grateful you did come after Meredith and me that night. The match would have been a mistake. It's Phoebe I want."

"You're certain of that?"

"Quite certain."

At three the following afternoon, Phoebe sat uneasily upstairs in her bedchamber and waited to be summoned to the library. The household had been so subdued since yesterday's events that one would have thought there had been a death in the family.

Phoebe knew full well what was happening. Her mother had told her earlier that Gabriel was going to offer for her and that Clarington would accept. It was clear her family's objections to Gabriel had been dropped.

Phoebe was grateful for that, but she could not seem to sort out her own conflicting emotions. A part of her rejoiced at the thought of being married to the man she loved. She longed to seize the opportunity. She wanted him as she had never wanted anyone or anything in her life.

But another part of her was extremely uneasy. She had no indication yet that Gabriel truly loved her. She was very much afraid he was making his offer out of a desire to protect her from the sort of incident that had occurred yesterday.

It was highly probable that Gabriel was marrying her out of a misguided sense of chivalry.

True, he was rather fond of her, she was certain of that much. He gave every indication of being physically attracted to her. And they did have interests in common.

But there had been no talk of love.

Phoebe glanced at the clock. It was almost three-thirty. What on earth was there to talk about that took half an hour? she wondered.

She got to her feet and began pacing the room. This was ridiculous. A woman had the right to be present when her future was being discussed.

This business of waiting meekly upstairs in her bedchamber while the men dealt with something as important as marriage was aggravating in the extreme. Men did not have a good grasp of such things.

They would not understand, for example, that she had no wish to be married because Gabriel's lofty notions of chivalry demanded it.

She had vowed long ago that she would only marry for true love, the sort of love that guided the knights and ladies of medieval legends. Nothing less would do for her.

At three forty-five, Phoebe decided she had had enough of playing the dutiful daughter. She marched out of her bedchamber and went downstairs to the library.

The door of the library was closed. The butler stood firmly planted in front of it. When he saw Phoebe, his expression turned wary, but determined.

"Step aside, please," she said to the butler. "I wish to join my father."

The butler drew himself up bravely. "Forgive me, madam, but your father left explicit instructions that he did not wish to be disturbed while in conference with Lord Wylde."

"Pssst, Phoebe." Lydia stuck her head around the corner of the drawing room and waved frantically to get Phoebe's attention. "Don't go in there. Men like to handle this kind of thing all by themselves. It makes them feel as if they are carrying out their responsibilities."

Meredith, hovering behind her mother, frowned delicately at Phoebe. "Wait until you are summoned, Phoebe. Papa will be most upset if you interrupt."

"I am already upset." Phoebe strode forward.

The butler wavered. It was all the opportunity Phoebe needed. She opened the door herself and walked into the library.

Gabriel and her father were seated near the fireplace. They each held a glass of brandy. Both men looked up with forbidding expressions as she entered.

"You may wait outside, my dear. I shall summon you in a few minutes," Clarington said firmly.

"I am tired of waiting." Phoebe came to a halt and glanced at Gabriel. She could tell nothing from his expression. "I want to know what is going on."

"Wylde is making an offer of marriage," Clarington said. "We are discussing the details. You need not concern yourself."

"You mean you have already accepted the offer on my behalf?" Phoebe demanded.

"Yes, I have." Clarington took a swallow of brandy.

Phoebe shot Gabriel a questioning look. He arched one brow in response. Her gaze went back to her father. "Papa, I wish to speak to Gabriel before any announcements are made."

"You may speak to him when I have finished settling matters."

"But Papa — "

"Leave us, Phoebe," Gabriel ordered quietly. "We will talk later."

"I want to discuss this now." Her hands

tightened into small fists. "It is my future that is being bandied about in here. I have a few thoughts on the subject. If the two of you think you are going to tie all the details into a neat little package and expect me to accept it without comment, you are quite wrong."

Clarington peered at her. "Very well, my dear, what is your chief objection to all this?"

Phoebe took a deep breath, opened her clenched fists, and dried her damp palms on the skirts of her gown. "I have always made it very clear that I will only marry for love. To be perfectly blunt, Papa, Wylde has never once mentioned love to me. I will not be rushed into marriage until I am certain there is true love on both sides. I will not be married simply because Wylde's sense of chivalry demands it."

"Phoebe," Clarington said wearily, "you are behaving like a romantical schoolgirl. Wylde is quite right. After what happened yesterday, you can no longer be allowed to continue in your rash, impulsive ways."

"He said that?" Phoebe glared at Gabriel.

"Yes, he did, and I agree with him," Clarington declared. "He claims he is willing to take on the task of managing you and I must say, I am grateful to be able to turn the responsibility over to him."

Phoebe was outraged. "What if I do not wish to be 'managed' by a husband?"

"I know of no better way to settle you down and rein in your eccentric manners than to marry you off," Clarington retorted. "It is time you were married, young lady. For God's sake, you are nearly five and twenty. The fact that you are an heiress puts you at terrible risk. Only think of what happened yesterday."

"Papa, what happened yesterday was not my fault."

"It most certainly was," Clarington shot back. "Who knows how many others of Kilbourne's sort are lurking out there? Wylde is correct when he says that sooner or later your impulsive ways will land you in serious trouble. I want you safely established under the guidance and protection of a husband."

A sense of desperation welled up in Phoebe. "Papa, please. I must have time to think about this. Wylde and I must discuss it."

Gabriel gave her a cool glance over the rim of his brandy glass. "As far as I am concerned, there is nothing that needs to be discussed at this moment. Go on upstairs to your bedchamber. We shall send for you presently."

Phoebe was speechless. To be banished upstairs to her bedchamber by the man whom she had considered a gallant knight, the man she had secretly viewed as a soul mate, the man she *loved*. It was too much.

"My lord," she whispered, "you are no better than Kilbourne."

There was a short, awful silence.

"Phoebe," her father thundered. "You will apologize at once. Wylde is no fortune hunter."

She dashed the back of her hand across her eyes to get rid of the moisture. "I did not mean to imply that he was. But he is certainly just as much of a pompous, over-bearing prig as Kilbourne ever was." She gave Gabriel one last anguished glance. "I thought you were my friend. I thought you understood how I felt about matters of love and marriage."

Before either man could respond, she whirled and fled from the room.

Out in the hall she dashed past the concerned faces of her mother and sister. She picked up her skirts and raced up the stairs. When she reached the privacy of her bedchamber, she threw herself down on the bed and surrendered to the tears.

Fifteen minutes later the storm had passed, leaving in its place an unnatural calm. She dried her eyes, washed her face, and sat down to wait.

Twenty minutes later, when she was finally summoned to the library, she was composed and solemn. She walked sedately down the stairs, waited politely for the butler to open the door, and then stepped inside.

Her father was still seated in his chair. He appeared to have started on another glass of brandy. Gabriel was standing near the fireplace, one arm resting along the mantel. He watched her intently as she came gravely into the room.

"You sent for me, Papa?" Phoebe asked with excruciating civility.

Clarington cast her a suspicious glance. "It's settled, my dear. You and Wylde will be married at the end of the Season."

Phoebe's stomach lurched, but she managed to keep her expression serene. "I see. Well, then, if that is all, I shall return to my room. I am not feeling very well."

Gabriel's black brows drew together in a severe line. "Phoebe, are you all right?"

"I believe I have a slight headache, my lord." She turned and walked back out of the room.

Shortly before dawn the next morning Phoebe dressed in her best traveling gown and tossed two large bags out her bedroom window. Then she threw a rope composed of knotted bedsheets over the sill.

She descended via the makeshift rope into the garden, collected her two bags, and walked around the front of the big house.

She mingled with saloop vendors and milk carriers in the early morning London traffic. At that hour the streets were teeming with country folk and their wagons full of market produce. No one paid much attention to her.

By seven o'clock Phoebe had boarded the stage that would take her into the heart of Sussex. Squashed between a plump woman in a gray turban and an odoriferous country squire who was swigging gin from a bottle, she had plenty of time to reflect on her fate.

Chapter 11

Gabriel called on every ounce of self-control he possessed to deal with the rage that threatened to consume him. He could not believe Phoebe had run from him like this.

Clarington and his family sat in funereal silence, their eyes following Gabriel as he paced back and forth across the drawing room.

It was nearly ten o'clock. No one had missed Phoebe until an hour ago, when her maid had gone to her room with her tea. Gabriel had received the cryptic summons shortly thereafter. When he had arrived at the Clarington town house, he had found the entire clan gathered here in the drawing room to deliver the news that Phoebe had fled.

"Look on the bright side," Lydia suggested. "As far as we know, she ran off by herself. There does not appear to be another man involved here."

"As far as we know," Anthony said morosely.

Gabriel shot him a furious glance. The last thing he wanted to do this morning was entertain the possibility that Phoebe had run off with another man. Matters were bad enough as it was. "You believe she's on her way to Sussex?"

"There was a note," Meredith said quietly. "She said she would be spending some time with an aunt in Sussex."

"It could have been a clever ruse," Lydia offered. "She might want us to think she has gone in one direction while in truth she has dashed off to somewhere else entirely."

"No." Meredith held herself very still. Her eyes never left Gabriel. "She knew we would worry, so she told us where she was going in hopes that we would not fret."

"Not fret?" Clarington turned red. "*Not fret?* The chit takes off before dawn without a word to anyone and she doesn't want us to fret? What in God's name does she expect us to do?"

Lydia put a hand on his arm. "Calm yourself, my dear. All will be well. Phoebe is quite capable of taking care of herself."

"Oh, is she, now?" Clarington gave his wife a scathing look. "And tell me, how will she take care of her reputation after news of this incident gets out, pray tell? I would not blame Wylde for calling off the marriage."

Meredith gasped. "Papa, you must not say that."

"Why not?" Anthony muttered. "What man in his right mind wants a wife who is going to cause him this kind of trouble?"

"Phoebe is frightened." Meredith leaped to her feet and faced Gabriel and the others. "Don't you understand? She ran away because she was being pushed into this marriage without so much as a by-your-leave. No one even bothered to ask her opinion."

Clarington scowled. "She likes Wylde. Leastways, I thought she did. What the devil is the matter with that creature? She makes no sense at all."

Meredith lifted her chin. "I'll tell you what the matter is. She discovered that her entire future was being settled by you and Wylde, Papa. She felt like a horse that was being sold to the highest bidder."

Gabriel's jaw tightened.

"Nonsense," Clarington said.

"It's the truth," Meredith said. "I know exactly how she felt because I felt precisely the same way eight years ago. The difference between Phoebe and me was that I asked someone to assist me in my escape. Phoebe, being Phoebe, arranged her own escape all by herself."

"What in hell does she even want to escape?" Anthony demanded. "Papa is right. She likes Wylde."

Meredith stamped her foot in exasperation. "Really? And how does Wylde feel about her?"

Gabriel frowned. "Phoebe knows how I feel about her."

"Is that so?" Meredith rounded on him. "You have declared your affections for her, then, sir? You have told her you love her?"

"For God's sake, Meredith," Gabriel muttered. "That is none of your business."

"Ah-hah. So you have not. Pray, sir, do you love her?"

Gabriel was suddenly very conscious of the others watching him intently. "Phoebe and I understand each other."

"I doubt that," Meredith said. "I'll wager you have the same sort of understanding between you that Trowbridge and I had eight years ago. Which amounts to nothing at all."

Gabriel was incensed. "That's not true."

Meredith narrowed her eyes in a most un-Meredith fashion. "You have as good as admitted that you have not told Phoebe that you love her. What did you expect her to do when she found herself on the brink of marriage?"

"She's not a green girl," Gabriel said through his teeth. "She had no business running off like this."

Meredith lifted her chin disdainfully. "If you ask me, she was practically obliged to run off. She had no reason to think you would behave any differently if she stayed and meekly agreed to all the plans you and Papa made for her. Phoebe is very strong-minded."

"Too headstrong by far," Gabriel said.

"You should have talked to her first about this marriage," Meredith said. "You should have told her of your feelings."

Lydia sighed. "Somehow I cannot believe any good will come of this strange notion that men and women should talk to each other about such intimate matters. Everyone knows men are not much good at that sort of thing. They get frustrated and irritable when they attempt such complicated discussions. Something to do with their brains, no doubt."

"No doubt, madam." Gabriel had had enough. He faced Phoebe's family. "Very well, then, as you appear to have lost my fiancée on the very day the notices are due to hit the papers, I must be on my way."

Anthony got to his feet. "What do you intend to do?"

"What do you think I'm going to do? Go after her, of course. She is not going to escape this easily." Gabriel started toward the door.

"Wait. I'll come with you," Anthony said.

"No, you will not. I have secured a special license. Phoebe and I shall deal with this matter alone."

"You're going to marry her?" Meredith looked alarmed. "Wylde, hold a moment. There is something I must say to you."

"What?" Gabriel was already at the door. He was seething with impatience.

Meredith gave him a pleading look. "You will be kind to her when you catch up to her, will you not? Please try to comprehend her feelings. I know she seems a bit impulsive, but the truth is, she is a creature of very delicate sensibilities. She needs understanding."

"She needs a strong hand applied to her backside," Gabriel said. He went out the door.

But Meredith's parting words haunted him as he made hurried preparations for leaving town. He remembered the look on Phoebe's face yesterday afternoon when Clarington had finally summoned her to the library to hear that her future had been settled. She had been much too distant and far too calm.

Gabriel realized now that Phoebe's demeanor had been a very unnatural one for her. He should have suspected all was not well. But it had never occurred to him that she would run off like this in order to avoid marriage to him.

You are no different than Kilbourne.

She had run from him. The knowledge cut into Gabriel like a knife. He realized that for some reason he had come to believe that his feisty, outrageous Phoebe would never leave him.

She had made a terrible mistake. Phoebe acknowledged that before the stage had gone fifteen miles.

What an idiot she was. She was running away from the man she loved.

What did it matter that Gabriel did not yet love her? She had the remainder of the Season to devise a plan to teach him to love her. It would be her new quest.

The sudden, violent lurching of the coach and the startled shouts of the passengers interrupted her anxious thoughts.

"Broke a wheel, by God," the man with the gin flask announced. "That'll slow us down a bit."

As far as Phoebe was concerned, the broken wheel was nothing less than an act of God. She had never been so grateful for a carriage accident in her life.

The crippled vehicle managed to make it to a nearby inn. Phoebe alighted from it along with the other passengers, collected her luggage, and made her way indoors.

She pushed her way through the crowd of passengers gathered in front of the innkeeper's desk and asked for a seat on the London stage.

"Won't be any seats available, ma'am," the innkeeper's wife said without any show of sympathy. "Sold all the tickets yesterday. I can sell you a seat on the ten o'clock stage tomorrow morning."

"But I must get back to London tonight," Phoebe said.

"You'll have to wait until tomorrow." The woman gave her a speculative look. "I've got a room I can give you for the night."

"No, thank you. I shall certainly not be spending the night here." Phoebe began to comprehend the true extent of the disaster. Her reputation was going to be ruined if anyone discovered that she had been obliged to spend the night alone in this inn.

She tugged her veil more firmly down over her face and limped into the inn's dining room for a bite to eat. She needed to think and she could not do that while she was starving.

She was aware that she was the object of

several rude stares when she sat down at a table. Ladies traveling alone were always vulnerable to that sort of thing. It would get a lot worse once night fell.

She wondered if Gabriel had been informed that she had run off. The thought drove her further into her gloomy mood. If he found out she had left Town, he might simply wash his hands of her entirely.

She had to get back before he discovered she was missing. What an idiotic impulse this had all been. Perhaps she could throw herself on the mercy of some family traveling to London by private coach. Assuming such a family chose to stop for a rest at this inn. But that would mean revealing her true identity. She dared not do that.

Phoebe's sense of desperation grew rapidly. She had to find a way out of this tangle. She covertly studied the other people in the tavern, wondering if any of them might provide assistance. Surely some of them were on their way to London. She might be able to buy a ticket for double or triple the price.

At that moment an odd little sensation rippled through her. She glanced around quickly and was stunned to see Gabriel striding through the door of the dining room.

Gabriel was here.

A rush of joyous relief swept over Phoebe.

He had come after her. Hard on the heels of that thought came the realization that he had never looked more dangerous. His face was as forbidding as a hawk's and his eyes were chips of green ice. He stood still for a moment and surveyed the crowded room.

Phoebe's stomach fluttered. This was no gallant lover who had ridden in pursuit of his beloved in hopes of convincing her to return to him. Gabriel definitely did not look as if he were in a mood to declare undying love and devotion.

For an instant Phoebe sat frozen, caught between an impulse to throw herself into his arms and an equally strong urge to flee. In that split second of indecision, Gabriel's eyes came to rest unerringly on her veiled face.

He appeared to recognize her instantly. Perhaps it was because of her vivid violet traveling gown. He walked straight toward her, his mud-spattered boots loud on the wooden floor. Several heads turned curiously as he went past. Gabriel looked neither to the right nor to the left. His gaze never left Phoebe.

By the time he reached her table, she hardly dared breathe.

"I'm disappointed in you, Phoebe," Gabriel said without any inflection. "It's not like you to run away from a problem. You generally stand your ground and fight."

It was too much. Phoebe leaped to her feet as rage poured through her. "I was not running away. As a matter of fact, I am waiting for the next stage back to London."

Gabriel's brows rose. "Is that so?"

"Yes, it is. You may check with the innkeeper's wife, if you do not believe me. She will tell you that I attempted to purchase a ticket."

"Attempted?"

"It was not my fault that there was no seat available on the next stage," Phoebe snapped. "I was planning to purchase someone else's ticket."

"I see." Gabriel's voice warmed a few degrees. His eyes lost their hard glitter. "Well, it does not matter whether or not there is a seat available. You will not be needing one."

She eyed him warily. "Why not?"

"You will not be using public transport." Gabriel took her arm.

"You are going to drive me back to London?"

"No, madam. I am going to take you home with me."

"Home?" Her eyes widened behind her veil. "You mean to your home?"

"Yes." His eyes softened almost imperceptibly. "I have a special license with me, Phoebe. We shall be married at once. By the time we reach Devil's Mist, you will be my wife."

"Oh, dear," she whispered. "I'm not at all certain that is a sound notion, my lord."

"Do you believe you can keep this day's events quiet?"

She looked up at him out of the corner of her eye as he led her out of the public room. "I've been thinking about this, my lord. I believe that if we are very cautious we might be able to sneak safely back to Town."

"Phoebe, allow me to tell you that you do not know the meaning of the word *cautious*. Nor is there any reason to delay the marriage in the hopes that you will talk me out of it. The notices have already appeared in the morning papers. There is no escape for either of us now. We may as well take care of the matter at once."

Phoebe winced. "You are quite certain you wish to marry me, Wylde?"

"Yes."

She took hold of her courage with both hands. "Because you love me?"

Gabriel scowled and glanced meaningfully around the crowded inn lobby. "For God's sake, madam, this is hardly the time or place to discuss such matters. Wait here while I see to the horses and your luggage. You do have luggage with you, I presume?"

Phoebe sighed. "Yes, my lord. I have luggage with me."

There was something not quite real about the rest of that day. At times Phoebe was convinced she was dreaming. At other moments she would find herself filled with a strange, hopeful excitement.

She became Gabriel's wife in a short, hurried ceremony that lacked any semblance of romantic trappings. Once Gabriel had produced the special license, the village parson was interested only in his fee.

A strange, uneasy silence descended afterward as Gabriel handed Phoebe up into his phaeton. He vaulted up onto the seat beside her and picked up the reins.

Phoebe kept reminding herself that this was her wedding day and that she had just married the man she loved, but she could not bring herself to believe it.

The sense of unreality grew more oppressive as dusk fell. Fog rolled in from the sea, blanketing the Sussex landscape in a gray mist. Phoebe shivered, aware of the chill that was seeping through her heavy traveling gown.

She was trying to think of a way to break the hard silence between herself and Gabriel when she spotted the hulking outline of an old castle looming up out of the mist. In the odd evening light, it might have been an illusion, an enchanted castle out of a medieval tale.

Phoebe straightened with sudden interest. "Good heavens, Gabriel. What is that?"

"That's Devil's Mist."

"Your home?" She turned to him in delight. "You live in a castle?"

His mouth curved faintly for the first time since he had plucked her out of the tavern's public room. "I had a feeling it would appeal to you."

Phoebe felt her spirits revive like flowers in the sun. "This is wonderful. I had no notion you lived in such a marvelous place. Although now that I think about it, it suits you."

"It suits you, too, Phoebe."

"Yes," she agreed, utterly enthralled. "I have always wished to live in a castle."

Phoebe was still bubbling over with enthusiasm an hour later as she and Gabriel sat down to dinner. Gabriel hid a smile of satisfaction as he studied her. His new wife already looked very much at home here in his cavernous dining room.

His wife. A fierce anticipation gripped Gabriel as he gazed at her. Soon she would be his.

Phoebe's soft, gently rounded shoulders and the upper swells of her breasts were as pale as moonlight in the glow of the candles. The fiery highlights in her dark hair gleamed. Her topaz eyes were brilliant and mysterious. He could see the slight flush on her cheeks and he knew she was thinking about the wedding night that lay ahead.

He had a sudden fierce urge to pick her up in his arms and carry her straight upstairs to bed. *Soon,* he promised himself. Very soon she would be completely his.

"I love Devil's Mist, my lord," Phoebe said as the butler poured wine into her glass. "I cannot wait to see all of it in the morning."

"I shall take you on a tour after breakfast," Gabriel promised. "You shall see everything, including the catacombs below."

"Catacombs?" Phoebe was clearly fascinated.

"At one time they were no doubt used as storage rooms and dungeons," Gabriel explained. "But I call them catacombs because that is what they remind me of. The only rule is that you must never go down there alone."

"Why not?"

"It's dangerous," Gabriel explained. "It's full of secret passageways and doors that can only be opened and closed by hidden mechanisms."

Phoebe's eyes widened. "How exciting. I cannot wait to explore the place."

"Immediately after breakfast, my dear." Breakfast would be very late tomorrow, he vowed to himself. He had no intention of rising early, not with Phoebe in his bed.

"Wherever did you acquire all that wonderful armor in the main hall?" Phoebe asked as she accepted a portion of veal pie from the footman. "I vow it is the most wonderful collection I have ever seen."

"Here and there."

"And that motto carved over the door. *Audeo.* Is that the traditional motto of the earls of Wylde?"

"It is now," Gabriel said.

Phoebe looked up sharply. "You mean you invented it yourself?"

"Yes."

She smiled, vastly pleased. "It means 'I dare,' does it not?"

"Yes."

"I must say it is a perfect motto for you, my lord."

"I believe it suits you, too, madam," Gabriel said deliberately.

Phoebe glowed. "Do you really think so?"

"Yes."

"That is very flattering, my lord." She chuckled. "But I had the impression that you were not quite so pleased with my daring earlier today. Do you know, I rather thought you were going to be extremely unpleasant about the whole thing. Well, that business is all behind us now, is it not?"

Gabriel sent the butler and the footman from the room with a small nod. When the door closed behind them, he leaned back in his chair and picked up his wineglass.

"About that business, Phoebe," he said quietly.

"Yes, my lord?" She seemed suddenly very occupied with her veal pie.

Gabriel hesitated, remembering the thoughts that had tormented him as he chased after Phoebe. "I am not really as bad as Kilbourne, you know."

Phoebe's fork paused halfway to her mouth. She slowly lowered it. "That was unkind of me. Of course you are not as bad as Kilbourne. I would never have married you if I thought you were as nasty as he is."

"You might have been forced to marry him if he had succeeded in carrying you off." Gabriel heard the edge on his own words, but he could not keep it out of his voice. Every time he thought of Kilbourne attempting to kidnap Phoebe, he went cold inside.

"I would not have married Kilbourne, regardless of whether or not he had kidnapped me," Phoebe said with a tiny shudder. "I would have preferred to live the rest of my life as a recluse in disgrace."

"Your family would have insisted that you marry him."

"They might have insisted, but I would never have agreed."

Gabriel narrowed his eyes. "You tried to avoid marriage to me, but you did not succeed."

Phoebe blushed and looked down at her plate. "I did not try very hard, my lord."

Gabriel's fingers tightened on his wineglass. "You ran away from me, Phoebe."

"Only because I wanted some time to think. I did not like the way everyone seemed to be making decisions for me. But by the time the wheel broke on the stage, I knew I had made a mistake."

"What convinced you that you had made a mistake?"

Phoebe toyed with her food. Then she looked up and her eyes met his. "I realized I was not opposed to the notion of marriage to you."

"Why not?"

"I think you know the answer to that, my lord."

He smiled whimsically. "Let me guess. You married me in order to acquire access to the contents of my library?"

Phoebe's eyes lit with amusement. "Not entirely, my lord, although now that you mention it, I must admit your library is one of your most interesting assets."

Gabriel pushed aside his plate and folded his arms on the table. "Did you marry me because you want to experience more of what you felt that night in Brantley's maze?"

Phoebe turned pink. "As I said at the time, that was very pleasant, my lord, but I would not have married for the sole purpose of repeating the experience."

"Then why did you marry me?"

Phoebe took a very large swallow of wine. She set the glass down with a small touch of defiance. "Because I am extremely fond of you, my lord. As you very well know."

"Fond of me?"

"Yes." She fiddled with her fork.

"Are you more fond of me than you were of Neil Baxter?"

Phoebe frowned. "Of course. Neil was very kind to me and he was interested in medieval literature. But the truth is that I did not love him. He was never more than a friend as far as I was concerned. That is one of the reasons I feel so guilty about his fate, you see. After all, he left England because he was determined to find a way to win my hand."

"Phoebe, your father paid Baxter a handsome sum to leave England," Gabriel said bluntly. "That's the reason Baxter went off to the South Seas. His courtship of you was a ploy to get money out of your family."

Phoebe did not move. Her eyes widened in bewildered distress. "I do not believe you."

"Then ask your father." Gabriel took a swallow of wine. "Clarington was the one who told me the truth. He was trying to buy me off at the time and rather casually mentioned that the technique had worked on Baxter."

"My father never said anything about paying Neil to leave England."

"Your father was no doubt attempting to protect your feelings," Gabriel said gruffly. "He probably knew you would be hurt if you discovered Baxter had never had any honorable intentions toward you. Of course poor Clarington does not know you've been on a quest to find the man you think killed Baxter. If your father had known that, he might have told you the full truth."

Phoebe's eyes were full of stunned shock.

"Are you certain of this?"

"Absolutely certain. Baxter used you to get money out of your family. That was his only interest in you. He deserved everything he got out there in the South Seas."

"But for an entire year I have felt terrible because I believed he went out there to make his fortune so that he could continue to woo me. He called himself my Lancelot. He claimed he wished to serve me forever. I would always be his Lady in the Tower."

"You need no longer feel any guilt on account of Baxter," Gabriel said. "Forget him."

"Finding his killer has been my quest for months."

"Forget the damn quest."

"I feel as though I have been living in an illusion," Phoebe whispered. "If what you say is true, I have wasted so much time. So much energy. So much emotion."

"Forget him, Phoebe."

Phoebe's fingers trembled as she folded her napkin and placed it carefully on the table. "Such a mistake makes one question one's judgment."

Gabriel shrugged. "We all make mistakes when it comes to matters of that sort. Hell, even I made a similar mistake eight years ago when I tried to run off with your sister."

"Yes, you did, didn't you? And now I have risked a great deal by marrying you."

He did not care for the strange expression in her eyes. "Phoebe, I only told you the truth so that you could put your silly quest behind you. I do not fancy being married to a woman who is bent on tracking down a killer. Very inconvenient."

"I see." She looked at him. "You knew the truth about Neil almost from the start?"

He hesitated. "Your father told me about him shortly after I arrived in London."

"Yet you led me to believe you were helping me on my quest. How long would you have let me go on believing that your intentions were honorable, sir?"

"My intentions were honorable. Eventually." Too late Gabriel saw the trap he had set for himself. "Phoebe, I can explain everything."

Phoebe stood up. "I do not believe there is anything to explain, sir. You lied to me. You told me you were assisting me on my quest to find Neil's killer. But you never had any intention of helping me find the pirate who murdered him, did you?"

Gabriel was trapped. He could hardly explain about his short-lived notions of vengeance. That news would only upset her further. "I did not lie to you."

"Yes, you did. Tell me, why did you marry me?" she demanded, her eyes fierce.

"Because I think we shall suit each other very well." Gabriel tried to make his tone reasonable and soothing. "Once you have settled down and stopped giving in to your reckless impulses, that is."

"Reckless impulses? You mean like the reckless impulse that led me to marry you today?" Phoebe started around the edge of the table. "I assure you, my lord, I have certainly learned my lesson. I will not succumb to any further reckless impulses."

Gabriel realized she was going to walk right out of the dining room. "Phoebe, come back here. I am talking to you."

"You may finish the conversation by yourself. I doubt there is anything meaningful that I can contribute. You seem to have all the answers."

"Damnation, Phoebe, I said come back here."

"I do not wish to do so, my lord."

"I am your husband," Gabriel reminded her grimly. "And this is our wedding night. If you are finished with dinner, you may go upstairs. I shall join you shortly."

She had her hand on the doorknob. Her eyes glittered with anger as she glanced back at him over her shoulder. "Forgive me, my lord, I am not in the mood to have any more illusions shattered tonight."

Gabriel set his teeth as she slammed the door. Silence descended.

She would not dare lock her door against him tonight, he thought. She was his wife.

But even as he tried to reassure himself on that score, Gabriel knew Phoebe was quite capable of refusing to grant him his rights as a husband.

Hell, she was capable of almost anything.

An hour later he discovered that she had not locked her bedroom door. She was not even in her bedroom.

Gabriel tore the castle apart, looking for her. He finally realized she had retreated to the tower room he used as a study. She had locked herself inside.

Gabriel pounded on the door. "Phoebe, what the hell do you think you're doing?"

"I am going to spend the night in here, Gabriel," she called back. "I want to think. I must sort this all out for myself."

Gabriel remembered the copy of *The Lady in the Tower* that was sitting in one of the bookcases. If she found it, she would probably never speak to him again.

She would never understand why it was in his possession. She would believe the worst. And in this case the worst was the simple truth. He had been responsible for Neil Baxter's death.

Gabriel went cold at the thought of the impending disaster. That was when he discovered that he, too, was capable of almost anything.

Chapter 12

Phoebe lit the fire that had been laid on the hearth. Then she got to her feet and surveyed the small stone room in the light of the flames. She knew at once that this had to be Gabriel's study.

She felt like a trespasser, but at the same time she was irresistibly intrigued by the knowledge that this room was so intimately connected to Gabriel. She could feel the heart and soul of him in here.

She had stumbled onto the tower room by accident when she had set out searching for a refuge. She had brought a pillow and a quilt with her because she fully intended to spend the night here. There had been no doubt in her mind but that Gabriel would try to exercise his marital rights tonight. He was, after all, a very sensual man. He was also not a man to ignore a clear challenge, and she had virtually issued him one.

It was always a mistake to issue a challenge to a knight-errant.

Perhaps if she had tried explaining herself

to him, she might have avoided the confrontation, Phoebe thought. But it was too late now. The damage had been done. Besides, she had not been in a mood to explain anything. She had been too hurt and too angry.

When she thought of the months she had wasted feeling guilty because of Neil Baxter, she wanted to scream. Had he really lied to her? It was difficult to believe. Surely there was some explanation for what had happened.

When she thought of how Gabriel had tricked her into believing he was going to help her on her quest, she wanted to cry. Gabriel definitely had lied to her. That was what hurt the most.

Of course, if she were perfectly honest with herself, she had to admit she had kept him in the dark about one or two matters right from the start. Not that she had ever intended to mislead him, she thought. It had just sort of happened due to an unfortunate set of circumstances over which she'd had little control.

As far as she could determine, Gabriel had no such excuse. But perhaps he did not see it in that light.

It was all too much to deal with on top of everything else that had happened today. She needed time to reflect. Time to decide what to do next. Somehow she had to find a way to make her marriage work.

She sat down behind Gabriel's desk. This was where he wrote, she realized. She felt oddly close to him as she sat there in the firelit room. She reached out to pick up one of his pens. He used these to create legends. The knowledge awed her.

A scraping sound outside the window jolted her out of her reverie. Startled, Phoebe dropped the pen and got to her feet. Her hand went to her throat when she heard the noise again.

It was not a tree branch rasping against the stone, she realized. This room was three stories off the ground and there were no trees outside the window.

The sliding, scraping sound came again. Phoebe swallowed uneasily. She did not believe in ghosts, she reminded herself. But this was a very old castle and it had certainly seen its share of violence and bloodshed.

There was a soft thud as a dark shape landed on the narrow ledge. A hand shoved hard against the window. Phoebe backed quickly toward the door fumbling for the lock. Her mouth opened on a scream.

The tower window slammed open and Gabriel vaulted into the room. A long, thick rope drifted in the opening behind him.

Phoebe realized it was suspended from the roof. She gazed at him in open-mouthed amazement and dawning horror.

"Good evening, madam wife." Gabriel's eyes glittered in the firelight as he coolly removed his gloves. He was not even breathing heavily. He had removed his jacket and cravat to make the descent. His white shirt was streaked with dirt and his boots were badly scuffed. "I suppose I should not be surprised to learn that your taste in wedding nights runs toward the bizarre."

Phoebe finally found her voice. "*Gabriel.* You bloody idiot. My God, you could have been killed."

She rushed past him and leaned out the window. The heavy rope dangled from high overhead. It was a very long way to the ground. Phoebe closed her eyes as terrible images appeared in her mind. She could easily visualize Gabriel's body lying broken on the courtyard stones.

"I'm glad you have the fire going." Gabriel held his hands out to the flames. "It's rather chilly out there tonight."

Phoebe ducked her head back inside the window and whirled to face him. "You came down from the roof."

He shrugged. "It was the only way. The door to this room appeared to be locked.

An accident, no doubt."

Phoebe lost her temper. "You risked your neck just to exercise your husbandly rights?" she yelled.

Gabriel's eyes roved possessively over her. "I cannot think of a better reason."

"Are you mad?" Phoebe wanted to throw something. "Of all the stupid, witless, brainless things to do. I cannot believe this. Have you no common sense?"

"That is a rather odd accusation, coming from you."

"This is not funny. You could have been killed."

He shrugged. "It was no worse than climbing a ship's mast."

"Good grief. 'Tis a scene straight out of the tale of *The Lady in the Tower*." Phoebe charged across the small space separating them and came to a halt directly in front of him. "You must never, ever do anything like this again, do you hear me?"

Gabriel's eyes burned. He caught her face between his palms. "I will do it again if you run from me again."

"Gabriel, you scared me to death. Every time I close my eyes I can see your body lying on the stones. You must not take such foolish chances."

He cut off her protest with a quick, hard

kiss. *"Promise me you will never run from me again."*

She splayed her fingers on his chest and searched his harsh face. "I promise. Do you vow that you will never do anything so wickedly reckless again?"

His thumbs traced the line of her cheekbones. "Do you care so much about me, then?"

Her lower lip trembled. "You must know that I do."

"Then you will not run off again or lock yourself away from me. Because if you do, I will come after you, even if it means descending a castle wall on a rope."

"But Gabriel — "

"Even if it means climbing down into hell itself," Gabriel vowed softly.

Phoebe felt her insides melt. "Oh, Gabriel . . ."

"Come here, my lady in the tower." Gabriel pulled her closer against his hard body. His palm slid down her back, pressing her into the cradle of his muscled thighs.

When Phoebe made a tiny sound, Gabriel brought his mouth back down on hers in a kiss that scorched her from head to toe. Warmth welled up inside her. It was mingled with a sense of longing that was so acute it brought tears to her eyes. She lowered her lashes, twined her arms around his neck, and gave herself up to the heat.

"This is the way it was meant to be between us, my sweet," Gabriel breathed. "I knew it from the first time I met you."

"Did you really?" Phoebe could hardly stand now. She clung to him, touching her lips to the strong line of his jaw. She turned her head and kissed the inside of his wrist. "I have been afraid to hope that you might feel for me some of the things I have been feeling for you."

He smiled against her cheek. "And precisely what have you been feeling for me?"

She shuddered against him. "I love you."

"Ah, my sweet Phoebe." His hands tightened on her, drawing her down onto the quilt she had spread on the carpet in front of the fire.

Phoebe felt the room whirl around her. Then she was lying on her back, her skirts foaming at her knees. She was aware of Gabriel stretching out beside her. His leg tangled with hers, urging her thighs apart, pinning her gently to the floor. When she opened her eyes, she found him gazing intently down into her face.

"Gabriel, I have done a great deal of thinking about this aspect of things."

"Have you?" He brushed his mouth lingeringly over her lips, seeking a response.

"Yes. I like your kisses very much. And I like the way you touch me."

"I'm glad." Gabriel dropped a warm kiss into the curve of her shoulder. "Because I definitely enjoy touching you."

"Nevertheless," Phoebe said quickly, "I cannot help but believe that it might be best if we waited a while before we consummate our marriage."

"I had the impression you were no longer angry with me." He nibbled at her earlobe.

"I'm not," she confessed. How could she be angry when he was making her burn like this? "But there are many matters we need to clear up between us. Matters such as those that came up during dinner tonight. Gabriel, there is still so much we do not know about each other."

"I thought we agreed you would not run from me again."

"I would not run away," she assured him quickly. "We would live as man and wife. I simply meant that perhaps we should become better acquainted before we actually become man and wife. If you see what I mean."

He trapped her head between his hands again. Phoebe stared up at him through her lashes. The firelight sharpened the edges of his hawklike face and deepened the mystery of his eyes.

"Tell me again that you love me, Phoebe."

"I love you," she whispered.

He smiled slowly. "And we are wed. There is no need to wait."

Phoebe gathered her courage. "But I am not precisely certain yet how you feel about me, Gabriel. I ran away this morning because I feared you were offering marriage out of a misguided sense of chivalry."

He took her earlobe between his teeth again and bit down just hard enough to startle her. "Trust me, madam, it was not a sense of chivalry that led me to offer marriage."

"Are you absolutely certain?" she persisted. "Because I truly do not want to feel you were obliged to marry me."

He looked down into her eyes. "I want you more than I want anything else on the face of the earth."

She read the desire in his eyes. "*Gabriel.* Do you mean it?"

"I will show you how much I mean it." Gabriel crushed her mouth gently beneath his own. His tongue plunged between her lips, inviting her to taste him as he was tasting her.

With a flash of feminine intuition, Phoebe realized that this was Gabriel's way of telling her of his feelings. He loved her. He could not make love to her like this unless his emotions matched her own.

Gabriel found the tapes of her gown and undid them in several short, swift motions. A moment later Phoebe felt the warmth of the fire on her bare skin as she was freed from the dress and the petticoat she had worn beneath it. Gabriel's palm moved across her breasts.

The feel of his roughened fingers against her nipples startled her. Her eyes widened in shock as she realized she was utterly naked except for her stockings.

"It's all right, sweet. You are so lovely." Gabriel's hand drifted over her, testing, stroking, exploring. "My God, you are beautiful." He bent his head and dropped a series of warm kisses in the valley between her breasts.

Phoebe arched against him, her embarrassment fading quickly beneath the impact of the urgent need she sensed in him.

His hand closed around her calf and then moved up along the length of her leg to her thigh. He did not untie her garters. Phoebe found it very odd to be wearing only her stockings.

She turned her face into his shoulder and slid curious fingers into the opening of his shirt. She touched the crisp hair there and

281

was enthralled. Impulsively she put the tip of her tongue to his warm skin. Gabriel sucked in his breath.

"You taste good," she whispered.

He gave a soft, hoarse laugh that dissolved into a husky groan. He cupped her buttocks and squeezed gently. "I have been wanting you for weeks."

Phoebe felt the hard length of his manhood pressing against the fabric of his tight breeches. The proof of his desire filled her with a sense of womanly power. She was caught up in a golden, glittering illusion. But this was no dream, she reminded herself. This was real. "I've loved you for weeks."

His fingers slipped into the triangle of hair at the apex of her thighs, seeking out the plump, moist folds. Phoebe cried out softly when he tested her with his finger.

"Yes," Gabriel breathed. "Yes, my sweet." He withdrew his hand from between her legs. He shifted slightly away from her and shrugged impatiently out of his shirt.

Phoebe watched through half-lowered lashes as he yanked off his boots. Then he got to his feet to remove his breeches.

Phoebe stared at his fully aroused body. She had never seen a man in such a condition. Her mouth went dry and her eyes flew up to meet his.

Gabriel knelt beside her and pulled her to a sitting position. He held her close against his chest. "Don't be afraid of me, Phoebe. Whatever happens, don't ever be afraid of me."

She wrapped her arms around his waist and hugged him tightly. "I'm not afraid of you."

"Trust me?"

"Yes. Always. Forever."

"I'm glad." He kissed the nape of her neck and then settled her back down on the carpet.

"It's just that I had not expected you to be quite so . . ."

"Quite so what?" he asked, nibbling at her throat.

"Quite so *legendary* in your proportions," she managed weakly.

Gabriel laughed. Phoebe felt herself turning a very bright shade of red.

"We shall spin ourselves a fine legend tonight, my sweet. One worthy of any medieval bard."

His mouth was like a warm drug on her skin. It soothed her, teased her, and then goaded her into a response. His hands moved over her, exploring her with a startling intimacy. Even though he was pressing her into the hard floor, she reveled in the weight of him as he sprawled across her.

Experimentally she stroked the contours of his strong back and then dug her fingers into the firm muscles of his hips. He was so strong, she thought, yet he shuddered every time she even grazed him with her fingertips.

Phoebe discovered she could not get enough of his response. No matter where she touched him, he reacted as if she had set fire to something deep inside him. His manhood pushed heavily against her inner thigh.

"I swear I cannot wait any longer." Gabriel's voice was thick with passion. "Open yourself for me, my sweet wife. I need to be inside you or I shall go mad."

She parted her trembling legs. He settled himself firmly between her thighs and eased himself upward until his shaft was pressing against her. Phoebe moved her head restlessly on the carpet as she realized just how large he was.

"Gabriel?"

"Wrap yourself around me, Phoebe." He put his hands under her knees and lifted them. Then he guided her legs into position. "Yes, like that. Now put your hands on my shoulders. Hold on tight, Phoebe. As tight as you can."

She clutched his sleek, powerful shoulders.

She had never felt so vulnerable. But she loved him, she reminded herself, and she ached for this union as much as he did. They were as one in this passion, just as they were in their love of old medieval legends.

"That's it." Gabriel kissed her throat and pushed himself more insistently against her passage. "You're very tight, but you're also very wet. I don't know how stormy this first sailing will be, but you must trust me. All will be well."

"It's all right, Gabriel." She lifted herself tentatively against him. "I want you."

"I'm never going to get enough of you after this." He reached down, opened her with his fingers, and guided himself slowly into her snug channel.

Phoebe held her breath, not certain what to expect, but needing the feel of him inside her. She had to have him. Instinctively she tightened her legs around him.

"Phoebe, wait, I don't want to hurt you."

Gabriel's face was a stark mask of self-imposed restraint. But when Phoebe lifted her hips once more, something seemed to give way inside him. "Yes. Oh, God, *yes.*" He surged into her in one powerful stroke.

Shock and surprise slammed through Phoebe. She was suddenly too full, too tight, too trapped beneath Gabriel's heavy weight. *He was inside her.*

She could not tell if there was any pain. She did not know what she was feeling. The sensation was literally indescribable. She gave a soft exclamation and clutched Gabriel's shoulders.

Gabriel shuddered again. "Go ahead. Sink your little claws into me. God knows I have sunk myself so deeply into you I may never recover."

Phoebe swallowed quickly. "I think that is far enough," she said in a small voice. "Perhaps we should stop now."

"I could not stop now if the earth opened up and swallowed me alive." Gabriel eased himself partway out of her and then pushed slowly, relentlessly back into her. "You feel so incredibly good, my sweet. Nothing has ever felt this good."

Phoebe kept her legs wrapped around Gabriel's waist. The sensual spell she had been under earlier had been shattered. She was uncomfortable but not in any real pain. It was a very strange sensation having Gabriel inside her like this. He was obviously finding pleasure, however, and she loved him too much to deny him the satisfaction he sought.

"Hold me." Gabriel's voice was raw. "Hold me, Phoebe. I need you."

She tightened her arms around him, clinging to him, offering herself up to him until he suddenly gave a muffled shout and went absolutely rigid above her. The muscles of his back and buttocks were like steel beneath his skin as he pumped himself into her.

Then he collapsed along the length of her.

For a long while Phoebe lay quietly beneath Gabriel and listened as he recovered his breath. She stroked his back slowly and felt the dampness there. He was like a stallion after a hard race, she thought.

Her stallion.

After a while Gabriel groaned and eased himself reluctantly out of her. He rolled to one side, put his arm across his eyes, and gathered her against him. "Next time it will be better for you, Phoebe. I promise."

"It was not bad this time," she said honestly. "Rather odd, but not bad."

He chuckled weakly. "Next time you will scream with pleasure. You have my oath on it. I shall make a quest out of the business and I shall not rest until I have successfully completed it."

Phoebe smiled and folded her arms on top of his damp chest. "I would never do anything so unladylike as to scream."

"Wait and see." He took his arm away from his eyes and threaded his fingers through her tangled hair. "The fire in your hair burns just as hot in the rest of you. You are an amazing creature, madam wife."

"Am I?"

"Most definitely." He closed his eyes again. "We shall rest for a few minutes and then we'll get dressed and go downstairs to my bedchamber."

"I like it up here," Phoebe said.

Gabriel did not open his eyes. "I have no intention of spending the rest of my wedding night on the floor of my study."

But he was asleep within a few seconds, his arm still locked around Phoebe.

She lay looking at him for a long while, vaguely aware of a host of new impressions. There was some soreness between her legs and the musky scent of his maleness was on her. She felt sticky and warm and a little restless.

So this was what it was like being married. She could deal with it, Phoebe decided. She rather liked the warm intimacy of it all, even if the actual act of lovemaking was nothing to get excited about. The preliminaries were certainly quite pleasant. But the real joy in the thing was the glorious knowledge that Gabriel was now hers.

She was married to the man she loved and he clearly loved her, even if he did have trouble saying the words. Many women, she knew, were not so lucky. For most people marriage was a practical matter entered into for the sake of property, social position, and inheritances.

She was one of the rare, fortunate women in her world who had married for love. And to think she had almost spoiled everything this morning by running off. Perhaps Gabriel had a point when he called her reckless.

Phoebe stretched carefully, aware that she was getting stiff. Gabriel's arm slid off her breast. He did not waken. The man was obviously exhausted. He'd had a hard day, to say the least.

She sat up slowly and gazed around the study. She was wide awake and strangely alert. The last thing she wanted to do right now was sleep. The contents of Gabriel's bookshelves beckoned.

She rose carefully from the quilt and slipped into the white lawn nightgown she had brought with her. Then she went over to the nearest bookcase.

She studied the row of leather-bound volumes behind the glass and was very impressed. When she reminded herself that this was only a small portion of his magnificent collection, she shook her head in amazement. One of the pleasures of being married to Gabriel, she thought smugly, was that she now had access to his library.

She stood on tiptoe to read the spines of the next row of books. The breath went out of her lungs when her gaze fell upon a familiar-looking volume. She stared, unwilling to believe her eyes. But there it was, inscribed in gilt: *The Lady in the Tower.*

It was her copy. She was almost certain of it.

Stunned, Phoebe glanced back over her shoulder at Gabriel. He had not moved, but his eyes were open now. He watched her, his expression unreadable in the flickering glow of the fire.

"I told you that I would complete the quest," he said quietly. "I promised to see to it that you found your copy of *The Lady in the Tower* before the end of the Season."

Phoebe turned slowly to confront him. "You found it but you neglected to tell me? Gabriel, I do not understand." She brightened as the obvious truth dawned on her. "Wait. It was to be my wedding gift, was it not?"

"Phoebe, listen to me."

But Phoebe was certain she knew what had happened. "What a wonderful surprise. I am so sorry I ruined it for you, but never fear. I am thrilled. Where did you find it? Who was the owner?"

He sat up slowly, heedless of his nakedness. The firelight danced on his broad shoulders, turning his skin to burnished gold. He raised one knee and rested his arm on it. His emerald eyes were full of brooding shadows.

"I am the owner of the book, Phoebe."

Phoebe swallowed uncertainly. "What do you mean? How did you acquire it?"

"I removed it from Baxter's cabin after we boarded his ship." Gabriel's voice was curiously lacking in inflection. "Baxter chose the sea rather than hanging. He went overboard and disappeared. He was presumed drowned."

"You boarded his ship?" Phoebe discovered that her knees suddenly felt weak. She sank down slowly onto the window seat and clasped her hands very tightly together in her lap. "Dear God, Gabriel, are you telling me you were a pirate in the South Seas? I refuse to believe it."

"I'm glad. Because I was no pirate. Merely a hardworking businessman trying to make a living in the pearl trade. Baxter was the one who took up pirating when he reached the islands."

"Impossible," Phoebe said quickly. "He would do no such thing."

"It does not particularly matter whether you believe it or not. It's the truth. Apparently he found it easier and more efficient than entering into a legitimate shipping venture. He became something of a nuisance to my company and to others. Someone had to get rid of him."

"A nuisance," Phoebe echoed, her mind spinning.

Gabriel's expression was grim. "He managed to acquire control of a ship of his own. He boarded two of my firm's ships, killing a number of men in the process. He stole a large quantity of goods, including an extremely valuable set of jewelry made of black pearls, gold, and diamonds. After that incident I decided to find him before he did any further damage."

Phoebe gazed at Gabriel in stunned amazement. "Good lord. This is incredible. I cannot believe I was so wrong about Neil."

"Because he played the part of Lancelot while he set up his scheme to blackmail your father? Baxter was a clever bastard. You were not the only woman he succeeded in deceiving."

Phoebe's face flamed. "You make me sound like a fool."

Gabriel's expression softened. "You are no fool, my sweet, but you are naive. Women are vulnerable to men such as Baxter. They long to believe the illusion he creates."

Phoebe's hands tightened in her lap. "You speak as if you have known other women who believed he was Lancelot."

"Out in the islands Baxter managed to pass himself off as a prosperous man engaged in legitimate shipping. He mingled freely with those of us who were in the shipping business, gaining information that he then used to set his traps for our ships." Gabriel's gaze hardened. "He preyed on the women, seeking details on cargoes and routes."

"The women?"

"Wives and daughters and . . ." Gabriel hesitated briefly, "others. He charmed them and they willingly told him what he wanted to know."

"I see." Phoebe was silent for a moment, working through the logic of the situation. "You have had my book all along. You were the object of my quest."

"In a manner of speaking, yes."

She looked at him. "Why did you not tell me?"

"There were a number of reasons. Chief among them was that you thought the owner of that book was a murderous pirate."

She smiled tremulously. "Of course. Naturally you were afraid to admit you had the book, for fear I would think the worst of you."

"Bloody hell." Gabriel's eyes narrowed. "It was not that I was afraid to admit it, rather that I had other plans."

"What other plans?"

"I have had enough of this nonsense," Gabriel said grimly. " 'Tis past time we had everything out in the open. Let us begin from the beginning. After I met you on that lane in Sussex, I decided I wanted you. The book was the key to getting you."

Phoebe's eyes widened. "You mean you knew you wanted to marry me right from the start? Gabriel, that is so romantic. You really ought to have told me."

Gabriel got to his feet and slammed his palm against the mantel. "Damn it, woman, why do you insist on seeing me as a heroic knight filled with honorable intentions?" He turned his head to glare at her. "I said I wanted you. To be perfectly blunt, I had no thought of marriage. Not at the beginning of our relationship. I wanted you in my bed. That was as far as matters went."

"Oh." She did not know what to say to that. At least he had wanted her, she thought. "So you agreed to help me in my quest as a way of getting to know me better?"

"As a way of getting you into my bed, damn it."

She smiled hopefully. "Well, your intentions might not have been, strictly speaking, entirely honorable at the start."

"You may be certain they were not."

"But you changed them quickly; that is the important thing. Your intentions became honorable when you got to know me."

"Damnation. You will not see the truth when it is before your very eyes." Gabriel reached for his breeches and put them on with quick, savage movements. "My intentions did not improve after I discovered you were Clarington's daughter. If anything, they became worse."

"Worse?"

He made a small gesture of disgust. "Phoebe, when I learned your true identity, I sought you out with the express purpose of using you to gain revenge against your family. I was going to seduce you in order to humiliate your father. There. Now do you comprehend?"

She blinked back tears and smiled bravely. "Perhaps revenge was your initial goal, but you did not go through with your scheme, did you? You married me instead."

He faced her, his hands on his hips. "So I did."

"Which means that your inherently noble nature ultimately guided your actions," Phoebe concluded.

"Damnation. If that's what you want to believe, who am I to contradict you?"

"You married me because of your naturally chivalrous nature." Phoebe caught her trembling lip between her teeth. "But you do not love me, do you, my lord?"

His eyes glittered. "Do not accuse me of having misled you on that score. That is one sin you cannot lay at my door. I never claimed to love you. I told you I wanted you, and that is the truth. The whole truth."

"You married me to save me from a potential scandal."

"I assure you I am not that noble," he growled. "All my knightly impulses were burned out of me eight years ago. Life in the South Seas did nothing to revive them. I am no heroic champion of love and justice."

"Then why did you marry me?" she shouted.

"I married you because I think you will make me a good countess," he roared back. "Your bloodlines are impeccable. More importantly, your reckless ways, as irritating as they are, bespeak courage and daring. Those are qualities I intend to breed into my sons. Furthermore, I find you vastly more interesting than any other lady I have encountered in recent memory. And I want you."

"But you do not love me."

"I never claimed to love you."

"No, but I hoped you could learn to do so," Phoebe explained. "That is why I took the biggest risk I have ever taken in my life today."

He gave her a disbelieving look. "You call marrying me the biggest risk you have ever taken?"

"Yes."

"That's a damned insult," Gabriel said. "I fully intend to be a good husband to you."

"Do you?"

He took a step forward, looming over her. "Yes, I do. And in return I expect a proper wife, by God."

Phoebe tilted her head to one side, studying him intently. "What constitutes a proper wife in your eyes?"

He caught her chin on the edge of his hand. His gaze glittered with outrage. "I do believe you are deliberately provoking me, madam. Nevertheless, I shall tell you precisely what I want from you. I want the respect and obedience a *proper* wife is expected to show her lord."

"I do respect you, Gabriel. But obedience has never been my forte."

"Well, you can bloody well learn the skill."

"For goodness' sake, Gabriel, you needn't look so threatening. We both know you aren't going to beat me into submission."

"You think not?"

She smiled fleetingly and stepped back from his hand. "Your naturally chivalrous nature would prevent you from using violence against a woman."

"For your own sake," he bit out, "I suggest you stop trying to convince yourself that I possess a chivalrous nature."

"I do hope you will not deprive me of my one remaining illusion." She went to the bookcase and opened the glass doors.

"What the devil do you mean by that?" Gabriel demanded.

"You have told me that Neil Baxter, the only man who ever claimed to love me with a pure and noble heart, lied to me." Phoebe plucked *The Lady in the Tower* off the shelf. "I find myself married instead to a man who claims he does not love me at all, the one fate I have always vowed to avoid. All things considered, my lord, it has not been the wedding day of my dreams."

"Phoebe — "

"Good night, my lord." Clutching the heavy volume to her breast, Phoebe walked to the door.

"*Damnation*, Phoebe, I wish to talk to you."

"About what? The nature of chivalry? Believe me, I am now well acquainted with it. I have no need of further instruction on the matter."

She unlocked the door and started down the spiral staircase. The stone steps were very cold beneath her bare feet.

Chapter 13

Why the devil hadn't he kept his mouth shut? Gabriel tossed aside his pen and gave up trying to write. He got to his feet and went to the window. It was raining. The rope he had used to descend from the roof last night still swung lazily against the glass.

Yes, he should most definitely have kept his mouth shut last night when he had awakened and seen Phoebe staring at her copy of *The Lady in the Tower* in his bookcase.

He was right to have told her the truth about how he had acquired *The Lady in the Tower* and about Neil Baxter, but he should never have told her the rest.

He winced as he recalled his short lecture on respect and obedience. Reminding a wife of such things on her wedding night was probably not the best way of convincing her that her marriage had been a brilliant match.

If she wanted to believe he had fallen in love with her at the start and that his intentions had been honorable all along, who was he to disabuse her of the notion?

Why had he felt the need to shatter all her illusions about him? he wondered.

Gabriel had been brooding over the matter all day and he was still not entirely certain of the answer.

He had been furious when she had run off yesterday morning. He had been angrier still when she had locked herself in the tower room last night. And with the anger there had been fear. He could not deny it. He had been afraid that she would see *The Lady in the Tower* before he could explain everything to her.

He did not want her crediting him with a noble heart and a chivalrous nature, but he did not want her to believe that he had been a murderous pirate, either.

He simply wanted there to be honesty between them, Gabriel told himself.

His jaw tightened as he turned away from the window. For better or worse, she now knew the truth. There was certainly plenty of honesty between them after last night.

She had married a man who initially had intended only to bed her and who had then decided to use her for revenge. In the end he had married her because of her bloodlines, her courage, and the fact that she would make him an interesting companion.

If that was not enough to shatter a lady's

most cherished illusions of love, nothing else would. Gabriel winced. He should have kept his mouth shut. Matters would have been so much simpler.

But perhaps it was better this way. After all, he prided himself on his pragmatic, realistic approach to life. He was no longer a sentimental, trusting, romantic youth. He was a man who dealt with the world as it was.

It was important that Phoebe understand she could not continue to lead him about on her adventures as if he were a pet dog. He had been playing the role of her knight-errant long enough. She was his wife now and she needed to know the true nature of her husband.

Gabriel went back to his desk and picked up his pen. He occupied himself for a few minutes sharpening the nib with a small knife. Then he sat down and tried to tidy up one or two passages in *A Reckless Venture*.

An hour later, surrounded by several sheets of discarded foolscap, Gabriel gave up the effort. He went downstairs to see what Phoebe was doing.

He finally located her in the library.

He opened the door soundlessly and studied her for a moment, his insides tightening as he remembered the events of his wedding night.

Phoebe was curled up in a chair near the window, her slippered feet tucked under the skirts of her pumpkin-colored gown. The watery sunlight filtering in through the narrow windows formed a warm halo around her dark hair. There was a prim little white ruffle around her throat.

Gabriel felt the sharp stab of guilt. She had probably been crying all morning.

"Phoebe?" he said gently.

"Yes, my lord?" She did not look up from the book in her lap.

"I came to see what you were doing."

"I am reading." She still did not look up. She seemed totally consumed by whatever it was she was studying.

"I see." Gabriel closed the door and walked forward. He came to a halt near the fireplace and stood gazing down at her bent head. He realized he did not know what to say next. He sought desperately for the right words. "About last night . . ."

"Hmm?"

Her obvious lack of interest in the subject left him floundering again for words. He took a deep breath. "I apologize if it was less than you might have wished for in a wedding night."

"You must not blame yourself, my lord," she said, head still bent over the book. "I am certain you did your best."

Her condescending tone took him back slightly. "Yes. Well, that is true. Phoebe, we are husband and wife now. It's important that there be complete honesty between us."

"I understand." Phoebe turned the page in her book. "I had not planned to complain, mind you, because you really did try very hard to make the experience a pleasant one. But since you believe so keenly in honesty, I am willing to be blunt."

He frowned. "You are?"

"Of course. To be perfectly frank, my lord, it was all something of a disappointment."

"Yes, I know, my dear, but that is only because you had some highly unrealistic notions about married life."

"I suppose so." Phoebe turned another page and studied an illustration. "But that was partly your fault. After what happened that night in Brantley's maze, I'm afraid I assumed I would experience the same interesting sensations when we actually engaged in the marital act. I had quite looked forward to it and no doubt my expectations were far too high."

Gabriel felt himself turn a dull red as it struck him that she was talking about his lovemaking, not the conversation which had followed. "Phoebe, for God's sake, I'm not discussing that."

"Weren't you, my lord?" She looked up at last, her gaze politely quizzical. "I'm sorry. What were you discussing?"

He wanted to shake her. "I'm talking about the conversation we had after you found *The Lady in the Tower.*"

"Oh, that."

"Yes, that. Damnation, woman, as far as the lovemaking is concerned, you need have no fears on that account. I told you it would improve mightily for you the next time."

Phoebe pursed her lips in a considering fashion. "Perhaps."

"There is no perhaps about it."

"Then again, perhaps not."

Gabriel narrowed his eyes. "*Perhaps* I should take you straight upstairs to your bedchamber and demonstrate."

"No, thank you."

"Why not?" Gabriel's hand clenched around the edge of the mantel. It was either that or he would find himself wrapping his fingers around her throat. "Because it's the middle of the afternoon? Don't tell me my reckless Veiled Lady has suddenly turned prim and proper. Have I married a little prig?"

"It's not that." She returned her attention

to her book. "It's simply that I do not believe the experience will improve until I can be certain that you truly love me. I have therefore decided there will be no more such incidents until you have learned to do so."

His fingers were clamped so fiercely around the mantel that it was a miracle he had not cracked the marble. He stared at her angelically bent head. "You little devil. So that is your game, is it?"

"I assure you I am not playing any games, my lord."

"You think you can continue to manage me the way you did before our marriage? I am no longer your personal knight-errant, madam. I am your husband."

"I have come to the conclusion that knights-errant are a great deal more fun than husbands."

He must not lose his temper, Gabriel told himself. He must not let his self-control slip. If he was to gain the upper hand in this domestic skirmish, he was going to have to stay cool under fire.

"You may be right, madam," Gabriel said evenly. "I have no doubt that a headstrong, willful female such as yourself would find an obedient knight-errant vastly more amusing than a husband. But it is a husband you have got now."

"I would prefer to keep the relationship in name only."

"Hell and damnation. Have you gone mad? There is absolutely no possibility of that. I will not allow you to manipulate me in such a fashion."

"I am not trying to manipulate you." Phoebe finally looked up from her book. "But I am determined that you learn to love me before you make love to me again."

"You do realize men have beaten their wives for less cause than this?" Gabriel asked very politely.

"We have already been through this, Gabriel. You will not beat me."

"There are other ways of exercising my husbandly rights. I found a means last night, did I not?"

She sighed. "I was under a misapprehension last night. When you took that terrible risk of climbing down from the roof, I thought you were proving your love for me. In future I will not be so easily fooled. You need not bother to risk your neck again in that fashion."

"I see." Gabriel inclined his head with icy civility. Two could play at this game, he decided. "Very well, then, madam. You have made your position clear. You may be certain I will not force myself on you."

She looked surprised. "I did not think you would."

He took a grip on his temper. "When you are ready to resume your duties as a wife, be so good as to let me know. In the meantime, rest assured you will receive every courtesy as a guest here at Devil's Mist." He started toward the door.

"Gabriel, wait, I did not mean to say I considered myself a guest in your home."

He paused briefly, careful to hide his satisfaction. "I beg your pardon? I thought that was the sort of relationship you wished."

"No, of course it isn't." She scowled in consternation. "I want us to get to know each other better. I feel certain you can learn to love if you will only give yourself a chance. I mean for us to live as man and wife in all other respects save in the bedchamber. Is that too much to ask?"

"Yes, Phoebe, it is. As I said, let me know when you are ready to be a wife. In the meantime I shall consider you a guest."

Gabriel went out into the hall without a backward glance and stalked through the rows of armor suits to the staircase. He was going to get some writing done this afternoon if it killed him. He was determined that the day would not be a total loss.

Three days later Phoebe retreated again to Gabriel's magnificent library and curled up in her favorite chair.

She gazed out a window and acknowledged that she was in serious danger of losing the grimly polite war that was going on between Gabriel and herself. Indeed, she did not know how much more she could stand of it. Gabriel's will was proving more than a match for her own.

Perhaps she had been doomed to lose from the beginning simply because she was more vulnerable than he. After all, she loved him with all her heart and he knew it. The knowledge definitely gave him the advantage, she realized glumly. Gabriel was clever enough to reason that if he simply waited, her defenses would collapse.

The worst of it was that as far as Phoebe could tell, she was not making any headway at all in teaching Gabriel to love her.

It was not that he was ignoring her, she reflected. It was that he insisted on treating her with an awful politeness that almost brought her to the point of tears. He no longer argued with her or lectured her or complained about her lack of wifely obedience.

He was treating her as a guest, just as he had said he would, and it was enough to make Phoebe grind her teeth in frustration.

Yesterday, in search of common ground, she had attempted to discuss a volume she had discovered in his magnificent library. She had brought the matter up at dinner.

"It is an absolutely magnificent copy of Malory's *Morte d'Arthur*," she remarked as she nibbled at her boiled rabbit smothered in onion sauce.

"Thank you," Gabriel said. He forked up a bite of boiled potato.

Phoebe tried again. "I recall that on the night we visited Mr. Nash you asked him if he had a specific copy of Malory's book. One that had an inscription on the flyleaf. Why would you want that particular book when you have such a fine copy of your own?"

"The copy I asked Nash about was the one my father gave me when I was ten," Gabriel said. "When I left England I was forced to sell it."

Phoebe was stricken. "You had to sell a book your father had given you?"

Gabriel looked at her, his eyes cold. "I was obliged to sell all the books I had inherited from him as well as the entire contents of my own library. I needed the money to finance my trip to the South Seas and to set myself up in business there."

"I see."

"A man who intends to survive cannot afford to be overly sentimental."

"How terrible for you to have to sell off the things that meant the most to you."

Gabriel had shrugged. "It was all part of the lesson I learned at the time. The bullet your brother lodged in my shoulder and the manner in which your father crushed my investment ventures concluded my instruction. I have never again allowed my emotions to rule my head."

Phoebe sighed as she recalled the conversation. Teaching Gabriel to love was going to be a more formidable task than she had first imagined. She stared out the library window into the gray mist and wondered if there was any hope at all of convincing Gabriel to trust his emotions again.

After a moment she got up and went to sit behind Gabriel's desk. It was time she sent a note off to Mr. Lacey. He would no doubt be wondering what had happened to her. Left to his own devices, Lacey would quickly drive the flourishing little publishing business back into oblivion. The man was interested only in gin and the craft of running his beloved printing press.

Lacey could be difficult at times, but Phoebe had known the instant she met him that he was the perfect business partner for her. In exchange for her financial support and editorial expertise he was content to keep silent about their association. There were other printers and publishers she could have approached when she decided to go into business for herself. Most had far greater literary pretensions than Lacey did. But Phoebe was afraid that most of them would not have been able to resist the urge to gossip. Being in business with the youngest daughter of the Earl of Clarington was simply too choice a tidbit for most people to conceal. Lacey, on the other hand, hated to waste his precious time talking, let alone gossiping.

A knock on the door interrupted her reverie. She closed a desk drawer and looked up to see a maid whom she did not recognize. A new member of the staff, Phoebe supposed. The woman was surprisingly pretty with her blond hair and lush figure, but she looked rather old to still be a housemaid.

"Who are you?" Phoebe asked curiously.

The maid blinked as if she had not expected such a question. "I'm Alice, ma'am. I've been sent with a message."

"What is the message, Alice?"

"His lordship would like to show ye an interestin' part of the castle, ma'am. He says he'll meet you down in the catacombs. I'm to show ye the way."

"Wylde has sent for me?" Phoebe leaped to her feet. "I'll come at once."

"This way, ma'am. We'll need candles. It's very dark down there. And filthy dirty, too. Would ye like to change yer clothes first?"

"No," Phoebe said hastily. "I do not wish to keep his lordship waiting."

Gabriel had sent for her. Phoebe was over-joyed. He was going to show her the mysterious passages below the castle. In his own awkward way he was attempting to break down the icy wall that he had erected between them.

Alice led the way down a dark stone stair-case at the rear of the huge hall. At the bottom of the dusty steps she removed a key from a hook on the wall and unlocked a heavy timbered door.

A dank, musty odor wafted upward from the darkness. Phoebe sneezed. She plucked a handkerchief from her pocket.

"Good grief," Phoebe muttered as she blew her nose. "When was the last time these passages were cleaned?"

Alice struck a match and lit the candles she and Phoebe held. The weak light flickered on the gray stone walls. "His lordship said there weren't no point in cleaning the cat-acombs."

"Well, I suppose he's right about that." Phoebe stuffed her handkerchief back into her pocket and looked eagerly around. "My goodness, how fascinating."

They were standing in a narrow, windowless tunnel that appeared to run the length of the castle. In the frail, wavering light Phoebe could see dark openings in the tunnel walls that marked doorways and passages. The air was fetid and motionless with an underlying tang from the sea.

"They says in the kitchens that in the old days the lord of the castle used some of these rooms as dungeons." Alice started forward, moving warily down the subterranean passage. She looked nervous as she led Phoebe past a yawning black opening. "They says if ye go into some of these horrid little cells, ye can still find the bones of some of the poor wretches who was chained down here."

Phoebe shivered and shielded her candle with her palm. This was more atmosphere than she had envisioned. "Where is his lordship planning to meet us?"

"He said to bring ye to the end of this passageway and he'd show ye the rest. I don't mind tellin' ye that I'll be glad to get back upstairs."

"This is amazing." Phoebe raised her candle to peer into one of the dark passages that led away from the main tunnel. A handful of what appeared to be ivory-colored sticks gleamed in the shadows of a small cell. She swallowed heavily and told herself they could not possibly be bones. "Just think of the history that this castle has witnessed."

"Beggin' yer pardon, ma'am, but I don't think that history, whatever it was, would make pleasant listenin'. Here we are."

Phoebe gazed ahead into the shadows and saw nothing except more of the stone passage. She thought she could hear the distant roar of the sea reverberating through the stone. "Where is Wylde?"

"I don't rightly know, ma'am." Alice stared at her with a strange expression in her eyes. She retreated a step. The candle in her hand flickered ominously. "He said to bring ye to this spot and he would meet us. I've done as I was told, I have. I want to go back upstairs now."

"Run along, then," Phoebe said, impatient to get on with the adventure. "I can wait for his lordship by myself." She stepped forward into the darkness, holding the candle aloft. "Wylde? Are you here, my lord?"

The sudden and terrible shriek of metal on stone behind her caused Phoebe to nearly drop the candle. The shriek was followed by a clanging thud. A scream formed on

Phoebe's lips as she whirled around.

She saw to her horror that a solid iron gate now barred the passageway from floor to ceiling. She was trapped on the far side.

Phoebe realized the gate must have been hidden in the wall. Something had triggered the mechanism that activated it. She ran forward and pounded on the thick metal wall.

"Alice. *Alice,* can you hear me?"

There was no answer. Phoebe thought she heard the faint sound of fleeing footsteps in the distance, but she could not be certain.

She took a calming breath. Alice had no doubt gone for help. Phoebe studied the stone walls, looking for some evidence of a concealed mechanism that might open the gate. She saw nothing.

She took a few more steps into the darkness of the stone passage. The distant roar of the sea was louder now.

"Wylde? Are you here? If you are, kindly answer me at once. Do not tease me, sir. I know I have offended you, but I swear I do not deserve to be tormented like this."

Her voice echoed down the stone passage. There was no response. Phoebe looked back at the iron gate. Surely it would not take Alice long to get help.

Fifteen minutes later there was still no

sign of rescue. Phoebe glanced down at her candle and saw that it was burning quickly. When it went out, she would be in pitch darkness.

It occurred to her that there was only one thing she could do to help herself. She must explore the remainder of the passage in hopes of finding an exit. Surely this long tunnel had been constructed with some other door than the one that led up into the main part of the castle.

Phoebe nervously started down the corridor. There were no more doorways cut into the stone walls. That seemed odd.

Aware that the candle was burning precariously low, she quickened her pace. The smell of the sea was stronger and it seemed to Phoebe that the air was not quite so dank now. Her spirits rose. She would find her own way out of the catacombs.

She heard the soft lapping sound of water a moment later. Encouraged, she rounded a bend in the stone passageway and found herself in a cavernous room. A narrow wedge of daylight shone in the distance.

Phoebe held the candle higher and looked around. She was standing on the stone quay of what appeared to be a tiny subterranean dock. Seawater lapped at the stone. Rusted iron rings embedded in the quay gave evidence that this cavern had once been used to moor boats.

She had found a secret escape route from the castle. It had no doubt been designed by the original owner for use during a siege. The tiny slit of daylight at the far end of the cavern was the exit.

The only problem was that there was no longer an escape boat tied up at the dock. A large volume of black water stood between Phoebe and daylight.

The candle sputtered. Phoebe glanced down at it. She saw that she had no more than a few minutes of light left. Soon she would be trapped in this dark tomb.

She looked back over her shoulder. There was no sound behind her. She had to assume that her rescuers were unable to move the heavy iron gate. It occurred to her that perhaps it had been designed to seal the passageway permanently shut. If the lord of the castle and his family were attempting to escape via this route, they would want to be certain they were not followed.

The candle hissed and wavered. Phoebe made up her mind. She could not bear to wait here in the darkness in hopes of a rescue that might not come.

She would have to swim for it.

Phoebe set the candle carefully down on

the edge of the quay. Then she unfastened the tapes of her gown and removed her ruffled chemisette.

Dressed in only her chemise, she sat down and slid her legs cautiously into the dark, cold water. For an instant raw terror gripped her as her feet disappeared into the black depths. She had no way of knowing what creatures made their home beneath the surface.

It took more courage than she had known she possessed to drop down into the water. The last flicker of the candle was a definite inspiration. When the frail light vanished, Phoebe's only thought was to get to the wedge of daylight that awaited her up ahead.

She struck out, swimming strongly at first toward the beacon in the distance.

She was horrified at how quickly her energy diminished in the cold water. By the time she was halfway to her goal, she was gasping for air and praying for strength. Her weak left leg was tiring rapidly.

It seemed to take forever to reach the cavern entrance. It was as if the water were deliberately trying to pull her down beneath the surface. Phoebe began to swim mechanically, like a clockwork toy. She dragged air into her lungs with every other stroke and used her fear of the invisible depths to propel her legs.

When her fingers scrabbled painfully against barnacle-encrusted rock, she nearly collapsed with relief. Gasping for air, she clutched fiercely at the rock and gazed eagerly out into the sunlight, hoping for a glimpse of the nearby shore.

It was then she realized that she had only completed a portion of her journey. The hidden cavern entrance jutted several yards out from the shoreline. No one would see her from the cliffs if she stayed where she was. Her cries for help would not be audible above the roar of the waves.

She would have to swim to the rocky beach.

Phoebe clung to her perch a moment longer, telling herself that at least she was in the sun now. It was not quite so cold. And there was only a short distance to go.

If only she were not so exhausted. If only she could rest longer.

But she did not dare hesitate. The water seemed to be getting colder in spite of the sunlight pouring down on her. She could only pray she had enough strength to swim the rest of the way.

"Gabriel," she whispered as she struck out toward shore, "where the devil are you when I need you?"

Chapter 14

"Where the devil is she?" Gabriel roared.

Rollins, the butler, wavered under fire but did not collapse. "I regret to inform you, sir, that I do not know where Lady Wylde is at the moment. The last I knew, she was in the library, as is her custom at this hour."

"And at every other hour," Gabriel muttered. Lately Phoebe seemed to spend every spare minute hiding from him in the damned library. "Assemble the staff immediately."

"Yes, my lord."

Within minutes the staff was clustered in the main hall. No one knew where Phoebe was. Everyone agreed that she had most recently been ensconced in the library. The last time anyone had actually seen her had been nearly two hours earlier.

Gabriel fought down his rising uneasiness and the fear that lay beneath it. Nothing was ever accomplished by giving way to strong emotion, he reminded himself. "I want every inch of the castle and the grounds searched at once. Rollins, you will direct the staff. I will take the cliffs. We will meet back here in an hour."

"Yes, my lord." Rollins hesitated. "Forgive me, sir, but do you believe that something dreadful has happened?"

"She has probably gone for a stroll and gotten lost," Gabriel said, not believing his own words for a minute. "She does not know the countryside around here. Start the search at once."

"Yes, my lord."

Gabriel headed out the front door and down the steps. Driven by a terrible restlessness, he strode through the courtyard and out through the castle gates.

She had promised she would not run from him again.

Gabriel reached the cliffs and stood gazing down at the rocks and driftwood that cluttered the narrow strip of beach. Surely if she had gone for a walk she would have stayed up here on the cliffs. She would not have tried to climb down to the water's edge.

But Phoebe was unpredictable. She was also capable of taking great risks. He still shuddered whenever he recalled how and where he had first met her. *At midnight on a lonely country lane, for God's sake.* The woman was a menace to herself.

When he found her, he was going to put

her on a very short rein. He had had enough of this nonsense.

Enough of this gut-wrenching fear.

He forced himself to calm down and recall the color of the gown Phoebe had been wearing that morning. It had been a rather glaring shade of citron yellow. With a ruffled chemisette. She had looked very bright and cheerful in it.

Not at all like a woman who was plotting to run away from her husband.

Gabriel started walking along the cliff edge. He would not allow himself to believe she had run off until he had exhausted every other possibility.

He frowned as he caught a glimpse of white on the water-lashed rocks. For a moment he thought it was the reflection of sunlight on sea foam. Then the patch of white moved, heaving itself higher up onto the rocks. Pale legs and arms and a tangle of wet, dark hair spilled over the stone.

Phoebe.

Gabriel's stomach went cold. For an instant he wondered if the little fool had gone swimming. Then he realized she was fighting for her life in the churning surf.

"Phoebe. Hold on. I'm coming for you," he shouted, plunging down the cliff path, heedless of skittering pebbles and shifting sand. He jumped the last few feet, landed on the beach, and splashed into the thigh-deep water.

"Phoebe. For God's sake."

The tangle of drenched hair moved as he waded toward her. Phoebe turned her head, her cheek pillowed against the barnacles. She clung to the rock, half in and half out of the water. Her eyes opened partway and she smiled with a soul-deep weariness.

"I knew you would come eventually, Gabriel."

"Hell and damnation, what are you doing down here?" Gabriel lifted her off the rock and cradled her in his arms. Her wet chemise was virtually transparent. He could see the dusky flowers of her nipples as clearly as if she were nude. "Where are your clothes? What in bloody hell has happened?"

"Went looking for you." Her voice was frighteningly weak. She lolled in his arms like a rag doll. Her eyes fluttered shut.

"Phoebe, open your eyes." Gabriel heard the rough edge of fear in his voice. "Open your eyes at once and look at me."

Obediently she lifted her lashes. "Why? I am safe now, am I not?"

"Yes," he whispered as he carried her up onto the tiny beach. "You are safe."

She had not run from him.

An hour later Phoebe lay propped up against the pillows in her bed. Under Gabriel's supervision she had been immersed in a warm bath and fed endless cups of hot tea. He had not been satisfied until the color had returned to her lips and cheeks.

When she had started to resist the tea and complain about the fussing that was going on around her, he knew she was all right. He sent the last of the maids from the room with a curt command.

He had almost lost her. The terrible weight of that fact gnawed at his insides, making him short-tempered and edgy. He had almost lost Phoebe.

He forced his seething emotions back under control. It was an almost impossible task. He used a blanket of anger to contain everything else he was feeling, including the fear.

"Now, then, madam wife," he said as the door closed behind the last maid, "perhaps you would care to explain what the devil happened to you today? What was all that nonsense about looking for me?"

She patted away a tiny yawn. "Alice said you had sent for me."

"Who is Alice?"

"One of the maids."

"Which maid?"

Phoebe stared at him from beneath drooping lashes. "Well, I really don't know. I thought I was acquainted with all the staff by now, but this is such a huge place and there are so many names and faces to learn."

"Describe her," Gabriel said abruptly.

"She had pale blond hair and a rather pretty face. I remember thinking she seemed a little old to still be a housemaid. One would have thought she would be at least a chambermaid by now."

Gabriel was very still. "What did this Alice tell you?"

"That you wished to meet me downstairs in the lower part of the castle. She said you were waiting down there to show me the catacombs." Phoebe paused. "I was very excited."

"She took you down there? Showed you the way?"

Phoebe nodded. "But we could not find you. Alice was getting nervous, so I sent her back and continued along the passageway on my own. Then the most awful accident occurred."

"What accident?"

"A massive iron gate slid out of the wall and sealed the passageway. I was trapped on the other side. I could hear no sounds of rescue and assumed no one could get the gate open. So I looked for another exit."

"And found the secret quay?" Gabriel was incredulous. "Damnation. You swam all the way out of the cavern and back to the shore?"

"I really did not see an alternative at the time."

Gabriel's jaw clenched. "Where the devil did you learn how to swim?"

Phoebe smiled slightly. "Once when I was very little I jumped into the pond at our country estate. It was a very hot day and I wanted to cool off as Anthony and his friends were doing. Anthony had to pull me out of the water. Mama said that he had better teach me how to swim, as there was no telling when I would take it into my head to jump back into the pond."

"Thank God for your mama," Gabriel muttered.

"Remember that when she asks for a loan to cover her gaming losses," Phoebe said dryly.

Gabriel scowled. "What is this about gaming losses?"

"Didn't I tell you?" Phoebe yawned again. "Mama is very fond of cards. She tends to view her sons-in-law as potential bankers."

"Good God."

"I would have warned you about Mama's passion for gaming before you offered for my hand if you had had the courtesy to consult me before you consulted Papa."

Gabriel smiled briefly. "So it's all my own fault if I end up having to cover your mother's losses?"

"Yes, my lord, it is." Phoebe was thoughtful for a moment. "Do you know, I believe it would be best if we did not mention this unfortunate incident to the members of my family. It would only alarm them and I seem to do that often enough as it is."

"I won't tell them about it, if that is your wish."

She flashed him a relieved smile. "Thank you. May I go to sleep now?"

"Yes, Phoebe. You may go to sleep." Gabriel moved away from the window and went to stand at the foot of the bed.

"You have an odd expression on your face, Gabriel. What are you going to do while I sleep?"

"Find the missing Alice."

Phoebe lowered her lashes and snuggled down into the pillows. "What will you do when you find her?"

"At the very least, I shall turn her off without a reference," Gabriel said.

Phoebe opened her eyes very wide. "That would be most cruel, sir. She would be unlikely to find work at her age without a proper reference."

"She may consider herself fortunate if I do not summon the magistrate and press charges. As far as I am concerned, she very nearly got you killed."

Phoebe looked up at him, her gaze intent. "Are you saying you did not send her to summon me this afternoon, my lord?"

"No, Phoebe," Gabriel said gently. "I did not."

"I see." She looked very forlorn. "I was afraid of that. I was rather hoping you had sent her to fetch me, you know. I thought it meant . . ."

He frowned. "What did you think it meant?"

"That you wanted to tear down the wall that you have put between us."

"I did not put the wall between us, Phoebe. You did. It is up to you to tear it down." He walked to the side of the bed and tugged the quilt up over her shoulders. "Get some rest, my dear. I shall have your dinner sent up to you."

"Gabriel?"

"Yes, Phoebe?"

"Thank you for saving me." Phoebe gave him a misty smile. "I knew you would."

"You saved yourself, Phoebe," he said. The stark reality of that fact was going to be with him for the rest of his life. *He had almost lost her.* "If you had stayed in the passageway, it might have been a very long time before I thought to look for you down there. I have standing orders that no one is to go down into the catacombs unless I accompany him or her. The door is always kept locked."

She gave him a searching glance. "Then why would Alice take me down there?"

"An excellent question, my dear. I shall not rest until I discover the answer."

Gabriel walked out of the room and closed the door quietly behind himself. Out in the hall he summoned Phoebe's maid.

"Stay with her while she sleeps," he instructed. "I do not want her left alone even for a moment."

"Yes, my lord. Is madam all right?"

"She will be fine. But do not leave her side until I return."

"Yes, my lord."

Gabriel went quickly down the stairs. He found Rollins hovering in the main hall.

"Is madam all right now?" Rollins asked anxiously.

"Yes. Bring Alice the housemaid to me at once."

Rollins looked uncertain. "Alice?"

"Blonde, rather pretty, and rather old to

still be in her position."

"I do not believe we have an Alice on staff, my lord. But I shall check with Mrs. Crimpton."

"Do that. I shall be at the foot of the stairs that lead down into the catacombs."

"Yes, my lord."

Gabriel collected a candle from the library and walked to the far end of the great hall. He descended the narrow, twisting stairs and stopped short when he saw that the heavy door at the bottom was locked.

Ten minutes later Rollins returned. His face was very sober. "There is no housemaid named Alice, sir."

Gabriel felt another chill run through him. "There was a woman in this house today who claimed her name was Alice and that she worked here."

"I regret to say, sir, that I do not know of her. May I ask why you are looking for her?"

"Never mind. I am going into the catacombs." Gabriel took the key down from the wall hook.

"Perhaps I should accompany you, sir."

"No, Rollins. I would rather you stayed up here and kept an eye on things."

Rollins drew himself up. "Yes, my lord."

Gabriel opened the heavy door and stepped

into the dark stone passageway. The candlelight revealed two sets of footsteps in the dust on the floor. Someone had definitely accompanied Phoebe into this tunnel. Someone who had claimed her name was Alice.

Gabriel strode swiftly along the passage, following the footsteps. When he saw the iron gate blocking his path up ahead, he set his back teeth. The thought of Phoebe being trapped on the other side and obliged to risk her life swimming to freedom enraged him anew.

He forced his anger back under control and reached down into his boot for the knife he always carried there. He seemed to have need of it rather frequently since meeting Phoebe.

Gabriel inserted the tip of the blade between two stones in the wall and tripped the hidden lever housed there. A moment later a secret panel in the wall opened up to reveal the mechanism that operated the gate. The gate itself was opened and closed by pushing on certain stones in the passageway.

Gabriel studied the ancient pulley arrangement. The wheels and chains were all in excellent working order. He, himself, had spent hours down here tinkering with the machine after he had discovered the secret of the gate.

He had taken great satisfaction in getting the old mechanism functioning again. He had even been inspired to insert a similar hidden mechanism into *A Reckless Venture*. It was a pity his mysterious editor and publisher had not had an opportunity to read his latest manuscript. She might have recognized the device and remembered the secret.

Gabriel had taken pains to ensure that all the members of his staff knew how to open and close the gate. Although he had given orders that no one was to explore the passageways without him, he'd had enough experience of human nature to know he could not depend on everyone following instructions. He had not wanted anyone to get accidentally trapped down here on the wrong side of the gate.

Everyone in the castle knew how the gate worked except Phoebe. The mysterious Alice could have learned the secret from a footman or a stable lad.

But why would she want to terrorize Phoebe? Gabriel wondered as he raised the gate. It made no sense.

The iron gate clanged and groaned as it slowly slid back into position in the wall. Gabriel walked down the remainder of the passageway until he came to the hidden quay.

The sight of Phoebe's crumpled citron-colored gown and the burned-out candle sitting beside it filled him with a helpless, smoldering rage. He stared at the black water that lapped against the stone and thought about Phoebe sliding into it. He knew many stalwart men who would have been paralyzed with fear in such a situation.

His reckless lady had the courage of a valiant knight.

And he had very nearly lost her.

The water was sucking at her, trying to pull her under. *A curse on he who would steal this book. May he drown beneath the waves.* Phoebe swam harder, kicking out frantically in a desperate effort to avoid the darkness behind her and the black depths below. She was surrounded by an endless night. Her only hope was the slip of light up ahead. She had to reach it. But the water was tugging at her, hampering her, trying to trap her.

Just when she thought she could not swim another stroke, a man's hand reached out of the darkness. She was about to grasp it when she saw the hand of another man reaching for her. Both men promised safety. One was lying.

Phoebe knew she had to choose. If she made the wrong choice, she would die.

She came awake to the fading echo of her own scream.

"Phoebe. Wake up. Open your eyes." Gabriel's voice was harsh with command. His hands closed tightly around her shoulders. He gave her a small, impatient shake. "You're dreaming. For God's sake, woman, wake up. That's an order. Do you hear me?"

Phoebe surfaced from the last remnants of the dream. She realized she was in bed. Moonlight poured through the window. Gabriel, dressed in a black silk dressing gown, was sitting beside her. His face was stark in the pale light.

She stared mutely up at him for a second and then, without a word, burrowed into his arms.

"Bloody hell." Gabriel's arms tightened fiercely around her. "You gave me a devilish start. Kindly don't do it again. That scream was enough to wake the dead."

"I was dreaming."

"I know."

"I was back in the cavern, trying to swim toward the light. For some reason part of the curse at the end of *The Lady in the Tower* was going through my head. It got all mixed up with the dream."

He raised her face so that he could look down at her. "What is this about the curse?"

"Don't you remember?" She quickly blinked back the tears of fear and relief that had formed. "At the end of *The Lady in the Tower* there is the usual scribe's curse. Drowning beneath the waves is part of it."

"I remember. Phoebe, it was just a dream."

"Yes, but it seemed very real."

"Given what you went through today, I have no doubt but that it did. Would you like me to send for something to help you sleep?"

"No, I'll be all right." *As long as you're holding me like this,* Phoebe added silently. She pressed herself against him, trying to absorb Gabriel's strength.

There was something amazingly reassuring about his size and power tonight. She remembered the way he had plucked her from the rock and carried her out of the heavy surf. The last terrors of the dream retreated back behind locked doors somewhere inside her.

"Phoebe?"

"Yes, Gabriel?"

"Do you think you can sleep now?" Gabriel's voice sounded strained.

"I don't know," she said honestly.

"It's very late. Nearly two in the morning."

"Yes."

"Phoebe . . ."

She wrapped her arms around his waist and turned her face into his shoulder. "Please stay here with me."

The sudden tension in him was palpable. "I don't think that's a particularly good idea, Phoebe."

"I know you are angry with me. But I really do not want to be alone."

Gabriel's hand clenched in her hair. "I am not angry with you."

"Yes, you are, and I cannot blame you. I have not been a very good wife to you thus far, have I?"

He dropped a small kiss into her hair. "You have been a very unconventional wife thus far, I'll grant that much."

Phoebe took a deep breath and hugged him more tightly. "I have been very non-sensical about the whole thing. I see that now. I am ready to be a proper wife to you, Gabriel."

Gabriel did not respond to that immediately. "Because you are afraid to be alone tonight?" he finally asked.

Phoebe was incensed. "Certainly not." She raised her head swiftly, colliding with Gabriel's chin in the process. She ignored his muffled groan. "How dare you imply that I would invite you to exercise your husbandly rights simply because I was afraid to stay by myself? You may leave at once, my lord."

"I don't think I can do that." Gabriel gingerly massaged his jaw. "If I try to stand up, I shall probably collapse. I vow I am dazed from that facer you just gave me. Have you been taking lessons from Gentleman Jackson, by any chance?"

Phoebe was alarmed. She touched his jaw lightly. "Did I really hurt you?"

"I shall recover." He reached for her, bearing her back against the pillows. His smile was wicked with sensual promise as he loomed over her. "And with any luck, I shall do so in time to teach you a very important lesson."

Phoebe smiled tremulously. "What lesson would that be, my lord?"

"That a wife can enjoy exercising her rights just as much as a husband can enjoy his."

Phoebe twined her arms around his neck. "I shall pay close attention, my lord."

"Don't worry. If you do not grasp the basic concepts this time, we shall keep practicing until you do."

Gabriel took her mouth in a slow, lingering kiss that seared Phoebe's senses. She responded with complete abandon, hungry for the deep intimacy she longed to share again with Gabriel. It did not matter if he could not yet love her, she told herself. He gave her a part of himself when he took her in his arms. She could work with that, build on it until the tiny flame blossomed into love. The thought made her clutch at him.

Gabriel chuckled softly against her cheek. "Not so fast, my sweet. This time we are going to get it right."

"I do not understand. Have we not been doing it right?"

"Only bits and pieces." He eased her nightgown open, baring her breasts. "This time we shall put it all together."

Phoebe gasped as she felt his tongue touch her nipple. Instinctively she tightened her hands in his hair.

"Do you like this, Phoebe?"

"Yes."

"You must be certain to tell me precisely what you like at every point along the way."

She licked her lips as he suckled gently. A delicious tension began to build deep inside her. "This . . . this is very nice."

"I agree." He lifted himself slightly away from her and shrugged out of his dressing gown. His hard, muscled body gleamed in the moonlight.

Phoebe stroked his powerful shoulders, aware of a sense of joyous delight. "You are very handsome, my lord."

"No, love, I'm not. But if you are under the illusion that I am, who am I to complain?" Gabriel slid slowly down the length of her, gently easing her gown off, dropping hot kisses over her breasts and across her soft stomach. "You, however, are definitely very beautiful."

She wanted to laugh at that bit of outrageousness, but her senses were rapidly falling into complete disarray. The laughter turned into a soft sigh of desire. "I am glad you think so, Gabriel. When you kiss me, I feel very beautiful."

"Then I shall be certain to kiss you frequently." Gabriel parted her legs and settled himself between them.

Phoebe trembled when she felt his mouth on the inside of her thigh. When his lips traveled higher, she gasped.

"Gabriel, wait, what are you doing?"

"Remember, you must tell me if you like this." He dropped a kiss into the thatch of curls that shielded her secrets.

Phoebe recoiled in shock. "Gabriel, stop that." She reached down and grabbed fistfuls of his hair. "What on earth do you think you are about?"

"Don't you like this?" He touched his tongue to the sensitive little nub of flesh.

Phoebe shrieked. "Good heavens, no. Stop

that at once." She yanked hard on his hair.

"Ouch. First a severe blow to my chin, and now you would tear out my hair. Making love to you is definitely a challenge, my dear."

"You said you would stop if I told you I did not enjoy something," she gasped.

"No, I did not. I said you must tell me what you like along the way."

"Well, I certainly cannot like this sort of thing. It is far too . . ." Phoebe broke off as she felt his tongue on the bud of delicate female flesh. Another soft cry tore through her. Unable to resist, she arched against him, seeking more of the incredible sensations. "Oh, my God, Gabriel."

"Tell me you like it, sweet." He continued the relentless assault on her most intimate secrets. He began to stroke his finger in and out of her passage as his tongue rasped her swollen flesh.

"Gabriel, stop, I cannot — "

"Tell me you like it." He sucked her gently between his teeth.

Phoebe could hardly breathe. "I cannot bear it."

"Yes, you can. You are a very adventurous woman." He inserted another finger into her, stretching her tenderly.

Phoebe twisted beneath him as the unbearable kisses continued to devastate her. She was beyond protest now. All she could do was surrender to the flood tide of passion.

"Tell me you like this, Phoebe."

"Gabriel, I cannot . . . I cannot . . . Yes. Yes, I like it. Very much. Dear heaven, you are driving me mad." She clutched at him, this time holding him to her as she lifted herself for the hot kisses. She felt his fingers slide into her once more and then she felt the sensual tension in her lower body reach a critical point.

"Gabriel."

"Yes," he whispered. "Now. Just like that. Give yourself up to it. I'll keep you safe."

He kissed her again and Phoebe came apart into a thousand little pieces. She was hardly aware of Gabriel's triumphant groan. She felt him slide up along the length of her. She was startled at the taste of herself on his mouth as he covered her lips with his own. And then she felt his engorged shaft forge deeply into her tight, convulsing body.

Even as she adjusted to the invasion, the tiny ripples of excitement seemed to intensify. Phoebe clung to Gabriel as tightly as she had clung to the surf-lashed rock that afternoon.

She was safe.

Chapter 15

The gray light of dawn was reflecting off the sea and pouring in through the window when Gabriel woke. He instinctively tightened his arm around Phoebe, assuring himself that she was still safely tucked against him.

She was exactly where she was supposed to be. The sweet, ripe curve of her bottom was cuddled against his hip and her small, shapely foot was lying alongside his leg. His fingers cupped her gently rounded breast.

Gabriel savored the simple, newfound pleasure of awakening in the early morning light with his wife in his arms. The unfamiliar sense of intimacy was deeply satisfying.

She was truly his at last, he thought. In the middle of the night she had given him the surrender he had been seeking. Her response had been complete and uninhibited. Except for one niggling little detail, Gabriel realized, he finally had everything he wanted.

The tiny, unimportant detail was that she had not told him she loved him. Even in the heat of her passion when she had shivered mindlessly in his arms and cried out his name, she had not said the words.

Not that it mattered, Gabriel assured himself. After all, she had confessed her love in a thousand different ways last night. He remembered how she had touched him, tentatively at first, and then with growing confidence. She had stroked him gently as she learned the shape and feel of him. He felt himself growing hard again at the memory.

"Gabriel?"

"Mmm?" He turned on his side and tugged the quilt down until her rose-tipped breasts peaked up at him.

Phoebe wriggled impatiently and yanked at the quilt. "I'm cold."

"I'll keep you warm." He kissed one soft breast and then the other.

She looked up at him, wide-eyed now. "This is very strange, is it not?"

"What?" He was preoccupied with the taste of her nipple.

"Waking up in the morning with someone else in one's bed."

Gabriel raised his head. " 'Tis your husband in your bed, madam, not just *someone*."

"Yes, I know, but all the same, it seems odd. Not unpleasant, mind you, just rather odd."

"You'll soon grow accustomed to the sensation," Gabriel vowed.

"Perhaps," she agreed, sounding unconvinced.

"Trust me. You most definitely will get used to it." He rolled onto his back and pulled her across his chest. His fully erect shaft pressed against her thigh.

"Good heavens, Gabriel." Phoebe's brows drew together in a disapproving frown as she glanced down at his heavy arousal. "Do you always wake up in this condition?"

"Are you always this chatty in the mornings?" He grasped her leg and drew it across his hips so that she was astride him.

"I don't know. As I said, I am not accustomed to waking up with someone else. . . . Gabriel, what are you doing?" Phoebe gasped as he found her softness with his fingers and began to stroke gently.

He felt the warm honey start to flow almost at once. He grinned. "I am learning to manage my managing little wife. You must admit I am an excellent student."

He guided himself to the humid entrance of her feminine passage, clamped his hands around her hips, and eased her firmly downward.

"Gabriel."

"I am right here, my sweet."

Some time later Gabriel reluctantly tossed aside the covers and got to his feet.

"It is still very early," Phoebe observed in a drowsy voice. "Where are you going, my lord?"

"I am going to get dressed." He leaned over the bed and gave her a gentle, thoroughly proprietary pat on her bare buttock. "And so are you. We shall be leaving for London directly after breakfast."

"London?" Phoebe sat up abruptly. "Why on earth are we going back to London? We have only been here a few days."

"I have business to attend to in Town, Phoebe. You may recall that our wedding took place in a rather unplanned fashion."

"Yes, I know, but surely there is no need to rush back."

"I was obliged to drop several important matters in order to chase off after you, madam wife." He picked up his dressing gown. "I can no longer ignore those matters."

"What can be so important that we must rush off like this? I like it here at Devil's Mist."

He smiled ruefully. "I'm glad you like your new home. But I must insist we leave today."

Phoebe lifted her chin. "My lord, I believe

we should discuss this further over breakfast before making a decision."

Gabriel cocked a brow. "Phoebe, you are a wife now. My wife. That means you will be guided by my decisions in matters such as this. We leave for London in two hours."

"The devil I will." Phoebe scrambled out of bed and grabbed her chintz wrapper. "Gabriel, I must warn you that if we are to enjoy a peaceful marriage, you will have to learn to discuss things with me before you make sweeping decisions. I am twenty-four years old, not a green girl who can be ordered about at your whim."

He turned in the doorway that connected her bedchamber to his, propped one shoulder against the frame, and folded his arms. "We leave for London in two hours. If you are not dressed and packed, you will be put into the carriage just as you are. Is that quite clear?"

Phoebe's soft mouth tightened mutinously and her eyes narrowed. "I will not be dragged across the landscape just because you are in the mood to do so."

"Would you care to make a wager on that?"

She started to fire back a response and then she hesitated. Gabriel groaned inwardly as he saw realization dawn in her eyes. He

347

had known all along there were drawbacks to having an intelligent, strong-minded female as a wife.

"Wait a minute," Phoebe said slowly. "You are doing this because of what happened yesterday, are you not?"

Gabriel exhaled wearily. There was no longer any point in trying to convince her he was merely being arbitrary. "I think it's for the best, Phoebe. I want you away from Devil's Mist for a while."

Phoebe hurried forward, her expression anxious. "But Gabriel, it was an accident."

"Was it?"

She shook her head, bemused. "What else could it have been?"

"I'm not certain. All I know is that this mysterious Alice deliberately committed a grave act of mischief. One that could have gotten you killed. I will talk to the local magistrate before we leave and tell him what has happened. He may very well know who Alice is. But until she is found, I want you safely away from here."

Phoebe frowned thoughtfully. "Perhaps the poor woman is mad."

"Then she must be locked up in a hospital for lunatics. I certainly do not want her running about the countryside around here," Gabriel said. "Two hours, Phoebe."

He straightened and walked into his own bedchamber. It struck him that he was not accustomed to explaining himself. Out in the South Seas, the only thing that had been required was the ability to enforce his own orders. He had been quite capable of doing that.

Having a wife who questioned every reasonable command was going to be trying.

Meredith winced at the sight of the bolt of scarlet silk. "Phoebe, that is positively the most unfashionable color I have ever seen. Please, I beg you, don't have it made up into a gown."

"Are you certain you don't care for it? I thought it rather attractive." Phoebe touched the brilliant silk, captivated by its fiery color.

"It is totally unsuitable."

"Well, if you are absolutely certain."

"I am absolutely positive it will look perfectly outrageous on you."

Phoebe sighed reluctantly and looked at the shopkeeper. "I suppose I shall have to select another color. Perhaps something in purple or yellow?"

"Certainly, madam." The mercer reached for another bolt. "I have some wonderful purple satin and there is this rather striking yellow Italian silk."

Meredith shuddered. "Phoebe, I do wish you would consider the pale blue muslin or the pink satin."

"I prefer bright colors. You know that."

"I know, but you are a countess now."

"What difference does that make?" Phoebe asked in surprise.

"For your husband's sake, you must begin to pay more attention to fashion. Try that pink and white sprigged muslin," Meredith suggested. "Pastels are all the rage."

"I do not care for pastels. I have never cared for pastels."

Meredith sighed. "I am only trying to guide you, Phoebe. Why must you always be so stubborn?"

"Perhaps I am stubborn because people have been trying to guide me all of my life." Phoebe fingered a brilliant purple velvet. "This is rather interesting."

"For a ball gown? You cannot be serious," Meredith exclaimed.

"I was thinking of it for a medieval costume." Phoebe draped a piece of yellow silk over the purple to study the effect. "I have decided to give a house party at Devil's Mist during the summer."

"Wonderful. Now that you are the Countess of Wylde, you must start entertaining. But what is this about a costume?"

Phoebe smiled. "I want the theme to be that of a medieval tournament."

"A tournament? You mean with men dressed in armor and dashing about on horseback?" Meredith looked seriously alarmed.

"Devil's Mist is the perfect place for such an affair. We shall see that no one will get hurt. We will have archery contests and a grand ball. I shall hire actors who will play the parts of jesters and troubadours. Everyone will wear appropriate costumes, of course."

"Phoebe, that will be a massive undertaking," Meredith said carefully. "You have never given so much as a small soiree. Are you certain you want to take on this sort of project?"

"It will be great fun. I think Wylde will enjoy it."

Meredith eyed her closely. "Forgive me for asking, but have you actually discussed this with Wylde?"

"Not yet." Phoebe chuckled. "But I am certain he will approve. It is just the sort of thing that will appeal to him."

"You are certain of that?"

"Quite certain."

Twenty minutes later Phoebe and Meredith left the shop. The footman they had brought with them carried two lengths of fine cloth, one purple, the other bright yellow. Phoebe was quite satisfied with her purchases. Meredith appeared resigned to the inevitable.

"We must stop in at Lacey's Bookshop while we are in the vicinity," Phoebe said to Meredith. "It is only a short distance from here."

"Very well." Meredith was quiet for a moment as they walked toward the bookshop. Then she moved a bit closer to Phoebe. "There is something I must ask you."

"Yes?" Phoebe could not wait to get to Lacey's. Gabriel had casually mentioned at breakfast that he had sent his newest manuscript off to his publisher that morning.

Phoebe had almost confessed to Gabriel that she was his publisher. She had tested the waters cautiously by suggesting that she should read his manuscript first.

"Absolutely not," Gabriel had said. "I have a very firm policy on that subject. No one reads my manuscripts except myself and my publisher." Then he had smiled with infuriating condescension. "Besides, what would you know of judging modern novels? Your expertise is in much older works, madam."

Phoebe had been so annoyed that she had brushed aside the guilt she felt about not having confided her secret activities as an editor and publisher to Gabriel.

Meredith hesitated. "Phoebe, dear, are you

happy in your marriage?"

Phoebe looked at her in surprise. Meredith's lovely eyes were filled with anxiety. "For heaven's sake, Meredith. Whatever makes you ask that?"

"I know you felt rushed into this alliance. I am well aware that you wanted time for Wylde to get to know you." Meredith flushed. "The thing is, everyone was extremely upset the day you ran off."

"Were they, indeed?"

"Yes. We were all quite dispirited except for Wylde. He was in a cold rage. I worried that when he caught up with you he would still be angry. I was not certain what he would do, if you see what I mean."

"No, Meredith, I do not see what you mean. What are you trying to say?"

Meredith's flush deepened. "The thing is, because of my experience with Wylde eight years ago I know something of his temperament. Phoebe, I have worried so that he was not kind or patient with you."

Phoebe frowned. "He has not taken to beating me, if that is what concerns you."

"Not exactly." Meredith glanced quickly around and apparently decided the footman was not within hearing distance. "What I am trying to say is that I know he has probably not been, strictly speaking, a gentleman in the bedchamber. He always was somewhat rough around the edges, and I feared that if he were angry he would not be considerate of a lady's natural sensibilities."

Phoebe stared at her in amazement. "Good lord, Meredith. If it is Wylde's performance as a lover that concerns you, set your mind at ease. It is one of the few things he has got right thus far."

At Lacey's Bookshop, Phoebe told her sister that she wanted to view a special volume that was being held for her in the back of the shop. Neither the clerk nor Meredith were surprised. Phoebe frequently viewed "special volumes" that were being held for her at Lacey's.

"I'll browse out here while you see to your old books," Meredith said. "But do hurry, Phoebe. I want to visit the glove-maker's this afternoon."

"I won't be long."

Lacey, an oily rag in his hand, was hovering over his big printing press with the attentiveness of a lover. He looked up, squinting, as Phoebe let herself into the back room.

"Is it here, Mr. Lacey?"

"Over there on the desk. Came about an hour ago." Lacey pulled his gin bottle out of his apron pocket and took a swallow. He wiped his mouth on the back of his hand

and regarded her with greedy speculation. "Reckon we'll make a tidy sum on it, do ye?"

"I am sure of it, Mr. Lacey. I shall see you later."

Phoebe snatched up the bundle on the desk and breezed out of the back room.

Meredith glanced at the parcel in her arm and made a tut-tutting sound. "You decided to buy another book, I see."

"This one is very unique," Phoebe assured her.

Three nights later at a huge ball given by longtime friends of the Earl and Countess of Clarington, Phoebe ran into her mother.

Lydia peered at her. "There you are, my dear. I've been looking for you. Where is your husband?"

"Wylde said he would arrive later. You know he is not particularly fond of balls and soirees."

"Yes, I know." Lydia smiled blandly. "Speaking of Wylde, I suppose it is rather too soon to be asking him for a small loan to cover some of my recent losses? Ran into a bit of a bad patch yesterday at Lady Rantley's card party. I'll soon come about, of course, but in the meantime I'm rather short of funds to cover my little debt of honor."

"Ask Wylde for anything you like, Mama. Just do not ask me to ask him for you."

"Really, Phoebe, I hardly think that it would be appropriate for me to go directly to him."

"I don't see why not. How did you happen to lose a large sum at Lady Rantley's? I thought you generally won when you played at her house."

"And so I do," Lydia said, not without a touch of pride. "But yesterday the gossip was just too delicious and I wound up concentrating on it rather than my cards. Always a mistake."

"What gossip?"

Lydia leaned closer. "It seems that Lord Prudstone has been seen rather frequently of late in a fashionable brothel known as the Velvet Hell. His wife has found out about his visits there and she is furious. Word has it she may be plotting revenge."

"And so she should," Phoebe declared. "What is this Velvet Hell place? I have never heard of it."

"I should think not," Lydia murmured. "But now that you are a married woman, it is time you learned a bit more of the world. The Velvet Hell is said to be one of the most exclusive brothels in London. Patronized only by very *tonnish* gentlemen."

"If I ever hear of Wylde stepping foot in the place, I shall throttle him."

Lydia started to respond to that but stopped short, her mouth open in shock. "Good lord. Phoebe, look behind you. Quickly. I do not have my spectacles on, but there is something very familiar about that gentleman."

"Which gentleman, Mama?" Phoebe glanced over her shoulder. The sight of the sandy-haired, hazel-eyed man moving toward her through the throng hit her like a blow in the stomach. "My God. It's Neil."

"I was afraid of that." Lydia grimaced. "He is supposed to be dead. Your father was quite right about him. Baxter has no consideration for others."

Phoebe was not listening. Still in shock, she took a step forward. She could hardly speak. "Neil?"

"Good evening, my beautiful Lady Phoebe." Neil took her gloved hand and bent over it with grave gallantry. His smile was sadly rueful. "I understand I must say Lady Wylde now."

"Neil, you're alive. We thought you were dead."

"I assure you, I am no ghost, Phoebe."

"My God, I cannot believe this." Phoebe was still too dazed to think clearly. She stared at him, shocked to see the physical changes in him. The Neil she had known three years ago had been a much softer-looking man. Now there was a bitterness in his eyes and in the lines around his mouth that had not been there before. In addition, he looked stronger. There was an indefinable coarseness about him that she did not recall from the past.

"Will you dance with me, my lady? It has been too long since I have known the pleasure of having my beloved Phoebe so near."

Without waiting for a response, Neil took her hand and led her out onto the floor. Phoebe went into his arms as the strains of a slow, dignified waltz filled the room. She danced mechanically, her mind whirling with questions.

"Neil, this is incredible. I cannot tell you how happy I am to see that you are alive and well. You must tell me what happened." She remembered what Gabriel had told her about Neil's activities in the South Seas. "There have been dreadful rumors."

"Have there? I have no doubt they were spread by your new husband. When he learns that he did not succeed in murdering me, he will probably create even more slanderous tales."

Phoebe's mouth went dry. "Are you telling

me that Wylde has lied about you? You were not a pirate?"

"Me? A pirate? How could you believe such a thing about your own true Lancelot?" Neil's gaze turned very grave. "I am frightened for you, my love."

"I am not your love, Neil. I was never your love." She hesitated. "Why are you frightened for me?"

"My dearest Phoebe, you have married one of the bloodiest buccaneers who ever sailed the South Seas. The man was the scourge of the shipping routes. He captured my small vessel and looted it. Then he gave every man on board the option of death by the sword or the sea. I chose the sea."

"No. I cannot believe that. Neil, you must be mistaken."

"I was there. I nearly died. Trust me, my dearest, it is the truth. Every word of it."

"What happened to you? How did you survive?"

"I drifted for days on a bit of wood before washing ashore on an island. I was driven nearly mad from thirst and hunger and the sun. Only the memory of your sweet face kept me clinging to life."

"Dear heaven."

Neil's mouth tightened. His hazel eyes glittered briefly with rage. "It took me months to get off that damned rock. And when I finally succeeded in getting to a port town, I had no money. I was ruined when Wylde sank my ship. Everything I had was invested in it. It has taken me all this time to gather sufficient funds to return to England."

Phoebe stared at him. "Neil, I don't know what to say or what to believe. None of this makes any sense. I was told that my father paid you to leave England."

"We both know your father was not pleased with our growing friendship," Neil reminded her gently.

"Yes, but did he pay you to stay away from me? That is what I want to know."

Neil smiled grimly. "An anonymous benefactor paid for my passage to the South Seas. I never learned his name. I assumed it was an old friend who came to my aid. Someone who knew I needed to make my fortune so that I would be worthy of you. Naturally, I seized the opportunity."

Phoebe felt dizzy, and not because of the sedate dancing. She tried frantically to deal with the implications of what she was hearing. "I do not understand any of this, Neil."

"No, my dearest, I am aware of that. But I understand only too well. Wylde has returned to England with eight years worth of plunder and has set himself up as a respectable member of the Social World."

"He was not a pirate," Phoebe insisted. "I know him too well now to believe that."

"Not as well as I do," Neil said softly. "He has taken from me the only woman I ever wanted to marry."

"I'm sorry, Neil, but you know I would never have married you. I told you that eight years ago."

"I could have convinced you to love me. Never fear. I am not angry with you. This marriage to Wylde is not your fault. You were led to believe I was dead."

"Yes." There seemed no point informing him yet again that even if she had believed him to be alive, she would not have waited for him. She had never intended to marry him and she had always tried to make that clear to him. She had wanted Neil as a friend, not as a lover or a husband.

"Like the pirate he is, Wylde has taken everything I valued. My ship, the woman I love, and the one memento I treasured above all others."

Phoebe's eyes widened as a dreadful premonition struck her. "Memento?"

"He took the book you gave me, my dearest. I saw him steal it that day he boarded my ship. He stripped my cabin bare of all my small valuables and then he found *The*

Lady in the Tower. I was nearly killed trying to prevent him from stealing it. Its loss grieved me more than I can say. It was all I had of you."

The niggling sense of guilt that was plaguing Phoebe grew worse. "Neil, I am so confused."

"I understand, my love. You have been fed some very finely spun lies and you do not know what to believe. All I ask is that you remember what we once were to each other."

A terrifying thought struck Phoebe. "What will you do now, Neil? Are you going to try to get Wylde thrown into prison? Because if so, I must tell you — "

"No, Phoebe, I will make no effort to see that Wylde meets the fate he deserves, for the simple reason that I can prove nothing. It all happened thousands of miles away and he and I are the only ones who know the truth. It would be my word against his. And he is now an earl. Furthermore, he is as rich as the devil himself and I am nearly penniless. Who do you think the court would believe?"

"I see." Phoebe sighed with relief. That was one problem she did not have to worry about at the moment.

"Phoebe?"

"Yes, Neil?"

"I know that you are trapped in this marriage."

"I am not exactly trapped," she muttered.

"A wife is at the mercy of her husband. And I pity any woman who is at Wylde's mercy. You are very dear to me and I shall continue to love you for the rest of my days. I want you to know that."

Phoebe swallowed. "That is very kind of you, Neil, but you must not pine for me. Truly, you must get on with your life."

He smiled. "I will survive, dearest, just as I survived all those days at sea. But it would give me great solace if I could have the book you gave me when I left England."

"You want *The Lady in the Tower*?"

"It is all I will ever have of you, Phoebe. I assume Wylde brought it back with him along with the rest of his booty?"

"Well, yes." Phoebe scowled. "That is to say, he brought it back with him from the South Seas along with his fortune."

"The book belongs to you, my love. It is yours to give or withhold. If you have any pity or affection left at all for your devoted Lancelot, I beg you to allow me to keep *The Lady in the Tower*. I cannot tell you how much it means to me."

Panic gripped Phoebe. "Neil, it is very gallant of you to want to keep *The Lady in the Tower,* but I really do not think I am in a position to give it to you."

"I understand. You must be cautious around Wylde. He is an extremely dangerous man. It would be best if you did not tell your husband that I want my keepsake back. There is no knowing what he might do. He hates me."

Phoebe frowned. "I would prefer that you not make personal comments about my husband. I do not wish to listen to them."

"Of course you don't. A wife must contrive to believe the best of her husband. It is her duty."

"It is not that precisely." Phoebe was irritated at the mention of wifely duty. "It is only that I cannot bring myself to believe Wylde was a pirate."

"Surely you do not believe that I was one?" Neil asked gently.

"Well, no," she admitted. "It is very difficult to picture you as a bloodthirsty buccaneer."

Neil inclined his head. "Thank you for that much, at least."

Phoebe was aware of Gabriel's presence in the ballroom before she saw him. A strong sense of relief washed through her. But when she turned her head and realized he was striding straight toward her, she had a change of heart.

She had a horrible feeling there was going to be a dreadful scene.

Gabriel looked every inch the hawk tonight. His green eyes were as pitiless as any raptor's. His black evening clothes emphasized the stark lines of his face and the predatory quality of his body. His gaze never left Phoebe and Neil as he approached.

When Gabriel reached them, he took Phoebe's hand off Neil's shoulder and pulled her to his side. His voice was lethally soft as he confronted Neil.

"So you survived your swim, after all, Baxter."

"As you see." Neil gave a mocking little bow.

"Take some advice," Gabriel said. "If you would go on surviving, stay away from my wife."

"It seems to me that what happens is up to Phoebe," Neil said. "Her position is very similar to that of the legendary Guinevere's, is it not? I believe I find myself playing Lancelot to your Arthur, Wylde. And we all know what happened in that tale. The lady betrayed her lord and gave herself to her lover."

Phoebe was outraged at the implication that she would betray Gabriel. "Stop this nonsense at once, both of you. I will not have it."

Neither Gabriel nor Neil paid her any heed.

"Unlike Arthur, I am prepared to protect my lady," Gabriel said quietly. "Arthur made the mistake of trusting Lancelot. I won't make that mistake because I have the advantage of already knowing you are a liar, a murderer, and a thief."

Neil's eyes flickered with fury. "Phoebe will realize the truth soon enough. Her heart is pure. Even you could not corrupt her, Wylde."

He turned on his heel and walked away.

Phoebe realized she was holding her breath. When Gabriel made to drag her off the dance floor, she felt her left leg buckle. He caught her instantly.

"Are you all right?" he demanded.

"Yes, but I would appreciate it if you would cease hauling me across the room like this, Wylde. People are starting to stare."

"Let them stare."

Phoebe sighed. He was going to be impossible. "Where are we going?"

"Home."

"Just as well," Phoebe said. "The evening has certainly been ruined."

Chapter 16

How in bloody hell had Baxter survived? Gabriel wondered. By rights the man should have been dead.

Gabriel watched Phoebe closely as the carriage rumbled through the crowded streets. He did not have a clue as to what she was thinking. The realization that he did not know how she was reacting to the fact that Baxter was alive alarmed him as nothing else could have done.

It seemed to Gabriel that he had been doing battle with Baxter's ghost since the first time he had met Phoebe. Baxter had always been there, hovering in the background. It had been bad enough dealing with Phoebe's memories of him. Now Gabriel found himself dealing with the man in the flesh. Why couldn't the bastard have stayed dead?

Gabriel's fingers tightened on the carved grip of his walking stick. He was impatient to get Phoebe home, but they were not making swift progress. Elegant lacquered coaches and fancy gigs of all sorts clogged the path. It was nearly midnight and the *ton* was in full motion, moving from one soiree to another in a frenzy that would not end until dawn.

It would have been a good deal faster to walk home, but Phoebe was wearing only a pair of satin dancing slippers that would have been cut to ribbons in minutes on the pavement. And, too, there was always the problem of footpads. The streets were not safe, Gabriel reminded himself.

And neither were the ballrooms.

Of the two, Gabriel decided, he would have preferred to take his chances on the streets.

Baxter was supposed to be dead.

Gabriel eyed Phoebe's unreadable expression. "What did he say to you?"

"He did not say very much," Phoebe said slowly. She was staring out the window. "To be perfectly frank, I had difficulty taking in what he did say. It was such a shock to see him there. I could not believe it."

"Phoebe, tell me exactly what he said to you."

She turned her head and met his eyes. "He said he was not a pirate."

Gabriel glanced down at his hand and saw that he had clenched it into a fist around his walking stick. He forced himself to relax his fingers. "He would deny it, of course."

"Yes, I suppose so. What pirate would admit to his villainy?"

"What else did he say to you?"

Phoebe caught her lower lip between her teeth. Gabriel was coming to know that expression well. It meant she was thinking. He groaned inwardly. Phoebe was always at her most dangerous when she was thinking. The lady was far too intelligent for her own good and she had an imagination which rivaled his own.

"He said," Phoebe murmured, "that you were the scourge of lawful shipping in the islands, not him."

Gabriel had known this was coming, but the foreknowledge did nothing to lessen his fury. "Damn the man. Damn him to bloody hell. He is a liar as well as a murderer. You did not believe him, of course."

"No, of course not." Phoebe's gaze slid away from his. She went back to studying the dark, crowded streets.

Gabriel's stomach clenched. It was not like Phoebe to avoid his gaze. He reached out and caught hold of her gloved hand. "Phoebe, look at me."

She glanced at him through her lashes, her eyes clearly troubled. "Yes, my lord?"

"You did not believe him, did you?" Even as he said the words, Gabriel knew they sounded more like a command than a question.

"No, my lord." She looked down at her hand, which had been swallowed up in his. "Gabriel, you're hurting me."

He realized he was crushing her fingers. He released her hand reluctantly. He must stay calm and in control. He could not allow emotion to cloud his judgment and influence his actions. There was far too much at stake. He forced himself to lean back in the seat and assume what he hoped was a bored expression.

"Forgive me, my dear. Baxter's return from the dead has been unsettling for both of us. The man always was something of an inconvenience."

"Gabriel, I must ask you a question."

"Yes?"

"Is there any possibility, any chance at all, that you were perhaps wrong about Neil's occupation out there in the islands?"

Goddamn the man. In the space of one waltz he had accomplished a great deal. But then, Baxter had always had a way with women.

"No," Gabriel said, willing her to believe him. "Baxter was a damned pirate. There is no question about it."

"I was rather hoping there had been some sort of terrible misunderstanding."

"If you had seen the bodies of the dead men Baxter left behind when he had finished with his work, you would not suggest there had been a misunderstanding."

Phoebe looked stricken. "Dead men?"

"I regret that you are forcing me to be unpleasantly blunt about this. If you do not wish to hear any more of the details, you must accept what I have told you. Baxter was a cutthroat. Did you think such men went about their business in a gallant fashion?"

"Well, no, of course not, but — "

"There is nothing in the least romantic about piracy. It is a bloody business."

"I realize that."

But he could see the doubt in her eyes. Obviously she could not envision her precious Neil Baxter as a monster. "Phoebe, pay close attention to me, because I do not want to have to repeat this. You are to stay away from Baxter. Do you understand?"

"I hear you, my lord."

"You are to have nothing to do with him."

"You make yourself very plain, sir."

"The man is a consummate liar. And he hates me. It is perfectly possible he will try to use you in some fashion to avenge himself on me. You heard what he said about playing Lancelot to my Arthur."

Phoebe's eyes flashed with anger. "I am not Guinevere, my lord. I would not betray you with another man, regardless of the circumstances." Her expression softened. "You can trust me, Gabriel."

"I have always found that it is better not to put such delicate things as trust to the test. You are not to go anywhere near Baxter. You will not dance with him again. You will not speak to him. You will not acknowledge his presence in any fashion. Is that clear?"

Phoebe veiled her eyes with her lashes. "My family once tried to give me similar orders regarding you, Gabriel."

He raised his brows. "And you did not obey them. I am very well aware of that fact. But you will obey me in this. You are my wife."

"I may be your wife, but I wish to be treated as an equal. Anyone can tell you I do not respond well to commands."

"You will respond to my commands, Phoebe. Or there will be bloody hell to pay."

He'd handled her badly.

Gabriel examined the conversation he'd had

with Phoebe over and over again after he dismissed his valet. He poured himself a glass of brandy and began to pace back and forth across his bedchamber.

The bald truth was that he could not think of any other way that he might have dealt with the matter. He had seen the uncertainty in her eyes. Baxter had put doubts into her mind.

Gabriel knew he had to keep Phoebe away from Neil Baxter at all costs. The only way to do that was to forbid her to have anything to do with the man she had once thought was her own true Lancelot.

Unfortunately, Phoebe did not take orders well.

Gabriel's groin throbbed with a sudden, fierce need to possess her. He was consumed with a desperate urge to sink himself into her softness. When she gave herself to him in bed, he felt completely certain of her. During that hot, wet time when he was deep inside her, he knew she was his.

Gabriel stopped pacing and put down the brandy glass. He went to the connecting door and opened it.

Phoebe's room was shrouded in darkness. He took a step toward the canopied bed and frowned when he realized she was moving restlessly on the pillows. She was asleep, but she was making tiny little sounds of protest. He could sense the fear in her and knew at once that she was in the grip of another nightmare.

"Phoebe, wake up." Gabriel sat down on the edge of the bed, took hold of her shoulders, and shook her gently. "Open your eyes, sweet. You are dreaming again."

Phoebe's lashes fluttered. She came awake with a gasp and levered herself up on her elbows. For an instant her eyes were wild in the shadows. Then she focused slowly on him. "Gabriel?"

"You're safe, Phoebe. I'm here. You were having another nightmare."

"Yes." She shook her head, as if trying to clear it. "It was the same one I had at Devil's Mist after I swam out of the cavern. I was in a dark place and two men were reaching out for me. Each said he could save me. But I knew one of them was lying. I had to choose."

Gabriel pulled her into his arms. "It was only a dream, Phoebe."

"I know."

"I'll help you forget it, just as I did last time." He eased her back down onto the pillows. Then he stood up.

She did not protest when he unfastened his dressing gown and dropped it carelessly on the floor. Her eyes were solemn and watchful as she took in the sight of his heavily aroused body. But she did not resist when he pulled back the covers and slid in beside her.

"Come here, my sweet." Gabriel reached for her, anxious to rekindle the desire that always flared so easily between them. He needed to know that she would respond to him tonight as she always had in the past.

A deep sense of relief shot through Gabriel as Phoebe's arms went slowly around him. He touched the soft swell of her breast, willing himself to take his time with her, wanting her to become as aroused as he was.

It was hopeless. The frantic urge to possess her overwhelmed all Gabriel's intentions. His willpower collapsed under the storm of driving need that was exploding inside him. He had to know that she was still his.

"Phoebe, I cannot wait."

"Yes. I know. It's all right."

He was on fire. The blood was roaring in his veins as Gabriel parted Phoebe's legs and lowered himself between her silken thighs. He used his hand to fit himself to her and then, with a husky, wordless exclamation, he surged into her.

Phoebe sucked in her breath, her body instinctively tightening around him. Gabriel looked down into her face and saw that her eyes were closed. He wanted her to look at him, but he could not find the words to ask her to do so. Nor was there any time to search for them. All that mattered now was slaking this overpowering need that raged within him.

He began to move quickly, driving again and again into Phoebe's snug warmth. She took him into her, wrapping him close, making him a part of herself. He reached down to find the small, sensitive bud of delicate female flesh.

"Gabriel."

Her soft cry put him over the brink. Every muscle in his body tightened in the penultimate moment. He arched his back and gritted his teeth and then he was pouring himself endlessly into her.

She accepted all that he gave her, holding him close as he shuddered above her. He felt her tiny convulsions ripple through her and then he was lost.

Gabriel lay awake for a long while afterward. He gazed into the shadows and put his mind to the task of figuring out how best to protect Phoebe from Baxter.

Phoebe arrived at her parents' town house promptly at eleven o'clock the following morning. She knew her father's habits well. She was certain she would find him hard at work on his latest mathematical device.

He was exactly where she thought he would be. When she was ushered into the study, she found him fussing over a large mechanical contraption composed of wheels, gears, and weights.

"Good morning, Papa." Phoebe untied her bonnet strings. "How is your mechanical calculation machine coming along?"

"Very nicely indeed." Clarington glanced at her over his shoulder. "I have hit upon a way of using punched cards to supply the instructions for the various calculations."

"Punched cards?"

"Very similar to the ones used by the Jacquard looms to establish weaving pattern."

"I see." Phoebe walked over and gave him a quick hug. "That is all very interesting, Papa. But you know I was never much good with sums and calculations."

"Probably just as well." Clarington snorted. "Got enough of that sort of talent in the family as it is. I wonder if Wylde would find this engine useful in his shipping business."

"I would not be surprised. Papa, I must talk to you." Phoebe sat down. "I have come to ask you a very important question."

Clarington looked wary. "I say, now, if this is a question about married life and your duties as a wife and that sort of thing, you will have to talk to your Mama. Not my field, if you see what I mean."

Phoebe waved that aside impatiently. "I am adjusting tolerably well to married life. That is not what I wished to discuss with you."

Clarington relaxed. "Well, then, what was it you wanted to ask me?"

Phoebe leaned forward determinedly. "Papa, did Neil Baxter leave England three years ago because you paid him to go? Did you buy him off because you did not want him making an offer for me?"

Clarington's bushy brows bunched together in irritation. "I say, who the devil told you that?"

"Wylde told me that."

"I see." Clarington sighed. "I suppose he had a good reason."

"That is not the point. Papa, I demand to know the truth."

"Why?" Clarington asked, his gaze turning shrewd. "Because Baxter is back in England?"

"Partly. And partly because I felt very guilty for a long time after I learned of his death. I told myself that if he had not gone off to make his fortune so that he would be able to ask for my hand, he would not have been killed."

Clarington gazed at her in astonishment. "Good God. What rubbish. I had no notion you were harboring such thoughts."

"Well, I was."

"Utter nonsense. My only regret is that the bloody bastard didn't have the decency to stay dead," Clarington muttered. "But that's Baxter for you. Went out of his way to be difficult."

"Papa, I must know if it's true that you gave him money to stay away from me."

Clarington shifted uncomfortably and tinkered with a mechanical wheel. "Sorry, my dear, but it's true." He glowered at her. "Not that it matters now. You're safely married to Wylde, and that's that, eh?"

"Why didn't you tell me?" Phoebe demanded.

"About bribing Baxter to get out of the country? Because I didn't want you to know."

"Why not?" Phoebe asked tightly.

"Because I thought you'd be hurt," Clarington snapped. "Not very pleasant for a romantical young female to learn that a man has only been toying with her affections in order to blackmail her father. You've always been the sentimental type, Phoebe. You saw Baxter as a young Sir Galahad or some such nonsense."

"Lancelot," Phoebe said softly. "I always thought of him as Lancelot."

Clarington scowled. "Beg pardon?"

"Never mind." Phoebe sat rigidly in the chair, her shoulders very straight. "You should have told me the truth, Papa."

"Didn't want to upset you."

"Well, it would not have been very pleasant to learn the truth, I'll grant you that," Phoebe said, "but at least I would not have spent the past year feeling guilty."

"Now, see here. How was I to know you'd been feeling guilty? You never mentioned the fact to me."

Phoebe tapped her gloved fingers on the edge of the chair. She frowned, thinking of what Neil had said the previous evening. "Did you pay him off directly?"

"Good God, no." Clarington looked offended. "A gentleman doesn't dirty his hands with that sort of thing. I had my solicitor handle it."

"Neil says he does not know who paid his passage to the South Seas. He was told a mysterious benefactor arranged matters."

Clarington's scowl darkened. "Nonsense. The man knows full well who paid his passage, and a good bit more besides. We made a deal. I agreed to give the bounder enough to set himself up very nicely on condition he got out of England."

Phoebe sighed. "It's rather difficult to know exactly what to believe."

Clarington was affronted. "Are you saying I'm not telling you the truth?"

"No, Papa, of course not." Phoebe smiled placatingly. "I do not think you are lying. But I cannot help but wonder if different people in this little play may have interpreted matters in somewhat different ways."

"Damnation, Phoebe, there was nothing to misinterpret. When my solicitor offered Baxter a small fortune to leave the country, the man grabbed it with both hands. That was all there was to it."

"Perhaps." Phoebe hesitated uncertainly. "Perhaps not. I wish I knew what to believe."

Clarington's thick brows twitched. "You will believe your papa. And your husband, by God. That's whom you will believe."

Phoebe smiled sadly. "Do you know what the problem is, Papa? The problem is that everyone spends entirely too much time and effort trying to protect me. I am left with bits and pieces of the truth, not the whole truth."

"Been my experience you don't always deal well with the whole truth."

"Papa, how can you say that?"

"It's true enough, Phoebe. You've always

seen things in a different light, if you know what I mean."

"No, Papa, I do not know what you mean."

"You ain't always realistic, my dear, and that's a fact. Ever since you were a little girl, you've been different. You were never like the rest of us. I never really understood what you were about, if you must know the truth. You were always looking for adventure, always getting into scrapes."

"Papa, that's not true."

"As God is my witness, it is true." Clarington's eyes were grim. "Never knew quite what to do with you. Always terrified you'd get involved in a major catastrophe one day, no matter how I tried to protect you from your own reckless nature. You cannot blame a father for wanting to protect his daughter."

"I don't blame you, Papa. But sometimes I felt smothered by the rest of you. You were all so very clever."

"Clever, hah. That's a joke. The rest of us could hardly keep up with you." Clarington glowered at her. "I'll tell you something, Phoebe. As fond of you as I am, I'm damned glad that you're Wylde's responsibility now. It's his turn to try to pull in the reins, and he's welcome to the task. It's a relief to be able to stop worrying about you."

Phoebe looked down at her reticule in her lap. For some reason tears burned in her eyes. She blinked them away. "I'm sorry I've been such a problem for you all these years, Papa."

Clarington groaned. He went over to her and tugged her to her feet. "It was worth it, Phoebe." He hugged her with gruff affection. "Your Mama likes to say that you kept us all from turning into complete bores and maybe she's right. Life around you has always been interesting, I'll grant you that."

"Thank you, Papa. It's always nice to know one has a useful function." Phoebe dashed the tears from her eyes and smiled.

"Here, now, my girl, you're not going to cry or anything, are you? I ain't much good with crying females."

"No, Papa. I won't cry."

"Good." Clarington was clearly relieved. "Lord knows it hasn't always been easy and I may have made a few mistakes along the way. But I swear I only did what I thought I had to in order to keep you from coming to grief."

"I understand, Papa."

"Excellent," Clarington said. He patted her shoulder. "Excellent. Well, then. That's that, eh? No offense, my dear, but I'm rather glad you're Wylde's problem now."

"And he is definitely my problem." Phoebe retied her bonnet strings. "I must be off, Papa. Thank you for telling me what you know of the truth about the situation with Neil."

Clarington was alarmed. "See here, now, I told you the whole truth, not just bits and pieces."

"Good-bye, Papa." Phoebe paused at the door. "Oh, by the way, I am planning a wonderful house party at Devil's Mist at the end of the Season. I am anxious for you and Mama and everyone else to see my new home."

"We shall certainly be there," Clarington assured her swiftly. He hesitated. "Phoebe, you won't give Wylde any unnecessary trouble, will you? He's a good man, but I don't know how patient he'll be if you make life difficult for him. He's accustomed to issuing orders and having them obeyed. Give him time to get used to your ways."

"Do not concern yourself, Papa. I would not dream of giving Wylde any unnecessary trouble." *Only the absolutely necessary amount,* she added silently.

Phoebe was still mulling over the conversation in her father's study later that day when she alighted from the carriage in front of Green's Bookshop. George, the footman who had accompanied her on the shopping expedition, held the door open for her and her maid.

Phoebe glanced across the street as she was handed down from the vehicle. A small man in a green cap was watching her intently. When he saw her look at him, he jerked his eyes away from her and pretended to study the contents of a shop window.

"Betsy, do you know that man?" Phoebe asked as they started up the steps of the bookshop.

Betsy glanced at the small man and shook her head. "No, ma'am. Is somethin' wrong?"

"I don't know," Phoebe said. "But I am almost certain I saw him earlier when we came out of the milliner's. I had the feeling he was watching me."

Betsy frowned. "Shall I tell George to run him off?"

Phoebe eyed the little man thoughtfully. "No, let's just wait and see if he is still about when we come out of Green's."

Phoebe went on up the steps and into the bookshop. She forgot all about the mysterious little man as Mr. Green came forward to greet her. The elderly bookshop owner was smiling in satisfaction.

"Welcome, welcome, Lady Wylde. I am

delighted you have come so quickly. As I said in my note, I have the volume you requested."

"The precise copy?"

"I am certain of it. You may examine it at once."

"Wherever did you find it?" Phoebe asked.

"Through a contact in Yorkshire. Wait here and I shall fetch it."

Mr. Green disappeared into his back room and reappeared a moment later with an old volume bound in red Moroccan leather. Phoebe opened the book carefully and read the inscription on the flyleaf:

To my son Gabriel, on the occasion of his tenth birthday, in the hope that he will live by the honorable code of chivalry all of his life. John Edward Banner.

"Yes," Phoebe said as she reverently closed the copy of Malory's *Morte d'Arthur*. "This is the right book. I cannot thank you enough, Mr. Green."

"It was a pleasure," Green assured her. "I look forward to doing business with you again in the future."

The little man in the green cap was still about when Phoebe and her maid walked back out of the shop.

"He's still there, ma'am," Betsy hissed in a conspiratorial tone. "Standin' in front of the glass shop."

Phoebe glanced across the street. "So he is. I wonder what this is all about. I sense a mystery."

Betsy's eyes widened. "Perhaps he means to follow us home and murder us in our beds, ma'am."

"Perhaps he does," Phoebe said. "This has all the signs of a dangerous situation." She turned to the footman. "George, tell the coachman that I believe we are being followed by a thief who means to rob us. We must contrive to escape him in the traffic."

George stared at her. "A thief, ma'am?"

"Yes. Hurry along, now. We must be on our way. I want to make certain that little man is not able to pursue us."

"The streets are crowded, ma'am," George pointed out as he handed her up into the coach. "He can keep up with us easily enough on foot."

"Not if we are very clever." Phoebe thought quickly as she sat down. "Tell the coachman to turn left at the next street and then turn right and then left again. He is to continue such a pattern until we are certain there is no sign of that little man in the dark green hat."

"Yes, ma'am." Looking seriously alarmed, George closed the carriage door and vaulted up onto the seat beside the coachman.

A moment later the carriage lurched off at a brisk pace. Phoebe smiled at Betsy in satisfaction as the vehicle dodged a high-perch phaeton and swung to the left. "This ought to take care of the matter. Whoever he is, that man in the green hat will not be expecting us to turn into this street."

Betsy peered out the window. "No, ma'am, he certainly won't. I only hope he isn't quick enough to follow us."

"We shall soon be rid of him," Phoebe predicted. "Wylde will no doubt be extremely impressed by our brilliant handling of a potentially dangerous situation."

Chapter 17

"You lost her?" Gabriel stared at the little man in the green hat. "What the devil do you mean, you lost her? I'm paying you to keep an eye on her, Stinton."

"I'm aware of that, yer lordship." Stinton drew himself up and gave Gabriel an affronted look. "And I'm doin' me best. But ye didn't tell me her ladyship had a habit of dashin' in all directions. Beggin' yer pardon, but she's sorta unpredictable, ain't she?"

"Her ladyship is a woman of impulse," Gabriel said through set teeth. "Which is precisely why I hired you to look after her. You came highly recommended from Bow Street. I was assured I could entrust my wife's safety to your care, and now you tell me you could not even keep up with her on a simple shopping expedition?"

"Well, no offense, m'lord, but it weren't exactly a simple shoppin' trip," Stinton said. "I'm proud to say I kept up with her in the Arcade and managed to hang on to her in Oxford Street even though we was all over the place. The last stop was a bookshop. It was when she came out of there that she up and bolted like a fox runnin' from a pack of hounds."

It took every ounce of willpower Gabriel possessed to keep a grip on his temper. "Do not ever again refer to Lady Wylde as a fox, Stinton."

"Right ye are, yer lordship. But I got to say I never seen a lady move that fast. Fast as any pickpocket I ever chased into the rookeries around Spitalfields."

Gabriel was feeling more uneasy by the minute. "You are quite certain you saw no one else around her?"

"Just her maid, the footman, and the coachman."

"And when she disappeared, she was in her own coach?"

"Yes, sir."

"There was no sign of anyone else following her?"

"No, yer lordship. Just me. And, quite frankly, if I couldn't keep up with her, no one else could, either."

"Damnation." Gabriel's imagination was already conjuring up a hundred different calamities that might have befallen Phoebe. He reminded himself that she was not alone. She had her maid, a footman, and the coachman with her. Nevertheless, all he could think about was the fact that Neil Baxter was out there somewhere, no doubt plotting revenge. *Lancelot to his Arthur.*

Stinton cleared his throat. "Beggin' yer pardon, yer lordship, but will you be wantin' me to continue followin' her ladyship around?"

"I'm not sure there is much point." Gabriel was disgusted. "Not if you cannot keep up with her."

"Well, sir, as to that, next time I'll stay a bit closer. Now that I'm on to her tricks and all, I won't be surprised the way I was today."

"My wife does not play tricks," Gabriel said grimly. "She is merely somewhat high-spirited and impulsive."

Stinton coughed discreetly. "Yes, sir. If you say so, sir. Seemed a bit tricky to me, though, m'lord, if you don't mind my sayin' so."

"I do mind. I mind very much, as a matter of fact. Stinton, if you intend to keep on in this post, you had better stop making insulting statements about my wife."

A commotion in the hall interrupted Gabriel before he could get around to wringing Stinton's scrawny little neck. A wave of relief went through him as he heard Phoebe's voice.

The library door was flung open and

Phoebe rushed in, bonnet strings flying. She was carrying a package in her hand. The muslin skirts of her bright green-and-yellow-striped gown swung around her small ankles. Her face was alight with excitement.

"Gabriel, we have had the most amazing adventure. Just wait until I tell you about it. I believe we were very nearly followed home by a thief. He might even have been a murderer. But we foiled his plans quite brilliantly, I must say."

Gabriel got to his feet. "Calm yourself, my dear."

"But Gabriel, it was very odd. There was this little man in a green hat." Phoebe came to an abrupt halt as she caught sight of Stinton. Her eyes widened. "Good heavens, it's him. It's the man who was following us."

"Didn't do too good a job of it," Stinton said. He smiled with approval, displaying several gaps in his yellowed teeth. "Must say, yer ladyship managed to slip away with the sort of skill I usually see exhibited by professional villains."

"Thank you." Phoebe gazed at him with intense curiosity in her eyes.

Gabriel swore and turned on Stinton. "Kindly refrain from drawing comparisons between my wife and members of the criminal class."

"Yes, sir," Stinton said politely. "Didn't mean no offense, yer ladyship. You was right clever, you was, ma'am."

Phoebe gave him a pleased smile. "Yes, I was, wasn't I?"

"Almost caught up with you after that first turn, but I never stood a chance after you had yer coachman make that second turn."

"I plotted it all out quite carefully," Phoebe assured him.

"Like I said, it was real professional," Stinton said.

Phoebe smiled warmly. "I must admit, I had a bit of luck. After the third turn we were in strange territory. There's no telling where we might have ended up if the coachman had not been familiar with the streets."

"That," Gabriel interrupted, "is quite enough from both of you." He glanced at Stinton. "You may go."

"Yes, m'lord." Stinton rotated his green hat in his hands. "And will ye be needin' me in the future?"

"I suppose I have no real alternative. God help us, I'm told you're the best that's available. You will report to work tomorrow morning when Lady Wylde goes out."

Stinton grinned. "Thank ye, yer lordship." He clapped his hat on his head and walked to the door with a jaunty step.

Gabriel waited until he and Phoebe were alone before he pointed to the chair across from his desk. "Sit down, madam."

Phoebe blinked. "Gabriel, what on earth — "

"Sit."

Phoebe sat. She put her package in her lap. "Who was that little man, Gabriel? What was he doing following me today?"

"His name is Stinton." Gabriel sat down and folded his hands together on his desk. He would stay calm and rational about this if it killed him, he promised himself. He would not lose his temper. "I hired him to follow you about when you went out."

"You hired him to follow me?" Phoebe's lips parted in amazement. "And you did not tell me?"

"No, madam, I did not. I saw no reason to alarm you."

"Why should I have been alarmed? Gabriel, what is going on here?"

Gabriel studied her for a moment, wondering how much to tell her. The problem was that she was now aware of Stinton. He had no real choice except to explain the rest. She would pester him about it until he did. "I have hired Stinton to make certain you do not have any problems with Baxter."

Phoebe looked at him in stunned silence.

Her hands clenched around the package in her lap. "With Neil?" she finally managed, her voice sounding half strangled.

"I think it very likely Baxter will attempt to contact you at some time when I am not around."

"I do not understand, my lord."

Gabriel felt his grip on his temper start to slip. "I fail to see why it isn't perfectly obvious, Phoebe. Baxter is a danger to you because he hates me. I have already told you that. I am merely taking prudent steps to be certain he does not get close to you."

"You're afraid that I'll believe whatever he tells me, aren't you?" Phoebe's gaze was suddenly shrewd. "You don't trust me to accept your version of events out there in the islands."

"I'm not going to take any chances." Gabriel surged to his feet and stalked over to the small table where the brandy sat. "I know Baxter too well. The man is a consummate liar."

"But it does not follow that I would believe his lies."

"Why not?" Gabriel swallowed brandy and slammed the glass down on the table. "You did once before."

Phoebe got to her feet, clutching her package to her breast. "That's not fair. I was a much younger woman then. I had not had the experience of the world that I have now."

He swung around to face her. "Experience of the world? You think you have enough experience of the world to deal with men like Neil Baxter? You are a reckless, naive, impulsive little fool. Believe me when I say you're no match for the Baxters of this world."

"Do not talk to me like that, Gabriel."

"I will talk to you any way I wish."

"No, you will not. Furthermore, I do not want you hiring little men to follow me around without my knowledge. It is very unpleasant and I will not tolerate it. If you wish to have someone keep an eye on me, then you must discuss the matter with me first."

"Is that right?"

Phoebe's chin came up swiftly. "Yes, it is. I will decide if I want someone trailing around behind me. But I must say, since the only thing that concerns you is the thought of Neil talking to me, I do not see any need for Stinton."

"Then you are even more naive than I had thought."

"Bloody hell, Gabriel. I am perfectly capable of dealing with Neil."

Gabriel took a step forward and captured

her defiant little chin on the edge of his hand. "You do not know what you are saying, madam. You do not know your golden-haired Lancelot the way I do."

Her face flushed. "He is not my Lancelot."

"He was once."

"That was three years ago," Phoebe stormed. "Everything has changed now. Gabriel, you must believe me, I am not in danger of being seduced by Neil Baxter. You must trust me."

Gabriel saw the desperate appeal in her eyes and felt his resolution waver. "It is not a question of trust. It is a question of caution."

"That's not true. It *is* a question of trust. Gabriel, you have made it clear you do not yet love me. If you do not trust me, either, then we have nothing at all between us."

Nothing at all between us. Talons of anguish and rage gripped him, sinking deep into his gut, piercing his soul. Gabriel fought to hold on to his self-control. "On the contrary, madam. We have a great deal between us."

"Such as what?" she challenged.

"Such as a marriage," he said coldly. "You are my wife. You will do as I say and you will accept the precautions I deem prudent. That is all there is to the matter. Henceforth, you are not to attempt to evade Stinton."

She looked at him with reckless fury. "And if I do?"

"If you do, you will not be allowed to go out at all. I will confine you to the house."

Phoebe stared at him in dawning shock. There was anger and something else in her eyes. Gabriel thought that the other emotion might have been grief. For a moment she just stood there, clinging to the package she had brought with her.

"So it is true," she finally said, her voice dulled with intense sadness. "We do not even have trust and mutual respect between us. We have nothing at all."

"Goddamn it, Phoebe."

"Here. This is for you." She shoved the package into his hands. Then she turned on her heel and walked toward the library door.

"Phoebe, come back here."

She did not turn around. She went out the door without a word.

Gabriel stared at the closed door for a long while. Then he went back behind his desk and sank wearily down into his chair.

He was aware of a strange numbness somewhere deep inside himself. He looked at the package in front of him for a few minutes and then he slowly and mechanically unwrapped it.

When he had finished peeling off the brown

paper, he sat gazing at the familiar volume for a long while. It occurred to him that this was the first gift Phoebe had ever given him. No, he thought, that was not true. The first gift had been the gift of herself. This was the second gift she had given him.

To date he had not given her anything of importance at all.

Phoebe was still wide awake at midnight. Dressed in her nightgown and wrapper, she sat in the chair near the window and gazed out into the darkness. She had opened the window earlier to let in the cool night air. It helped her to think.

She had been thinking intently for hours.

She had stayed in her room all afternoon and evening and she was getting increasingly restless. She was rapidly coming to the conclusion that she was not much suited to sulking. Apparently she did not have the temperament for it.

Certainly she had had a good cry immediately after the scene in the library, but after that, she had gotten rather bored. When she had refused to go down for dinner, she had half expected Gabriel to pound on her door to order her downstairs. Instead he had seen to it that tea and toast had been sent to her room. As a consequence, Phoebe was now extremely hungry.

She was aware that Gabriel had dined at his club. He had been gone for some time before returning home a few minutes ago. She knew he was in his bedchamber now. She had heard him dismiss his valet. Phoebe glanced wistfully at the closed door that connected her room to Gabriel's. Her intuition told her he would not open it tonight. His pride would not allow him to do so.

Phoebe considered her own pride very carefully. It had seemed a very large obstacle earlier in the day, but now it did not appear to be quite so terribly important.

Gabriel was proving to be a perfectly infuriating husband, but there were mitigating circumstances. In his own way he had been trying to protect her. Her reasons for failing to appreciate that protection clearly baffled him.

It was obvious they each had a lot to learn about the other.

Phoebe got up slowly and went to the connecting door. She put her ear to the wood panel and listened carefully. There was no sound from the other room. Gabriel was probably in bed. It would likely never occur to him that he was the one who should apologize. The man could be incredibly dense about some things.

Phoebe drew a deep breath, gathered her courage, and cautiously opened the door. She peeked around the edge and saw Gabriel sitting in a chair. He was wearing his black dressing gown and he had a book open on his lap. He was reading by the light of the candle that sat on the small desk beside him.

He looked up as Phoebe walked slowly into the room. She saw that his shadowed face was marked with a dark, brooding intensity, and a small shiver went through her. Phoebe folded her arms together beneath her breasts and slipped her hands inside the sleeves of her wrapper. She came to a halt a few steps away from him and gently cleared her throat.

"Good evening, my lord," she said politely.

"Good evening, madam. I would have thought you'd be asleep by now."

"Yes, well, I could not seem to sleep."

"I see." Satisfaction gleamed briefly in his eyes. "Have you come to apologize for your loss of temper and several hours of sulking?"

"No, of course not. I had every right to lose my temper and sulk as long as I wished." She took a step closer and glanced down at the book in his hands. Her heart soared when she saw what it was. "I see you are reading Malory's *Morte d'Arthur*."

"Yes. I am extremely pleased to have it

back in my possession." Gabriel smiled slightly. "I do not believe I have thanked you properly."

"Think nothing of it." She was delighted to know he liked the gift. "I am glad I could find it for you."

Gabriel's eyes did not waver. "Rest assured I shall return the favor."

"We are more than even," she said. "After all, in a roundabout way it is because of you that I have *The Lady in the Tower* back, is it not?"

"One could see it from that point of view." Gabriel continued to eye her intently. "Why were you unable to sleep?"

Phoebe felt herself turning red beneath his burning gaze. She was very glad she stood in shadow. "I've been thinking."

"Have you, indeed? Did you find the exercise interesting?"

"You need not sound so sarcastic, my lord. I am quite serious. I have been thinking about our marriage."

Gabriel's gaze was unreadable. "Wondering if you have made a mistake, perhaps? It is a little too late for such qualms, madam. You know the saying about marrying in haste."

"And repenting at leisure? Yes, I am familiar with it, thank you. That was not what

I wanted to discuss."

Gabriel hesitated as if that was not quite the response he had been expecting. "Then what did you want to talk about?"

"Our future, my lord."

"What about it?"

"I am aware that you are distrustful of the emotion of love, Gabriel."

"I have never known that particular emotion to bring anything but trouble to a man."

Phoebe suddenly found the tension intolerable. To break it she began to move, trailing aimlessly around the room. She paused in front of the fireplace and examined the handsome clock that stood on it. "Yes, well, the thing is, Gabriel, I am not so fearful of such emotions as you are."

His mouth curved wryly. "I am aware of that."

"I was thinking about the differences between us in that regard," she persisted. "In the beginning I concluded that your unwillingness to indulge in the emotion of love came about because my sister changed her mind after she ran off with you. I knew you must have been hurt."

"I would have recovered soon enough from the blow," Gabriel said coolly. "Recovering from financial ruin and a bullet in the shoulder took somewhat longer. I admit the incident taught me a lesson about the dangers of allowing oneself to be governed by emotion, however."

"But that was not the only incident that taught you that lesson, was it?" Phoebe asked gently.

"What the devil are you talking about now?"

She moved on to his dressing table and stood looking at the handful of masculine items arrayed there. She picked up a small black lacquer box that was trimmed with silver. "I think you may have learned that lesson earlier in your life. You and I were raised in very different situations, were we not, Gabriel?"

"I think that is a safe assumption," he said. "Your father has a title that goes back several generations, and an enormous fortune. You have lived in luxury all of your life. Money and power make a great difference."

"That is not what I am talking about. I am talking about the fact that my family is very close. It is true that I have been treated as the baby all of my life. My family has always tended to be overprotective of me and in some ways they do not quite understand me. But they have always loved me. And I have always known that. You did not have that advantage."

Gabriel stilled. "What are you trying to say, Phoebe?"

She turned around to face him. "Your mother died when you were very young. You had only your father, and he, I think, preferred the company of his books. Is that not the way it was?"

"My father was a scholarly man." Gabriel closed the volume in his lap. "It was only natural that he devoted himself to his studies."

"I don't think it was so very natural," Phoebe retorted. "I think he should have devoted himself to you. Or at the very least, he should have given you the same degree of attention he gave his books."

"Phoebe, this is a pointless discussion. You have no notion of what you are talking about. I think it would be best if you went back to bed."

"Don't send me away, Gabriel." Phoebe hastily put the black and silver box back down on the dressing table. She went across the room to where Gabriel sat and came to a halt directly in front of him. "Please."

He smiled wryly. "I am not sending you away. I am sending you back to bed. There is no need to overdramatize the situation, my dear."

"I have been thinking about this matter all evening and I am convinced that the reason you are afraid of the emotion of love is because you do not trust it. And the reason you do not trust it is because too many people who have claimed to love you have abandoned you."

"Phoebe, that is rubbish."

"No, listen to me. It makes perfect sense and it explains so much." She flung herself down on her knees beside him and put her hand on his thigh. "Your mother loved you, but she died. Your father was supposed to love you, but for the most part he ignored you. You thought my sister loved you because she wanted to run away with you, but she was only seeking escape from another problem. No wonder you are distrustful."

Gabriel's brows rose. "This is the logic you have been working on all evening in your bedchamber?"

"Yes, it is."

"I regret to tell you that you have wasted your time, my dear. You would have done better to come downstairs and eat dinner. No doubt you are quite famished."

Phoebe stared at him. "You are an incredibly stubborn man."

"If by that you mean I am not going to be swayed by the sort of feminine logic you are employing at the moment, then yes, I suppose I am."

Phoebe was outraged. She jumped to her feet. "Do you know what I think? I think that in addition to being stubborn, you are also a coward."

"This is not the first time you have called me a coward," Gabriel said mildly. "It's fortunate that I do not take offense easily. Some men might take such a remark amiss. Especially from a wife."

"Is that so? Well, let me tell you something, Gabriel. It's fortunate that I am just as stubborn as you are. I still believe deep down that you love me. I think you are afraid to admit it, and that is why I call you a coward."

"You are, of course, entitled to your opinion."

"Damn you, Gabriel." Phoebe stamped her foot in frustration. "You are impossible at times." She whirled around and dashed back through the connecting door into her darkened bedchamber.

Safe on the other side, she slammed the door shut and began pacing her room. *Damn the man.* He was going to drive her mad with his stubborn refusal to surrender to the softer emotions. She knew he was not immune to them. She refused to believe she had been wrong about him.

The notion of having been wrong about Gabriel all these years was too staggeringly terrible to even contemplate. She was married to the man. Her future was now inexorably linked with his. She had to find a way to uncover the noble, idealistic knight she knew lay beneath the cynical exterior.

Raging at him and calling him a coward to his face was probably not a promising way to go about the task.

The object sailed through the open window without a sound. Phoebe was unaware anything had been thrown into the room from the street below until she heard a soft thud on the bed.

Startled, she swung around and stood staring into the shadows of the room. Whatever it was had rolled over to the edge of the mattress. For an instant she saw nothing at all. She sincerely hoped it was not a bat.

In the very next heartbeat there was a soft, muffled rush of sound. Without any warning, orange flames sprang up. They were curiously silent as they began feeding voraciously on the lace that edged the counterpane.

In another few minutes the fire would envelop the bed.

Phoebe broke through the shock that gripped her. She dashed across the room and seized the pitcher that stood beside the basin.

"Gabriel," she yelled as she hurled the contents of the pitcher over the flames.

The door slammed open. "What the hell . . . ?" He took in the sight of the leaping flames. "Christ. Get the pitcher from my room and then rouse the household. Quickly, Phoebe."

Phoebe raced into the other bedchamber, grabbed the pitcher, and hurried back. Gabriel already had the burning counterpane off the bed. He was smothering the flames by rolling them up inside the heavy fabric.

Phoebe handed him the pitcher of water and flew out of the room to wake the staff.

Chapter 18

The damage was minimal. Gabriel's fury was not.

An hour after the fire was safely out and the staff had returned to their beds, he was still inwardly raging against the near disaster. He sprawled in his chair, brandy glass in his hand, and stared broodingly at Phoebe. She was sitting on top of his bed, her feet curled under her. She had a thoughtful expression on her face as she sipped the brandy he had given her.

He had nearly lost her this time, too. The knowledge sent a shudder through Gabriel's soul.

All he could think about was what a near thing it had been. If Phoebe had been asleep, she might not have awakened in time to save herself. He might not have smelled the smoke here in his own room until it was too late.

Thank God she had been awake.

"I am not going to let you out of my sight again," Gabriel said, half under his breath. He downed the last of his brandy.

"What was that, Gabriel?" Phoebe glanced at him.

"It must have been that crazed housemaid who took you down into the catacombs at Devil's Mist."

"You mean Alice?"

Gabriel turned the brandy glass around in his hands. "That madwoman must have followed us to London. For some reason she wants to frighten you. Perhaps harm you. It makes no sense."

"Madness seldom does make sense. If it did, we would not call it madness."

"But why has she focused her madness on you? You don't even know the woman."

"The person who threw that lantern through the window might not have been Alice," Phoebe said slowly. "It could have been anyone. Perhaps a gang of villains were out on the town tonight, looking for trouble. You know how it is when the mob is in full cry. They throw rocks through windows, start fires, and cause all manner of destruction."

"For God's sake, Phoebe, there was no mob outside your window. We heard no noise."

"That's true," she admitted. She chewed reflectively on her lip. "I've been thinking about something."

"What's that?" Gabriel got to his feet and paced impatiently to the window. He had been examining the street below every few minutes in hopes of seeing someone or something that might give him a clue.

"This business with the fire tonight."

"What about it?"

"Well," Phoebe said slowly, "it bears a rather striking resemblance to the incident in which I escaped the catacombs by swimming out through the cavern."

Gabriel scowled over his shoulder. "In what way?"

"Don't you see? It's another of the curses spelled out at the end of *The Lady in the Tower*."

"Bloody hell. That's impossible. I refuse to drag the supernatural element into this on top of everything else. Damnation, Phoebe, I don't even use the supernatural in my own writing."

"Yes, I know. But remember how the colophon goes?" Phoebe jumped up off the bed and disappeared into her own room. She returned a moment later with *The Lady in the Tower*.

"Phoebe, this is ridiculous."

"Listen to this." Phoebe settled herself on the bed again and opened the old book to the last page. "A curse on he who would steal this book. May he drown beneath the waves. May he be consumed by flames. May he spend an eternal night in hell."

"Devil take it, Phoebe. That's nonsense." Gabriel paused. "Unless, of course, Alice knows about the curse and in her madness is attempting to make it come true."

"How would she know about it?" Phoebe closed the book carefully.

"*The Lady in the Tower* has been in my possession for the entire time I've been back in England. It's possible someone on my staff has taken the liberty of going through the contents of my library. He or she might have told Alice about it."

Phoebe's brows drew together. "Even if that were so, the curse is written in Old French. What are the odds that a member of your staff could read it?"

"A good question." Gabriel studied the dark street again. "And who the hell is Alice?"

"I do not know, Gabriel. I have wracked my brain and I am absolutely certain I have never met her."

"She didn't work in your parents' household at some point in the past?"

"No."

"There has got to be a connection."

"Gabriel?"

"Yes?" He did not turn around; his mind was whirling with conjectures and possibilities. A connection. There had to be a connection between the book and Alice and the incidents.

"I hesitate to mention this because I know you are already biased in your opinion of Neil, but — "

A cold chill sliced through Gabriel. He spun around and advanced toward the bed. "What the devil does Baxter have to do with all this?"

"Nothing." Phoebe straightened in alarm as he bore down on the bed. "At least, I do not think he has anything to do with it. No, I am certain he doesn't."

"But?"

Phoebe swallowed. "But he told me that night he danced with me that he wanted *The Lady in the Tower* back. He said he felt it was rightfully his and that as it was all he would ever have of me, the least I could do was give it to him."

"Goddamn his bloody soul."

"Gabriel, you must not jump to any conclusions. Only think, my lord, the first incident happened at Devil's Mist, before we even knew Neil was still alive. And it was Alice who took me down into those catacombs, not Neil."

"Then there is some connection between Alice and Baxter," Gabriel said with savage satisfaction. "All I have to do is find it."

"My lord, I really do not think we should assume there is a connection at this stage," Phoebe said quickly. "Neil's interest in the book is sentimental in nature."

"Baxter has all the tender sensibilities of a shark."

Phoebe's mouth tightened. "Whatever you may think of him, the fact is he would have no reason to harm me."

"He has a reason to harm me and he is smart enough to know he can use you to do it."

"You cannot prove anything, Gabriel."

"I shall find the connection between Alice and Baxter. When I have that, I shall have my proof."

"Gabriel, you are obsessed with casting Neil in the role of the villain. You frighten me."

Gabriel chained his anger and sense of unease. "Forgive me, my dear. I don't mean to alarm you." He reached down and scooped her up in his arms. He set her on her feet beside the bed and turned back the quilt. "Let us get some sleep. In the morning I shall set Stinton to investigating the mysterious Alice."

"What about me?" Phoebe asked as she obediently scrambled into bed. "I thought you intended to have Stinton follow me around."

"He cannot be in two places at once."

Phoebe's eyes brightened. "Does this mean you have decided to trust me, after all? You no longer believe you need someone to keep an eye on me?"

"It means," Gabriel said as he blew out the candle and got in beside her, "that you will not need anyone to follow you about tomorrow because you are not going anywhere."

She stilled, eyes widening in the shadows. "You cannot mean that, my lord. I have engagements tomorrow. I am going to visit my sister."

"Your sister can come here to visit you." Gabriel reached for her. "You are not going anywhere until this matter is settled."

"Anywhere at all? Gabriel, you simply cannot do this."

"I can and I will. I realize the concept of obedience to anyone, let alone your poor husband, is quite foreign to you. But in this matter I intend to be obeyed." Gabriel felt her whole body stiffen in reaction. He tried to soften his tone, willing her to understand. "I'm sorry, my dear, but I cannot take any

416

chances. You must stay here in the house unless I am free to escort you or unless Stinton is available."

Phoebe struggled to sit up. "My lord, I refuse to be kept a prisoner in my own home."

Gabriel pressed her down into the bedding and came down on top of her. She wriggled angrily until he threw a heavy leg over her thighs and captured her defiant face in his hands.

"Be still, Phoebe," he said gently. "This is not another exciting adventure you are having. This is a very dangerous situation. You will be guided by me."

"Why should I be guided by you?"

"Because I am your husband. And because I know a great deal more about this kind of thing than you do."

She glared defiantly up at him, searching his eyes, testing his strength of will. He stayed silent, praying she would submit.

The struggle for the upper hand lasted only a moment or two and then it was over. Phoebe relaxed beneath him and Gabriel knew he had won. For now, at least. His sense of relief was almost overwhelming.

"There are times, my lord, when I find this business of marriage extremely irritating," Phoebe said.

"I know you do," Gabriel whispered.

She was not happy with her own acquiescence, Gabriel realized. Moonlight streaming through the window illuminated the resentment in her eyes.

He was suddenly reminded of the first time he had seen her features revealed by moonlight. That night on the lonely lane in Sussex he had lifted her veil, taken one look at her shocked, defiant face, and he had known he wanted her. Something in him had known that he would stop at nothing to make her his own.

Audeo. I dare.

Now she was his. But she was so very vulnerable and so very impulsive. He had to protect her because he could not trust her to protect herself.

"My God, Phoebe," he said against her mouth. "You do not know what you do to me. I swear I do not comprehend it myself. But I do know that you are mine and I will do whatever I must to keep you safe."

He crushed her lips beneath his own, drinking in the essence of her, trying to capture her soul as well as her sweet body. After a moment Phoebe made a soft little sound and wrapped her arms around his neck.

"What the devil is going on?" Anthony

418

grabbed the bottle of claret off the end table and poured himself a glass. He glowered at Gabriel as he dropped into a chair across from him.

"Keep your voice down." Gabriel flicked a meaningful glance around the club room. It was still early in the afternoon and the club was only sparsely populated as of yet, but one or two of the members were standing close enough to overhear a loud conversation. "I do not particularly wish to announce my affairs to the world."

Anthony subsided in annoyance. "Very well," he said, lowering his voice, "tell me what this is all about. Why the urgent summons?"

"Someone is trying to hurt or, at the very least, terrify Phoebe." *Someone might even be trying to kill her,* Gabriel added silently. But he could not bring himself to say the words aloud.

"Good God." Anthony stared, thunder-struck. "Are you certain?"

"As certain as I can be."

"Who is it? I'll kill him."

"I'm afraid you must wait your turn. I have first claim on that pleasure. As it happens, I believe the person directly responsible is a woman named Alice. She is either mad or a member of the criminal class who has some acting talent. She was able to pass herself off to Phoebe as a housemaid. I believe there is a strong possibility that Neil Baxter is involved." He briefly summarized events.

Anthony listened in fulminating silence. When Gabriel finished, he nearly exploded. "Goddamn it, man, Baxter is supposed to be dead. You assured us he was."

"Believe me, I am vastly more disappointed than you are that he is not."

"What the devil are you going to do about him?"

"Get rid of him again," Gabriel said. "But this time I intend to make certain he stays out of my way in future."

Anthony's eyes narrowed. "He truly is a cutthroat?"

"I was told by some of the survivors on my ship that he even seemed to enjoy the business of cutting throats."

"Why the attacks on Phoebe?"

"I believe they are Baxter's way of taunting me."

"Why is he using this Alice person?" Anthony persisted.

"Perhaps so that there will be no proof that he is behind the attacks." Gabriel frowned, thinking it through. "If anyone is caught, it will be her. If she is truly mad, she will not be able to point the finger of blame at Baxter. If she is a professional villain and chooses to confess, her word will not mean much against Baxter's."

"Perhaps she does not even know Baxter's identity," Anthony said slowly. "He might have hired her to do his dirty work without letting her know who he was."

Gabriel nodded. "Possible. But I am going to try to find out if there is a connection between the two."

"How will you do that?"

Gabriel leaned forward and lowered his voice even further. "I am having a Runner look into it. I have instructed him to find out if Baxter has a mistress or some connection to the criminal class."

Anthony studied him for a moment. "If you cannot prove Baxter is behind these acts of violence against Phoebe, what will you do?"

Gabriel shrugged. "I would prefer to be able to prove that Baxter is causing the trouble, if only to convince Phoebe that he is not the Sir Lancelot she believes him to be. But one way or another, I shall have to get rid of Baxter. In the end I may be obliged to do it without being able to prove what I know to be true."

"Phoebe will want proof. She does not turn on old friends easily. She is very loyal."

"I know." Gabriel kept his face expressionless with effort. "But Baxter is potentially too dangerous to be allowed to hang around her much longer. He is fully capable of charming an innocent such as Phoebe. Out in the islands he seduced more than one wife into telling him her husband's business secrets. And more than one mistress into betraying her lover's plans."

Anthony arched a brow. "Your mistress, perhaps?"

"Not exactly. She was the woman to whom I was engaged," Gabriel said quietly. "She was the daughter of one of my partners. Her name was Honora. Ironic, is it not? If ever a woman had less sense of honor than Honora Ralston, I have not had the misfortune to meet her."

"She gave information to Baxter?"

"He made himself her lover. Convinced her I was a dangerous pirate masquerading as a legitimate businessman. He said he was trying to trap me."

"I see." Anthony hesitated. "You eventually realized what was going on?"

"Yes."

Anthony stared at him. "What did you do?"

Gabriel shrugged. "The obvious. I tricked Honora into giving Baxter false information

422

and then I set a trap for him."

"I hesitate to ask this, but what, exactly, happened to Honora?"

"When her father found out she had given herself to Baxter and nearly ruined the company in which he had shares in the process, he married her off very quietly."

"To whom?" Anthony asked curiously.

"An aging partner in the shipping venture."

Anthony narrowed his gaze. "Any chance she's the mysterious Alice? Out for revenge?"

"Not likely. The last I heard, she was pregnant with her second child and still living out in the islands. The elderly partner has apparently decided to found himself a shipping dynasty."

"So that leaves us with the mysterious Alice and a possible connection to Neil Baxter." Anthony reflected on that for a moment. "What about Phoebe?"

Gabriel reluctantly pulled himself away from his thoughts. "What about her?"

"You are quite certain she is safe while you go about the business of trying to find Alice?"

"Yes, of course. Did you think I would leave her unprotected?"

"No," Anthony said. "But I thought that by now you would have realized it is rather difficult to protect Phoebe if she is not inclined to be cooperative. Where is she?"

"At home. The staff has been alerted not to allow any strangers into the house under any pretext."

Anthony scowled. "Phoebe's agreed to stay in the house all day?"

"She will stay there as long as it is necessary. I have given her instructions not to leave unless I accompany her or unless Stinton is free to keep an eye on her."

Anthony's jaw dropped. "You've confined Phoebe to the house?"

"Yes."

"Indefinitely?"

"Yes."

"She's agreed to this?" Anthony demanded warily.

Gabriel drummed his fingers on the arm of the chair. "Phoebe will do as she is told."

"Devil take it, man. Are you mad? This is Phoebe we're talking about. She does exactly as she wishes. What makes you think she'll obey you?"

"She's my wife," Gabriel said.

"What difference does that make? She never went out of her way to obey her father or me, her older brother. Phoebe has always been guided by her impulsive nature. My God, she could be riding merrily off into danger at this very moment. She's probably convinced herself she's on another quest to find the mysterious Alice."

Gabriel got to his feet, unwilling to reveal how uneasy Anthony was making him. "I gave her strict orders to stay at home today. She knows better than to flaunt those orders."

"Brave words," Anthony growled. "But this is my sister we're talking about. She ran away from you once before, if you will recall."

Gabriel winced. "That was a different matter entirely."

"So you say. I'm going to call on her at once. I want to be certain she is at home."

"She will be there."

Anthony shot him a derisive look as he headed toward the door. "Ten pounds says she's not. I know Phoebe. She is too headstrong by far to take orders from a husband."

"I'll accompany you on this call you intend to pay on my wife," Gabriel said. "And make no mistake, I fully intend to collect my ten pounds."

"And if she is not at home? What will you do then?" Anthony challenged.

"Find her and lock her in her bedchamber," Gabriel vowed.

"Phoebe's very good at knotting bedsheets together," Anthony reminded him.

★ ★ ★

Meredith and Lydia arrived at the town house within half an hour after Phoebe sent her messages to them. They hastened into the drawing room, expressions of grave alarm on their faces.

"What is this about Wylde confining you to the house?" Lydia demanded as she pulled her spectacles out of her reticule and ran a worried eye over Phoebe. "What has happened? Has he beaten you? I vow your Papa will not stand for that. And neither will I. We agreed to allow him to marry you because we thought he could deal with you, but he goes too far, by heaven."

Meredith gave Phoebe an anxious look as she untied her bonnet strings. "Has he hurt you, Phoebe? I warned you he was not a patient man. Nevertheless, rest assured we will not let him get away with abusing you."

Phoebe smiled serenely and reached for the teapot. "Please be seated. It is a very exciting story. And as I am longing to tell someone the tale, I decided to send for you and Mama."

Lydia eyed her warily as she seated herself. "Phoebe, this is not some sort of jest, is it? When I got your note, I was extremely worried. Are you or are you not confined to the house?"

"I have been forbidden to leave unless

Wylde escorts me." Phoebe wrinkled her nose. "Or unless a certain Mr. Stinton is available to follow me about. It is most annoying, I assure you."

"Then it's true? You have been confined against your will?" Meredith searched her face as she accepted her cup of tea.

"It certainly was not my choice," Phoebe said.

"Then why, might one ask, are you staying put?" Lydia asked bluntly.

"Because Wylde is extremely worried about my safety." Phoebe sipped her tea. "Actually, I take it as a rather hopeful sign, if you must know the truth. I think he is worried because he loves me. Not that he will admit it, of course."

Meredith exchanged glances with Lydia and then turned back to Phoebe. "Perhaps you had better start from the beginning."

"Perhaps I should," Phoebe agreed. She ran through the tale quickly. "The thing is, we do not know who, precisely, this Alice is. Nor do we know how she came to learn of the curse in the back of *The Lady in the Tower*. Gabriel suspects Neil Baxter is involved somehow."

"Good grief," Lydia said. "Will we never be free of that abominable man?"

Phoebe pursed her lips. "I am not at all

certain Neil has anything to do with this. I feel it's quite possible that Wylde is leaping to conclusions simply because he does not have any liking for Neil and because he may be just a tiny bit jealous."

"Ah, that would explain his reaction, wouldn't it?" Meredith murmured.

"I like to think so," Phoebe agreed cheerfully. "However, the fact remains that Wylde has forbidden me to even communicate with Neil, so I cannot talk to him to get his side of the story."

"Just as well, if you ask me," Lydia said. "Well, then, what are Meredith and I to do? Entertain you during the course of your imprisonment?"

"Mother, really." Meredith frowned at her. "She is hardly a prisoner."

"Yes, I am," Phoebe said.

"Yes, she is," Lydia agreed.

Meredith scowled at both of them. "Wylde is quite right to keep you safely tucked up here until he can determine what is going on, Phoebe. I do not blame him in the least."

"I'm sure he means well," Phoebe said. "Wylde generally does mean well. It is just that he tends to go about things in a rather heavy-handed fashion. But I expect I shall be able to correct that bad habit in time."

"Excellent attitude." Lydia smiled with

428

maternal approval. "Always knew you'd make a clever wife, Phoebe."

Meredith's lovely brow creased in another gentle frown. "You should not be plotting to correct your husband's habits, Phoebe. You should be grateful that he is able to guide you."

"I suggest we change the subject," Phoebe said determinedly. "Now, then, I asked both of you to come here today for a reason. I have every intention of getting myself out of prison as quickly as possible."

Lydia's brows rose. "And just how do you plan to do that?"

Phoebe smiled. "With your help, of course."

Meredith gasped. "You surely cannot mean you want Mama and me to help you sneak out of the house. Phoebe, it would not be right to go against your husband like that. Not when all he is trying to do is protect you. And Wylde would be furious if we did get you out."

"I do not intend to defy Wylde in this," Phoebe said.

"Thank heaven." Meredith sagged with relief.

"What I intend to do," Phoebe continued smoothly, "is help Wylde solve the puzzle of who is behind these strange occurrences."

"Oh, my God," Meredith murmured.

Lydia gazed intently at Phoebe. "Just how do you plan to solve this puzzle?"

"First," Phoebe said as she poured more tea, "we must discover the truth about Neil. I wish to know for certain if he is truly a villain or merely the victim of unfortunate misunderstandings and circumstances."

"How do you propose to learn the truth?" Lydia's eyes were alight with curiosity behind the lenses of her spectacles.

"I believe you are in a very good position to help, Mama." Phoebe smiled. "I want you to question your card-playing friends very carefully and with great subtlety. They are always a wonderful source of gossip. Let us see if they know anything about Neil and a woman named Alice."

"That," Lydia exclaimed, "is not a bad notion."

"I suppose there would be no harm done," Meredith agreed slowly.

"And as for you, Meredith," Phoebe said, "I believe you are in a position to make inquiries, also."

Meredith's eyes widened. "You mean because of the amount of entertaining I do?"

"Precisely. And because people talk to you freely. When they look at you, they see only a demure paragon of womanhood."

"You needn't go into details," Meredith said. "I am well aware that most people do not believe I have a brain in my head. And I will admit that perception is useful at times. I have had some experience picking up bits and pieces of information that Trowbridge has found helpful in his business affairs."

"You know very well your husband relies on you as an equal partner in his business affairs because of your skills. Will you help me?"

"Of course," Meredith said.

Lydia beamed with pleasure. "I really did a rather fine job of raising you two, if I do say so."

The drawing room door crashed open at that moment and everyone turned in surprise as Anthony and Gabriel stalked into the room.

Gabriel's eyes went first to Phoebe. She saw intense relief mingled with a great deal of masculine satisfaction reflected there. She arched one brow in a silent question.

"Told you she'd be here," Gabriel said to Anthony.

"Well, I'll be damned." Anthony chuckled. "So she is. My compliments, Wylde. I wouldn't have believed it if I hadn't seen it with my own eyes. Good afternoon, ladies."

"Good afternoon, my lords," Phoebe said politely. "We were not expecting you. Would you care for tea?"

Gabriel grinned as he went toward her. "That sounds delightful, my dear. I see you have summoned some visitors to keep you company while you pine away here in prison."

"Yes, Mama and Meredith were kind enough to visit today." Phoebe handed him his cup of tea. She was about to explain her brilliant plan when she heard a familiar footstep in the hall. It was accompanied by an equally familiar voice.

"Where the hell is my daughter?"

"That will be Clarington," Lydia murmured. "It's about time he got here."

Gabriel frowned. "What the devil does he want?"

The door burst open again and Clarington stomped into the room. He gave Phoebe a quick assessing glance and then rounded on Gabriel.

"I understand you have been beating my daughter, sir."

"Not yet," Gabriel said dryly. "I admit the temptation has been there on a couple of occasions, but thus far I have resisted."

"Damnation, what is this about, locking her up inside her own house, then?" Clarington demanded.

"Phoebe has become extremely interested

in domestic matters of late and has developed a preference for home and hearth," Gabriel said. He gave Phoebe a challenging smile. "Is that not right, my dear?"

"That is certainly one way of putting it," Phoebe said demurely. "Will you have a cup of tea, Papa?"

"No, thank you. On my way to a meeting of the Analytical Society." Clarington shot a sharp, questioning glance at each of the members of his family. "Everything all right, then?"

Lydia smiled sweetly. "Everything is just fine between Phoebe and Wylde, dear. But there appears to be a slight problem with that odious Neil Baxter."

Clarington glowered at Gabriel. "Damnation, man, why don't you do something about Baxter?"

"I intend to," Gabriel said.

"Excellent. I shall leave Baxter to you, then. You seem quite capable of dealing with that sort of problem. If you need my assistance, feel free to call on me. In the meantime, I must be off." Clarington nodded at his wife and walked out of the drawing room.

Phoebe waited until her father had left and then she smiled very brightly at Gabriel. "I have some wonderful news, Wylde. Mama and Meredith are going to help me track down the truth about Neil Baxter. Never fear, we shall get to the bottom of this."

"Bloody hell." Gabriel choked on the tea he had just swallowed. Anthony walked across the room and pounded him helpfully between the shoulders.

"Don't look so stunned, Wylde," Anthony said as Gabriel coughed and sputtered. "You should know by now that there is rarely a dull moment around Phoebe."

Chapter 19

Gabriel managed to restrain himself until his in-laws had finally departed. The moment the last of the clan was out the door, he confronted Phoebe.

"You will put this insane notion of investigating Baxter out of your brain immediately," he said. "I will not have you getting involved in this."

"I am already involved," Phoebe pointed out. "And in any event, it will be Mama and Meredith who do the investigating. I have been forbidden to leave the house, if you will recall."

He wanted to shake her. "You don't understand how dangerous Baxter is."

"Mama and Meredith are not going to take any risks," Phoebe said soothingly. "They are merely going to make a few inquiries. Mama will bring up Neil's name over a hand of whist and Meredith will mention it to some doddering old peer who is in his cups at one of her soirees."

"I don't like it." Gabriel started to pace

the drawing room. "I already have Stinton working on the matter."

"Stinton cannot move about in Society the way Mama and Meredith can."

"Your brother and I will deal with Society."

Phoebe shook her head. "You and Anthony will not be able to get gossip out of Mama's card-playing cronies. And Meredith can talk to people at her parties in a way you and Anthony could not. Admit it, Gabriel. My plan to investigate Neil is extremely clever."

Gabriel ran a hand through his hair and gazed at Phoebe in frustration. The worst of it was he knew she was right. Lady Clarington and Meredith could probe in ways that he and Anthony could not. "I still don't like it."

"I know you don't, Gabriel. It is because you are worried about me. It is very sweet of you."

"*Sweet?*"

"Yes. But I am perfectly safe here in the house and Mama and Meredith will not be in any danger so long as they merely ask a few discreet questions. Admit it."

"Perhaps," he said reluctantly. "But the thought of your family getting involved in all this makes me extremely uneasy."

Phoebe got to her feet and walked across the room to stand looking up at him. A gentle, rather wistful smile played about her soft mouth. "Do you know what your problem is, Gabriel?"

He eyed her warily. "What?"

"You are not accustomed to being part of a family. You have been on your own for so long you don't understand what it means to have others around who care about you. You don't know what it is to have people about who are always on your side, regardless of the circumstances."

"This is your family we are talking about, not mine," he muttered. "They are rallying around you, not me."

"It amounts to the same thing now. As far as they are concerned, you're a member of the family because you are married to me." Phoebe's smile widened. "You must face the fact that you are no longer alone in the world, Gabriel."

No longer alone. He looked down into her warm eyes and felt something inside him start to loosen and untwist. Instinctively he resisted the hint of weakness he sensed within himself. That way lay disaster. He must not let emotion rule him.

"You think this is just another grand adventure, don't you, Phoebe? None of you knows what Baxter is really like." Gabriel paused, thinking it through. "But I suppose there is little I can do to stop your mother and Meredith from asking their questions. Perhaps they will learn something useful. In the meantime, you are to stay here in the house."

Phoebe made a face. "Yes, my lord."

Gabriel smiled briefly, in spite of his dark, uneasy mood. He clamped his hands around Phoebe's shoulders, pulled her close, and dropped a quick, hard kiss on her forehead. "Remind me to add ten pounds to your quarterly allowance."

"Why are you increasing my allowance by ten pounds? I am not short of funds."

"I owe you the ten pounds. It is in the nature of a debt of honor." Gabriel released her and started toward the door. "Your brother wagered that amount that you would not obey my command to stay inside the house. As I fully intend to collect from him, I feel it's only fair to give the money to you. After all, I could not have won without your assistance."

Phoebe gasped in outrage. "You won a wager based on the fact that I obeyed you? How dare you." She launched herself across the room, grabbed an embroidered pillow off the sofa, and hurled it straight at Gabriel's head.

Gabriel did not bother to turn around. He

put up a hand and caught the pillow as it sailed past his ear. "I congratulate you, my dear. At the rate you are going, we shall soon turn you into a paragon of wifely virtue."

"*Never.*"

Gabriel grinned to himself as he went out the door. He hoped she was right.

Two hours later Gabriel was no longer grinning. He walked through the door of the nondescript tavern and quickly scanned the small, nearly empty room. Stinton was sitting at a table, waiting for him. Gabriel crossed the wooden floor and sat down in the chair across from the little man.

"I got your message," Gabriel said without any preamble. "What is this about?"

"I don't rightly know, yer lordship." Stinton lifted his mug and took a deep swallow of beer. "But you asked me to hire a boy to keep an eye on yer town house while I was tryin' to dig up information on Mr. Baxter. I took the liberty of usin' my son for the job. Might as well keep the income in the family, if you see what I mean."

"I don't give a damn who you hired. Has something happened?"

"Could be nothin' at all. Might be somethin' interestin'. Hard to know."

Gabriel made a bid for his patience. "What are you talking about, man?"

"My boy says a message arrived at the back door of yer town house about an hour ago."

"What sort of message?" Gabriel demanded, exasperated.

"Don't know. He just said a message was delivered. Thought you'd like to know."

Gabriel was disgusted. "It could have been anything. One of the maids might be exchanging love notes with a footman in another household."

"Don't believe this was a love note, yer lordship." Stinton looked thoughtful. "Or if it was, it weren't directed to one of yer maids. My boy heard the messenger say it was for the lady of the house."

Gabriel surged to his feet and flung a few coins on the table. "Thank you, Stinton. That will cover your beer. Keep working on the other matter."

"Not havin' much luck in that department." Stinton sighed. "No one seems to know much about Mr. Baxter. Appears to have disappeared sometime during the past few days."

"Dig deeper." Gabriel was already halfway to the door.

Twenty minutes later he went up the steps

of the town house. Shelton opened the door at once.

"Where is her ladyship?" Gabriel asked quietly.

"In her bedchamber, I believe," Shelton said. He took Gabriel's curly brimmed beaver hat. "Shall I send a maid to inform her you are at home?"

"That will not be necessary. I shall tell her myself."

Gabriel went past the butler and started up the staircase. He took the steps two at a time.

When he reached the landing, he strode quickly down the hall to Phoebe's door. He opened it without bothering to knock.

Phoebe, dressed in a bright violet gown trimmed in yellow, was sitting at her little gilt escritoire. She looked up, startled, as Gabriel stalked into the room.

"Gabriel. What on earth are you doing here? I did not know you were home."

"I understand you received a message a short while ago."

Her eyes widened in dismay. "How did you know?"

"That is not important. I would like to see the note, if you please."

Phoebe looked stricken. At the sight of her face, Gabriel's worst fears were confirmed. Whatever had been in the note was dangerous.

"My lord, I assure you, the note was insignificant. Merely a message from an acquaintance," Phoebe said quickly.

"Nevertheless, I wish to see it."

"But there is no need for you to concern yourself with it." Phoebe swallowed visibly. "Indeed, I am not certain I still have it. I probably tossed it away."

Gabriel's fears rose like flames, threatening to consume him. He quashed them beneath a cold, disciplined anger. "The note, Phoebe. I want it. Now."

Phoebe got to her feet. "My lord, I assure you, it would be better if you did not read it. I am certain it will only serve to annoy you."

"I appreciate your concerns," Gabriel said grimly. "But you will give me the note immediately, or I shall start searching for it."

Phoebe sighed. "I vow, my lord, you are turning into an extremely trying sort of husband."

"I am well aware I am not the man you once believed me to be," Gabriel said. "But as you yourself pointed out this afternoon, you are stuck with me now." He smiled thinly. "I am a member of the family, if you will recall."

"Only too well," Phoebe grumbled. She yanked open the small drawer in the center of her escritoire and pulled out a sheet of folded foolscap. "Very well. I was not going to show this to you because I knew it would alarm you, but since you insist . . ."

"I insist." He stepped forward and snatched the paper from her hand. He opened it and read the message swiftly.

My dearest Phoebe:

I grow increasingly concerned for your safety as each day passes. I recently learned how close you came to drowning and I know about the fire in your bedchamber. I fear for your life, my dear.

I have concluded your husband seeks to murder you in such a way that your family will believe it to be an accident. Like the pirate he is, Wylde wishes to seize your inheritance. He is using the methods spelled out in the curse at the end of *The Lady in the Tower*. Have you noticed?

You have married a cruel and dangerous monster who has always had a taste for the macabre. Just ask any of the handful of men who survived his vicious attacks at sea.

My dearest Phoebe, I must speak with

you. I must have a chance to explain everything. I have no doubt but that Wylde has told you nothing but lies about me. I know you will not believe his malicious tales, but you undoubtedly have questions. For the sake of what we once meant to each other, let me answer those questions. I have proof. Let me save you from him.

I remain your most devoted admirer,
Lancelot

"Bastard." Gabriel crumpled the note savagely in his fist. He narrowed his eyes as he gazed down into Phoebe's anxious face. "You do not believe him, of course."

"Of course not." She stared at him as if she were trying to see beneath the surface of his skin. "Gabriel, are you angry?"

"What do you think? Baxter is attempting to seduce you into believing that he is innocent and that I am a villain who is attempting to murder you for the sake of your inheritance. Furthermore, he makes it clear he is still determined to play the role of Lancelot."

"I told you once, I am no Guinevere," Phoebe said proudly. "I am a great deal smarter than she was. Gabriel, you must trust me."

He smiled grimly. "Really? Tell me, my dear, when would you have gotten around to showing me this note?"

She paled. "I told you that I did not wish to alarm you with it."

"I assure you, I am far more alarmed by the fact that you had no intention of showing it to me."

"You don't understand."

"I understand only too well," Gabriel said. "I have got to find Baxter. And I must do so quickly. I must put a stop to this nonsense."

A knock on the door of Phoebe's bedchamber broke the tension in the room.

"What is it?" Phoebe called.

The door was opened by a maid who gave a quick curtsy. "Beggin' yer pardon, madam. Lady Clarington is downstairs askin' to see you at once."

"I'll be right down," Phoebe said. She glanced at Gabriel as she started toward the door. "Perhaps you should come also, my lord," she said coolly. "Mama may have news for us."

"Phoebe, wait." Gabriel started to put out a hand to restrain her and then changed his mind. He knew he had hurt her again, but he did not know what to do about it. *Damn Baxter,* he thought. *This is all his fault.*

Without a word Gabriel went downstairs with an equally silent Phoebe. She brightened up at once, however, as they walked into the drawing room.

Lydia, a vision of high fashion in soft peach, was seated on the sofa. She was bubbling over with eagerness. "There you are, Phoebe. I am glad Wylde is here, too. This should interest him."

"Good afternoon, Lady Clarington," Gabriel said formally.

"Mama, what have you found out?" Phoebe demanded as she seated herself.

"I played cards at Lady Clawdale's this afternoon," Lydia said. "Lost two hundred pounds, but it may have been worth it. I brought up Baxter's name very casually in the course of the conversation."

Gabriel frowned. "What did you learn?"

Lydia's eyes sparkled. "It seems that Lady Rantley recalls something about Neil Baxter having a mistress shortly before he left London three years ago. Apparently the woman was an actress."

"A *mistress*." Phoebe was plainly insulted. "Do you mean to say that while he was playing the part of my devoted Lancelot, he was keeping a mistress? Of all the bloody nerve."

Lydia met Gabriel's eyes and winked. Gabriel smiled ruefully. He definitely owed his mother-in-law a favor, he thought. She had done more to demolish Baxter's reputation in Phoebe's eyes in the past ten seconds than he had succeeded in doing in the past several days.

"Did Lady Rantley know anything specific about Baxter's bit of muslin?" Gabriel asked. He was aware that Phoebe was silently fuming.

"Not much," Lydia said. "Only that she later went on to bigger and better things after Baxter left town."

"What bigger and better things?" Phoebe asked.

Lydia smiled triumphantly. "Apparently she opened one of the more popular brothels. Lady Rantley did not know where it was, naturally. But I have given the matter some thought and I see no reason why it would have closed. I'll wager it's still doing business." She looked at Gabriel. "Perhaps if you locate it and talked to Baxter's ex-mistress, you might learn something of import."

"I might, indeed." Gabriel was already heading toward the door. This was definitely information that could narrow the search.

"Hold one minute, my lord," Phoebe ordered. "Where do you think you are going?"

447

"To find out what I can about Baxter's mistress."

"But that means you will be going to a brothel. Perhaps more than one," she protested. "I do not want you anywhere near such a place."

Gabriel gave her an impatient look. "Have no fear, madam. I do not intend to sample the wares. I am merely going to look for information."

"I do not want you going alone," she said quickly. "I shall go with you."

Lydia groaned. "Don't be an idiot, Phoebe. There is no way you can go with him."

"Your mother is right," Gabriel agreed immediately, grateful for Lydia's support. He walked over to Phoebe and took her hand in his. He could not help smiling at her obvious jealousy. It warmed his heart. "Calm yourself, my dear. I appreciate your concerns, but there is nothing in this that need alarm you. Trust me."

Her brows rose coolly. "I am to trust you even though you do not trust me? That does not seem particularly fair, Wylde."

Gabriel dropped his smile and her hand. "I shall no doubt be late getting home tonight. You need not wait up for me."

Phoebe glowered at him. "Lovely. I can look forward to another jolly evening at home alone with the servants. I am getting fed up to the teeth with this business, Wylde."

"That reminds me," Lydia interrupted smoothly. "I was wondering if you might consider releasing Phoebe from prison for the evening, Wylde. Meredith and I are going to the theater. Anthony will accompany us. Is there any reason Phoebe could not join us?"

Phoebe brightened. "No reason at all." She turned to Gabriel. "I shall be perfectly safe in the bosom of my family, my lord. Surely you cannot object."

Gabriel hesitated. He did not like the idea, but he realized he had no sound reason to forbid her from going out tonight. She would be surrounded by her family, and her brother would be along in the event of trouble.

"Very well," he said reluctantly.

Phoebe made a face. "Your gracious generosity quite overwhelms me, my lord. Who would have thought that I would find myself in the position of having to beg my husband's permission to go to the theater? I vow, you have changed my life, sir."

"Then we are even," he said. "Because you have certainly changed mine." He glanced at Lydia. "I am in your debt, madam."

"I know." Lydia chuckled. "Never fear, I shall collect."

Phoebe groaned aloud and rolled her eyes toward the ceiling. "Never say I did not warn you, Wylde."

Gabriel grinned ruefully. He inclined his head toward his bright-eyed mother-in-law. "I believe you said you lost two hundred pounds in the course of gaining the information about Baxter's mistress, madam. You must allow me to cover your losses."

"I would not dream of it," Lydia murmured.

"I insist," Gabriel said.

"Well, in that case," Lydia said, "I suppose I shall have to let you do as you see fit. And to think that some would have us believe the age of chivalry has gone."

Phoebe glared at Gabriel. "Some are going out of their way to bury it. Wylde, I do not care for this business of you investigating brothels."

"Think of me as being on a quest, my dear." Gabriel went out the door.

Phoebe gazed out at the crowded theater with satisfaction. "I vow, an evening at the opera has never seemed quite so entertaining before," she said to Meredith.

Meredith, seated beside Phoebe in the plush box, adjusted the pale blue skirts of her evening gown. "I suspect it merely seems more entertaining than usual because you have been feeling somewhat confined of late."

"That is putting it mildly," Phoebe said. "I have been imprisoned of late."

"Come, now, Phoebe." Meredith smiled. "You make it sound as if you have been held captive for months rather than a mere day. Besides, you know Wylde was only doing what he thought was best."

"I fear I am fated to be surrounded by people who think they know what is best for me." Phoebe studied the rows of boxes full of glittering theatergoers. "What a crush. We shall be an hour waiting for the carriage after the performance is over."

"Not unusual at the height of the Season," Lydia observed. The pink plumes that decorated her satin headband bobbed as she raised her opera glass to her eyes. "I do believe I see Lady Markham. I wonder who that handsome young man is with her. Certainly not her son. I wonder if she has acquired another paramour. I am told she has only just got rid of the last."

Meredith looked disapproving. "Mother, you are always a source of the most amazing gossip."

"I do my best," Lydia said proudly.

The velvet curtain at the back of the box twitched as Anthony entered. Phoebe's brows rose when she saw that he was scowling. "Did you bring us some lemonade?"

"No, I did not. A much more pressing issue has arisen." Anthony dropped down onto one of the velvet-cushioned chairs. "I just ran into Rantley. He and two of his friends were talking about Wylde."

Phoebe asked. "What were they saying?"

Anthony's mouth hardened. "They changed the topic the moment I arrived, but I overheard their earlier remarks. They were discussing the possibility that your husband may have made his fortune as a pirate rather than as a legitimate businessman while out in the islands."

"How dare they?" Phoebe stormed. She shot to her feet. "I shall find them and correct that notion at once."

"What's this?" Lydia lowered her opera glass and frowned at Phoebe. "Sit down, my girl. You are not going anywhere."

Meredith gave Phoebe a quelling glance. "Mother is quite right. Sit down at once. Do you want people staring at this box and wondering what is going on?"

Phoebe reluctantly sat. "We must do something about this dreadful gossip. I cannot stand by and allow people to speculate about Wylde in this manner."

"You will accomplish nothing by chasing

452

after the gossip mongers," Lydia said sternly.

"What do you suggest I do?" Phoebe snapped.

Lydia's smile was filled with the happy anticipation of battle. "We shall let them come to us, of course."

Phoebe blinked. "I beg your pardon?"

"Mama is quite right," Meredith said calmly. "It is always preferable to fight the enemy on one's own ground."

Phoebe looked helplessly at Anthony. "Do you know what they are talking about?"

Anthony chuckled. "No, but I have utmost respect for Mama and Meredith when it comes to dealing with this sort of thing."

Lydia nodded with satisfaction. "I doubt that we will have long to wait for the first skirmish." She raised her glass to her eye again. "Ah, yes. Lady Rantley is leaving her box at this very moment. I'll wager she's on her way over here."

"Do you think she intends to ask rude questions about Wylde's past?" Phoebe demanded.

"I think it highly likely, given that her lord is talking about it to his friends." Lydia assumed a thoughtful expression. "The interesting thing about Eugenie is that she is the one who makes all the financial moves in the Rantley household. Rantley merely carries out her instructions. You will remember that when she gets here, won't you?"

"Yes, Mama," Meredith said.

Anthony grinned. "I understand."

"Excellent." Lydia paused. "I wonder who started that rumor of piracy."

"Baxter, no doubt," Anthony said. "Wylde really is going to have to do something about him. He's becoming more than a nuisance. Wylde says he has a mesmerizing effect on females. Apparently his former fiancée fell under Baxter's spell."

Phoebe stared at her brother. "What former fiancée?"

Anthony winced. "Sorry. Shouldn't have mentioned it. It's all finished. She's married to someone else."

"*What former fiancée?*" Phoebe repeated grimly.

"Just someone he was engaged to for a while out in the islands," Anthony said in soothing tones. "Wylde mentioned her in passing. It was not important."

Phoebe felt slightly ill. "Not important," she repeated under her breath. "Today I find out Wylde is pursuing a woman who runs a brothel and tonight I learn he was previously engaged to another woman. Someone he has never bothered to mention."

"There are two types of men in the world,

Phoebe." Lydia peered through her glass. "The type who talk about their pasts incessantly and the type who rarely mention the subject. Be grateful you have got the latter sort. The former tend to become a bore over time."

"Nevertheless," Phoebe muttered, "it is unnerving to learn that my husband was rather recently engaged to another woman."

"Not so recently," Anthony said. "The engagement ended about a year ago. Right after Wylde learned that his fiancée was passing information on sailing dates and cargoes to Baxter."

"Oh, my God," Phoebe said. "What was she like?"

"The fiancée?" Anthony shrugged. "He did not describe her. I gather she was rather naive and not particularly loyal. Apparently Baxter had no difficulty seducing her."

Phoebe sighed. It seemed that every time she turned around, she discovered yet another reason why Gabriel hesitated to trust anyone. There were moments when she almost despaired of fulfilling her quest. How could she teach him to love if she could not even teach him to trust?

Bleakly she recalled the cold anger in his eyes that afternoon when he had stalked into her bedchamber, demanding Neil's note. He had obviously assumed the worst from the start.

For her part, she had been so busy recovering from the shock of the message that she had not had time to think about how to respond, let alone how to deal with Gabriel. Her first instinct had been to hide the note and she had done so. She had known Gabriel would be enraged, that he would worry she might believe Neil's lies.

Obviously she had chosen the wrong tactic. Gabriel was probably more wary now than ever of trusting her. Everything she did around Gabriel seemed to misfire.

"Good evening, Lydia."

Phoebe turned at the sound of the booming voice. Eugenie, Lady Rantley, sailed into the box with all the aplomb of a large vessel coming into port. She was garbed in an amethyst-colored satin gown that strained across her enormous chest and broad hips. Huge artificial flowers graced her turban.

Anthony got to his feet and Meredith nodded politely.

"Good evening, Eugenie." Lydia did not do anything more than glance over her shoulder. "Have you seen Milly's new paramour? He appears to be a charming young man."

"Milly has no doubt brought him here to put him on display," Lady Rantley said.

"That is not what I wanted to talk to you about. Have you heard the rumors, Lydia?"

Phoebe started to speak, but Meredith caught her eye and silently hushed her.

"What rumors would those be?" Lydia continued to scan the audience with her opera glass.

"About Wylde, of course." Lady Rantley glanced at Phoebe. "They are saying the man made his fortune as a pirate."

"Are they, indeed?" Lydia said calmly. "How very exciting. I have always thought that every family needs a pirate or two somewhere in the family tree. It invigorates the bloodlines, you know."

Lady Rantley stared at Lydia. "Are you saying you are aware of the possibility that Wylde might have actually been a pirate?"

"Of course. Anthony, Lady Cressborough has brought her daughter with her tonight. I want you to take a look at her. I believe she would make you an excellent wife."

Anthony grimaced. "I danced with her the other night at the Tannershams' ball. She has not got a brain in her head."

"Oh, dear. Well, that's that, then. I could not bear to have a stupid daughter-in-law," Lydia said dryly. "Got to think of the bloodlines, you know."

Lady Rantley cleared her throat loudly.

"I beg your pardon, Lydia, but am I right in concluding that you are making a joke out of this extremely alarming gossip?"

Meredith smiled vaguely at Lady Rantley. "My husband assures me that Wylde is richer than Croesus and has extensive shipping interests."

"So I hear," Lady Rantley said ominously.

"Trowbridge also says Wylde is starting up a new venture that is expected to be highly profitable." Meredith's smile grew even more bland. "All of Wylde's ventures are profitable, he says. I believe Wylde will be selling some shares in the project. Trowbridge is buying several."

Lady Rantley's gaze sharpened abruptly. "Is that so? Shares will be available, you say?"

"Yes, indeed." Meredith fanned herself gently. "I never pay much attention to that sort of thing, of course. But if you think your husband might be interested in some shares in Wylde's project, I might be able to prevail upon Trowbridge to see if he can convince Wylde to sell him some."

"I would appreciate that," Lady Rantley said quickly.

"I'm not so certain that will work," Anthony said with a meditative air. "You know Wylde, Meredith. He does not take kindly to gossip. If he discovers that Lord Rantley

458

is spreading the pirate story about, he is quite likely to refuse to let him into the venture."

Meredith gave Anthony a concerned look. "You are quite right." She turned back to Lady Rantley with a regretful expression. "I had better withdraw my promise to speak to Trowbridge on your behalf. Wylde will no doubt be extremely annoyed at anyone who spreads the rumors of piracy."

"No, wait," Lady Rantley said urgently. "I have no notion where this dreadful pirate story came from, but I will undertake to quash it at once."

"Very wise of you, Eugenie." Lydia finally put down her opera glass and beamed at Lady Rantley. "It is wonderfully amusing pretending to have a pirate in the family, but we are not at all certain that Wylde will be quite as amused as the rest of us are if he hears the tales. And when Wylde is annoyed, he can be extremely difficult."

"And on top of that, there is no telling what Papa would do if he discovered rumors were going around about his new son-in-law," Meredith said with a troubled look. "Papa is so fussy about that sort of thing. He might feel obliged to limit all his business dealings to gentlemen he felt he could trust not to repeat such stories."

"Quite true," Lydia murmured. "Eugenie,

I believe Rantley has recently bought shares in a mining venture that Clarington has started, has he not?"

"Yes, as a matter of fact he has. We are quite hopeful of success," Lady Rantley allowed cautiously.

"It would be a shame if Clarington concluded he could not do business with Rantley."

Anthony looked extremely grave. "Very unfortunate."

"I understand." Lady Rantley rose majestically. "Rest assured that the rumor will be put to rest at once." She sailed grandly back out of the box.

Phoebe smiled happily at her mother, brother, and sister. "I always knew that there must be some use for all that boring business information you are all forever discussing."

"I know that from time to time you find us extremely stuffy and tiresome, Phoebe," Anthony said. "But we are not stupid."

"I have never made the mistake of thinking you are," Phoebe assured him. "Thank you for your support of Wylde tonight. He is not used to it, you know."

Lydia swept her opera glass across the audience one last time. "He will become accustomed to it. After all, he is a member of the family now."

Chapter 20

"Good heavens, what a crush." The crowd outside the theater was every bit as bad as Phoebe had envisioned. "I was right when I said we would be forever waiting for our carriage."

"It's raining," Meredith exclaimed. "That will make it all the longer."

"I'll see what I can do about hurrying things along," Anthony said. "You three wait here. I'll find one of the footmen."

He detached himself and disappeared into the throng of elegantly dressed theatergoers. Phoebe stood with Lydia and Meredith beneath the roof at the lobby entrance and watched the crowd milling about in front of the theater.

Carriages jammed the street, vying for position. Tempers were flaring. Coachmen yelled at one another as they tried to force their vehicles into a more advantageous location. Two or three people were arguing a short distance away from Phoebe.

"Well, then, Phoebe." Lydia smiled in satisfaction. "Did you enjoy your brief respite from incarceration?"

"Very much. I am forever indebted to you for your efforts on my behalf Mama."

Meredith looked at her. "In truth, I was rather surprised Wylde let you out even for a short while tonight."

Phoebe grinned. "So was I. Mama convinced him to do so."

At that moment the argument which had been brewing a short distance away erupted into a loud shouting match. One of the men punched the other. The second man roared with rage and shoved the first man aside.

"Get out of my way, you bastard. I saw that hackney first, by God."

"The devil you did."

The first man used his fists to drive home his claim to the hackney. Someone else yelled as the first man's punch went wild and struck a bystander. A fourth man screamed abuse.

Meredith frowned. "Let's move out of the way. I wish Anthony would hurry."

Phoebe started to retreat back into the lobby with her mother and sister, but the argument was exploding all around them now. People were pushing and shoving. Ladies shrieked. The sound of ripping silk caused Phoebe to glance over her shoulder. A woman was slapping furiously at two rude young bucks who were using the commotion to take liberties.

Phoebe swung her reticule at the head of the nearest dandy. He staggered as the small purse found its mark. With amazing speed, he snagged the reticule and angrily started to tug it out of Phoebe's hand.

She jerked hard on the strings of the reticule. They snapped. The little beaded bag disappeared forever beneath the feet of the crowd.

The woman who had been defending herself from the two men used the momentary distraction to dash toward the safety of the lobby.

Phoebe turned around and discovered that she had been separated from her sister and mother by the surging throng. She glanced about anxiously. People heaved about like flotsam on a stormy sea, making it impossible for Phoebe to see anyone.

A drunken young man reeled into her just as she stood on tiptoe to see over the nearest heads. Phoebe's left leg buckled and she lost her balance.

"Devil take it." Phoebe staggered awkwardly but managed to keep her feet. She gathered her skirts close around her and tried to forge a path toward the lights of the theater lobby.

A man's arm closed around her waist.

Phoebe yelled in outrage and tried to pry herself free of the arm. "Let me go, you blundering fool."

The man did not respond. He began to drag Phoebe relentlessly through the crowd. Phoebe yelled again, this time much louder. There were people all around her, but no one paid any attention to her shouts for help. Everyone was too busy trying to protect himself or herself from the crowd that was threatening to turn into a mob.

A second man materialized near the one who had a grip on Phoebe.

"Ye sure this be the right gel?" he hissed as he grabbed Phoebe's flailing arm.

"It better be," the man snarled. "Wearin' a yellow and green dress, just like we was told. I'll tell ye one thing, I ain't goin' back into that lot to find another gel."

Phoebe lashed out with her hand. Her fingers found a man's bewhiskered cheek. She dug in her nails, raking his skin fiercely. The man growled in outrage.

"Damn little bitch."

"She's a right 'andful," the first man complained. "Is the carriage where it's supposed to be?"

"It's there. Bloody 'ell."

"What happened?"

"She kicked me."

"We're almost there. Get the door open." The first man heaved Phoebe upward.

Phoebe grabbed at the open door of the carriage. Her gloved fingers scrabbled on the wood. She braced herself, but the effort was useless.

Someone shoved her forcefully between the shoulder blades and she was thrown inside the cab. She landed in a heap on the floor between the cushioned seats.

The first man yelled at the coachman, then vaulted up into the cab. The second man followed.

Phoebe felt the coach lurch forward. She screamed furiously and kicked wildly until rough hands succeeded in binding her wrists and feet. A dirty piece of cloth stuffed into her mouth cut off her shouts for help.

"Sweet bloody Jesus," one of the men said in exasperation as he collapsed onto a cushion. "What a little hellcat. If she was mine, I'd teach her to keep her mouth shut."

The other man chuckled lewdly. He prodded Phoebe's hip with the toe of his boot. "I expect she'll be singin' a different tune by mornin'. A night at Alice's place is enough to make even a hellcat mind her tongue."

Phoebe froze on the floor of the carriage. *Alice's place.*

She forced herself to calm down and think logically. There was nothing she could do while she was trussed up here in the carriage, but sooner or later she would have her chance. In the meantime she silently went to work trying to wriggle her wrists free from the hastily tied rope that bound them.

The crowded streets slowed travel to a crawl. It seemed ages before the carriage eventually came to a halt. When it did, one of the two men shoved open the door and then reached inside to assist his partner. Together they lifted Phoebe out of the cab and carried her up a flight of steps.

She glanced around, trying to orient herself as she was carried down a long hall. She was carted past several doors, all of them firmly closed. A woman's laughing shriek sounded from behind one of them. The slap of a whip on flesh followed by a man's anguished groan emanated from behind another.

"What 'ave ye got there?" a woman's drunken voice demanded. "A new girl?"

"That's right. And it ain't none of yer business," one of the men carrying Phoebe said.

"Didn't know Alice was 'avin' to pick 'em up off the street these days," the woman muttered as she went on past. "Always plenty of applicants for a job 'ere in the Velvet 'ell."

"This one's special. Alice says she has a customer with peculiar tastes," one of the men said.

Phoebe heard a door open. She was carried into a dark room and dropped on top of a bed. She lay still, struggling to get her bearings in the shadows.

"That's that, then," one of the men said in relief. "Time to collect our pay and get out of 'ere."

The door closed behind them with a solid, chunking sound. A few seconds later Phoebe heard a key turn in the lock. Footsteps went down the hall.

Silence descended.

Phoebe sat up slowly. Her pulse was racing and her heart was pounding. For an instant she thought she would suffocate because of the gag. The fear that was rippling through her made everything worse. The dark world spun around her. She wondered in alarm if she might actually be going to faint.

Slowly and with great difficulty she managed to rein in the terror that threatened to turn her into a madwoman. She had to stay calm or all was lost.

The first step was to get free of the gag and the ropes that bound her wrists and ankles.

Phoebe wriggled to the edge of the bed and swung her feet down to the floor. Surely where there was a bed there would be a table nearby to hold such necessities as a candle and perhaps some useful implements. She would dearly love to find a knife.

The small table was right where one would expect. Phoebe managed to hook the drawer knob under her gag and pry the dirty cloth out of her mouth. She sucked in a great gulp of air and turned her back to the drawer. She fumbled with it, using her bound hands to pull it open.

Inside the drawer was a small bottle of the sort that usually held laudanum.

The sound of a key scraping in the lock interrupted Phoebe's awkward search. She hastily closed the drawer and tumbled back down onto the bed.

Light from the hall splashed onto the counterpane as the door of the chamber opened. A woman stood in the opening.

"Welcome to the Velvet Hell," the woman said. "I'm glad you are here. And none too soon. I have wasted enough time and money on this venture."

She walked into the room and closed the door behind her. Phoebe heard the candle on the table being lit. When the flame flared, it revealed a halo of golden blond hair and the pretty face of the mysterious Alice.

"I see you are getting on in the world, Alice," Phoebe said quietly. "I assume running a brothel pays better than the position of housemaid."

"A great deal better." Alice smiled thinly. "A woman in my position must make the most of her opportunities."

Phoebe eyed her warily. "What are you going to do with me?"

"I had what I thought was a truly clever plan." Alice came to the edge of the bed and stood looking down at Phoebe. "But I fear time is running out. Neil is close to discovering what has been happening, so I must give up my original scheme and proceed in another manner."

Phoebe did not move. "What are you talking about? What was your original plan?"

"Why, to frighten you into selling the book, of course. I count more than one or two collectors among my clients here at the Velvet Hell and I have discovered they tend to be an eccentric, superstitious lot."

"You tried to make the curse come true, didn't you?"

"Yes. Neil had told me all about it, you see. He talked a great deal about that damn book. After I carried out the second part of the curse, I intended to send you a note. I wanted you to believe that an anonymous collector was offering to buy *The Lady in the Tower*. I thought that by then you would be happy to sell the thing just to get rid of it."

"Were you Neil's mistress three years ago?"

"Oh, yes," Alice said bitterly. "I was Neil's mistress all the while he pretended to be your devoted Lancelot. He told me he had a plan to get money out of your father. He told me that he would marry me as soon as he achieved his goal. He claimed it was me he loved, not you. And fool that I was, I believed him."

"This is all so confusing," Phoebe whispered. "I do not know who or what to believe. How did you know about the catacombs?"

"Servants' talk in the little village near Devil's Mist." Alice sat down in a chair, her posture as graceful as that of any lady. "I am a fair actress. It was easy enough to play the part of a tavern wench for a few days. I learned everything I needed to know about the castle."

"I see."

"At first I had intended merely to push you over the cliffs into the sea. But when I learned of the catacombs and the secret passage, I was intrigued with the notion of using them instead. I did not actually want you dead, you see. Merely frightened."

"You could have killed me the night you started the fire in my bedchamber."

"Not likely." Alice shrugged. "I assumed your husband would be with you and that you would not be asleep yet. You are, after all, a recently married woman, and the rumors are that Wylde is besotted with his new bride."

"What do you intend to do now?" Phoebe demanded.

"Hold you for ransom, of course. Your husband will receive a message saying that he can have you back in exchange for the book. Things will be a bit more difficult this way, but I really have no choice. As I said, Neil has learned of my plans and time is running out."

Phoebe gazed at her intently. "Why do you want the book, Alice? What is so important about it?"

"I don't know," Alice said simply.

"You're going to all this trouble and you don't know why?" Phoebe asked in disbelief.

"I only know that Neil wants *The Lady in the Tower* very badly. That is enough for me." Alice's fingers tightened on the arm of the chair and her eyes gleamed with barely suppressed rage. "He has talked of nothing else since his return except getting that stupid book back. Well, now he will have to deal with me in order to get his hands on it and I shall extract a very, very high price."

Phoebe wondered if she were, indeed, dealing with a madwoman. "I think Neil only wants the book for sentimental reasons."

"There is more to it than that," Alice said. "There must be. Neil could not possibly harbor any great, undying devotion for you. It is all an act, I know it is."

"Alice, I believe you have become crazed with your desire for revenge against Neil," Phoebe said gently.

"Perhaps." Alice rose to her feet and went to stand near the bed. "A woman in my profession spends a great many nights in hell. It is enough to drive anyone mad. Only the strongest of us survive."

"You have survived."

"Yes," Alice whispered. "I have survived. And one of the things that has kept me going is the hope of gaining my revenge on Neil Baxter. He is the one who condemned me to the Velvet Hell."

Phoebe stared at her. "What will happen to me?"

"You?" Alice gave her a speculative look. "I suppose it might be amusing for me to make the last part of the curse come true for you, as it has for me."

"What are you talking about?"

"How does the last part of the book curse go?" Alice leaned closer. "Something about spending an eternal night in hell. I could make you spend an eternal night in hell, Lady Wylde. One night in this place serving my customers would certainly seem like a night in hell to a woman like you."

Phoebe said nothing. Her mouth went dry. She held Alice's half-wild eyes and did not look away.

"But I do not hate you that much," Alice continued softly. "You are merely the means to an end." She reached down, grasped the flimsy bodice of Phoebe's bright gown, and tore the delicate silk dress all the way to the hem. Within seconds Phoebe was lying amid the shredded fabric, wearing only her petticoat.

"Why did you do that?" Phoebe demanded furiously.

"Just a precaution. I doubt you will be able to free yourself from the ropes, but in the event you did, the lack of a decent gown will keep you from attempting to escape."

"You think so?"

Alice gave her a chilling smile. "You never know whom you will meet in the halls of the Velvet Hell, madam. Chances are excellent you will run into some old friends of the family. Your husband will not thank you if you crucify his honor and your own reputation by being seen here. And what will you do when you reach the street?"

Phoebe had to admit she had a point. "Alice, listen to me — "

"Use your common sense. Stay here and do not cause any trouble until your lord ransoms you."

Alice dropped the shredded silk on the floor and walked out of the chamber. She closed the door very softly behind her. Phoebe heard the key turn in the lock.

Phoebe waited until she was sure the woman had gone down the hall. When all was quiet, she sat up again on the edge of the bed. She turned around and fumbled with the drawer in the bedside table. A moment later her fingers closed around the little bottle of laudanum.

She dropped the bottle, deliberately smashing it into several pieces. Crouching down, she leaned back and carefully picked up one of the shards of glass.

It took forever and there was blood on her hands before she finished, but Phoebe managed to sever her ties. She hurriedly undid the ropes that bound her ankles, and stood up.

Drunken laughter sounded out in the hall.

Phoebe shuddered. She had to get out of the chamber as quickly as possible, but Alice was right. She dared not risk being seen in the hall.

She opened the door of the wardrobe, hoping to find clothing. It was empty.

She went to the window and looked out. There was nothing but a sheer drop to the dark alley far below. She would surely break her legs if she tried to jump.

Phoebe turned around and studied her shadowed surroundings. There was nothing she could use to escape the horrid chamber.

Except the sheets on the bed.

She dove for the bed.

Less than ten minutes later she had two large sheets securely tied together. She secured one end of her makeshift rope to the bedpost and draped the remainder out the window.

She levered herself up onto the sill, took a firm grip on the knotted sheets, and began to lower herself down the wall into the alley.

"Phoebe." Neil Baxter's voice rose softly from the depths of the alley. "For God's sake, have a care, my love. I'm coming to get you."

The shock of Neil's voice nearly caused Phoebe to lose her grip on the sheets. She stopped her awkward descent and peered down into the alley. "Neil? Is that you?"

"Yes. Hold on. I'll have you safely down in a minute." He moved into a shaft of moonlight.

Phoebe stared down at him. "What are you doing? How did you know I was here?"

"When I got word Alice had kidnapped you, I came straight here. I had some notion of trying to save you, but it appears you have already taken steps to save yourself. You always were a clever girl. Come on down, my love, but be careful."

Phoebe hesitated. She clung to the bedsheets and tried to read Neil's handsome face. She could see little of his expression in the darkness.

As she dangled there, torn with indecision about what to do next, she heard the door open in the chamber above her.

"Phoebe?" Gabriel's voice was muffled but unmistakable. "Phoebe, are you in here?"

"Gabriel?" she called tentatively.

"Damnation, Phoebe, where are you?"

"It's Wylde," Neil hissed. "Phoebe, I beg of you, my darling, let go of the sheets. He will have you in another minute."

"It's too far to drop," Phoebe protested.

"I'll catch you," Neil promised. He sounded desperate. "Hurry, love. I have information that he means to kill you. I can prove it."

476

Gabriel leaned out through the open window above Phoebe. His hands clamped around the sill. "*Phoebe*. Bloody hell, woman, come back here." He took hold of the knotted sheets and started hauling them upward.

"Phoebe, you must trust me," Neil called. "If you let him drag you back through that window, you will be signing your own death warrant." He held up his arms. "Let go. I'll catch you, my love. You'll be safe with me."

Phoebe's arms were straining with effort. Her shoulders ached and her fingers were clenched so tightly in the sheets, they were trembling. She did not know how much longer she could maintain her death grip.

"If you let go of the damn sheet, I swear I shall lock you up for a year," Gabriel vowed.

"Phoebe, save yourself." Neil's arms were lifted upward in a pleading manner. "For the sake of what we once meant to each other, I beg you to trust your loyal Lancelot."

"You are my wife, Phoebe." Gabriel continued to haul in the sheet. "You will obey me in this. *Don't let go of the sheet.*"

It was just like her dream, Phoebe realized as she was hoisted inexorably upward. Two men were reaching out for her, both promising safety. She had to choose between them.

But she had already made her choice.

She clung tightly to the sheet until she was less than a foot below the windowsill.

"Hell and damnation, Phoebe, you're going to be the death of me yet." Gabriel reached down, caught hold of her wrists, and dragged her through the window. "Are you all right?"

"Yes, I think so."

He dropped her unceremoniously onto the floor and leaned out over the sill. "Goddamn the bastard. He's getting away."

Phoebe picked herself up off the floor and straightened her torn chemise. "Gabriel, how did you find me?"

He spun around, his face very fierce in the moonlight. "Stinton and I have been keeping an eye on this house since we located it earlier today. We saw you being carried in earlier, but we were too far away to stop the villains. We had to bide our time. Come on. We've got to get you out of here."

"I cannot walk out dressed in my chemise." Phoebe crossed her arms protectively over her bosom. "Someone is bound to notice."

Gabriel scowled. "Maybe there's a dress in the wardrobe."

"It's empty."

"We can't stay here. Come on." He grabbed her wrist and opened the door. He glanced up and down the hall. "There's no one about. I think we can make it to the back stairs."

Phoebe clutched at the front of her chemise as she limped quickly after Gabriel. She felt terribly exposed in the fine lawn undergarment. "How did you get in?"

"I came up the back steps, the same way you were brought in. No one saw me."

A roar of masculine laughter sounded from the main staircase at the far end of the hall. A woman giggled.

"Someone's coming," Phoebe said. She glanced over her shoulder. "He'll see us as soon as he reaches the top of the stairs."

"In here." Gabriel turned the knob on the nearest door. Mercifully it opened. He tugged Phoebe into the chamber.

A young woman wearing only a cascade of red hair and a pair of black stockings turned around in surprise. She held a whip upraised in one hand. She had obviously been applying it vigorously to the plump buttocks of the stout man who was tied facedown to the bedposts. The man on the bed was wearing a black blindfold over his eyes.

Gabriel held his fingers up to his lips to indicate silence. The redheaded woman cocked a brow. Her mouth curved in cynical amusement at the sight of Phoebe's shocked expression.

"Don't stop, my little tyrant," the man on the bed pleaded. "We must finish this quickly or all is lost."

The redhead obligingly plied the whip. Phoebe flinched.

"Harder," the man cried. "Harder."

"Of course, my love," the redhead purred. "And are you sorry yet, my dear?"

"Yes, yes, I am sorry."

"I do not believe you are sorry enough." The redhead picked up the pace of the whip, making a fair amount of noise in the process.

The man on the bed groaned in rising ecstasy.

Gabriel tossed several notes down onto the dressing table and indicated the wardrobe. The redhead glanced at the money and nodded. She did not pause in her task. The whip sang and the man groaned in a rousing crescendo of sound as Gabriel quietly opened the wardrobe.

Phoebe forgot all about the bizarre sight she was witnessing when she saw the array of spectacular dresses in the wardrobe. She stared in awe at the brilliantly colored gowns.

"Choose one," Gabriel mouthed silently.

It was an impossible choice. Phoebe loved them all. But with Gabriel standing there looking so impatient, she knew she could not hesitate. She grabbed a brilliant crimson satinet gown and tugged it on over her head.

The groans of the man on the bed grew louder and more impassioned. Gabriel reached into the top of the wardrobe and removed a curly blond wig. He shoved it down on top of Phoebe's head. She found herself gazing up at him through a veil of blond ringlets.

The redhead nodded toward a drawer built into the wardrobe. Gabriel followed her gaze and pulled it open. He picked up a black lace mask and handed it to Phoebe. She donned it quickly.

Gabriel took her hand, nodded his thanks to the hardworking courtesan, and silently opened the door. The man on the bed gave a warbling cry of satisfaction just as Phoebe and Gabriel stepped out into the hall.

They nearly collided with a portly gentleman who lurched into their path. Phoebe stared at him through her mask, stunned to realize she recognized him. It was Lord Prudstone, a cheerful, grandfatherly sort who had occasionally chatted with her at various soirees.

Prudstone gave a start when he saw Gabriel; then he grinned knowingly and slapped him on the shoulder.

"Here, now, Wylde. Didn't expect to see you here so soon after the nuptials. Don't tell me married life has gotten boring already."

"I was just leaving," Gabriel said.

"And taking some of the merchandise with you, I see?" Prudstone chuckled as his gaze rested appreciatively on the extremely low neckline of Phoebe's crimson gown.

"Special arrangements with the management." Gabriel's voice held a poorly concealed edge that could have cut glass. "You must excuse us, Prudstone. We're in something of a hurry."

"Off you go, my little lovebirds. Enjoy yourselves." Prudstone wove his way back down the hall, waving merrily.

Gabriel practically dragged Phoebe toward the back stairs. He slammed open the door and hurried her down the darkened steps.

"Good heavens, Gabriel," Phoebe whispered, "that was Lord Prudstone."

"I know."

"How dare he assume you would come to a place like this. You're a married man."

"I know. Believe me, I know. I have never been so aware of that fact as I am tonight. Christ, Phoebe, you gave me a scare. Watch out for the body at the bottom of the steps."

"Body?" Phoebe tried to come to a halt, but Gabriel tugged her ever downward. "There's a dead man somewhere on these steps?"

"He's unconscious, not dead. He was guarding the back steps."

"I see." Phoebe swallowed. "You rendered him unconscious, I take it?"

"No, I asked him if he'd care to play a hand of whist," Gabriel said in a voice that indicated he was at the end of his patience. "Where the hell do you think I got the key to your room? *Move*, Phoebe."

Phoebe moved.

Five minutes later they were safe inside an anonymous hackney carriage. Stinton was on the box, handling the reins. Gabriel did not speak on the journey home.

When they reached the town house, he snatched off Phoebe's blond wig and tossed aside her mask. In the light provided by the carriage lamps his eyes were unreadable.

"You are to go straight upstairs to your bedchamber," he said. "I shall be up shortly. I must speak with Stinton and then I shall have a few things to discuss with you."

Chapter 21

Gabriel stood on the town house steps and gave Stinton his orders. "Try to find Baxter. If you do find him, stay with him, but don't let him know you're around. Whatever you do, don't lose him."

"Aye, m'lord. I'll do me best." Stinton, still perched on the hackney box, tipped his hat respectfully. "I'm right glad the little lady is safe. Got plenty of bottom, she has, if ye don't mind my sayin' so."

Gabriel winced at the slang but forbore to give Stinton another lecture. There was no time. "I shall tell her ladyship you have great admiration for her courage," he said dryly.

"Yes, sir, plenty of bottom. Just like I said. Don't meet many ladies of her stamp in my business." Stinton slapped the reins lightly and the carriage rolled off down the street.

Gabriel went back inside the house, closed the door, and took the stairs two at a time to the upper level. His mind was whirling

484

and his body was still pulsing with tension. He strode down the hall to Phoebe's bedchamber door and then paused, his hand on the knob. He realized he was not quite certain what to say to her.

She had chosen him.

As long as he lived he would never forget that moment when he had found Phoebe dangling from a rope of bedsheets, suspended between the two men who wanted her.

She had chosen him.

The realization roared through him like fire. He had never even told her that he loved her, let alone admitted to her that he trusted her. Yet she had chosen him, trusted him, not her golden-haired Lancelot.

Gabriel twisted the knob, opened the door, and walked softly into the room. He stopped short when he saw Phoebe standing in front of her dressing mirror. She was admiring herself in the gaudy crimson dress he had purchased for her from a whore.

"Gabriel, thank you so much for this gown. I always sensed that I could wear red, even though Meredith insisted it would be awful on me." Phoebe whirled around, her eyes alight with excitement. "I cannot wait to wear it to a soiree. I vow there will not be another woman dressed in such a fashion."

"I think that's a reasonably safe assumption." Gabriel smiled slightly as he took a close look at the gown. The cheap, shiny, crimson material was so bright it lit up the room. Deep ruffles edged the scalloped hem, which exposed far too much of Phoebe's legs. Huge black lace flowers that barely concealed her nipples decorated the exceedingly low neckline.

"I wonder if that redheaded woman at the Velvet Hell would give me the name of her dressmaker," Phoebe mused. She turned back to the mirror to adjust the tiny sleeves of the gown.

"We'll never know, because you are most certainly not going to ask her." Gabriel reached out and caught hold of her shoulders. He swung her back around to face him. "Phoebe, tell me everything that happened tonight. I know it was Alice who had you kidnapped. What did she say to you?"

Phoebe hesitated. "She was going to hold me for ransom."

"She wanted money?"

"No. She wants *The Lady in the Tower*."

"Good God, why?" Gabriel asked.

"Because Neil wants it and she will do anything to get revenge on him. He did not keep his promise to marry her, you see. He left her in hell while he went off to the South Seas. She will never forgive him."

"Damnation," Gabriel whispered, trying to sort it all out. "There have been two people, not one, after the book all this time."

"So it appears."

"It was probably Baxter who searched my town house library before our marriage." He searched her face. "Why in God's name were you climbing down those sheets into Baxter's arms?"

"I was trying to escape. I didn't know he was in the alley until I had started down the side of the wall. Gabriel, what is this all about?"

"Revenge, I think. But there's something more. Something to do with that damned book." Gabriel forced himself to take his hands off Phoebe's bare shoulders. He paced across the room to the window.

"It always comes back to *The Lady in the Tower* doesn't it?"

"The thing is," Gabriel said, thoroughly frustrated, "the book simply isn't all that valuable. It's not worth this kind of trouble."

Phoebe considered that for a moment. "Perhaps it's time we took a closer look at it."

He glanced around sharply. "Why? There's nothing unusual about it."

"Nevertheless, I think we should look at it again."

"Very well."

Phoebe crossed the room and took *The Lady in the Tower* from the bottom drawer of her wardrobe.

Gabriel watched as she put the book on the table and leaned over to examine it closely. Candlelight gleamed on her dark hair and lit her intelligent face. Even in a whore's red dress she looked like a lady. There was an innate, womanly nobility about her that no gown or circumstance could alter. This was a woman a man could trust with his life and his honor.

And she had chosen him.

"Gabriel, there truly is something different about this book."

He frowned. "You said it was the very one you gave to Baxter."

"It is, but something has been done to it. I believe the binding has been restitched in places. See? Some of it looks new."

Gabriel examined the thickly padded leather covers. "It was not this way when you gave it to Lancelot?"

Phoebe wrinkled her nose. "Don't call him that. And to answer your question, no, it was not this way. The stitching was uniformly old when I gave it to Neil."

"Perhaps we had better have a look beneath the leather."

Gabriel took a small penknife from

Phoebe's escritoire and carefully slit the newly stitched leather. He watched intently as Phoebe lifted one edge. She peeled it back slowly to reveal soft, white cotton.

"What on earth?" Phoebe cautiously lifted aside the cotton.

Gabriel saw the gleam of dark moonlight, diamonds, and gold, and knew at once what he was looking at. "Ah, yes. I wondered what had become of it."

"What is it?" Phoebe asked in amazement.

"A necklace I had made up in Canton using some very special pearls." Gabriel lifted the glittering thing out of the book. "With any luck there will be a matching bracelet, a brooch, and a set of earrings."

"It's beautiful." Phoebe stared at the gems. "But I have never seen pearls of that color before."

"They're very rare. It took me years to collect this many of this quality." He held the necklace close to the candle flame. The diamonds sparkled with an inner fire, but the pearls glowed with a mysterious dark light. It was like looking into an endless midnight sky.

"I thought at first they were black pearls," Phoebe observed. "But they are not black at all. It's almost impossible to describe the color. They are some fantastic combination of silver and green and deep blue."

"Dark moonlight."

"Dark moonlight," Phoebe repeated in wonder. "Yes, that's a perfect description." She fingered one gently. "How extraordinary."

Gabriel looked down at her candlelit skin. "They will look magnificent on you."

She looked up quickly. "This necklace truly belongs to you?"

He nodded. "It did once upon a time. Baxter took it when he attacked one of my ships."

"And now you have it back," Phoebe said with satisfaction.

He shook his head. "No. You found it, my sweet. As of now it belongs to you."

Phoebe stared at him, obviously flustered. "You cannot mean to give me such a gift."

"But I do mean to give it to you."

"But Gabriel — "

"You must indulge me, Phoebe. I have given you very little thus far in our marriage."

"That's not true," she sputtered. "Not true at all. Why, just this evening you bought me this beautiful gown."

Gabriel looked at the awful gown and started to laugh.

"I fail to see what is so amusing about this, my lord."

Gabriel laughed harder. A fierce joy crashed through him as he gazed at Phoebe in her cheap, gaudy dress. She looked so incredibly lovely, he thought. Like a princess out of a medieval legend. Her eyes were huge and luminous and her mouth promised a passion that he knew belonged only to him. She was his.

"Gabriel, are you laughing at me?"

He sobered quickly. "No, my sweet. Never that. The necklace is yours, Phoebe. I had it made for the woman I would someday marry."

"The fiancée who betrayed you in the islands?" she asked suspiciously.

He wondered who had told her about Honora. Anthony, most likely. "At the time I had it fashioned, I was not engaged. I did not know whom I would marry," Gabriel said honestly. "I wanted to have a suitable necklace to give my future wife, just as I wanted a suitable motto for my descendants."

"So you invented the family jewels, just as you did the family motto." She glanced at the necklace and then back at him. "I'm certain you mean well, as usual, but I do not want such a spectacular gift from you."

"Why not?" He took a step toward her and stopped when she retreated an equal distance. "I can afford it."

"I know you can. That's not the point."

He took another step forward, crowding her back against the wall. He clasped the necklace around her throat and then braced his hands on either side of her head. He kissed her forehead. "Then what is the point?"

"Damnation, Gabriel, do not try to seduce me now. 'Tis not a necklace I want from you, and you know it."

"Then what do you want?"

"You know very well what I want. I want your trust."

He smiled slightly. "You don't understand, do you?"

"What don't I understand?" she breathed.

"I trust you, my sweet."

She gazed up at him, her eyes full of dawning hope. "You do?"

"Yes."

"In spite of all our little misunderstandings?"

"Maybe because of them," he admitted. "No woman who was deliberately trying to deceive me would make such a hash of it time after time. Leastways not a woman as clever as you are."

She smiled tremulously. "I'm not certain that is a compliment."

"The problem," Gabriel said, his voice

roughening, "is not whether I trust you. What has torn my guts apart for days is that I didn't know whether you would continue to trust me."

"Gabriel, how could you think I would lose my faith in you?"

"The evidence was mounting against me. I did not know in the end if you would choose to believe your golden-haired Sir Lancelot or your increasingly short-tempered, overbearing, dictatorial husband."

Phoebe slowly twined her arms around his neck. Her eyes gleamed with love and mischief. "I could say that I came to a conclusion similar to your own. After all, surely no man who was out to charm and beguile me into trusting him would have been so appallingly heavy-handed."

He smiled ruefully. "You think not?"

"Let me put it this way. I was not certain if Neil was the victim of a misunderstanding, but I have never doubted you, Gabriel. I knew which man to trust tonight when I found myself suspended between you and Neil."

Gabriel was exultant. "What gave you the clue?"

Phoebe brushed her lips lightly against his. "Neil made the mistake of playing the chivalrous, gallant knight right to the very end."

"I heard him," Gabriel muttered.

"You, on the other hand, were acting much more like a genuinely frantic husband trying to save his wife. In that moment you did not even try to charm me. You were far too desperate to think of such a ruse."

Gabriel eyed her with a disgruntled expression. "I suppose that is true enough."

Phoebe laughed softly and reached up to frame his face between her soft hands. "I believe, my lord, that in all the ways that truly count, we do trust each other."

At the sight of the tender warmth in her eyes, an aching hunger seized Gabriel. "Yes. God, yes, Phoebe."

With a low exclamation he scooped her up and carried her over to the bed. The crimson skirts of her tawdry gown billowed around his boots as he covered her body with his own.

Phoebe's eyes were brilliant as she looked up at him through her lashes. Gabriel thought he would drown in that gaze. He kissed her with a desperate passion. His tongue surged into her mouth in an act of possession that presaged the even more intimate one that would soon follow.

"I will never be able to get enough of you," he whispered thickly. He lowered his head to taste one rosy nipple that had been

revealed by a shifting black lace flower.

Phoebe arched herself against him with a sensual generosity that seared Gabriel's already inflamed senses. He tugged the bright crimson gown down to her waist so that he could savor the sight and feel of her breasts. Phoebe opened his shirt and twisted her fingers gently in the hair on his chest.

"I love you," she said against the side of his face.

"For God's sake, don't ever stop loving me," Gabriel heard himself plead in a tortured voice he hardly recognized. "I could not bear it."

He pushed the red skirts up over her thighs so that they bunched at her waist. The cheap satinet gleamed as richly as Italian silk in the candlelight. He looked down at the soft curls that shielded her softness and closed a hand over them for a moment. She was already damp.

Phoebe shivered at his touch. He could feel the rising heat in her. He could also feel his manhood straining against his breeches. He reached down to unfasten his clothing, freeing his shaft.

"Gabriel? Aren't you even going to take off your boots?"

"I cannot wait that long for you." He moved between her soft thighs and fitted himself to her. "Hold me and do not let go. Ever."

He eased himself carefully into her hot, snug passage. He felt her tighten around him as he lowered his head to recapture her mouth. Her arms wrapped him close and her legs gripped him. She gave herself up to him and Gabriel was overwhelmed by the gift.

He drove himself deeply into her as if he could somehow become a part of her.

And for that moment out of time, he was.

Phoebe stirred a long while later. She was conscious of Gabriel's strong, warm thigh lying alongside hers. His arm curved around her. She realized he was awake.

"Gabriel?"

"Ummm?"

"What are you thinking about?"

He squeezed her gently. " 'Tis nothing, sweet. Go back to sleep."

"There is not a chance of that." She sat up abruptly. The crushed satinet of her crimson gown made a rustling noise. She glanced down in horror. "Oh, no, Gabriel, look at my beautiful dress. I hope it is not ruined."

He folded his arms behind his head on the pillow and eyed the gown with amusement. "I imagine it was constructed to withstand rough treatment."

"Do you think it will be all right?" Phoebe scrambled off the bed and slipped the gown down over her hips. She stepped out of it, shook out the folds of the crumpled satinet, and studied the dress with an anxious gaze.

"I think it will survive. If it does not, I shall buy you another."

"I doubt if we shall find another one in this beautiful shade of red," Phoebe said wistfully. She spread the gown out carefully on the foot of the bed. "It's a little rumpled, but otherwise intact."

Gabriel's gaze slipped over her body, which was clad only in her thin chemise. "Do not concern yourself about the dress, Phoebe."

She straightened and glanced at him, her eyes searching his face. "What were you thinking about, Gabriel?"

"It isn't important. Come back to bed."

She sat down on the edge of the bed instead. "Tell me. Now that we have declared our trust in each other, we must tell each other everything."

Gabriel winced. "Everything?"

"Absolutely."

He smiled. "Very well. I suppose you will find out sooner or later, anyway. I was thinking about the best way of setting a trap for Baxter."

Phoebe stilled. "The way you did the last time?"

"Not quite." Gabriel's mouth hardened and his eyes went cold. "This time he will not escape."

A tiny shiver went through Phoebe. "How will you do it?"

"He does not know we have discovered the necklace inside *The Lady in the Tower*," Gabriel said slowly. "I have no doubt but that he will make another try to get his hands on the book. I am thinking of making it easy for him."

"You intend to capture him when he makes his next try?"

"Yes."

"I see. How do you plan to lure him into this trap?"

"That's the difficulty."

Phoebe brightened as a thought struck her. "I know how we could lure him into this trap of yours."

Gabriel cocked a brow. "Yes?"

"Use me as bait." Phoebe smiled triumphantly.

Gabriel stared at her. "Have you gone mad? That is absolutely out of the question."

"But it would work, Gabriel. I know it would."

He sat up, swung his booted feet to the

floor, and stood. Hands on his hips, his shirt hanging open, he leaned over her with an expression as forbidding as midnight. "I said," he repeated evenly, "that using you as bait is absolutely out of the question. I meant it."

"But Gabriel — "

"I do not want to hear another word on the subject."

She glared up at him. "Really, Gabriel. That is going a bit too far. It was only a suggestion."

"A damned ridiculous suggestion. Don't even think of mentioning it again." He walked over to the table and stood gazing down at *The Lady in the Tower.* "I need to find a way to make Baxter believe the book is vulnerable."

Phoebe considered that. "You could arrange for it to be sold."

"What did you say?"

"If Neil thought we had sold the book, he might try for it when it was transferred to its new owner. It would be vulnerable then."

Gabriel's smile was slow and wicked. "My dearest wife, allow me to tell you that you would have done very well hunting pirates in the South Seas. That is a truly brilliant notion."

Phoebe was filled with an elated warmth. "Thank you, my lord."

Gabriel began to pace the room, his face intent. "I suppose we could arrange to sell the book to our old friend Nash. His insistence on doing business in the middle of the night might be extremely useful. If Baxter thought the book was being taken by carriage along a lonely country lane at midnight to be delivered to an eccentric collector, he might try his hand at a little road piracy."

"You mean he might try to waylay the carriage?"

"Precisely. We would, of course, be ready for him."

"Yes, indeed." Phoebe was filled with enthusiasm for the project. "I could wear men's clothing and pretend to be the agent hired to take the book to Nash. You could be disguised as the coachman. When he stopped the carriage, we would be ready for him."

Gabriel came to a halt directly in front of her, clamped his hands around her shoulders, and hauled her up off the bed. "You," he said, "are not going to be anywhere near that damned book when Baxter makes his try. You will not be involved in this scheme in any way whatsoever. Understood?"

"Gabriel, I want to share this adventure

with you. I have a right to do so."

"A *right?*"

She glared up at him mutinously. "*The Lady in the Tower* belongs to me."

"No, it does not. I took it from Baxter after I attacked his ship. It's mine by right of the law of the sea."

"Gabriel, that is not a valid argument, and you know it."

"Then I claim the bloody book as part of your dowry," he growled. "There. Does that satisfy you?"

"No. I still insist on being part of this plan to trap Neil."

"You may insist all you like. I will not allow you to be put in danger." He kissed her roughly and set her aside. "Now, then, I must think some more on this. Your idea of selling the book is sound, but I'm not certain I like the notion of trying to trick Baxter into waylaying the carriage. Too many uncontrollable elements in the situation."

Phoebe glared at him resentfully. "Well, don't expect me to come up with any more brilliant notions. Not if you intend to keep me from sharing in the adventure."

He ignored her. "Yes, I like the idea of selling the book." He paused by the table, picked up the knife, and began cutting through the stitching of the back cover binding. "Perhaps to someone else besides Nash, however. A book dealer here in London might work."

"That's true," Phoebe agreed, unable to resist working on the plan even though she was annoyed at being told she would not be allowed to help implement it. "Neil might believe he could steal it rather easily from a bookshop."

"We could let it be known through the gossip mills that you have decided to sell the book because you have become superstitious about it."

"It would be easy to get such gossip out. Mother and Meredith could handle that part for us."

"It just might work." Gabriel had finished cutting through the back binding.

Phoebe watched in fascination as he peeled the leather aside. He reached into the cotton padding and removed a handful of glittering stones.

"We would make the transaction in broad daylight," Gabriel continued. "The bookshop owner would be warned in advance. He would be told that I will be watching the shop, waiting for Baxter to make his move."

"I could help you keep watch," Phoebe said quickly.

"Not a chance, my sweet." Gabriel opened

his palm and revealed a bracelet, earrings, and brooch that matched the necklace. "I shall ask your brother to assist me. And perhaps Stinton."

"Oh, very well." Phoebe folded her arms beneath her breasts. "Honestly, Gabriel, I do hope this is not an indication of how you intend to conduct yourself in the future. I do not want to be shut out of all the adventures."

He smiled faintly. "I give you my word, I shall endeavor to occupy you with other sorts of adventures, my dear."

"Hah."

He chuckled softly. "Trust me."

Phoebe pursed her lips. "You will need a cooperative bookshop owner."

"Yes."

"Someone who will be willing to go along with your scheme. Not every shopkeeper would want his establishment set up as a target for a thief."

Gabriel frowned thoughtfully. "True enough."

Phoebe paused delicately. "I have a suggestion."

He glanced at her curiously. "Yes?"

"Why don't you ask your publisher, Lacey, if he will let his bookshop be used for this purpose?"

"That old sot? I suppose he might be persuaded to go along with the scheme."

Phoebe slanted Gabriel an assessing look. "I am sure he could be persuaded."

"What makes you so certain of that, my dear?" Gabriel's eyes gleamed in the shadows.

Phoebe tore her gaze away from his and focused on her bare toes. "There is something I have not had an opportunity to explain, my lord."

"Is that so?" He crossed the room and wrapped one hand around the bedpost. "And what would that be?"

Phoebe cleared her throat, very conscious of him looming over her. "I kept meaning to tell you, but somehow the opportunity never arose."

"I cannot believe that, my sweet. We have had ample opportunity to discuss the most intimate matters."

"Yes, well, the truth is, I was not precisely certain how to bring up the subject. I knew you would not be pleased, you see. And the longer I kept it from you, the more I feared that you would think I had deliberately deceived you."

"Which you most certainly had."

"Not really. I just didn't mention the matter, if you see the difference. The thing is, you told me at the beginning you had a distaste for deception. And you already had such difficulty trusting me and it all got increasingly awkward. And on top of everything else I did not want my family to discover my secret and you have been on extremely close terms with them lately. You might have felt obliged to tell them what I was doing."

"Enough." Gabriel shut off the flow of words by clamping one hand gently over her mouth. "Suppose you allow me to make this latest confession easier for you, madam."

She gazed up at him over the edge of his hand and saw that his eyes were gleaming with laughter.

"Now, then." Gabriel removed his hand cautiously from her mouth. "Let us come at this from a slightly different tact. What do you think of *The Reckless Venture*, Madam Editor?"

"It is incredibly wonderful, my lord. I loved it. The first-print run will be at least fifteen thousand copies. And we shall increase the price, too," Phoebe said gleefully. "People will be standing in line outside of Lacey's shop to purchase it. All the circulating libraries will want copies. We shall make a fortune — " She broke off abruptly and stared at him in shock.

Gabriel leaned against the bedpost, folded

his arms across his chest, and smiled his dangerous smile.

"You knew all along?" Phoebe asked weakly.

"Almost from the beginning."

"I see." She peered at him closely. She could read nothing in his expression. "Would you care to tell me precisely how annoyed you are to learn that I am your editor and publisher, my lord?"

"I believe I would rather show you."

He swooped down on her, tumbling her onto her back. He caught her up and rolled with her across the rumpled bed until she lay on top of him.

Phoebe was breathless. "I do hope you won't think you can use this technique in future to influence my opinion of your work."

"That depends. A desperate author will do almost anything to get his books published. Would this technique of influencing you be successful, do you think?"

"Very likely," Phoebe murmured.

"In that case, you may definitely expect me to use it frequently."

Chapter 22

A heavy fog shrouded London on the second night of the vigil outside Lacey's Bookshop. The gray tendrils drifted through the streets like an endless parade of ghosts. In the course of their passage they absorbed what little light was provided by the oil lamps that were mounted at intervals on iron stands. The new gas lights that illuminated Pall Mall and St. James had not yet been installed in this section of town.

Gabriel had no doubt that his decision to allow Phoebe to accompany him and Anthony while they kept their midnight watch was a serious error in judgment. But he had been unable to resist her logic or her unrelenting pleas. His lady was every bit as stubborn as he himself was. It was difficult to deny that she had a right to be present when he closed the trap around Neil Baxter.

At least he had succeeded in crushing her many and varied suggestions to use herself as bait, he thought. Some of her notions had been disconcertingly creative. But he had put a heavy, booted foot down on every one of them. He was not about to risk her neck to catch the son of a bitch who had caused all this trouble.

The compromise he and Phoebe had arrived at after numerous arguments, pleas, and impassioned speeches was that she would be allowed to watch events from the safety of the carriage.

He glanced at her now as she sat beside him in the darkened vehicle. Garbed in a black, hooded cloak, she looked as mysterious and ethereal as the fog. She was gazing intently at Lacey's Bookshop through a small gap in the curtains that covered the window.

Although she had been bubbling with excitement earlier in the evening when they had first parked the carriage on the side street, she had grown pensive during the last hour. She had done the same thing last night when they had waited in vain for Baxter to show. Gabriel wondered what she was thinking.

Some part of her, he suddenly realized, was destined to remain a mystery to him. Perhaps it was always that way between a man and a woman. Perhaps that was part of the magic. He only knew that no matter how many times he possessed Phoebe, no matter how often he laughed with her or quarreled with her, he would never learn all of her secrets. Even though he knew she was completely and irrevocably his, he also knew that she would remain forever his tantalizing, intriguing, intoxicating Veiled Lady.

He also knew with a deep sense of satisfaction that he could enjoy the occasional hint of the unknown in her because he trusted her as he had never trusted anyone else in his life. She would never leave him.

So be it, Gabriel thought. Every writer needed a muse. Phoebe would be his. She would also be his editor and publisher. That was a far more unsettling notion. But it would make for some interesting dinner table conversations, he reflected with a fleeting grin.

"Not having second thoughts about trapping Lancelot tonight, I trust," he said quietly, to break the long period of silence.

"No. I am convinced that Neil is everything you said he was and more."

"More?"

"I was not the only woman he deceived. He treated Alice very cruelly. He allowed her to believe in him when he had no intention of rescuing her from hell."

Gabriel could not think of anything to say to that. He briefly considered all the men who had cheerfully taken their pleasure from innumerable Alices and then abandoned them to the hellish life of a brothel. "He was a master of illusion."

"No, not a master," Phoebe said slowly. "He did not succeed in everything he attempted. He did not fool my father three years ago. Nor did he succeed in making me fall in love with him, although he tried. And he did not get away with piracy indefinitely."

"Most importantly he did not succeed in seducing you into believing that I was a bloodthirsty pirate who was only after your inheritance," Gabriel muttered.

"Of course he did not. I always knew what kind of man you were." She glanced at him over her shoulder. "Do you think he will show tonight, Gabriel? There was no sign of him last night."

"By now he knows he must make his move either tonight or tomorrow night. The gossip we invented has made it clear that *The Lady in the Tower* will be going into the collection of a powerful collector the day after tomorrow. The three nights it spends in Lacey's Bookshop are the only nights when it will be vulnerable."

A small tapping sound came from the roof of the closed carriage. Gabriel stood up and raised the trapdoor. Anthony, heavily shrouded in a hackney driver's hat and caped cloak, sat huddled on the box. He was doing an excellent job of imitating a dozing coachman.

"Any sign of Baxter?" Gabriel asked softly.

"No, but I'm getting a bit concerned about Stinton. He should have been back from his little foray into the alley by now."

Gabriel searched the fog, looking for signs of the missing Stinton. He had dispatched the Runner earlier to check the alley behind the shop. "You're right. I think I'd better have a look. Keep an eye on Phoebe."

"Why don't you just chain her to the inside of the carriage, to be on the safe side?" Anthony suggested dryly. "I don't want the blame if she takes a sudden notion to see what's happening."

"I resent that," Phoebe said behind Gabriel. "I have agreed to follow instructions."

Gabriel swore softly. "You will both stay here while I check on Stinton."

Phoebe touched his arm as he opened the carriage door. "Be careful, my love."

"I will." He picked up her hand, kissed the delicate inside of her wrist, and then went out through the door.

As soon as he was on the street, he moved into the deep shadows of the nearest building. The fog was as useful to him as it would be to Baxter, he thought. He glided through a particularly thick patch of it as he crossed the empty street.

There was no sign of anyone else in the vicinity. The shops were dark and silent. A cat appeared briefly, flashed across Gabriel's path, and then vanished back into the mist.

Gabriel sensed the wrongness as soon as he reached the alley entrance. He stood quietly for a moment, letting his senses feel what he could not see. Then he reached into the pocket of his greatcoat and removed the pistol he had brought with him.

He went into the alley slowly, staying close to the wall. There was almost no light here at all and he did not want to go back to the carriage for a lantern. If Baxter was near, he would be warned by the light.

Gabriel took another step into the darkness and caught the toe of his boot on something that felt suspiciously soft. He looked down and saw a bundle of what appeared to be old clothes at his feet.

He had found Stinton.

Gabriel crouched beside the fallen man, feeling for the pulse that indicated life. He found it. Stinton was unconscious, not dead.

There were two possibilities. Either a footpad had come upon Stinton in the fog or Baxter had managed to slip unseen into the alley and was even now in the bookshop.

Gabriel moved silently across the cobble-stones until he found the back entrance of the shop. The door stood ajar. He slipped inside the dark room, aware from his earlier visit that he was in the room where Lacey operated his printing press. There was just enough light seeping in from the windows to reveal the outline of the machine.

A deep, jangling sense of danger sliced through his senses an instant before he heard the scrape of a boot on the floor behind him.

Gabriel whirled around, but it was too late to avoid the figure that lunged at him out of the dark. He went down beneath the impact, rolling swiftly in an effort to shake loose his assailant. The pistol was knocked from his hand.

"You damned bloody bastard." Neil's up-raised arm slashed downward toward Gabriel's throat. A gleam of light glanced off the knife in his hand.

Gabriel managed to block the blow. He wrenched himself out from under Neil and rose to a crouching position. He reached down into his boot for the knife he carried there.

"You won't stop me this time," Baxter snarled. "I'm going to cut your throat for you."

513

He leaped toward Gabriel, knife extended. Gabriel danced backward and found himself trapped against the heavy iron press. He slid to the side as Baxter lunged again.

"Think twice before you try that again, Baxter. I am not unarmed."

"I heard your pistol fall to the floor." Baxter's teeth flashed in the shadows like those of a shark in the depths of the sea. "You're empty-handed, Wylde. This time you're a dead man."

Neil launched himself forward again, the knife aimed at Gabriel's midsection. Gabriel swung his heavy greatcoat off his shoulders and directly into Neil's path. Neil roared with rage as he became tangled up in it.

Gabriel kicked out swiftly. His booted foot caught Neil on the thigh, throwing the other man off balance. Neil yelled again as he tripped and went down.

Gabriel stepped forward, bringing his boot down on Neil's outflung arm. "Drop the knife."

"No, goddamn you."

Gabriel leaned down and held the tip of his own knife to Neil's throat. "This is not Excalibur and I am not Arthur. I would just as soon finish this right now, and the hell with the rules of chivalry. Let go of the blade, Baxter."

Neil went still. "You won't use it, Wylde."

"You think not?"

Neil's fingers unclenched from the handle of the knife. He glared up at Gabriel. "Phoebe would never forgive you for slitting my throat, and you know it."

"Phoebe no longer thinks of you as her fair Lancelot. The illusion you created was shattered for all time when Phoebe and Alice met. Apparently my wife does not approve of the way you abandoned your mistress. Lancelot was supposed to rescue the ladies, not leave them in hell."

Baxter stared up at him. "You're mad. Why would Phoebe give a damn about a whore?"

The light of a lantern fell across the two men. "Why, indeed?" asked the woman who stepped through the doorway from the alley. She had a pistol in her gloved hand. "You certainly did not care about me, did you, Neil? You gave me nothing but lies. And I believed them all."

"Alice." The yellow light from the lantern revealed the shock on Neil's face. "Alice, for God's sake, make him drop the knife. Use the pistol. Hurry, woman."

"I'd sooner use it on you, Neil." Alice held the lantern higher. "Where's your precious book?"

"For God's sake, Alice, help me. I'll get the book if you'll just shoot Wylde."

"I have no interest in killing Wylde," Alice said calmly. "If I kill anyone, it will be you. Where is the book?"

"I don't know," Neil said quickly. "Wylde interfered before I found it."

Gabriel looked at Alice. "It's in that desk over there in the corner."

"Thank you," Alice said. She kept the pistol trained on the two men as she went over to the desk.

"The second drawer," Gabriel said.

Alice opened the drawer. "I see. You are most cooperative, Wylde. I appreciate that."

She backed toward the door through which she had entered. Her pistol never wavered. "I shall be leaving now."

"Alice, my dearest love, you must help me," Neil whispered thickly. "You were the only woman who ever really mattered to me. You know that."

"You should have taken me with you when you left England with Clarington's money," Alice said.

"How could I subject the woman I loved to the harsh conditions of a trip to the islands?" Neil said.

"Did you think I enjoyed the conditions of a brothel more? I am not precisely certain

516

why this book is so important to you, but as you have been obsessed with finding it since you returned to London, I intend to find out."

"Help me and I'll show you why it's important," Neil pleaded.

Alice shook her head and took another step back.

Gabriel saw Anthony step into the doorway behind her. Alice retreated one more step and came up against him. Anthony's arm closed around her throat.

"I regret the inconvenience," Anthony murmured as he snapped the pistol from her hand. "Set the lantern down carefully."

Alice hesitated.

"Do it," Gabriel advised. "And then leave us. We have no interest in you. It is Baxter we want."

Alice lowered the lantern to the floor. Anthony released her and stepped into the room.

"Now the book, if you please," Gabriel said softly. He saw Alice's hand tighten around the old volume. Her gaze went to Neil.

At that moment Phoebe's cloaked figure appeared in the doorway. Gabriel swore softly. He should have guessed there would be no way to keep her out of this.

"I would like for Alice to keep the book," Phoebe said.

Gabriel sighed. "Very well, she may keep the damned book. I want her out of here."

"No, wait," Neil shouted. "None of you know what you're doing. I will tell you the secret of the book if you agree to release me. I promise you, the book is worth a fortune, but only if you know the secret."

"You refer to the jewels you had hidden inside, I assume?" Gabriel smiled briefly. "You needn't concern yourself over their fate, Baxter. We found them."

"Goddamn you." Baxter gave Alice a look of black despair. "Goddamn you all." His desperate eyes went to Phoebe. "You must listen to me, Phoebe. Wylde is everything I said he was and worse. I was only trying to save you."

"I saw how you *saved* Alice," Phoebe said.

"Alice is a whore," Neil raged. "Nothing but a whore."

"Alice is a woman, and so am I. You lied to her and you betrayed her. What makes you think I would trust you?"

"Didn't you hear me? She's nothing. A bit o' muslin who got above herself. A bloody whore."

"A true knight does not betray those who trust him," Phoebe said quietly.

"You and your endless, stupid chatter about knighthood and chivalry. Are you crazed, you silly bitch?"

Gabriel ground his boot down on Neil's wrist. Neil screamed in agony.

"I think that will be enough conversation," Gabriel said. He glanced at Alice. "I told you that you were free to go. Be off with you."

Alice clutched the book to her breast and turned toward the door. Phoebe stepped into her path.

"One moment, Alice. I want you to have this." Phoebe opened her gloved hand and revealed the pearl and diamond brooch.

Alice stared at it. "What are those strange silvery stones?"

"Dark moonlight," Phoebe said softly. "Pearls unlike any you have ever seen. Very, very rare."

Alice's gaze met Phoebe's. "That's what was hidden in the book?"

"One of several pieces that Neil had stolen and stashed inside the binding. Wylde gave them all to me. I'm keeping the other pieces, but I want you to have this brooch."

"Why?" Alice asked.

"Because even though I was in your power and you had reason to hate me, you were willing to spare me a night in hell."

Alice hesitated. Then she reached out and took the brooch. "Thank you. I shall use it to help buy my own way out of hell," she whispered. She handed Phoebe the book. "Here. I shall not be needing this now."

She stepped around Phoebe and disappeared into the night.

Fierce pride surged through Gabriel. He looked at Phoebe. "My lady, allow me to tell you that you are, in Mr. Chaucer's words, a 'verray parfit gentil knight.' "

Phoebe favored him with her brilliant smile and Gabriel realized quite suddenly that he loved her with a devastating intensity that would last as long as he had breath in his body. He longed to tell her so.

But this was not the time.

"Phoebe," Neil pleaded, "you must listen to me. I beg of you, for the sake of our great, undying love, you must help me."

Phoebe did not look at him.

"We had better see if we can rouse Stinton so that he can take Baxter into custody," Gabriel said to Anthony. "I grow weary of dealing with a pirate."

Two hours later Phoebe lay back against the pillows of Gabriel's massive bed and watched him shed the last of his clothing. The candlelight gleamed on the powerful contours of his back and thighs.

"You really are quite magnificent, my lord," she said.

He laughed softly as he climbed into bed beside her. He reached for her, pulling her down on top of his chest. "You are the magnificent one, my love."

She blinked. "What did you say?"

"I said you are magnificent."

"No, after that," she said impatiently. "What did you call me?"

He smiled. "I believe I called you my love."

"Ah, yes. I like the sound of that."

"It's true, you know," Gabriel said. "I do love you. I believe I have loved you from the day I opened the first letter you sent to me."

"I'm glad," she whispered.

He framed her face in his palms. "You do not seem overly astonished by my monumental confession of undying love."

She ducked her head and kissed his throat. When she looked up again, her eyes were glowing. "I admit that I began to suspect you might love me when you kept overlooking all my tiny, insignificant little adventures."

"I should have been somewhat suspicious myself," he said dryly. "Because your little adventures were not all that tiny, insignificant, or accidental. Your recklessness is enough to turn a man old before his time."

"I regret every single one of them," Phoebe declared passionately. "And I swear there will never be any more."

Gabriel laughed softly. "I am, of course, delighted to hear that." He wrapped his hand around the back of her head and brought her mouth close to his. "In the meantime, just keep telling me that you love me and I vow I will not mind the occasional bout of recklessness. So long as I am with you to look after you, that is."

"I love you," Phoebe whispered.

"I love you," Gabriel said against her lips. "More than life itself."

Phoebe scheduled the grand tournament at Devil's Mist to coincide with the publication of *A Reckless Venture*. Both the event and the book were successful beyond her wildest dreams.

On the night of the tournament ball the great hall of Devil's Mist was thronged with people in medieval costume. The columns of old armor looked very much at home amid the gaily dressed crowd. Music echoed off the old stone walls. All in all, Phoebe thought proudly, the castle looked quite as

522

it must have appeared several hundred years ago when medieval knights and their ladies had gathered here for a festive occasion.

"What a clever daughter I have," Lydia said with satisfaction as she surveyed the great hall. "You, my dearest Phoebe, have achieved an absolutely brilliant social coup."

"You mean the staging of the mock tournament this afternoon?" Phoebe smiled. "That was rather clever of me, wasn't it? I couldn't have done it without Wylde's help, however. I must admit he handled most of the details. I was rather worried that horses might accidentally crash into each other or someone might actually hit someone else with one of the battle-axes. But it all came off perfectly."

Lydia's brows rose in amusement. "The tournament was great fun, but that is not the coup I was talking about. Your stroke of brilliance, Phoebe, was in being able to present the author of *The Quest* to the Social World. Your stature as a hostess is assured for years to come."

"It wasn't easy," Phoebe confided. "Wylde was very set against being identified as the author of such a successful book. I believe that when it comes to that sort of thing he is rather shy. Amazing, is it not?"

"Most amazing," Lydia agreed. She smiled

at her husband as he ambled over. "There you are, my dear. Are you enjoying yourself?"

"Quite." Clarington took a sip from the champagne glass he was holding and gazed about the room. "Fascinating old place. Looked at some of the armor earlier. Very ingeniously made. Did I tell you that this morning Wylde demonstrated the workings of an extremely unusual machine down in the cellars? It's hidden in the wall and it contrives to open and close a gate. Have you seen it, Phoebe?"

Phoebe shuddered at the memory. "Yes, Papa, I have seen it."

"The pulley system is quite advanced in design. Especially when you consider that it was fashioned several hundred years ago."

"I know, Papa." Phoebe broke off as Meredith and her husband approached.

Meredith was radiant as always in a pale pink gown edged in silver. Trowbridge, handsome in his tunic costume, smiled at Phoebe.

"Most unusual affair, Phoebe," Trowbridge said. "Vastly entertaining. Highly successful, I should say."

"Yes, indeed," Meredith agreed. "You have made a stunning debut as a hostess, Phoebe. And I must tell you that everyone is commenting on your unusual jewelry. You are the envy of every woman here."

Phoebe smiled, aware of the weight of the Wylde necklace around her throat. "Do you like it?"

"Very much," Meredith said. "Not everyone could wear those strange pearls, but on you they are perfect. And they go wonderfully well with that rather bright red gown of yours."

"Thank you." Phoebe glanced down at the skirts of her crimson red dress. "I had another red gown I wanted to wear, one that Wylde purchased for me. But he reminded me that it was not precisely medieval in style. I had this one made instead."

Anthony appeared out of the crowd. "You had better see to your husband, Phoebe. He wants rescuing from several admirers. They appear to have trapped him over there near the door."

Phoebe stood on tiptoe until she saw Gabriel. He was standing beneath the arched doorway, surrounded by several eager-looking people. He caught Phoebe's eye and sent her a look that held desperate appeal.

"Excuse me," Phoebe said to her family. "Anthony is right. I must go and rescue Wylde."

She picked up her skirts and forged a path through the crowd until she reached Gabriel's side. He grabbed her hand.

"I wonder if I might have a word alone with my wife," he said to the group gathered around him.

The small gaggle of admirers took the hint and reluctantly moved off into the crowd. Gabriel turned on Phoebe.

"I told you this was an extremely unsound notion," he said. "I do not like this business of being a famous author."

"Nonsense," Phoebe said. "Most of the time you will be safe enough here at Devil's Mist. Surely you can handle a few admirers on the rare occasion such as tonight."

"The occasions had better be extremely rare," Gabriel warned. His eyes gleamed.

"They will be," Phoebe promised. She gave him a gloating smile. "And just think of what it will do for your career. I'll wager we shall have to go back to print for another five or six thousand copies after this lot returns to London. Everyone here cannot wait to inform his or her friends of the true identity of the author of *The Quest.* Lacey's Bookshop will make another tidy little fortune."

"What a mercenary mind you have, my dear."

"It's in the blood," she assured him cheerfully. "In my case it just took a bit longer to reveal itself."

"When are you going to tell your family that you are Lacey's partner?"

"Eventually." Phoebe laughed up at him. "But first there is something I wish to tell you."

Gabriel eyed her warily. "Another little secret you have forgotten to mention?"

"A very little secret." Phoebe blushed. "I believe I am with child, my lord."

Gabriel stared at her for a few dumbfounded seconds. His green eyes became very brilliant and he gave her a slow smile. "I did not think I could be any happier than I already am, my love. But I see I was wrong." He pulled her into his arms.

"For goodness' sake, Gabriel." Phoebe was shocked in spite of herself. She hastily glanced around in alarm. "What on earth do you think you are doing? You would not dare kiss me here in front of all these people."

Gabriel looked up at the motto etched in stone above his head. AUDEO. He grinned. "Now, that is where you are wrong, my love. I would most certainly dare. And what is more, you will kiss me back because you are just as daring and just as reckless as I am."

He captured her mouth, kissing her with the love he had been saving up all of his life. Phoebe wrapped her arms around his neck and kissed him back.

"I think," she whispered, "that I would like to name our first son Arthur."

"Of course," Gabriel agreed, warm, loving laughter gleaming in his eyes. "What else would we call him? And when we have our Arthur, we shall set about creating an entire Round Table to accompany him."

"So long as you don't mind the fact that some of our young knights will be female," Phoebe stipulated.

"Not in the least." Gabriel's arms tightened around her again. "I won't pretend that I don't find the idea of having several daughters who take after their reckless lady mother somewhat daunting, but I expect I will rise to the challenge."

"I am sure you will, my lord. You always do."